Barry Gray

My Married Life at Hillside

Barry Gray

My Married Life at Hillside

ISBN/EAN: 9783337095536

Printed in Europe, USA, Canada, Australia, Japan

Cover: Foto ©Andreas Hilbeck / pixelio.de

More available books at **www.hansebooks.com**

MY MARRIED LIFE AT HILLSIDE

BY

BARRY GRAY

WITH ILLUSTRATIONS BY McNEVIN

NEW YORK
PUBLISHED BY HURD AND HOUGHTON
1871.

RIVERSIDE, CAMBRIDGE:
STEREOTYPED AND PRINTED BY
H. O. HOUGHTON AND COMPANY

TO

ALBERT BIERSTADT,

AS A SLIGHT TESTIMONIAL OF ADMIRATION FOR HIM AS AN
ARTIST, RESPECT FOR HIM AS A MAN, AND
REGARD FOR HIM AS A FRIEND,

This Volume

IS INSCRIBED,

WITH THE KIND WISHES OF THE AUTHOR

CONTENTS.

CHAPTER I.

CHAPTER II.

CHAPTER III.

CHAPTER IV.

CHAPTER V.

CHAPTER VI.

CHAPTER VII.

CHAPTER VIII.

CHAPTER IX.

CHAPTER X.

CHAPTER XI.

CHAPTER XII.

CHAPTER XIII.

CHAPTER XIV.

CHAPTER XV.

CHAPTER XVI.

CHAPTER XVII.

CHAPTER XVIII.

CHAPTER XIX.

CHAPTER XX.

CHAPTER XXI.

CHAPTER XXII.

CHAPTER XXIII.

CHAPTER XXIV.

CHAPTER XXV.

CHAPTER XXVI.

CHAPTER XXVII.

CHAPTER XXVIII.

CHAPTER XXIX.

CHAPTER XXX.

CHAPTER XXXI.

CHAPTER XXXII.

CHAPTER XXXIII.

CHAPTER XXXIV.

CHAPTER XXXV.

CHAPTER XXXVI.

CHAPTER XXXVII.

CHAPTER XXXVIII.

CHAPTER XXXIX.

CHAPTER XL.

CHAPTER XLI.

CHAPTER XLII.

CHAPTER XLIII.

CHAPTER XLIV.

ILLUSTRATIONS.

PREFATORY LETTER.

To my Readers.

When, ten years ago, I commenced the publication, in the "Home Journal," of the larger part of the contents of this volume, in a series of sketches contributed from week to week, I had no intention of "making a book"; but as by degrees they grew in number under my hand, and were received with favor by my readers, I came to think it would not be amiss for me to collect them into a volume. Having been deterred, however, from fulfilling this purpose until the present time, I trust that the interest, expressed by those who read them in a serial form, will not entirely have passed away, and that they will be pleased to renew their acquaintance with the various characters introduced to them so long ago. By thus waiting, also, I trust that I have gained a new and fresh class of readers, and one, too, which will find in my bachelor friends, my old soldiers, my exemplary parson, my eccentric editor, my borrowing neighbors, my mischievous little black boy, and the estimable Mrs. Gray herself, characters which will both amuse and interest them. Many of these personages were drawn from life, and all, I believe, have forgiven me the liberty I took in putting them into print. Of my bachelor friends, most of them are no longer bachelors. Only Frank, who is afar off in Japan, winning a name and fortune, still clings to single blessedness; the rest have taken to themselves wives, and are no longer permitted to visit the Female College, but are required to stay at home and attend to the wants of their little ones. The little black boy, who, as all little black boys will, who are not cut off in the bloom of youth, grew to man's estate, and profiting by the instructions he received while "doing chores" at Hillside, became a trustworthy and industrious man. It grieves me, however, to record the fact that he is no more. He fell, bravely fighting, before Petersburg, and now fills a soldier's grave. Peace to his memory!

I would, if I dared, point out the truth and the fiction in this book; but I stand in wholesome fear of Mrs. Gray's reproaches should I separate, as I have sometimes been requested to do, for the gratification of my readers, the one from the other. My whilom bachelor friends, and all married men, indeed, will have little difficulty in deciding which portion is drawn from actual experience, and which is purely imaginary.

For the illustrations in this volume I am indebted to my friend Mr. J. M'Nevin, who has succeeded in catching the exact spirit of the text, and conveying it in his drawings in a graphic and admirable manner. The graphotype process, by which these illustrations are executed, is entirely new, and this is the first book published in this country, with original designs produced by this mode. Through this process two desirable advances are made over wood-engraving: one is rapidity of execution, and the other a saving of at least one half in the expense. Still another advantage is, that every line made by the artist is faithfully reproduced. Each touch is his, and no intervening graver comes in to mar his handiwork. The process is most simple, and can be accomplished by any one accustomed to the handling of a brush. A brief description will suffice to show that when the artist makes the drawing, he at the same time effects the engraving. A thin plate of zinc, on which a coating of plaster composition is first spread, is subjected to hydraulic pressure, and afterwards kiln-dried. A surface as smooth and polished as plate glass is the result, and on this, with a camel's hair-brush, the drawing is made, with a metallic ink. This ink has the property of hardening the composition wherever it touches, so effectually as to permit of the untouched part being brushed away with a velvet buffer, without breaking or disturbing the lines drawn, which remain in relief. The plate is then effectually hardened by a chemical liquid, and a plaster cast taken of it, which is the matrix from which a stereotype is made, and from this the engraving is printed.

In these grave and thoughtful times, when war dwells in the land, and few households are without a vacant chair, I have yet thought fit to bring this volume before the Public, believing that to turn for a little while from the contemplation of war and its horrors to the simple story of a quiet country life, as herein set forth, is good for the heart and mind.   **B. G.**

New York, *March* **17, 1865.**

MY MARRIED LIFE AT HILLSIDE.

CHAPTER I.

SENT to the city for some wines, and then, when they came, I got married. It was a grave thing for a bachelor of my age to marry. It required considerable nerve and resolution on my part to relinquish the careless life I had been leading for thirty odd years, and assume the responsibilities devolving upon a married man. I smoked a large number of cigars, and drank a great many bottles of Scotch ale, before I finally decided to take the step I did. I, moreover, took the precaution of visiting several of my intimate friends who were married and had families, with a view to learn whether they were as happy in their new position as they had been in the olden one. But, bless me! I could n't tell anything about it. They were all prepared for my coming; — the husbands put on their most gracious tones, and the wives their prettiest ways, while the children were severally drilled into an extra degree of politeness. I was company, and therefore was treated as such.

I even went so far, in my extreme cautiousness, as to

write a strictly private letter to my brother-in-law, who lives "Out West," asking his advice in the matter; and I must confess his reply was most encouraging and highly satisfactory, — though I afterward discovered that his wife, my respected sister, had dictated, word by word, the answer.

Aside from love, there were certain reasons, I am free to confess, which had weight in influencing me to marry. In the first place, the lady who had the honor to be the object of my respectful admiration, and who is now my wife, knew how to make coffee. I will say that she excelled in that particular accomplishment. Nowhere have I ever found any coffee worthy of being compared to that she concocted. In fact, it was a cup of coffee that she made which caused me first to think of asking her to be my wife. I am very fond of coffee, — no man can be more so. It is as food, clothes, and books to me. Deprive me of it, and I am but a common man, a mere cipher, an unknown individual; but feed me with it, and I am, at the lowest, a poet, and with every cup grade upward a step higher. While under the influence which that first cup of coffee produced, I addressed some lines to my intended, which were published in the "Home Journal." These I sent to her anonymously; but when next we met, I thought I discovered, by her manners, which were most pleasing, that she suspected me of being the author. In a confidential conversation, which took place one night since our marriage, between us, I learned that this supposition of mine was correct, and that she not only suspected, but fully believed I was the author, from the circumstance that the handwriting of her address, which accompanied the lines in question, was a perfect fac-simile of one I had previously sent her. It seems very strange to me now that this little fact escaped my attention at that time.

That I might obtain a cup of excellent coffee, then, was one reason why I decided to marry; and another reason was — buttons. I had a mind above buttons, therefore

I would not sew them on myself, and it was not perfectly convenient for me to keep a tailor at my elbow. A tailor in one's house is, perhaps, an excellent institution ; but when, like myself, you have no house, and only one room, six by nine, it may not accord exactly with your ideas of economy to keep a tailor, especially as he would expect to share your bed, and, most likely, desire to use your brushes and combs, razors and towels, and similar articles of your personal property. Rather, therefore, than submit to so great an inconvenience as that of owning a tailor, I would prefer to take to myself a wife, even if she possessed no more than the necessary articles of her toilet.

With me, things — especially my pantaloons — were fast arriving at a crisis. I should soon be in no condition to visit among "our best society," but should be obliged to emigrate to some sunny isle like Typee, where, after all, I might be obliged to wed a deserted Fayaway. Preferring, therefore, — either to a tailor or Typee, — a wife, I resolved to become a Benedict.

Between the arrival of the wine and the wedding-day, though but a brief season, I accomplished much. I settled an account at my washer-woman's ; I sold a fighting-dog, which an inconsiderate sporting friend left me when he died ; I burnt a package of old letters, tied with faded blue ribbons, which had been in a secret corner of my writing-desk many years ; I cast to the winds several ringlets of once glossy hair ; I rubbed out three daguerreotypes ; I exchanged several little articles of jewelry, that, somehow, chanced to be in my possession, for a plain gold ring ; I presented my night-key, with a few appropriate words of advice, to the young man who was to occupy my place at "our boarding-house" ; I read up Mrs. Caudle's " Curtain Lectures " ; I inquired the price of meat at the butcher's, and was astonished to find it so high, — the same of bread at the baker's, and also of various groceries at the corner-store. Then I remembered that I was going to live in the country, and I felt very thankful that there were no shops of any kind near by. I have an indistinct recollection, moreover, of drinking sundry glasses of ale, about that time, with bachelor friends, and making several little speeches — farewell addresses, I may call them — pertinent to the occasion, — some of which, I believe, were reported in the daily papers at the time, and attracted considerable attention.

At last the day came, and with it the parson, the ring, the cake, the champagne, and all that sort of thing. After the parson had read the service, and the ring was put on, and the cake cut, and the champagne opened, we, that is my wife and her husband, departed in the cars. Yet for all this it did not seem to me as though I were a married man. I mentioned as much to Mrs. Gray, who, in reply, stated it did not seem to her that she was a married woman. I deemed this a very singular coincidence, and made a note of it, at the time, in my memorandum-book. I could but think that all that had passed, and was passing, would prove to be simply a dream, and nothing more, and that when the cars stopped I should wake from it, and lose the little hand which I held clasped so closely in mine, and hear no longer the sweet-toned voice that was music to my ears, and see no more the joyous face which was beaming upon me. But none of these things, I am pleased to say, happened, though it seemed none the less a dream.

When a few days afterwards, however, I read a notice of our marriage in the newspaper, I felt that it might be true. Nevertheless, I took the precaution, for the sake of future reference, if at any time doubts should arise respecting it, to cut the article in question out of the paper, and preserve it in my pocket-book. I took occasion to read this little notice aloud to my wife many times during the day, and its perusal each time gave me infinite and peculiar satisfaction. It seemed to me that the phraseology of it was excellent. Indeed, viewed simply in a literary point of view, it was perfect; much superior, I remarked to Mrs. B. G., than the general run of such articles. She fully coincided with me as regarded its merits, and expressed herself highly pleased with it. My wife also mentioned to me that there did not appear to be anything else worth reading in the paper, and after a careful examination my-self, I could see nothing of interest in its columns. This surprised me exceedingly, as in general I considered the paper a very readable one.

Not, however, till our return home from the wedding-tour, and I had obtained from the parson who performed the ceremony a marriage certificate, which I have had framed and hung in a conspicuous place in our chamber, did I fully realize that I was a husband.

The honeymoon, which promises to be a very long one, has not yet passed, though the summer has fled and the autumn is fast wasting away. Mrs. Gray already calls me by my Christian name, although, as yet, I have not dared to venture upon so much familiarity with her, but hope to be able so to do somewhere about Christmas.

CHAPTER II.

My Wife. — Envious Bachelors. — Mrs. G.'s Remarks thereon. — Deprivations. — Mr. Hayward done for. — Dr. Philtre. — Carving. — My Children in Utopia. — Confidence. — A Breakfast. — Spring Chickens *versus* Old Red.

T is a fine thing, I find, to be a married man. There is something peculiarly gratifying to one's own feelings in being able to speak of "my wife." When I am among my bachelor friends, I take great delight in thus alluding to Mrs. Gray. It tells with remarkable effect. It seems to me that my old companions treat me with more respect now than they did previous to my marriage. I sometimes think that they look on me with feelings almost akin to envy; especially when they meet me in the street accompanied by Mrs. Gray, or when they see her seated by my side as we ride to church. For my own part, — and I am free to confess it, — I am pleased that they should thus regard me. I mentioned as much to Mrs. G., and was astonished to find that she did not coincide with me in this matter; for, as she very truly, and I think, feelingly, remarked, " You know, Barry, that it would not be possible for me to marry all of them; and envy is a passion which should not be tolerated in any Christian's bosom." Of course, I acknowledged the propriety of this remark, but at the same time it did not in the least change my feelings.

It is a fine thing, I repeat it, to be a married man. There are, to be sure, sundry habits, which, though irregular, still are permissible in the bachelor, that the husband is expected to resign. For instance, I am no longer permitted to smoke after dinner, while lingering at the table, nor yet in the parlor of an evening, though at my old boarding-house such acts were not considered improper. Then, again, I am not allowed even to drink a glass of ale, except when prescribed by our family physician. This, to me, is a great deprivation. I had not thought I should be required to give up this trifling source of enjoyment. I came very near getting eight dozen of Scotch ale on my hands. I had gone so far as to write to my friend Richard Haywarde, inquiring the price of said beverage. When his reply came, I was foolish enough to show it to Mrs. B. G. "If," said she, "as this wine-merchant writes, ' half the ale which is sold in this market for Scotch never saw the land of Burns,' then I recommend to you, Mr. Gray, not to purchase any ; for," continued she, " if you take his own word for it, four dozen of that you propose buying would, of course, be manufactured in this country." There was a roguish sparkle in Mrs. G.'s eyes, as she said this, which was delightful to behold. Her rejoinder, I thought, was complete ; and as I could not gainsay it, I forgot to send the order as I had intended. Living out of town as I do, too, it is no easy matter for me to see our family physician, Dr. Philtre, to get him to prescribe for me every time I am ailing. Sometimes, when I go to the post-office for my letters, I avail myself of the opportunity to call on him for medical advice. It is surprising how well he understands the nature of my complaint. His prescriptions I have no hesitation in following implicitly. In these Maine-law days how good a thing it is to find, not only a conscientious, but an accommodating physician, — as is my friend, Dr. Philtre !

Notwithstanding these, and certain other little drawbacks upon the liberty of a husband, yet it is a fine thing to be a married man. To find one's self the head of the household ! To sit at the top of the table, opposite one's wife, and carve ! Sometimes, at my boarding-place, when the white-haired old gentleman who occupied, by courtesy of the landlady, this post of honor, was absent, I have been invited to take his place ; but it was always with a degree of nervousness which rendered the position anything but agreeable. Now, however, it is different. Seated at my own board, with only Mrs. Gray to watch me, I am fast becoming a skilful and scientific carver. To be sure, on Thanksgiving Day, when a young physician and his wife took dinner with me, I managed to deposit the turkey I was carving upon the floor ; but that was entirely owing, I believe, to the fork slipping from its proper place, and not in any degree to my awkwardness or lack of skill.

It is, as I said before, a fine thing to be a married man. There is a prospect in the future before him, which the bachelor can never behold ; or, at least, is seen by the latter only as through a glass, darkly. I refer to beholding in one's house what the poet calls "a well-spring of pleasure." I took the liberty of saying as much to Mrs. Gray. She replied, "that I would much oblige her if I would refrain from ever again alluding to that subject." Since then I have. with one exception, passed over the matter in silence. About a year since I wrote a little story for one of the newspapers, entitled "My Children in Utopia." Some of you, perhaps, may have seen it. Mrs. G. had not. One evening, as we were sitting comfortably before the blazing wood-fire, with a plate of apples and some cider on the table beside us, I chanced to think of this story, and, with little forethought, asked my wife if she had ever seen "My Children in Utopia." She answered, with some asperity and shortness, "No!" adding, after a pause, "that, if they were in the place I said they were, she hoped they 'd stay there." It required nice management on my part to mollify Mrs. B. G. and satisfy her that I referred only to fictitious beings, creatures solely of my imagination. After I had read to her the story, she said it was very pretty, but that she wished, from the bottom of her heart, I would not write any more like it !

Is it not a fine thing to be a married man? To possess unlimited confidence in your buttons; to feel certain that there are no holes in your coats — no rents in your pantaloons; to be able to put on your stockings without stopping to darn them; to have warm water to shave with, and a looking-glass somewhat larger than a tea-plate in which to admire yourself; to know you can have your favorite meat for dinner, and to possess the privilege of investigating the pantry just before retiring at night; to find, when you come into the house, your easy-chair drawn up in front of the fire, your slippers lying beside it, and your dressing-gown resting on its back; lastly, and best of all, to be greeted with a pleasant word, a sunny smile, and, if you are deserving of it, something more beside.

It certainly is a fine thing to be a married man; especially if one lives in the country and keeps house. It is pleasant to have your friends visit you; and a breakfast in the country is delightful. It does n't cost much either to get one up: a pair of spring chickens, some fresh eggs, new butter, rich cream, Mocha coffee, and a few light rolls, are all that are necessary; and the pleasure you take in seeing your friends more than compensates you for all the trouble. Looking on the affair in this light, I took the liberty, shortly after I was married, without consulting Mrs. Gray in the matter, to invite a half-dozen of my bachelor friends to breakfast. When I told Mrs. G. what I had done, I supposed she would be as pleased as I was with the arrangement. I found, however, the reverse to be the case. I had evidently committed a serious blunder. For, instead of a smile, I saw, almost, a frown. I began to fear the honeymoon was over. " Who," asked Mrs. G., " of all your boon companions, Mr. Gray, have you been pleased to invite?" When I had enumerated their names, she made some striking comments in regard to them. I had always thought they were good fellows; but my confidence in them thenceforth was shaken. I wondered how I could have been so blind to their numerous faults. It was certainly astonishing. I was sorry that I had invited such men. Then, too, I found that I had selected for the occasion what my wife was pleased to term " washing-day." This is an institution which, in my bachelor calendar, was entirely unknown, and is, I have since learned, purely of a domestic character. It may not be, perhaps, worth while to state all that passed between Mrs. Gray and myself at this lamentable period. Suffice it to say that the breakfast in question did not pass off as pleasantly as I hoped it would. The chickens proved to be tough ; the eggs were boiled at least three minutes longer than they should have been ; the butter lacked salt ; the rolls were undone ; only the coffee merited praise ; and, to crown all, my wife was afflicted with a nervous headache that morning, and, consequently, did not make her appearance. After breakfast, when I took my friends out to the barn-yard to show them my fowls, especially the " Old Red," I discovered he was missing. Upon questioning the black boy in regard to his whereabouts, he replied that he " guessed the gentlemen had eaten him for breakfast." This accounted for the particular toughness of one, at least, of what I supposed were spring chickens. He must have broken shell, however, many springs ago. I considered him the patriarch of the barn-yard, — the identical " cock that crowed in the morn, to wake the priest all shaven and shorn," — the chanticleer who was the envy of all other chanticleers in the vicinity, and the pride and glory of the hens for miles around ; who had spurs three inches long, and whose voice, in the early morning, rang out like the clarion trumpet. When my friend Frank took from his pocket a spur, which I identified as belonging to my gallinaceous favorite, I felt that there was no longer any doubt as to what had become of him ; especially when Frank said he was preserving it as a memento of the breakfast which he had partaken, and also as a sample of what my spring chickens were capable of producing.

It is scarcely necessary for me to add that I have given no more breakfasts to bachelor friends. I do not think that, in the long run, they will "*pay.*" I fear, too, that Mrs. Gray does not regard them in a favorable light, else why did she have so severe a headache? In consideration of these points, therefore, Mrs. G. and myself usually take this meal alone together. Yet, notwithstanding all this, I honestly believe that it is a fine thing to be a married man!

CHAPTER III.

Dining out. — Going home. — Curtain drops. — " Home, sweet Home." — How a Husband feels. — Little Black Boy. — Our Barn. — Angry Cook. Bells. — Belated Dinner. — Indignant Wife. — Honeymoon returns.

RECEIVED an invitation a day or two since, while in the village, to remain and dine with a friend. The person who invited me was one of my bachelor companions. I regard him in the light of a brother. Even Mrs. Gray alludes to him in favorable terms. He never smokes, nor drinks, nor talks in a boisterous manner, nor laughs aloud, — four things that my wife particularly dislikes. Had he been one whom Mrs. Gray does not admire, I should have declined; as it was, I had no scruples or hesitation in accepting. We dined at the hotel, where we had a cheerful time, and afterwards passed an hour in pleasant talk. On my way home, as I neared " Hillside," I confess to feeling a little uncomfortable. I had told Mrs. Gray that I should be home to dinner. Living in the country, as we do, we have adopted country customs, consequently our dinner-hour is one o'clock. It was then — for I looked at my watch just as I got in sight of the house — three forty, according to railroad time. I did really hope that my wife had not kept dinner waiting for me. I feared, if she had, that it was spoiled. I said so to the old black horse, as he went slowly up the hill. I have no doubt but he understood me, for he pricked up his ears and gave his tail a fling, and whinnied as though he feared his oats were spoiling. I then remembered, too, that Mrs. Gray asked me, just before I started for town, what hour she should have dinner on the table. I had replied, the usual hour. She said she was thus particular in inquiring because she intended to have for dinner a favorite dish of mine, namely, chicken-pie. I had forgotten this when I accepted Frank's invitation, but now it returned to my mind most forcibly. I would have given much if I had not dined abroad. I fervently hoped that Mrs. Barry had not waited for me, but had herself quietly partaken of the noontide meal. I feared, however, I was hoping against hope. I was certain of this when, as I entered the gate, I saw the curtain drop at the bay-window. I knew, then, that Mrs. Gray was watching me from behind it. I felt that I was blushing, and it vexed me to know it. I assumed a careless air, and struck the horse slightly once or twice with my whip. I even essayed to whistle a stave or two of " Home, sweet home ! " I felt, though, that it was a failure, it sounded so much like " Hark, from the tombs ! "

My wife usually opens the door for me on my return from the village. On this occasion, however, it remained obstinately closed. Fortunately, I was in no hurry to go in, so I followed my horse to the stable, and gave some directions, in regard to him, to the little colored boy who does the " chores." I spent some time in the stable and about the barn before I was ready to enter the house. It seemed to me exactly as if I were afraid to go in. I am not naturally a coward, nor even timid. I may be diffident and shy, but these feelings are entirely different from those I then experienced. I have no recollection of ever having had similar ones when I was a bachelor. I am satisfied, indeed, that it is only the husband who can thus feel. It took me a long while to make up my mind to seek my wife. Before I did, I sent the little black boy in to get of Mrs. Gray some saddler's sewing-silk, intending, while I was in the stable, to repair one of the reins. When the colored boy came back, I asked him if Mrs. Gray had sent any message to me. He replied, " No ! " I confess I was disappointed. I had hoped that she would at least have asked as to what was detaining me from her side. Her silence seemed ominous of evil. As a general thing, she is fond of my society. I thought so before we were married, and up to this time I had fully believed it. I began to feel very badly.

After a few minutes' consideration, I concluded to try her again. "She'll be sorry," I said to myself, "that she did not inquire about me, and will wish she had; I'll give her another opportunity." So I sent the above-mentioned colored lad to her for some wax. This time he did not come back. I grew weary of waiting for him. The sun was getting low and the air chilly. I feared I was taking cold. It was not comfortable in the barn. It appeared to me to be even colder **than barns usually are.** I think the cracks between the boards must be wider **than can be found else-where.** When I looked through one of them towards the house, I discovered the little black wretch sawing **wood.** I stepped to the door and telegraphed with my hand for him to come to me; but he shook his woolly pate, and, showing his ivories, distinctly gave me to understand that I could not be favored with his presence, because, as he shouted, Mrs. Gray had set him to doing up his chores. I don't like to get angry. I don't think it conducive to health. Besides, I believe it, in a moral point of view, to be wrong. Yet I confess to feeling thus at that moment; and my resentment covered the whole world generally, and that little darkey in particular. When, a few minutes thereafter, just as the hens were going to roost, I went into the house, I accidentally trod on that little black boy, and I must say I hoped he would cry, but he didn't; he only grinned **at me in derision.** I made up my mind, then, to flog him the first opportunity. I hate little black boys. I think they suck eggs. Since my bachelor friends break-fasted with me, we've been short of eggs.

I took the precaution of entering the house by the back **way.** By so doing I escaped passing the room where I knew Mrs. Gray was sitting, probably with the door ajar. In avoiding Scylla, however, I ran upon Charybdis, for, as I walked through the kitchen, the cook looked daggers at me. I think an angry cook is a terrible being. I believe my knees shook under me. I felt that a crisis was approaching. Instead of entering the sitting-room, I passed directly to the library. The fire was out, and the room cold ; yet I sat down, and tried to read "Maud." It was maudlin, to me : I could make nothing of it. In a few minutes I heard some one come down the hall on tiptoe, and stop near the library door. I thought it was my wife, and nerved myself to meet her. I grasped tighter the arms of my easy-chair, and half in joy, half in fear, I waited for the opening of the door. But I waited in vain. Instead, came the sound of a bell rung by my ebony friend. I felt certain it meant dinner. I know well the sound, and can never be deceived. I may hear it any hour of the twenty-four, and to whatever meal it calls I am sure to be able to tell. There is a sharp sound to the breakfast-bell, which speaks plainly of coffee ; and a lazy tinkle to the supper-bell, which is equally distinct as to tea ; while the dinner-bell has a full round tone that tells unmistakably of roasted beef. As a usual thing, I " admire " to hear the dinner-bell, except when, as this did, it speaks of an overdone chicken-pie and a deeply injured wife !

I looked at my watch, and found it was five o'clock. I could not help thinking it was a fashionable hour for dinner. As I entered the dining-room, I mentioned as much to Mrs. Gray, who already occupied her seat at the table. She wished to know whether I said that as a piece of pleasantry, or with an intention to insult her ! Of course I disclaimed all desire as to the last. I felt that the honey-moon was again in danger of setting. As I anticipated, the chicken-pie was done rather brown. Had the cutting of it required much skill, I should have blundered in it sadly. It was lucky for me that there was no gravy to spil'

on the cloth. I felt nervous. My hand trembled. I was
very thankful when Mrs. Gray and myself were helped to
the pie.

When I came to offer Mrs. Gray what I supposed, from
their appearance, were mashed turnips, she indignantly
denied them, and said they were potatoes. "Yes, Mr.
Gray, potatoes — but boiled to pieces."

There was a dish, however, which I felt sure contained
sliced turnips, so, placing a spoon within it, I said, " You
will at least allow me, my dear, to give you some turnips ! "

"Turnips, Mr. Gray? They are beets, though their
color has boiled away."

I gave it up then; and to whatever else I helped Mrs
Barry, I took the precaution to point at, and ask if she
would permit me to give her some of *this*. I was glad
when the meal came to an end. It had been a silent one,
though at first I tried to converse, yet, as Mrs. Gray replied to me only in monosyllables, I soon ceased to speak.

In a letter which I wrote, just before I was married, to
my brother-in-law, who lives "Out West," I asked him
what course he pursued with his wife when she was out of
humor. He replied that, for his own part, he kissed her
into good-humor, though an acquaintance of his pursued
a somewhat different plan, and swore terribly at his wife.
He did not himself know which was the better way, but
thought I might discover by experimenting. I confess
that his letter shocked me. I half suspected he was joking, only he seldom jokes. So I "might discover by experimenting" which was the better plan. I resolved, when
I read his letter, that I would do no such thing. I would
follow his course, and trust to its being a wise one.

So now I determined to adopt it. When, therefore, we
arose from the table, I took the liberty of kissing Mrs.
Gray. The effect was magical. Smiles overcame the
frowns, and the honeymoon returned in all its glory.

CHAPTER IV.

I propose a Christmas Dinner. — My Brother-in-Law's Plan. — Cost of a Dinner. — A Cart-load of Turkeys. — My Bachelor Friends. — The Strangers I wished to invite. — Mrs. Gray's Feelings. — Explanation. — The Dinner. — Abeline. — Act of Thankfulness. — My Speech. — Mrs. Gray's Opinion of it. — My Modesty.

DAY or two before Christmas I asked Mrs. Gray what she thought of our giving a Christmas dinner, and inviting thereto a few friends. She replied that she had not thought of it at all. The tone of voice in which Mrs. Gray answered was not in the least encouraging. It sounded to me very like as if she had said, "No! Mr. Gray; a breakfast to bachelor friends is all-sufficient, without thinking of a Christmas dinner." Most husbands would have felt discouraged at this reply, and would incontinently have dropped the subject. But I was not thus easily repulsed; so I continued, "Well, my dear, the affair is worth thinking about: a Christmas dinner, remember, can be given but once a year." Here Mrs. Gray remarked that, for her part, she was glad of it. "Though, to be sure, my love," I continued, not heeding her interruption, "every meal I partake of with you seems to me *like* a Christmas dinner." I noticed hereupon that Mrs. Gray smiled, though she said not a word. The smile, however, was a favorable one.

In a letter I received, a short time since, from my brother-in-law, who lives "Out West," he wrote that, by a little well-timed flattery, he could persuade his wife, my respected sister, to yield many points, which, as Elder Sniffles remarks, she had "set her face like a flint against." I thought it well to adopt such a course with Mrs. Gray, and it was in pursuance of this plan, therefore, that I allowed myself so touchingly to allude to our solitary repasts. Whether I had effected my purpose I could not immediately tell, for Mrs. Gray just then was called away by household duties.

That evening, however, at supper, the subject was resumed by my wife saying, "If we give this Christmas dinner, Mr. Gray, I fear we shall have nothing in the house for New-Year's Day. A dinner such as you would desire to set before your friends will cost money. It will be an expensive affair, and you know how ill we can afford it!"

It is as good as a small fortune for a man to possess an economical wife. I said as much to Mrs. Gray. She replied by handing me a bit of paper, on which, as she remarked, she had figured up the cost of a Christmas dinner. I must say that I was astonished at the amount required. I had no idea that a quarter of the sum named would be necessary. I pondered on it: I became lost in calculations, and was only recalled to consciousness by something my wife said about cold coffee. After I had straightened myself in my chair, and my cup had been replenished, I turned to Mrs. Gray and asked her what she proposed doing. In reply, she said, "Just think, my dear, of the many poor families who, with the money this banquet would cost, might be made happy by our sending each of them a turkey for their Christmas dinner, and yet we have one left for ourselves." After a little ciphering in my head, I found, to my surprise, that, at a cost of seventy-five cents per turkey, I could purchase with the above-named amount almost a cart-load. It would certainly be charitable, I thought, for me to follow out this suggestion of Mrs. Gray's; but then it is a pleasant thing to see one's friends around the Christmas board, — to believe that they are happy, and, so long at least as the dinner lasts, consider their entertainers in a favorable light. I had thought of this dinner for some time — long before I mentioned the subject to Mrs. Gray. Somehow, I kept putting off speaking to her about it, just as though I dreaded doing so, and was afraid she would raise objections. Had I waited eight-and-forty hours longer, there would have been no necessity for alluding to it at all, as Christmas then would have been over. As it was, I had deferred to the last minute introducing the matter to Mrs. Gray. I had even hinted to several of my bachelor friends, weeks previous, that such an affair was likely to occur at Hillside. Two or three, I knew, considered themselves as good as invited, and had casually asked me whether I had sent a Christmas order for wines to my wine-merchant, in town. It was provoking to think that, after all, they might have to go farther, and, perhaps, fare worse. I said so to Mrs. Gray. I think she was rather pleased than otherwise at the prospect before them. I felt that I had got myself into a dilemma. I saw that my wife was decidedly opposed to giving a Christmas din ner. I was certain that, if it came off, she would be prevented by a nervous headache from being present. But then, again, I knew that my friends would be dreadfully disappointed should it not take place, and, maybe, it might end in a duel. I told Mrs. Barry so; but she laughed outright, and said I need not fear them, and called them " arrant cowards." She added, too, that they were afraid of her, — and I believe it, for they don't come out to Hillside to see me, half so often as they used to. My mind was fearfully perplexed in the matter, how to decide; so I agreed with Mrs. Gray to let the affair lay over till the following day.

The next morning, therefore, at breakfast, I said to Mrs. Gray that the thing was settled ; and I felt that, under the circumstances, a Christmas dinner was indispensable. I saw that my wife was disappointed — I will not say displeased, for that is a harsh word — at my decision. I noticed her hand trembled slightly as she poured out my cup

of coffee, and the ribbons on her morning cap fluttered
more than usual. My own heart was troubled within me.
I half repented of my decision. After a silence between
us of some minutes, she asked in a faltering voice, which
she strove, however, to steady, who she might expect to
have the pleasure of dining with on the morrow. I replied
that I thought of inviting Hiawatha and Maud, Mr. and
Mrs. Sparrowgrass, together with Paul Fane, and Pocahontas, the Chieftain's Daughter. Somewhat perplexed
and astonished, Mrs. Gray remarked that she was not acquainted with these persons, and hoped, for goodness' sake,
that I would n't invite a lot of strangers. "At the very
worst, Mr. Gray," she continued, "I had thought to see
two or three of your abominable bachelor friends; and
now, to have to entertain a whole raft of people who I am
sure nobody knows, is altogether too bad, and I can't en-
dure it. If I were as strong and healthy as some ladies
are, Mr. Gray, it might be a different thing; but subject,
as you know I am, to nervous headaches, it is not right or
considerate in you to expect me to entertain company."

There were tears in my wife's eyes, as she made this little
speech, which affected me to behold: so I hastened to re-
lieve her mind on the subject. "My dear," I said, " permit
me to explain. I am joking — nothing more. Don't you
remember the poem about the Indian chief, Hiawatha, I
read to you the other evening, when you fell asleep in your
chair?" My wife nodded her head. "And Maud, too," I
continued; "you have not forgotten her — the young lady
who has received so many invitations lately through the
newspapers, to 'come to the garden.' I thought I'd ask
her to come to Hillside; but now that I see you feel so
badly about it, I won't send her the invitation." Mrs. Gray
still remaining in doubt, I explained further. "In regard
to Mr. and Mrs. Sparrowgrass, love, you know that they,
like ourselves, are 'living in the country'; Mr. S., you
will recollect, owns a 'playful horse,' so I thought like

enough he'd be pleased to drive him out here, and bring
Mrs. S. along." Mrs. Gray still appearing greatly perplexed, I continued my explanation. "As relates to Paul
Fane, why, I am free to confess, I know very little about
him. I have merely seen his name mentioned in the daily
journals, and, moreover, understand that Mr. Willis ac-
knowledges himself to be his father. How this is, I cannot
really say; but perhaps Mr. Willis will himself fully explain the matter to you. Of Pocahontas, the Chieftain's
Daughter, however, I can simply say that she once lived in
Virginia, and is a child of my friend, General Morris." It
was surprising to me, at least, how very long it was before
Mrs. Gray comprehended my joke. After I had rendered
her these explanations, she expressed doubts in regard to
the paternity of Mr. Fane and Miss Pocahontas, asking,
while a blush mantled her cheek, how they came to bear
names different from their fathers. I often grieve over
Mrs. Gray's slowness in understanding a joke. That she
is quick enough in some things, I am well convinced. Occasionally she makes a remark that, for brilliancy, sur-
passes anything of which her husband is capable. Even
after I supposed that all had been made clear to her,
she astonished me by exclaiming that she was glad
those strange people were not coming to Hillside, Christmas.

So it turned out that Mrs. G. and myself partook of our
Christmas dinner alone together. I was sorry, though,
that my friend, the doctor, was not present to mark the
improvement I had made since Thanksgiving-day in carving the turkey which graced our round table. After the
cloth was removed, I took the liberty of introducing on the
table, with the coffee, a bottle of old Madeira. It was during the imbibing of the wine that I addressed my wife in a
more familiar manner than I had ever before allowed myself to do, namely, by her Christian name — Abeline. At

the same moment I astonished her by seizing her hand across the table, and shaking it in a violent and unusual manner. Perhaps it will be as well here to state that, whenever I uttered her name during the evening, I repeated this little act of greeting each time, to the increased wonder and delight of Mrs. Gray. In a private conversation which I held with Mrs. G. during the watches of the night, I apologized for my conduct. And although she accepted it, and said "it was highly satisfactory to her matrimonial feelings," yet I am half fearful that it was not altogether agreeable to her. As my wife, however, I consider that I have a perfect right to address her as Abeline. Her cousin, a young man fresh from college, rusticated, I hear, for misconduct, does not scruple, even in my presence, to call her so. Her family generally speak to her thus. Even some letters she receives bear that superscription, though all packages from dry-goods stores, etc., I notice, are marked distinctly "Mrs. Barry Gray." Why, then, I wonder, cannot I say Abeline? I like the name — and to my ears it has a most musical cadence. I think I shall adopt it altogether hereafter, and make it a household word.

Before the night — Christmas night — closed in, and while yet the nuts and wine were on the table, after the health of the many uninvited guests had been proposed by me and drank, I made to Mrs. Gray, if I may take her word for it, a delightful little speech. It is barely possible that this gem may find its way, by and by, into the newspapers. My wife, when alluding to it at the "sewing society," a day or two thereafter, to a select circle of friends, including the parson's wife, convened in a corner, praised it very warmly, and said she thought it equalled, if it did not surpass, some sermons to which she had listened. I have, of course, my own private opinion as to its merits, yet I feel it due to my modesty to state that I think Mrs.

Gray takes rather high grounds as regards its excellence. But if a generous amount could be raised by subscription among my many admirers, to defray the expense of its publication, I think I might be induced to let a noble-hearted public judge for itself as to its beauty and worth.

CHAPTER V.

Mrs. Gray's Idea of a Sleigh-ride. — My Brother-in-law's Rule. — A Little Turn in the Yard. — Who laughed? — Stylish Sleigh-bells. — Fleet Steed. — Mrs. G.'s Churchmanship. — Picking Pockets. — The Parson. Slightly Jealous. — Original Remark.

E had a snow-storm at Hillside one night; and the next morning, while at breakfast, I proposed to Mrs. Gray a sleigh-ride. I am happy to state that my proposal met with her entire approbation. "It is so nice, Mr. G.," said she, "to go bounding over the fleecy snow, behind a fleet steed, well wrapped up in buffalo-robes, hearkening to the merry notes of sleigh-bells, and breathing an atmosphere which, though cold, is yet delightful." It struck me that my wife's remark was slightly poetical. I was in the act of raising a cup of coffee to my lips when she commenced speaking, but I paused, with the cup in mid-air, till she had finished. Even after she had concluded, I remained in the same position, regarding her with astonishment. I paused so long she reminded me that not only was my coffee cooling, but I was spilling it on the table-cloth. Replacing the cup carefully by the side of my plate, and leaning slightly forward, I begged Mrs. Gray to repeat what she had just uttered in regard to "fleecy snow." Her only reply was, that I certainly was the most provoking man she had ever met. Most persons who know me will conclude from this that Mrs. G. has met but few men in her life. This, however, I have many reasons for thinking is not the case.

In a private letter, written unknown to his wife, which I received, a few days since, from my brother-in-law, who lives "Out West," he remarked he had, early in his married life, adopted the rule of never replying to, nor contradicting his wife, my respected sister, when she chanced to make assertions of a nature to cause him unpleasant feelings. I know that my brother-in-law makes a very good husband; therefore, in many instances, I choose to adopt his rules as my own, and by so doing I reap a benefit.

Instead, then, of replying to Mrs. Barry's last ungenerous remark, as some husbands would have done, I contented myself with praising the coffee, at the same time handing to her my cup to be refilled. It is surprising how susceptible to praise or blame, in the matter of coffee, is the excellent Mrs. G. In the present instance, what I said brought to her face one of the sunny smiles which, when I was a bachelor, had so great an attraction for me. I really thought my second cup, partly sweetened as it was by her smile, surpassed any former one of Mrs. Gray's preparing. I mentioned to her as much. She replied that it was all my imagination, for she knew it was neither better nor worse than that she usually gave me. I am inclined to think, notwithstanding this assertion, that there was an extra egg used to settle the coffee in question.

In resuming the subject of a sleigh-ride, my wife asked me where we should go. I replied I thought the village as good as anywhere. She said she thought so too. This point being settled, I ordered the little black boy, whom I suspect of sucking eggs, to harness the "sorrel" to the cutter. "And," I added, "put some straw into the bottom of the sleigh; and bring out the buffalo-robes; and don't forget to put the bells on the horse." The little black boy gave me to understand that he would faithfully attend to my instructions. When he had retired, I told Mrs. Gray my suspicions in regard to him. She had herself, she remarked, noticed the small number of eggs the boy brought in from the hennery, but she supposed that it was owing to some of the hens ceasing to lay. "If the egg crop should fail entirely, Mrs. Gray," I said, "it would be a very bad thing." She replied that she guessed I would think so, if there were none to settle the coffee with. I resolved thenceforth to watch that little black boy more closely. I felt that it would be very wrong for us to be without eggs. Somehow, too, I was sorry that the "old red" was dead. Not that I connected him exactly with the "egg troubles," but because I thought that on a farm one ought to have an "old red."

Being ready a few minutes before Mrs. Gray, I thought I would take a turn in the yard with the horse and sleigh, before starting for the village. Our yard is a good yard for the kind; but there are two or three old stumps, standing here and there within the enclosure. I suggested, several times during the past summer, to Mrs. G. that it would be well to eradicate these aged stumps from the lawn, as they disfigured it sadly. My wife, however, thought otherwise. "They are nice," she said, "for vines to clamber over." I found, on the present occasion, that they were slightly in the way. Being hidden from sight by the snow, I accidentally drove upon the largest of them, and in consequence I was turned out of the sleigh, and nearly smothered in the snow. When I got up, I looked like a polar bear; and I am sure I felt just as savage. I thought, too, I heard some one laugh. I turned around to see who it was who dared to laugh at me; but there was nobody in sight except the little black boy; and he, with his face from me, was busily engaged in cutting pumpkins for the cows. I concluded, then, that it was a young rooster out at the barn trying to crow. I don't like incipient chanticleers, unless they are broiled. One "old red" would be worth a dozen of them.

When I went into the house, after leading the horse back to where I started from, Mrs. Gray asked me what I had been doing. I replied, "I have been taking a little turn in the yard." As Mrs. G. and myself rode past, I pointed out to her the exact spot where I took the turn. She said that it did not surprise her, for I was such a rash driver. She professed to be glad, however, that I was not hurt. She supposed though that one of these days I would be killed — I was so reckless. Just then one runner of the sleigh went into a hollow, and Mrs. Gray, grasping the lines from my hands, caused the horse to swerve a little, and — over we went. After we had scrambled up, and I had righted the sleigh and placed Mrs. G. within it, she commented freely on my manner of driving, laying, woman-like, all the blame of the turn-over on my shoulders.

We had proceeded but a short distance from the scene of our late disaster, when Mrs. Gray called my attention to the singular sound the bells sent forth. It was something entirely different, I thought, from what sleigh-bells are capable of doing. At my wife's request, I stopped the horse, to examine into the matter. To my surprise, I discovered that, in addition to the appropriate string of bells, the large house-bell and a smaller table-bell were ingeniously fastened upon the neck of the horse. I told Mrs. Barry what manner of sleigh-bells we had, and, to my astonishment, she laughed till I thought she would fall out of the sleigh. She said they were very stylish. For my own part, I was indignant. I had great difficulty in undoing those bells. My fingers got very cold; and I think that I had very wicked thoughts in my heart regarding our little black boy. But I thought it best to do nothing rash: I determined, however, to make him wear one of those bells around his neck for a week. When I told Mrs. Gray how I should punish him, she replied that it would be hard for her to hear the noise of the bell, but that she thought the boy himself would be rather pleased with it.

" Where," said I to Mrs. Gray, as we entered the village, " shall I drive our fleet steed ? " It may be as well to mention, that the " fleet steed " here referred to is what some would call a good family horse: one warranted to stand without tying; one never known to jog faster than five miles an hour; and which a child of tender years can manage. The time he makes on the road between Hillside and the post-office, a distance of three miles, varies from one to one and a quarter hours, — though I have, when I thought dinner was awaiting me and I feared Mrs. G.'s displeasure, accomplished the distance in forty-five minutes. But this is of so rare an occurrence as scarcely to warrant me in saying that he could do the like again. To the question propounded at the beginning of this paragraph, Mrs. Gray replied, without hesitation, "To the parsonage."

Of course it pleases me that my wife admires and loves the church. I have no objection even to her taking an active part in the "sewing circle" which is connected with the same. The interest she manifests in the prosperity of the parish school is, moreover, deserving of praise. Engaged, as the vestry is at this time, in raising funds to enable them to erect a very tall spire on the new church, it may be excusable in her to lighten my pockets, as she does every night, of any superfluous change which may chance to be in them; but after allowing all this, I do not perceive the advantage derivable of visiting the parsonage as often as Mrs. G. proposes. I have no hesitation in saying that I am myself a great admirer of the parson. I am indebted to him for several good things. When I was quite an infant, he baptized me. I shall ever be grateful to him for this. Then again, after I had arrived to manhood and began to be regarded as a bachelor, he performed another act, which it will be impossible for me ever to forget. I allude to the ceremony which made Mrs. Gray my wife. How grateful I am to him for this, I will not here say. I sometimes think that Mrs. G. is more grateful to him for this little act than it is really necessary for her to be. I was glad, therefore, when we called at the parsonage, to find that the inmates were abroad. I mentioned as much to Mrs. Gray. She replied that it was very wicked in me to say so.

As we slowly rode back to Hillside, Mrs. G. occupied the time with a little discourse — or, as I called it, sermon — on jealousy. An original remark that she made, beginning thus, " Trifles light as air," and closing with the words " holy writ," was, as she said, pertinent to the occasion, and, she added in conclusion, she hoped I would profit by it.

Several days have elapsed since the above recounted sleigh-ride came off. The little black boy is expiating his offence by wearing a bell, as I proposed ; he seems rather proud of it, however, and feels the punishment most when Mrs. Gray insists on his muffling the clapper : this I kindly allow him to do in consideration of her headaches. I am myself profiting by the original remark of Mrs. G., and have so far overcome my feelings as to invite the parson to a little tea-party at Hillside, which is set down for next Monday evening.

CHAPTER VI.

Mrs. Gray's Excitement. — What occasioned it. — Upon the Hay. — My
Audience. — His Opinion. — Fire and Smoke. — Oh, Abeline! — Mrs.
G.'s Remarks. — A Poem or a Sermon. — The Poem.

RS. GRAY returned from the village, a few days
since, in a high state of excitement. When Mrs.
G. becomes thus, which I am happy to say is
seldom, I notice that the little black boy performs his
"chores" with great celerity and exactness. On the present occasion he was unusually brisk in his movements.
Even the fat cook in the kitchen stepped very lightly in
her shoes. The farm-dog, Watch, who considers himself,
I think, an important member of the household, I perceived
making his exit from the backdoor, with drooping tail and
crestfallen air. Immediately after noticing this state of
things, I retired to my library, and commenced writing a
letter of inquiry to my brother-in-law, who, as I think I
have mentioned in former chapters, lives " Out West." I
experienced, however, great difficulty in concentrating my
thoughts on the letter in question. It appeared to me as
though I was in some way connected with the cause of the
house-warming then taking place. I wondered what the
trouble was all about. My excellent wife had said nothing
to me by which I could infer that I was, even in the most
remote manner, connected with the present difficulty ; but
I augured from certain looks she gave me that I was, after
all, at the bottom of the mischief. It is astonishing how
soon a man, after he becomes a husband, learns to interpret
aright the side-looks and glances which he is apt now and
then to receive from his spouse.

When Mrs. Gray, therefore, entered the library, I felt slightly uncomfortable. Nor was this feeling in the least toned down when she abruptly remarked that she never thought I would be guilty of doing such a thing. "What thing, Mrs. Gray," I humbly asked, "do you refer to?" "Why, writing those Hillside Sketches, Mr. Gray," she replied. "You know well enough," she continued, "how little truth there is in them, and yet everybody in the whole world will believe every sentence you have written." I was completely thunder-struck. I had no idea that my wife would ever have learned aught concerning them. I had not thought that any one within a hundred miles of Hillside would be likely to get hold of the papers containing them. It struck me, at the moment, that the "Home Journal," in which they were published, must possess a very wide circulation. The copy I receive I am particular to hide from Mrs. Gray. I generally retire to the barn when I read the numbers. I have a place up high on the hay where I sit. It is there that I keep the papers on file. The little black boy knows the exact spot. I am in the habit of reading them to him up there. He is my audience. He was so tickled with what I wrote about his sucking eggs that he tumbled off the hay upon the floor; but, as he struck on his head, no harm ensued.

When, at Mrs. Gray's earnest request, I gave up smoking in the house, it was to the hay-mow that I retreated. Here, with my cigar and newspaper, I passed many pleasant hours. Being questioned by Mrs. G. one day as to what I was doing in the barn, I replied that I was smoking. I may as well here confess that what I then heard in regard to setting barns on fire, effectually deterred me from carrying out my smoking arrangement. Since then, whenever Mrs. Gray asks what is engaging my attention in that cheerless barn, I reply that I am hunting for eggs. I felt satisfied in my own mind that she did not know about these letters. So that when she made the attack on me, as mentioned above, I was utterly unprepared to reply. It took me some time to collect my scattered thoughts. At first I could but murmur " Oh, Abeline !" This I repeated some five or six times. Afterwards I said, distinctly and with great emphasis, " Mrs. Gray, don't." Mrs. G., however, I am sorry to say, paid no attention to my request, but continued her remarks, saying, " Yes, Mr. Gray, it is not pleasant thus to have one's domestic privacy published to the world, so that all our acquaintances may know exactly what we are doing at Hillside. Why could n't you, Mr. Gray, if you would write these letters, have adopted some name, and not paraded Barry Gray at the head of each of them ? Never, Mr. Gray, in all my life, have I been so shocked as I was this afternoon, when a gentleman, a banker, Mr. G., said that he was sorry we did not give the Christmas dinner at Hillside, as we proposed. At first I thought one of your bachelor abominations, who had lost a good dinner, had reported some story about it ; but when he asked me if I had been troubled lately with nervous headaches, I tell you, Mr. Gray, I was angry enough. I wished to know what he meant ; and then — out the whole thing came. He found the papers for me, and there, in his office, I read them. When I had finished them, I told him I thought that they were just the meanest things I had ever read. He replied, he thought so, too : adding, also, that everybody in the village had seen them, and pronounced them ' quite idiotic.' " I could bear this no longer ; so I interrupted Mrs. Gray by saying, " Allow me, Mrs. G., to differ in regard to what everybody pronounces them to be, and to declare that I consider them remarkable productions ; and in this opinion, my dear, I am sustained by our little black boy."

" If," commenced Mrs. Gray, in a softer tone, thinking that, perhaps, my feelings were hurt by what she had said, — " if you would write some poetry, similar to that you used to write before we were married, love, and have it published, why I think that would be something worth while. Or, if you would compose a good sermon and present it to the parson, at his donation party, that, too, would be worthy of your attention ; but don't, for goodness' sake, Mr. Gray, write any more letters from Hillside."

Before I had time to answer Mrs. G., she was called away to attend to some household affairs. I was glad of it, for it gave me an opportunity to write in a style which I knew would please her, and at the same time be a source of delight to myself. She desired some poetry, and I resolved that she should have it. After a few minutes' consideration, I composed, much to my own satisfaction, the following lines, addressed

TO OUR LITTLE BLACK BOY.

Come hither, little black boy,
  For once let us agree ;
What dost thou most in life enjoy ?
  Reveal the truth to me.

Art thou most fond of gay attire,
  Blue jackets, waistcoats red ?
Or doth thy boyish mind aspire
  To own a horse and sled ?

Say, art thou proud of doing " chores "
  About my Hillside home ?
Or hadst thou rather out of doors,
  Through woods and meadows roam ?

Dost like full well, thou simple one,
  Amidst the hay to be,
And, all thy morning's labors done,
  Learn there thy A B C ?

Or hadst thou rather plague the cook ;
  Or tease old Watch, so brave ;
Or skate upon the frozen brook ;
  Or strive the cat to shave ?

No, no ; these things, my darkey **boy,**
   Though dearly prized by thee,
Are not what **most** thou dost enjoy,
   Nor most displeasest me.

But this it is — know all **my friends !** —
   Thou 'dst rather lose thy legs,
Take up with life's stray odds and ends,
   Than give up sucking eggs.

When I had completed this admirable poem, I invited into the library **my** excellent wife, and, with considerable feeling, read it aloud to her. She did not, however, compliment it as highly as I hoped she would. She said that it was not quite the thing she expected. She thought something more sentimental — something more particularly addressed to herself, as my wife — would be preferable ; but she added that it showed a desire on my part to please her, which, in itself, was gratifying.

Of course I shall write no more Hillside Sketches, unless the Editors of the " Home Journal " will promise me not to send their paper to this part of the country ; as it would never do for Mrs. Gray, subject, as she is, to nervous headaches, to find any more papers containing my productions.

CHAPTER VII.

Mrs Gray visits her Mother. — My Sorrow. — I invite a few Friends. — The Cook's Exodus. — Elevation of the Little Black Boy. — Equestrian Sports. My Regard for Mrs. G. — The Poem.

MRS. GRAY, my esteemed wife, has gone to visit her mother. I expect Mrs. G. will be absent from Hillside a month. When I went with her to the retired place where her mother resides, I had the forethought to inquire if the "Home Journal" was received there. To my surprise, I found that the paper was unknown in that vicinity, for the reasons that there was no post-office there, and that my wife's mother was the only person in the place who could either read or write! Hence I resolved that, on my return home, I would write one or two additional Hillside Sketches.

I am certain that Mrs. Gray will not see them during her absence; and as soon as she comes back, I will let her know about it. I question not but her joy at meeting me will be so great that she will willingly overlook the circumstance. Of course I deeply regret the absence of my estimable spouse. It was painful for me to consent to her going. I felt, though, that it was my duty. Our family physician recommended it. He thought a change of air would be of benefit to her. I trust that it will be the means of effectually curing the nervous headaches to which she is subject.

I found it very lonesome at Hillside the first few days after my wife's departure. I missed her very much indeed. I kept her daguerreotype constantly opened before me, when I was in the house during the day; and at night I slept with it under my pillow. I found it to be a source of great comfort to me. The little black boy, too, missed her exceedingly. He complained one morning to me of the coffee the cook gave him. He said it was not as good as that Mrs. Gray made. I believe he was right. I ventured to call the cook's attention to the matter. She told me, somewhat abruptly, that if it did n't suit me, I had better make it myself. I made no reply to this, but walked out of the kitchen in a very dignified manner. I remembered that my **wife said to me,** just before she left home, I had better not have **any words** with the cook; **and this is the** reason **why** I **kept silent.**

I never regretted any one's absence more than I did Mrs. Gray's. At first, I was very low-spirited. On the third day, my usual cheerfulness returned. So I rode down to the village, and invited several of my bachelor friends to stay with me during Mrs. G.'s absence. All, to a man, accepted my invitation. They were particular, however, to inquire the exact length of time Mrs. Gray would be absent. They came up from the village with me that evening to tea, and remained till after breakfast the following morning. They have done the like every day since. We have fine times together. We call ourselves "the happy family." My friends have the run of the house, generally, and the larder in particular. They kept the cook very busy. She was in a state of constant excitement. The fourth day after their coming, she left, with her bandboxes, for parts unknown. I did not consider this kind. When Mrs. Gray hired her, it was with the understanding that she should give us a week's warning before she went away. She did not, I am sorry to say, fulfil her contract. She stopped work in the middle of her month. Moreover, she overdrew her slender salary by two and sixpence, the night previous to her departure. I could not conceive why, on the following morning, the bell for breakfast was not rung.

At length I requested my friends to accompany me in a body to the kitchen, that I might hear the reason. From the little black boy we learnt, to our surprise, the state of the case. I immediately took prompt measures to get up a breakfast. I raised the little black boy, somewhat against his inclination, to the situation of cook. Should he follow that vocation a series of years, I have no doubt but that he would improve considerably. There is room, at all events, for it. Still, everything considered, I think we live quite well enough at Hillside. We have a pair of chickens every morning for breakfast; we cut a ham twice a week; we follow up the hens that lay eggs, very closely; we are extremely lavish with the cream; we use the butter with a liberal hand; there is no end to the buckwheat cakes we eat; and, in the matter of coffee, why I forget the exact number of pounds consumed per day, but it is a large quantity.

After the cook's departure, I found it quite a job to feed the work-hands; so I gave them a week's holiday. Of course, the horses would stand idle in the stable, only I allow my friends the use of them, in going to and from the village. When we go down on horseback, we make quite an imposing appearance. The first time we rode into the village, the small boys shouted to each other that the circus had come. We generally go out of our direct course a short distance, that we may pass by the Female College. It is my opinion that the young ladies in that institution are pretty well off in the item of white handkerchiefs. I sometimes think that I should like to have Mrs. Gray behold us. I believe she would be slightly astonished. I am not altogether satisfied, in my own mind, however, that she would be fully pleased to see us. I think my friends, if it were put to vote, would object to meeting her. I trust that she will write me when she is ready to return home, so that I can meet her at the depot. I should like, too, to have the house well aired, so that there shall be no tobacco-smoke lurking in the corners of the rooms. I should like, also, to find a good cook, who will take the place of the late departed one. There are several other little things which it would be only proper and decent in me to attend to, prior to Mrs. Gray's return. I do fervently trust that she will not come upon me unaware.

I pass the greater part of each day in the village with my friends. We take a slight repast at the "Arbour," about noon; but we save the bulk of our appetites till we return to Hillside, in the evening, when we partake of a hearty supper. We have rather exciting times going home. We get up private races on the road. My tall friend, Mr. P., on the pony, generally wins the race. It is a treat to see him assist the pony over the ground. When my tall friend asked me what I thought of his riding, I replied it was my opinion that six legs were even better than four. In this opinion I was fully sustained by my other friends.

I am sorry to say that I enjoy my present course of life very much. It seems to me as though my bachelor days had come back. I should not like, however, for Mrs. Gray to know the extent of my feelings in this matter. It is not probable she ever will. I believe that I am a very good husband to Mrs. Gray. It certainly is my intention so to be. I have written Mrs. G. several letters since I left her at her mother's residence. I have also addressed some verses to her, which I think will gratify her. I like to gratify my wife. I think it is the duty of every husband to gratify his wife, to a certain extent. If I can please Mrs. Gray by writing poetry, why, I will write reams of it, provided I have that much paper. Before I sent the lines in question to Mrs. G., I took the precaution of reading them aloud to my bachelor friends. The few amendments which they suggested, I readily made; and when I had done so, they individually expressed themselves highly delighted with the production. Simply to oblige them, and because they insisted on my doing so, I have included the

lines in the present chapter. I am free to confess that, as a
poetical composition, it falls far short of a great number of
chance poems which I have read. I may be allowed to say,
without overstepping the bounds of that modesty which
hedges me about, that it is far from approximating, in point
of excellence, even to some former pieces from my Muse.
The postscript, which was added by my friend Frank, seems
to me equal, if not better than the verses preceding it. In
fear and trembling, then, I confide these precious lines into
the hands of — the printer.

TO MY ABSENT WIFE.

There is a grief within my heart,
  A sorrow in my brain,
That causes foolish tears to start,
  And fills my life with pain.

It came the very hour you passed
  From out my loving sight;
And, till we meet again, 't will last,
  To shroud my soul in night.

The brightest day to me is dark;
  No evening shows a star;
And all too well my pulses mark
  How long the moments are.

I walk about our Hillside home,
  And listen for your voice;
But ah! no music tones will come,
  To make my soul rejoice.

I cannot enter any room,
  But something there I view,
Which, though it fills my heart with gloom,
  Reminds me, love, of you.

Some trifle, which your gentle hands
  Once worked, and laid aside;
The very collar, and the bands
  You wore when first my bride.

A bit of edging, dropped by chance
 Upon the chamber-floor;
The mirror which your sunny glance
 Has idly wandered o'er.

A dainty ruffle you had worn
 Around your throat so fair ;
The very spot where, night and morn,
 You kneel in silent prayer.

These things, and more, my darling **wife,**
 Bring freshly to my mind
Our early days of wedded life,
 Left far, alas ! behind.

'T is dark — all dark around me, now,
 Since **you, my** pride, have fled :
And I go up **and** down the house,
 Like spirit from the dead.

I do not laugh — I scarcely speak —
 My appetite is gone ;
The red has vanished from my cheek,
 And I am quite forlorn.

My whiskers go untrimmed, my **dear ;**
 My hair is turning gray ;
And soon my friends will mark, I fear,
 My buttons giving way.

Indeed, I live a hermit's life,
 And shall, till you come home.
Few men appreciate a wife
 Until abroad she roam !

Then, oh ! return, my precious one ;
 Yes, hasten, love, to me ;
And all the sparkling things I 've **done**
 You will be pleased to see.

POSTSCRIPT.

Still, if your mother wants you, **dear,**
 With her you 'd better stay,
Until the spring-time of the year ;
 Then come to

BARRY GRAY.

CHAPTER VIII.

State of Mrs. Gray's Health. — The Party. — Frank as Mrs. Gray. — Stampede of Bachelors. — The New Red. — The Little Black Boy's Friendship. — His Cooking. — His Tricks. — Puns. — Treating the Little Black Boy.

HAVE received several letters lately from Mrs. Gray. She writes very encouragingly in regard to her health. The nervous headaches, to which she is subject, are, I am happy to state, not as severe as they were formerly. She **says that she will** be ready to return home in the **course of a week,** provided I will go for her. I have doubts **as** to whether I shall be able to leave the farm **before next** month. Affairs at home, I think, **require** my strictest attention. Besides, it **would not be** polite **in me** to say to my bachelor **friends** that **they had** better go down town again, for I expected Mrs. Gray home; especially as I invited them to pass a month with me, **and** as yet but two **weeks have** elapsed. Moreover, it would be awkward for me to tell them to depart. They feel so much **at home,** that, really, I could n't do it. It would be like turning my brothers out of the house. Then, too, we have plans to be consummated, of very pleasing character. I **should** not like to be obliged to give them up.

At the earnest solicitation of my bachelor friends, I have consented to give a party at Hillside, and, in fact, have sent out the invitations. This little affair will come off, *Deo volente,* on **the evening** of Washington's birthday. It will be, I suppose, **a sort of** bachelors' ball. **My** friends' names, as managers, appear on the notes **of** invitation. The guests are expected to come in fancy costumes. I alone, being the host, do not intend to array myself in borrowed plumes. My friend Frank is to personate Mrs. Gray. He has shaved off his whiskers, and has purchased some flowing ringlets for the occasion. He is practising the character in private before me. The rehearsals are exceedingly amusing. Fortunately Mrs. G. did not take her party-dresses with her; all other articles, however, of feminine attire, I have been unable to discover. I fear the cook carried them away. Frank has been obliged, therefore, to borrow from his large circle of lady friends many garments, which, if Mrs. G.'s wardrobe were larger than it is, I should have been happy to supply him with. When he returned from the village the other evening, he brought behind him, on horseback, a pillow-case filled with the necessary garments. Had it not been for my superior knowledge in the matter, he would never have gotten them properly on. So well did he look and act the part of Mrs. Gray, that my heart beat fast as I gazed at him. The little black boy, coming into the room at the moment, was fearfully astonished. He turned quickly about at the sight, and running down-stairs, told my bachelor friends there assembled that Mrs. Gray had come, and they had better cut and run. There was considerable scampering among them, just then, and I was surprised to see them, through an upper window, making tracks for the gate. They were all bareheaded except one, and he had on my white hat, which had slipped down over his eyes. I thought, first, that the dog was after them; then I feared the house was on fire; and, afterwards, I wondered if the cook had returned. While they were endeavoring to unlatch the gate, I called to them, and asked what was the matter. My voice apparently reassured them, and, after a slight consultation which they held together, they came slowly and cautiously back — all, except my tall friend P., who had scaled the gate and reached the foot of the hill. I may as well here state that we saw nothing of Mr. P for two whole days thereafter.

Ever since the demise of the "Old Red," I 've felt badly. It did not seem right to live on a farm with no Red to wake one o' mornings. The crow they get up is a peculiar one. I honestly believe that the cock Peter heard was red. After travelling about the country for weeks, in search of a chanticleer to take the place of the "Old Red," I at last succeeded in finding one. The old lady who owned him was sorry to part with him, — he had been so long in the family, she said, that he seemed like one of 'em ; but the little inducement I offered, in the shape of a gold dollar, was all-sufficient to atone for his loss. When I inquired his age, the old lady took down a bundle of almanacs, and, turning to one of some years' standing, showed me the day, marked with a bit of red chalk, wherein, she said, he was hatched. Counting up the years on my fingers, I found they amounted to twelve. This I considered perfectly satisfactory. It is the age, too, of our little black boy. Of course, he and the "New Red" are great friends. In fact, they are intimate friends : so intimate that chanticleer has taught the lad to crow ; and the little black boy imitates him so perfectly that it is impossible to say which crows the more naturally. Sometimes I think the rooster excels, and then again I am constrained to award the palm to the Ethiopian. The other night, about twelve o'clock, the hour when all honest country folks are asleep, the whole house was alarmed by a series of crowings going on in the little black boy's apartment. Accompanied by all my friends, I marched resolutely up to his room. There I found the ebony youth, sitting on the cross rail of the bedstead, fast asleep, and crowing after the manner of the "New Red." I was in hopes that he would not be guilty of this offence a second time ; but there is scarcely a night wherein he does not arouse us with his untimely crowing. It is an old saying, that one good turn deserves another. I mentioned above that the rooster taught the little black boy to crow. As a set-off to this, I caught the little black boy one day with a number of the " Home Journal" and my copy of Worcester's Dictionary, unabridged, in his hands, teaching the Red to read.

My confidence in the African lad is returning. The hens appear to be coming in. Fresh eggs are quite plentiful. To what this state of things is owing, I can scarcely say. I think that the lines I addressed to the individual above referred to, and which I read to him one day in the barn, before sending them to the " Journal" for publication, had a good effect. I think by the time *Paus* comes, the supply of eggs will be large. It takes the little black boy to cook eggs. He gets them up for the table in a variety of forms. His favorite style is to scramble them. Any dish requiring considerable stirring, I notice, he "admires" to cook. Since I elevated him to the rank of cook, he has grown quite important. I discovered, the other day, that he was wearing one of my standing collars. I often see my boots going to the well when I certainly am not accompanying them. Coming home yesterday, quite unexpectedly, I caught the little rascal freshly lathered, and using my best razor on his sooty chin. The additional lathering he received, on account of this performance, however, was not applied to his face. While laboring under the excitement attendant on this correction, he struck, just before supper-time, for higher wages. I immediately checked his further demands by depositing him in a snow-bank. My friend Frank remarked that I should have given him a check on a bank of violets, payable in the spring. My equestrian friend P. thought that I drew rather too taut a check-rein on the lad; while Fred said that a negro's life was checkered enough under whosesoever reign he dwelt. After having rained these witticisms on me, they very prudently retired to their rooms. I wish Mrs. G. had been home : I think she would have checkmated them all.

When the little black boy had finished his chores for the day, and was preparing to go to bed, I called him into the library and lectured him severely on his misconduct ; and, in conclusion, I asked him if he were not ashamed of himself. To my surprise he distinctly gave me to understand that he was not ; adding that he only wished Mrs. Gray was home. His reply quite alarmed me. It sounded very much to my ears like a threat. I felt that it would never do for Mrs. G. to know everything that had taken place at Hillside during her absence. The knowledge might, I feared, be the means of bringing on again those terrible nervous headaches. So I resolved to adopt a more conciliatory tone with my ebony friend. I asked him if he slept warm, and told him to take an extra blanket from the closet as he went up-stairs. I also treated him to a slice of my own wedding-cake and a brandy peach, both of which he relished exceedingly. When he left me I heard him, as he passed through the hall, say to himself that this was pretty tall kind of feed for a little black boy. I feel satisfied now that I can depend fully on that child for a long time to come ; or, at least, so long as the cake and peaches last.

CHAPTER IX.

The Village Newspaper.—Washington's Birthday Ball.— Festivities at Hillside. — State of the House after the Party. — Loneliness. — Cowardly Bachelors. — Old Beaux. — Keeping Pasch. — A Rhymed Note of Invitation

THE following notice which I clipped from the columns of the village newspaper, issued the Monday following the 22d of February, fully describes the little affair that came off at Hillside on that glorious day. It is written in the peculiarly happy style for which the editor is famous, and is remarkable for its candor and truthfulness. A desire on my part to lay before my readers a satisfactory account of the festivities at Hillside on that occasion, induces me to transfer the article in question to these pages. The demand in the village for the number containing it has been immense, and though an extra edition was struck off, yet it has been found impossible to supply the call for it. I alone took thirty copies, and each of my bachelor friends twenty-five. The editor assured me, in a confidential chat which we held together in his *sanctum*, that he had made a very good thing out of it, and mentioned the exact amount he expected to realize by the operation. In a later number of his journal he published a very polite note, subscribed by himself and one or two other gentlemen connected with his printing-office, asking me to repeat the ball, — that is, give another one similar in every respect. For various reasons, — mostly of a private nature, however, and, therefore, best known to myself, — I have been obliged to refuse. The reason I gave him for thus doing, and which may be called the public one, was, that the party or ball being a strictly birthday festival given in celebration of the birth of Washington, — which anniversary unfortunately occurs but once a year, — I considered, therefore, that it would be impossible for me to oblige him.   I mentioned in my reply that I regretted this exceedingly, and concluded by quoting the following lines, wherein I substituted " Washington " for the name rightly belonging thereto : —

> "Long shall we seek his likeness — long in vain,
> And turn to all of him which may remain ;
> Sighing that Nature formed but one such man,
> And broke the die in moulding Washington."

The community about Hillside kindly attribute the above lines to my Muse, and commend them exceedingly, but persons better acquainted with English poetry will have no hesitancy in naming the author.

[From the Star Spangled Banner.]

FESTIVITIES AT HILLSIDE.

" We had the honor, on Friday evening the 22d February, of making one of the numerous and fashionable company assembled at Hillside to celebrate the anniversary of the birthday of General George Washington. By agreement, the invited guests met at an early hour at the Spread Eagle Tavern, where sleighs were in waiting to convey them to Hillside. The procession, when formed, made a most imposing appearance. The village band marched at the head of it, discoursing most elegant music ; while the committee, — Mr. Gray's particular bachelor friends, — mounted on magnificent chargers, brought up the rear. The company all appeared in fancy costumes. We and our better half sustained the characters of Punch and Judy. It was, perhaps, because we felt bound to keep up the character we had assumed that, during the evening, we devoted so much time to imbibing our own particular namesake, which we found cold on the sideboard in the East-room.

"But our attention was not exclusively confined to this noble beverage; for we recollect dipping freely into the oyster-soup, likewise into the ice-cream and brandy-peaches. We are not totally forgetful of the tenderness of the boned turkey, or the excellent flavor of the venison. Of smaller items — such as raisins, almonds, cakes, etc. — our provident spouse brought home, in her capacious pockets, enough to keep the children feasting several days. It is not true, however, that we, 'OURSELF,' had our hat full of hard-boiled eggs when we left Hillside; this is a base slander, and we cast it into the teeth of those who report it.

"It would scarcely be delicate in us to particularize the persons present. We mention a few, however, who kindly have given us permission to use their names. Among the first, we noticed Frank, who, as Mrs. Gray, acted her lady-ship to perfection. We were received by him as we entered, and supposed that it was Mrs. G. herself; nor did we discover our error until late in the evening. Mr. H—— enacted the part of 'Sam's around' in a most happy manner. Mr. C——, as a locomotive, was powerful; while the lady who hung on his arm as a 'tender,' was sweet. Messrs. P—— and S—— came together as the Siamese Twins; the deception would have been complete were it not for the difference in their height. Mr. Gray's equestrian friend, P——, appeared in the costume of a Highland chief, and produced a remarkable effect. These names are all that we are at liberty to mention. There are many more of whom we should like to have the public hear, but feel that it would not be safe for us so to do. We must not, however, forget the little black boy, who was a feature of the evening, — sustaining as he did the character of 'the New Red,' Mr. Gray's favorite rooster. It would be impossible to imagine it better done, even by the Red himself.

"In bringing this slight sketch to a conclusion, we will simply add that the festivities were kept up till a late hour, and the whole affair most creditably sustained. Too great thanks cannot be awarded to Mr. Gray and the committee for their part in the getting up of this delightful party."

Thus says the editor of the "Star-Spangled Banner." I feel — and I mentioned as much to my friends — that it would be needless for me, after transcribing this, to render any further account of the proceedings. "Enough is as good as a feast;" and in connection with this remark, I will add that we had enough left, after our birthday feast, to keep us from famishing for several days following. It is astonishing to me how wasteful people are on such occasions. How utterly regardless, too, of soiling and spoiling one's carpets. There was no apartment but exhibited some little memento of the supper, — a turkey-leg, a pickled oyster, a sandwich, a piece of cake, a bit of jelly, or something else of the kind, was scattered miscellaneously throughout the house. The way the little black boy and myself worked during the following week, "cleaning up," was worthy of a better cause. For my part, I feared that Mrs. Gray might return and find "things" around generally, which would not prove very agreeable, I felt certain, to either of us.

I am afraid, notwithstanding my efforts to the contrary, that Mrs. Gray will learn all about the party, and a number of other occurrences which have taken place at Hillside since her departure, which I should be sorry for her to know. I am beginning to wish, however, that Mrs. G. would come back; I think I should like to hear the sound of her voice once more. I know that I should like to feel the clasp of her hand, and press my lips to hers again. I am getting lonely up here. Since the party, my bachelor friends have deserted me. They say the snow is so deep and the weather so cold that they can't go to Hillside any more   I don't think the reason is a good one ; they used to come here when the snow was quite as deep, and the weather colder by twenty degrees. No ! I believe that they are fearful Mrs. Gray will return home and catch them. I can't imagine why they should be afraid of Mrs. G. She never hurt any one of them. It is n't like her to wish to do so. To be sure, as a general thing, she does not admire them, and speaks of them, I allow, in a very un-generous manner. But that is nothing. My brother-in-law, who lives " Out West," writes me that his wife, my amiable sister, used to act just so ; but after a spell she overcame it. I think that in time my own wife will like-wise overcome it. At all events, I hope so.

In the last letter received by me from Mrs. G., she named the day on which she should be home. A gentle-man, — one of her old *friends*, — she wrote, who was going to New York, would escort her to Hillside. I noticed in Mrs. G.'s letter that the word " friend " was quite blotted. On examining it closely, I found that some other word had been erased and friend substituted for it. I think the erased word was *flames*. Very likely he is one of my wife's old beaux. I hate Mrs. G.'s old beaux. What business have old beaux to be travelling about the country with married women for, I should like to know ! If he comes to Hillside, I think I 'll give the little black boy a holiday, and suggest to him the fun of pelting Mrs. G.'s old flame with eggs. The little black boy will do it, I know.

After all, I am sorry that Mrs. Gray will be home so soon. I think it would have been better for her health to have remained with her mother till after Easter. I have made some preparations for celebrating Pasch in the true Dutch style, with which, I fear, her coming may interfere. To be sure, I might celebrate the day in advance ; and then, too, a week-day would, after all, be the properest under the circumstances. I believe I shall adopt this plan ; and I will decide on the day before that which ushers Mrs. G. back to Hillside. I will notify my friends, therefore, to that effect; and, at the same time, I will send them, addressed as follows,

A RHYMED NOTE OF INVITATION TO MY BACHELOR FRIENDS.

Come up from the village, ye bachelors gay;
You 're welcome to Hillside this bright sunny day :
Though the buttons be off of your shirts and your coats,
And your chins all unshaven, and shaggy as goats.

Come up, though your sisters may fret and may pout,
And your fond mothers scold, when·they find you are out;
Though your sweethearts, by turns, be both tearful and cross
When they learn where you 're going to celebrate Paus.

Never mind what they do — never care what they say —
But to Hillside repair without any delay;
For the hens have come in, and the eggs are quite fresh,
And they 're better to-day than fish, pudding, or flesh.

But don't be alarmed, you 'll get plenty to eat,
For the larder is stored full of pastry and meat;
Fowls, oysters, and game — the last from the West —
My brother, who lives there, has sent me the best.

And down in the cellar are bottles of wine,
In original packages, line upon line;
With a barrel of cider — another of ale,
To keep our hearts mellow when sorrows prevail.

I know it is wrong, in these temperance days,
For me to be praising such things in my lays;
But a love for them runs through our family tree,
From my grandfather Timothy downward to me.

The evil, too, rests not so much in the glass
Which we drain to the health of some favorite lass,
As it does with ourselves, and 't is yours as 't is mine,
If we drink to excess of the blood of the vine.

Perhaps you would find, should you question me close,
I partake of these things as a medical dose;

For our family doctor is friendly to me,
And prescribes them whatever my symptoms may be.

Forgive this digression, ye bachelors gay !
It dropped from my pen in the easiest way ;
And so, to return to my subject, I 'll add,
To see you at Hillside will make me most glad.

My wife, as you know, has departed from town,
To visit her mother, the good Mrs. Brown ;
And I, left alone, have invited you all
To breakfasts, to suppers, and one little ball.

And now, as a close to this season of fun,
I propose a Paus dinner, and then I have done ;
For Mrs. Gray writes me, come sun, wind, or rain,
She 'll return on the morrow to Hillside again.

Then, farewell, my bachelor friends, for a while :
I shall dwell the next season in Mrs. Gray's smile,
Be careful of all I may say, drink, or eat,
And walk by her side with most circumspect feet.

CHAPTER X.

Mrs. Gray returns Home. — Our Meeting. — The Tall Man. — Mrs. G.'s Commiseration. — Her Discoveries. — Bribing the Little Black Boy Finding Eggs. — The Paus Dinner. — Postscript.

MRS. GRAY has returned home. The meeting between Mrs. G. and myself was of an affecting character. I met my estimable spouse at the depot. She came on the night express. It was exactly fifty-five minutes past eleven P. M. when I was aroused from a short nap in which I was indulging, in the "ladies' room," by the sound of the engine-whistle for the train to "break up." Three minutes thereafter I had the extreme felicity of welcoming Mrs. Gray. It is not necessary, however, for me to particularize the style of our greeting. Several of my bachelor friends, who were watching us from a safe distance, confessed to me afterwards that they quite envied me on that occasion. One of them, I hear, offered himself to a young lady the following evening. I regret to say, however, that she refused him. I understand that he speaks of that young lady now in terms anything but complimentary.

I noticed that a tall man assisted Mrs. Gray to alight from the cars. I perceived, moreover, that Mrs. G. immediately took the tall man's arm. As soon as I could work my way through the crowd to where Mrs. G. and the tall man stood, I did so. When Mrs. Gray saw me, she withdrew her arm from that of the tall man and stepped forward to meet me. Then it was that what followed made my bachelor friends envious. I felt glad that the tall man witnessed our meeting. I thought at the time that he did not consider it an agreeable sight, for he immediately said, that, as he had Mrs. Gray's checks in his possession, he would see about her baggage. As I had no objection to his collecting together her trunks, I did not offer any opposition. I simply directed the little black boy to keep an eye on the tall man, however, and show him the proper sleigh in which to place them.

While I awaited the little black boy's return, Mrs. G. told me the tall man's name; mentioning at the same time, seemingly in his behalf, that she had been acquainted with him a great many years. If there is anything I dislike hearing about, it is of Mrs. Gray's old acquaintances. It does n't seem proper to me that my wife should have been acquainted with any one previous to her knowing me. It is n't pleasant to sit and hear another than myself speaking to Mrs. G. of events that occurred ever so long ago, before I knew her, and of persons whom I don't know and don't care to know. And now here turned up this tall man —an old acquaintance, forsooth! and who, as I mentioned in a former chapter, I more than half suspected to be one of Mrs. Gray's old flames. I believe I had a very wicked wish concerning him.

When the tall man returned, Mrs. Gray introduced me. I told him I was happy to make his acquaintance! When, shortly afterwards, I thought of these words, I feared that I had not told the truth. Just then Mrs. G. suggested to me, in a whisper, that it would be no more than polite to invite her friend to Hillside. To this I assented, but remarked confidentially to my wife that the cook had absconded a few weeks since. That settled the matter; and Mrs. G. immediately thanked him for his kindness to her, and hoped the next time he visited E—— that he would not neglect to come to Hillside.

As we rode towards home, I revealed to my wife, so far as I considered it prudent, the state of affairs there. She said it was very wrong in the cook to have deserted her

post. She wished I had informed her of it; she feared I had fared poorly; she simply wondered I was not starved; she felt sorry for me; she thought I must have been very lonely; she greatly admired the "lines" I had sent her, — and to show her appreciation of them, she repeated them aloud for my gratification. She asked how I had occupied myself in her long absence? I told her that I had been studying Hebrew. She was astonished at it, and trusted I had not injured my health by too close application. I confessed to having invited one or two of my bachelor friends to dinner. Mrs. Gray thereupon said she was glad I had, for it must have been very tedious for me during her absence.

Several times, as we rode along, I thought I heard the little black boy laugh. I think it wrong for little black boys to laugh at their superiors. Considering the exalted position which that little black boy has occupied since he became a resident at Hillside, and the daily examples of politeness he has witnessed, I am astonished at his rudeness. Fortunately — for him, I mean — his laughter did not reach the ears of Mrs. Gray.

Before we got home I had lulled my conscience into a state of security, but no sooner did we enter the house than my peace of mind vanished. The instant the front-door was opened, Mrs. G. detected the scent of tobacco-smoke. I felt then that I was a lost individual. I had expended several dollars in the purchase of fumigating powders, and for thirteen hours prior to my wife's return had distributed them liberally throughout the house. For my own part, I could detect every imaginable odor except that of tobacco-smoke. I think that Mrs. G.'s sense of smell is altogether too acute.

The day after Mrs. Gray's return was one of considerable excitement. The discoveries she made regarding the domestic economy which had prevailed at Hillside during her absence, were astonishing. She wished to know if I had been keeping a hotel? The number of dishes broken

was immense. The loss, in the single item of goblets, was
enormous. Five silver tea-spoons, four dessert and two
table spoons, together with a silver punch-ladle, were missing. Of course I ascribed their disappearance to the cook;
but Mrs. G. suspects my honest bachelor friends.

Every carpet in the house, according to her views, is
completely ruined. Where all the butter that she packed
down has gone to, she can't imagine. She would think I
had lived on ham and eggs, if she could discover any beef,
or pork, or salt fish in the house. It would not surprise
her to learn that my blood was composed four fifths of
coffee; and as for tea, I must have fed it to the chickens.
She had hoped to have milk and cream, at least, in the
house, but there was not a drop of either; and the little
black boy had informed her that the cows were dry. The
cold meats and pies, however, which she found in the
various pantries, "would keep," as she solemnly informed
me, "a regiment of dragoons from starving for a month."
When Mrs. Gray discovered in the corner of a dark closet,
where I had hidden it, one of my old hats filled with hard-
boiled eggs, her astonishment was unbounded. The shells
of some of them were colored; and the little black boy,
when examined by Mrs. G. in regard to them, asserted
that the hens laid them just as they were.

I am afraid that Mrs. Gray will one day find out all that
occurred at Hillside while she was at her mother's. The
number of brandy-peaches and slices of cake I have been
obliged to give the little black boy to keep him from
telling tales, is telling upon his constitution. I fear I shall
have to discharge him. He grows too fast.

Each day my wife discovers something ruined or "missing." The opinion which she entertains of the cook, as
well as my bachelor friends, is anything but flattering. I
sometimes think that warrants will be issued for their ar-
rests. I hope none of them will think of visiting Hillside
for the present. Last evening, when I returned from the

village, (I pass a good deal of my time in the village now-adays,) Mrs. Gray informed me that some one — the cook, she thought — had had the audacity to wear her wedding-dress, and that there was a grease-spot on the front breadth, as large as a dinner-plate. I told her it was very likely, for I remembered of the cook's going to a wedding one night. Poor Frank! if Mrs. G. ever learns the truth, I shall pity him!

The day before Mrs. Gray's return home, the *Paus* dinner came off. The occasion was one of considerable interest. All of my bachelor friends were present. Several married men, — old compeers of mine, — eluding the vigilance of their amiable wives, graced my festive board. The speeches made were decidedly spicy. I regret that no reporter for the public press was present. The reading community, thereby, has lost many things of a brilliant character.

POSTSCRIPT. — Since writing the above, I have learned that the "Star-Spangled Banner" of the present week contains a glowing description of the *Paus* dinner. When I invited the editor of that newspaper on the occasion referred to, it was with the express understanding that the dinner, being strictly a private affair, nor in the least affecting the interests of the village, was not, therefore, to be used by him as capital for his newspaper. There existed other reasons, too, which I confidentially explained to him, why it would not be politic to make the affair public. When he gave me his word, as "Editor of the 'Star-Spangled Banner,'" that he would keep mum, I believed him. I think now that he meant "Mumm," as I noticed he paid considerable attention, throughout the evening, to the champagne of that particular brand.

The little black boy, whom I started for the village on one of the "chargers," for a copy of the "Star-Spangled Banner," has just returned, bearing with him the compliments of the editor, and a hundred copies of the paper.

CHAPTER XI.

Paper Clothing. — The Star-Spangled Banner's **Report**. — **Bill of Fare**. —
In the Cellar.

WHEN the little black boy returned from the village, with a basket filled with copies of the "Star-Spangled Banner," Mrs. Gray, who chanced to be in the library, asked what I wanted with so many newspapers? Her question took me by surprise. So I answered at random, that I proposed working them up into pantaloons for the little black boy. Hereupon Mrs G. regarded me with considerable astonishment, and, I noticed, took a step towards the door. I immediately explained to her that, by a simple, yet ingenious process, lately discovered by a Frenchman, very substantial clothing could be manufactured from common newspapers. She replied that I was a very credulous man, if I believed any such thing; that the newspapers were full of falsehoods, and that, for her part, she had no faith in anything they published. Moreover, if I persisted in putting that little black boy into such a ridiculous suit of clothes, she should think I was crazy. She then left the room in a very agitated frame of mind. When I directly took up one of the papers, and read as follows : —

[From the Star-Spangled Banner.]

CELEBRATION OF PASCH AT HILLSIDE.

"Again we take pleasure in recording, in our valuable journal, an affair that came off at Hillside the afternoon prior to that on which Mrs. Gray returned home. The gentlemanly host, Mr. Gray, celebrated Pasch — or, as the Dutch have it, Paus — in the most approved fashion. It became necessary, however, for Mr. G. to have this little affair take place a few days before that on which Pasch falls. By referring to our almanac, we find that Pasch occurs, this year, on Sunday; so that, after all, the course pursued by Mr. Gray was, perhaps, the very best.

" It was about five o'clock of the P. M. prior to Mrs. Gray's return, that some twenty individuals, including 'OURSELF,' advanced towards Hillside. A portion of the company was in sleighs, the balance on foot. We noticed that there was a good deal of snow about Hillside; also, that it was, in particular localities, considerably drifted; that the wind, which was blowing in our faces, was a little south of east, and that the thermometer marked twenty degrees above zero. It was tedious going, especially for the pedestrians; but we persevered, knowing what was before us. At least, we 'OURSELF' did; for we printed the bills of fare used on the occasion, and carried one in our pocket. We examined, several times during the day, that particular slip of paper with considerable delight. We marked with red ink several favorite dishes, of which we intended to partake. WE expatiated profoundly to OUR wife, during the eating of a light lunch, of which we partook sparingly, at noon. on the good taste displayed in getting up this bill of fare. Aside from its gastric excellence, its worth as . specimen of typographical art is unsurpassed. We subjoin it for the approval of all who may wish show-bills, circulars, or notes of invitation, got up in style.

. CELEBRATION OF PASCH AT HILLSIDE.

———

BILL OF FARE.

———

SOUPS.

Oyster Soup.	Chicken Soup.	Pea Soup

FISIL

Brook Trout à la Parson.   Lake Trout à la Sam.

Pickerel à la Black Boy.

EGGS.

Hard-boiled Eggs.   Soft-boiled Eggs.   Colored Eggs.

Scrambled Eggs.   Poached Eggs.   Fried Eggs.

Scolloped Eggs.   Roasted Eggs.

Omelette soufflé.

Omelette, plain.   Omelette aux herbs.

Eggs aux naturelle.

BOILED DISHES.

Cold Ham.   Cold Tongue.   Turkey, oyster sauce.

Beef à la Mode.   Stuffed Capons.   Leg of Mutton.

SIDE DISHES.

Oyster Pies   Broiled Chickens.   Pigeon Pies.

Prairie Hens.   Patés de Fois Gras.   Ham and Eggs.

ROAST DISHES.

Turkey, Beef, Pork, Duck, Mutton, Bear, Venison, Bison.

VEGETABLES.

Mashed Potatoes, Potatoes Lyonnaise, Beets, Turnips, Onions, Parsnips, Rice, Succotash.

DESSERT.

Mince Pie, Apple Pie, Pumpkin Pie, Apple Fritters.

Custards, Apple Dumplings, Quince Tarts.

Plum Pudding, Tapioca Pudding, Wheat Pudding.

Rice Pudding.   Charlotte Russe.

Ice-cream à la Fanny,

Jelly à la Nelly.

Floating Islands à la Mrs. Gray.

Walnuts, Almonds, Raisins, Figs.

Coffee.

Cigars and Toothpicks à la Prigs.

" At exactly six o'clock, the little black boy, throwing open the dining-room doors, announced, in a clear manly voice, that dinner was on the table. After we were seated, a very touching grace was pronounced by the Rev. Dr. Blank, when we immediately attacked the good things before us, which disappeared, under our charge, with wonderful rapid-

ity. After full justice had been done on all sides, the
cloth was dexterously removed by the little black boy, and
the wine generously placed on the mahogany. There were
several speeches made by different individuals, including
' OURSELF.' Many toasts were given ; and several songs,
of a highly effective character, were sung. We have an
indistinct recollection of having either sung a song, or
joined in the chorus of one, or else wept at the recital of
some pathetic story, but we cannot, however, for the life
of us, tell exactly which. Mr. Gray, we clearly remember,
sung a comic song, composed by himself, entitled, ' Come,
rest in this bosom, my own stricken dear,' the little black
boy whistling an accompaniment. The same little black boy,
whose name we don't know, recited a short poem, the first
verse of which only seems to have been preserved. It was
written, we understand, by Frank. Some day we trust to
be able to present it to our readers entire : —

FIRST VERSE.

" You 'd scarce expect a darkey lad,
Who, Topsey-like, don't know his dad,
To come before this festive throng,
With speech, or toast, or merry song.

" But it seems he did come ; and what he had to say, we
are bound to affirm, was well said. We consider that youth
to be a black diamond of inestimable value ; and we distinctly remember drinking said little black boy's health at
least a dozen times during the evening.

"In closing this leading article of our paper, we feel
called on to deny the accusation, made by some unknown
person, to the effect that we lost our way returning home,
and were found the next morning buried in a snow-bank
near the Female College. Neither did we, as has been
alleged, carry home, under our cloak, to our better half,
a boiled ham and a bottle of champagne. No, these things,
thanks to our paying subscribers, we have money enough

to purchase ; but we cannot afford to let our good name and deeds be trodden underfeet, like pearls cast before swine.

" In conclusion, with feelings of the highest respect, we propose the following toast. Circumstances, purely of a private nature, made it inconvenient for us, on the day of the Pasch dinner, to offer it in the presence of the assembled guests. We regret this the more, for the reason that we gave a good deal of time to composing and polishing the same ; and our worthy spouse had prophesied that it would be equal to any other toast of the evening : —

MY TOAST—OUR HOST.

" May he never be,
  On land or sea,
Without a sunbeam on his path,
A cricket on his hearth ;
A dollar in his purse,
And a wife to be his nurse."

So much for the " Star-Spangled Banner." I don't think that I shall ever again ask its editor to Hillside. It was with great difficulty that I could keep him out of the cellar. He came near breaking his neck several times, during the evening, by falling down the stairs that lead thereto. I can't imagine what he was after, unless it were cheese. To be sure I have an inner cellar, built during Mrs. Gray's absence, but the door of it is locked, and I keep the key in my pocket. Only my wine-merchant and myself know what it contains. I cannot but think, then, that he smelt cheese, and it was simply that that he wanted ; — though it is all in the rat-traps, and I fear he would have had a difficult time getting it. Foolish man that he was !

CHAPTER XII.

Our New Cook. — My Seriousness. — My Gayety. — My Wildness. — The Round Robin. — Mrs. G. at the Sewing Circle. — Her Considerateness. Her Valentine.

WE have got a new cook. She is "a colored lady," and traces her forefathers back to Ham. When Mrs. Gray came to question her closely, she discovered that they were both natives of the same village. They are, moreover, both acquainted with the same persons. The cook knows some of Mrs. Gray's old beaux. Mrs. G. was very much pleased when she learned this. She came straightway and told me of it. I remarked to her that she appeared to be as much delighted at the circumstance as if she had discovered a second cousin. She said that she was. I don't think I shall like the new cook. I fear Mrs. Gray will pass too much time in the kitchen, talking about her old flames. I spent many days looking up this "colored lady." The inhabitants of Slabtown began to view me with suspicious eyes. They feared I came for no good to them. It was with great trouble that I succeeded in getting our new cook, and I should be sorry now if I were obliged to part with her; but then she must n't talk about Mrs. G.'s old beaux.

Since Mrs. Gray's return, I have led a very exemplary life. No one would suppose, to look at me, that I was so lately a bachelor. On the contrary, my appearance denotes the married man of long standing. I have become very grave and dignified, — too dignified, I think, for my own comfort. To please Mrs. Gray, however, I am cultivating, to an alarming extent, this quality in my character. I am already " as grave as a judge." I intend, at a future period, to become a candidate for a judgeship. There is a sternness in my manners which is appalling to the little boys whom I encounter in the streets. When, accidentally of course, I behold myself in the mirror, my looks remind me of one of my schoolmasters, who was noted for his severity. Besides all this, I am getting up a terrible frown, — such a one as I have seen a great American tragedian employ with remarkable effect. I design using it on my bachelor friends, should I chance to encounter them during my pedestrian excursions with Mrs. G. At present, I am practising it on the little black boy. He does not, however, appear much to mind it. I am confident, though, that in the long run it will have an effect upon him. I overheard him, a day or two since, tell the new cook, that Mr. Gray looked awful.

It is natural for me to be gay. Perhaps, during Mrs. Gray's absence from Hillside, I was rather too gay. To atone for this, I am now quite serious. I resolved to be so the very day Mrs. G. came home. When I informed her of this resolve, she said she was glad of it ; " for," continued she, " you know, Mr. Gray, considering your age, your ' wild oats ' ought to have been sown long ago." The next Sunday morning, when Mrs. G. assisted me at my toilet, she pointed out to me a gray hair amid my whiskers. I was greatly astonished at the sight, and immediately determined to commence reaping the oats referred to by Mrs. Gray.

After the month of dissipation which I passed, it is a great relief for me to sit down quietly by the side of Mrs. Gray, and read aloud to her, while she busies herself with her needle. It is very comfortable to be alone with one's wife. At my earnest entreaty, Mrs. G. has promised that she will not leave me again to visit her mother. This is exceedingly gratifying to me. When I informed my bachelor friends of her intention, they declared it to be "too bad." They even went so far as to address a "round robin" to me, expressive of their displeasure. I took the liberty of showing to Mrs. G. that little document. What she said in regard to them, I should be quite unwilling to repeat in their presence.

As I anticipated and feared, Mrs. Gray has heard of nearly all the events which occurred at Hillside during her absence. As soon as she went to the sewing society — of which she is an humble member — she was duly informed thereof. Some, in whispers, revealed the matter to her, as they affirmed, purely from a sense of duty. Others, less conscientious, I suppose, spoke openly on the subject, and termed it a shameless affair. While one fair maiden lady advised Mrs. G. to apply for a divorce. When my wife mentioned to me this woman's name, I recognized her for an old sweetheart of mine, still remaining unmarried.

I confess I was somewhat surprised, and, withal, pleased when I found how considerate Mrs. Gray was in regard to these matters. The manner in which she alluded to them affected me deeply. She spake "more in sorrow than in anger." Had Mrs. G. been at all excited, it is probable that an "unfortunate misunderstanding" would have arisen between us. The course Mrs. Gray adopted, however, was clearly the proper one. Better than any other would have done — it touched my heart. In short, Mrs. G. felt that she herself was not altogether blameless in the matter. "My absence," as she sweetly expressed it, "was the cause of your loneliness. To dispel that loneliness, you invited a few friends to Hillside. Nothing improper in this, and, under the circumstances, Mr. Gray, worthy of praise." In my opinion, Mrs. Gray is a very remarkable woman. I admire and love her very much.

In a confidential talk which I held with Mrs. G., during the watches of the night, she informed me that while at her mother's she received a Valentine, containing simply these words, —

"When the cat 's away, the mouse will play."

From which she inferred that Mr. Gray was making the most of her absence; so that **she** was not, after all, quite unprepared to hear of the events which occurred at Hillside.

CHAPTER XIII.

My Life. — Tribulation of the Little Black Boy. — Quakerism. — My Great-
Grandfather. — Mrs. G.'s Tears. — My Readings. — Wood-Choppers. —
Snow-Shoes.— Perilous Situation. — Something Hot. — The Back Way.

T present it is extremely quiet at Hillside. **Mrs.** Gray and myself lead a very peaceful life. **Our** intercourse with the village is limited to the daily excursions which the little black boy makes on horseback. The post-office is his end and aim. He complained, however, to me the other day, that the horse he rode persisted **in stopping** at the " Arbor." I remember that my bachelor friend, John, often **rode the said horse during** his sojourn at Hillside. He, doubtless, taught the animal to stop there. The **little black boy feared that it would injure his reputa-** tion to be seen going there so frequently. **I told** him then that he had better ride by without stopping. **He** replied that he had tried **so** to do, but could not, for the horse would, in spite **of** his efforts, stop at a particular post. To appease the little black boy, I have given him the pony to ride. I am happy to state that the pony does very much better. My tall friend P. **never** went to such places.

I really enjoy my **present** manner of life exceedingly. There is a repose in **it which** is quieting to one's nerves. I feel my Quaker descent now very palpably. Occasionally I find **myself** using, quite unintentionally, the plain language. Abeline thinks that I utter " thee " and " thou " very prettily. She says it is a wonder I am not a " Friend." I should be one, I tell her, if it were not that my forefathers were sea-captains. As sailors, they learned to use **strange** words, and forgot the milder forms of speech their

mothers taught them. She thinks it a great pity. Perhaps
it is. Then I told her this

ANECDOTE OF MY GREAT-GRANDFATHER.

"My great-grandfather," Mrs. Gray, "was, by birth, a
Nantucketer ; but early in life he settled on the 'mainland.' After he had left the seas, and anchored his stanch,
though weather-beaten hull in the city he helped to build,
and which he saw rise from the primeval forest, he still
kept an eye on the flying clouds, noted the state of the
weather, and marked the changes of the wind. There were
watchmen in those days, who, during the night, called aloud
the passing hours ; and added, moreover, something concerning the weather, for the benefit of those who chanced
to be awake, and to wake those who, perchance, were
asleep.   But this alone did not satisfy my grandfather ; so
he paid the watchman a certain sum per month to shout
aloud, in addition to this desirable information, directly
beneath his chamber-window, the direction of the wind.
I distinctly recollect when a lad," — here Mrs. G. raised
a finger and pointed to the single gray hair in my
whiskers, which made me sigh, and wonder where all the
years had flown since then, — "when a lad," I continued,
after a short pause, "of listening nightly to the watchman,
crying aloud, for my grandfather's satisfaction, the fact that
it was 'past twelve o'clock, and a cold, clear night ; wind
nor' by nor'west.'

"If the old man happened to be asleep, but, awakened
by the familiar cry, did not quite understand the matter,
he would rise from his bed, and, opening the window, call
the watchman back, to shout the same thing over again ;
but, on the contrary, if he were awake, and clearly understood it, the watchman was duly notified thereof, by my
grandfather's deep but clear, 'Ay, ay, sir !'

"When my great-grandfather, close on a hundred years,
went out with the tide and a favorable wind, the boy — who

long afterwards married Mrs. Gray — missing the watchman's nightly call, and the old man's quick reply, would
turn restless and unsatisfied upon his pillow, till at last,
overcome by weariness, he would weep himself to sleep."

When I had finished, I saw traces of tears on Mrs. Gray's
cheeks ; but she straightway brushed the marks away, and
asked me if the above story were true. I replied I could
refer her to very respectable parties, who would vouch for
its truthfulness. She wished to know if my mother were
one of those "very respectable parties." I said that she
was. "Then," answered Mrs. G., "I am satisfied that you
have told me the truth." Soon afterwards I overheard Mrs.
Gray relating this anecdote, with slight additions, to the
Secretary of the Sewing Society, who just then called, for
the purpose of notifying Mrs. G. that a special meeting
would be held on the following evening. My wife, I am
happy to state, did not feel inclined to attend. She said
that she would rather remain at home to hear me read
aloud. I felt quite flattered by this remark. Not that I
think my wife appreciates, as she ought, my reading, for she
invariably interrupts me in the most affecting passages, by
speaking of something entirely irrelevant to the story which
should be occupying her attention. If I remonstrate with
her regarding her inattention, she promises me for the
future to be more careful ; but, at the same time, remarks
that she clearly understands all I have been reading.
When, however, I examine her at such times in relation to
the principal points of the story, she gives such a wonderful
account of it, made up partly of what I have been reading,
and partly gathered from her imagination, and told, withal,
so glibly, and with so much confidence, that I have to look
at the book again to see whether it is not as Mrs. Gray
states. My regard for Mrs. G. will not permit me to offer
any refutation to her account of the story, but I have my
own private opinion in regard thereto.

We have wood-choppers at work over the hill, on the other side of the farm. Once a month I go there to measure the wood they have cut. During Mrs. Gray's absence from Hillside, however, I neglected attending, as I should have done, to this little business; I let the thing run along for nearly three weeks. Having company at Hillside, the state of the weather, the deep snow, and, perhaps, my natural indolence, were the reasons I possessed for not doing my duty. At last the choppers appointed a committee of three to wait on me, and to "respectfully entreat" me to visit them. According to an agreement entered into between Mr. Gray, the party of the first part, and the wood-choppers, the parties of the second part, their pay for chopping was not to be rendered them till after each month's wood was measured. This, perhaps, may account for the anxiety displayed by them. I found, however, when I attempted to visit the forest, that, owing to the depth of the snow, it was impossible to get there, either by sleigh or on horseback. In this dilemma I bethought me of a purchase I made from an Indian, when at Niagara with Mrs. Gray, last summer. I refer to a pair of snow-shoes. I bought them more to please Mrs. G., who thought they would look well hanging against the library wall, than expecting ever to put them to a practical use. When I mentioned to Mrs. Gray my idea of wearing snow-shoes, she said that she was favorably impressed with it, and at the same time wondered why I had not thought of it before. Thereupon she immediately dispatched the little black boy to the library for them. When he returned with them, she found that they required considerable dusting. After she had satisfactorily performed this little household duty, I managed, with much difficulty, to get them properly adjusted to my feet. Mrs. G., however, persisted in saying that the toes pointed backward instead of forward. I informed the lady that she knew nothing about the matter.

When I was prepared to leave the house, I found it

troublesome to walk. The points of the shoes would get entangled in the hearth-rugs and door-mats, and slide in among the legs of the chairs, and catch on the rockers. At last, however, assisted by my wife and the little black boy, I reached the front-door. Directly before me was a snow-bank. Making a violent effort, I placed myself on the summit of said bank. The ground slopes from the doorway gradually down to the carriage way, nearly twenty feet distant. Unfortunately for me, there was a stiff crust formed on the snow. While I remained poised on the top of the bank, I did well enough, but with the first step I attempted to take I realized the falseness of my position, for I found myself sliding, in a very ungraceful manner, down the declivity. While I wondered if I should keep on till I reached the village, my wonderment ceased as I drove headlong into a drift that had been blown across my path.

When I had gathered myself up and looked around, I saw Mrs. Gray standing at the window, apparently laughing heartily. The little black boy, too, a short distance off, was indulging in a like exhibition of rudeness. As soon as I had taken in these several points, I immediately started for the little black boy, fully intending to annihilate him on the spot. But I directly found it was not as easy reaching him as I had supposed. My snow-shoes were anything but aids to me. They tripped me up repeatedly; while the little black boy, at my futile attempts to reach him, laughed the more. I could only shake my fist at him, at the same time giving him to understand how wonderfully he was exposing himself to a whipping. Mrs. G., also, I perceived, was freely indulging herself at my expense; and, to crown all, I saw the new cook, with arms akimbo, standing at her side, fairly crying. I think I hated, for the moment, the entire community. At last, completely worn out, I sank down in the snow, quite resolved to pass the day there. This plan had the desired effect. It obtained for me the sympathy of Mrs. G For, opening the windows, she en treated me to return to the house. I only shook my head, and plunged deeper into the snow. A moment afterwards she dispatched the little black boy with a small covered jug containing a hot preparation for me to imbibe. This revived me exceedingly; and after drinking Mrs. Gray's health, I resolved to continue my journey. With the assistance of a long pole, similar to those the Ravels use, I moved cautiously forward. Just as I passed around the corner of the house, I noticed Mrs. G. standing in the doorway, with one hand on her side, and waving with the other a white handkerchief, as if to encourage me to advance. As soon, however, as I had got out of sight I stopped, unstrapped the snow-shoes, and placing them under my arm, retreated quietly by the back way into the house, and thence, proceeding to the library, sat comfortably down and began a letter of inquiry to my brother-in-law, who lives "Out West."

CHAPTER XIV.

Spring and Green Peas. — Pea-nuts. — My Wickedness. — "The Husband's Appeal." — How it affected Mrs. Gray. — Speech of the Little Black Boy. — Brandy Peaches.

HEN I looked from my chamber-window the other morning, I found, to my surprise, that spring had arrived. The snow, which since last December encompassed Hillside, had now, thanks to the night's rain, almost entirely disappeared. I mentioned as much to Mrs. Gray. She simply replied, " Nonsense." Thereupon, to convince Mrs. G. of the truth of what I had asserted, I opened the window-sash and let in, not only the first breath of spring, but also some bird music, — " the matin songs," as I informed my wife, " of a robin and bluebird," which feathered warblers I noticed on the leafless elm at the side of the house.

Mrs. Gray being now convinced, said that she considered spring the delightfullest season of the year ; adding, after a pause, that she trusted we would have plenty of radishes.

" And peas, Mrs. G.," I remarked.

" Yes," she said, " peas of course ; and lettuce, and asparagus, and nasturtiums."

What nasturtiums were I had not the least idea ; but as my brother-in-law, who lives " Out West," had advised me, I resolved not to betray my ignorance. So I merely said, " Oh, yes, certainly."

In a private talk which I held, just around the corner of the barn, with the little black boy, I learned what they are. According to his report, I find they are a species of berry, somewhere between the strawberry and barberry. This, t/

me, is perfectly satisfactory. I feel myself under obligations to him. I consider his knowledge of " garden sauce " very extensive. I informed Mrs. G. of the opinion I entertain concerning him. She is very glad he is so learned in such matters. She hopes, after I have examined him more fully on the subject, that I will give him the situation of gardener. I have promised her to do so.

There is a patch of ground near the house, on which I propose raising a variety of vegetables. It is very convenient in the spring to own fresh vegetables. It saves the trouble of going to market for them. Not but what it is a pleasant thing, sometimes, of a spring morning, to go to market. When I was a boy, nothing pleased me better. My purchases, however, at that time, were small. They seldom exceeded a basket of strawberries or a bunch of radishes. Indeed, my family was so limited — only Barry Gray and myself — that it was unnecessary to purchase any large stock. Besides, I was obliged, for reasons best known to my mother, to be somewhat economical.

The little black boy is making great preparation, also, in regard to that patch of ground. He contemplates raising pea-nuts in the southern corner of the same. On examining his lot of seed pea-nuts, I found that the larger proportion of them were baked. I told the little black boy this; he replied he was glad of it, for he preferred those that were baked. I am afraid that my ebony friend will not realize all he expects to from his speculation.

I regret to say that I accidentally damaged the feelings of Mrs. Gray this morning while at breakfast. It did not seem to me that the coffee I was drinking quite equalled the first cup — the original one, I mean, that won my bachelor heart — prepared for me by Mrs. G. I have thought for a month past — in fact, ever since my wife returned from her mother's — that there was a gradual falling off in the quality of said coffee. This was effected so gradually, however, that it was impossible for me to detect the daily change. It was only by recalling to my blessed memory the peculiar flavor and fragrance of that early cup that I could satisfy myself in the matter. This morning, for the first time, it seemed to me that the coffee had gone through the process of boiling. By **boiling** coffee, it loses **that** delicate **flavor** which is absolutely necessary for it **to** possess, **that so** it may be **what** is called a fine cup of coffee.

I **mentioned to** Mrs. Gray my suspicions. **I did so in a** very **kind and** considerate manner. I had no intention, **by** so doing, of wishing **to break** her heart, as she ungenerously insisted that I had; neither was it my purpose to make her **cry, as** she sobbingly asserted it was. I had no thought either that what I said might bring on again an attack of nervous headache, although Mrs. G. said I had. Something, too, Mrs. G. remarked to me from behind her cambric, about paying **another visit to her mother.** This, of course, I can never accede to. It would **not do for** my wife to go away again from Hillside, **unless we went** together. I would not like **to suffer** from loneliness **as I did** during **her** late absence. No, I would rather drink **such** coffee as the neighbors might send in, than allow my wife to **leave** me. Before **I** could pacify Mrs. Gray, I was obliged to **drink** five cups of **the** coffee **in** question. I believe she saw **then** that I entertained no ill-will towards either her **or the** coffee.

I noticed that she **did** not deny my charge in relation to the boiling business. The little black boy haunts the kitchen about meal-time. From something he informed me, **after** partaking of a brandy-peach in the library, **I** am inclined **to** think that **I hit** the nail **on** the head. Still I am sorry **to have** hurt Mrs. G.'s feelings.

Immediately after breakfast, however, I retired to the library, where **I** wrote, on some delicate buff-colored paper, a few verses, which, after enclosing them in an envelope matching the paper, I dispatched to Mrs. Gray by the hand

of the little black boy. They read as follows, and are
entitled

THE HUSBAND'S APPEAL.

In my memory there dwelleth forms and faces most divine,
Which in boyhood's days I cherished, thinking I should make them
          mine :
Faces only seen in slumbers, or in fancy's golden dreams,
Or on stainéd oriel windows, when the sunlight through them
          gleams, —
Faces such as Raphael painted, — such as poets love to weave
In their sweetest, best creations, over which we joy or grieve.

But of all these lovely pictures, there is none that will compare
With the living, mortal woman, who is good as she is fair :
Lowly minded, pure, and earnest, serving God with all her heart,
And, like Mary of the Scripture, choosing well the better part.
She it is who sits beside me, — she who, trusting, gave her hand,
With the promise that together we would journey through the land.

I have walked with haughty damsels, walked with maids of low
          degree ;
Spoken words of praise to beauty, and to goodness bowed the knee ;
Felt my heart grow warm from glances cast by softest eyes of blue,
Felt my heart grow strong and earnest cheered by eyes of darker
          hue ;
Hoped and struggled—toiled and suffered, for some paltry gain in
          life, —
But in nothing found contentment till I found my blesséd wife.

Wife ! the word is full of beauty — full of purity and truth —
Whether now 't is present with us — whether still a dream of youth,
Unfulfilled — a hope — a something which may never come to pass ;
Or, a memory sweet, though faded, like the old year's faded grass.
Wife ! it speaks of home — of children — joys too sweet to be
          revealed :
One to love — to cherish — pray for, and from every grief to shield.

You, who have a wife to love you with a love that 's unsurpassed,
Treasure it as something precious, for you know not if 't will last.
Death may come within your dwelling, chase the sunlight from each
          room,

Turn the blazing hearth to ashes — fill your onward path with
    gloom.
Pray, then, that no word be spoken to her, which you may regret,
When the golden bowl is broken — when the light of home is set.

If you carelessly have uttered words that bore a bitter sting,
Ask yourself these simple questions, Can they break the marriage
    ring ?
Can they even dim the lustre which that marriage ring should
    bear ?
Can they fill her heart with sorrow, or enshroud her brow with
    care ?
If your cooler moments show you these or more may come to pass,
Quickly seek to be forgiven, ere life's sands shall quit the glass.

When the pleasant word is spoken, asking pardon for your sin,
How the upturned face is gladdened ! how rejoiced the heart within !
What low, tender words come flowing from the fountain you have
    stirr'd,
When your voice, in pleading accents, by the precious one is heard !
Oh ! 't is something good and noble thus to set a heart at rest,
Sending peace and sweet contentment back within the fluttering
    breast.

Oh, my darling wife ! I pray thee, list to what I have to say,
And forgive the mean suspicion entertained by Barry Gray.
It was foolish, idle, naughty, thus for me to speak to thee,
And 't were justice, love, to make me live a week on sloppy tea.
But if mercy tempers justice — and I know it will, my dear —
You 'll forgive me, and my coffee henceforth will be strong and
    clear.

When Mrs. Gray had perused the above verses, she was,
as she has since informed me, very much affected by them.
She proceeded directly to the library, where I was, and
winding her arms around my neck, gave way to tears. For
my own part, I could not refrain from joining her. I felt
quite weak and unmanned. Our proceedings quite astounded
the little black boy, who chanced to be in the room ; and
he came very near crying himself, but fortunately a fit of
laughter saved him from it.

When Mrs. G. had recovered her composure, and, with needlework in her hands, was quietly seated on a low stool just at my feet, she informed me of a piece of singular conduct on the part of the little black boy. In presenting to her the lines above quoted, he got upon a chair and attempted to make a speech. If it had not been, Mrs. G. remarked, for some extra efforts at politeness of his, she thinks he would have uttered something highly creditable. He, however, undertook too much. After every two or three words which he uttered he attempted a graceful bow, — what I call a dancing-school bow, — one which my friend Frank taught to him. The result was, that, in making one of these bows, after he had got as far in his speech to my wife, as saying, " Ladies and gentlemen," he fell from the chair, and dropping the note on the floor, which Mrs. Gray picked up, he retired into private life.

In questioning my ebony friend in regard to his conduct, from the confused manner in which he answered, I suspected that all was not right. In fact, I detected unmistakable signs in him of intoxication. Straightway I examined the jar containing brandy-peaches, when I discovered a wonderful falling off in the quantity therein. It seems that the little black boy had been occupied. during the time I was writing " The Husband's Appeal," in devouring my stock of brandied fruits. He could n't have eaten less, I judged, than thirty to forty peaches, to say nothing of the syrup accompanying them. This, then, was the reason that the lad attempted a speech. This was the cause, too, of his falling off the chair. I must take better care of my brandy-peaches. I can't afford to intoxicate him at the price this cost me. Besides, it made him very sick. He did no " chores " through the day. I was obliged to send for our family physician, and a stomach-pump, and a box of blue pills. He had an awful time — it nearly threw him into fits ; Dr. Philtre said it was because the little black boy had swallowed all the stones! I should judge from this that too many brandy-peach-stones don't agree with little black boys. When Master Ebony saw the doctor and the stomach-pump, he was very much frightened — so frightened that the kinks in his hair straightened out. During the height of his attack he solemnly promised, both the doctor and myself, never to eat any more brandy-peaches.

CHAPTER XV.

Interesting Times at Hillside. — Mrs. G.'s Industry. — My Brother-in-Law's
Letter. — My Dilemma. — Strange Woman. — A Precious Package. —
Bribing the Nurse. — Pin-cushions. — Clarence's Letter. — X.'s Baby.

E 'VE experienced highly interesting times at Hillside lately. Not altogether unexpected, however;
for from various little circumstances which came
under my notice, I more than half suspected how the matter would end. Sometimes, when I entered the house unexpectedly. I would discover my wife at work on rather
mysterious-looking articles. My desire to learn for what
purpose they were intended, was increased by the fact that
I thought Mrs. Gray endeavored to keep them out of my
sight. I felt certain they were not for any one then composing my family circle. What, and for whom they were.
thenceforth became to me a question of considerable interest. I revolved the matter in my own mind many times,
without coming to anything like a definite conclusion. At
last it occurred to me that I had better write a letter of
inquiry to my brother-in-law, who lives " Out West." I did
so ; and in it mentioned some small circumstances which I
thought might help to throw a light on the subject. I told
him my wife was engaged in making up several drawers of
strange garments. I confessed to him, however, that they
looked very pretty. There was a good deal of lace and
insertion and edging used in connection with them. They
consisted principally of muslins, cambrics, and such light
fabrics ; together with fine flannels, some of them, I noticed,
being embroidered with white silk very neatly. I also
mentioned — as being rather singular more than because

I thought it had anything to do with the subject in question — that Mrs. Gray had lately purchased several pieces of towelling ; and that, consequently, we were well off in the matter of towels, so that if he should come to Hillside, — as I knew he loved cleanliness above all things, — he would not find us short in the articles of rain-water and towels. I waited very patiently for his answer. At last it came. It was very brief, though not, it seemed to me, particularly lucid. It read thus : —

"Out West," April 1st.

Dear Barry, — Coming events cast their shadows before. Look out for a well-spring of pleasure. [See Tupper.] Your affectionate brother-in-law,

Mac.

After I had read it I was more puzzled than ever. "What," I asked myself, "if coming events do cast their shadows before? I know who said that long before my brother-in-law thought of it. 'T was a certain wizard warning Lochiel; but what in wonder has it to do with me?"

I confess, however, that the remaining portion of the letter considerably startled me. "Look out for a well-spring of pleasure!" It was as if he had said, "Look out for a locomotive." But where, in the name of the Old Woman who lived in a Shoe, and who, according to Mother Goose, had so many children that she did n't know what to do, was I expected to look for one. It did n't exactly seem clear to me, either, whether he wanted me to look out for one for myself, or whether it was a commission he gave me to select one for him. I rather inclined to the latter rendering of the sentence. I considered about it. I took the little black boy's opinion on the subject. He coincided, heart and soul, with me. I began to calculate the profits which would be mine if I succeeded in finding a well-spring of pleasure — whatever that might be — for my brother-in-law, who lives "Out West." Ten per cent. commission, I thought, would be about the fair thing. I carefully examined the "price current" of the New York market, as set forth in the papers, without finding therein the article of which I was in search. The price of well-springs, it seemed, was not quoted. I contemplated writing to Agassiz to learn if he could give me any information on the subject. I presumed a naturalist would know all about it. But who, I asked myself, is the individual named Tupper, whom my brother-in-law advises me, between brackets, to see. I asked Mrs. Gray if she could give me any information regarding one Tupper. She replied that he was the person who wrote the "Proverbial Philosophy." Thereupon I referred to the volume in question, in hope of obtaining the desired information. After a diligent search I read in its pages, "A babe in a house is a well-spring of pleasure." I was thunder-struck, but the riddle was solved.

Some time after this a very remarkable woman appeared at Hillside, where she made herself very much at home, taking possession of our best chamber, and ruling the cook with a rod of iron. The little black boy says that she uses the same rod with which to rule him, except that she heats it red-hot. She wanted the keys of sundry left-hand closets where I keep "medical stuff," and insisted on having the key of the inner cellar. I am happy to state that I was enabled to "stand out" against her overbearing wishes. When she found how decided I was, she held her peace. But she has a way of looking at me which is unendurable.

Somewhere about twenty-four hours after the arrival of said woman, there was another arrival. A small but precious package came to hand. I allude to the birth of my infant son. I feel very proud of this acquisition to my family. I have made a memorandum of the date of this event in my Hebrew Bible, — also in my Greek Testament; and as soon as I can obtain a large family Bible, I shall record it there in the proper place.

Of course I soon discovered what situation at Hillside the strange woman came to fill. I had no idea that nurses were so arbitrary as is this woman. I was scarcely permitted to set foot into my wife's chamber. I was exiled, as it were, out in the barn. It was only by giving the nurse a five-dollar bill that I was permitted, after three weary days, to look on the face of my infant son. When — as I several times each day insisted on doing — I went into my wife's chamber to press her pale cheek, and clasp her thin hand for a moment, while I whispered some endearing word, the baby was either "sound asleep and must n't be disturbed," or else he was " crying, and if I look'd at him 't would make him cry the more," that I began to think I might as well not be a father if I were never to be permitted the pleasure of holding my own child. Times, however, are changed since I gave the nurse the five-dollar bill; and I have, in several instances, held the child somewhat more than was necessary to my entire satisfaction.

I shall be very glad when the nurse takes her departure. I am inclined to think it will not be long before she does ; for there was a gentleman up here from the village, a day or two since, who held a private conversation with her, and who, I thought, expressed a desire to have her visit him.

When it became known that I was the owner of a baby, congratulations and presents began to drop in. The pincushion, which does duty so often on these occasions, was duly received the day before the event occurred. It was of white satin, trimmed with blue ribbon, and the pins were so placed as to read, " Welcome, little stranger." This came from my sister, who lives " Out West." In addition to this, an English lady, a resident of Montreal, sent me one with the motto " Up Guards, and at 'em !" Then, too, my friend Bustle got up a very pretty one, with the sentence, " See, the conquering hero comes." My bachelor friends in the village sent me a " round robin," expressive of their ap-

proval of the thing, and wishing me many returns of the
same. They also sent a silver spoon to " Little Barry," with
the compliments of the season. From my friend Clarence,
who lives " Over the Bay," I received the following **letter**.

" OVER THE BAY," Some Time in May.

MY DEAR BARRY, — You remember our mutual friend,
X., of boarding-school memory, — the chap who always wore
red flannel drawers, a blue shirt, and adorned his head o'
nights with a white cotton nightcap ? — we nicknamed him
tricolor, — and who, moreover, was continually talking about
" wumpusses " and " wows," because he could n't pronounce
the letter R ? Yes, of course you do. Well, X. got married one day, and, in due course of time, was blessed with a
baby, — and such a baby ! none of your pale, lily-complex-
ioned youngsters, but one as red, sir, when I saw it, as a
peony. To hear X. speak of it, you would have thought
't was the only baby in Christendom ; — babies have become
more common since then, I believe.

When it was a week old, X. coaxed me to go home with
him to see it ; I consented, and I must say I was considerably astonished by that, my first sight of an incipient young
man. Never, if I live to be more than very aged, shall I
forget it. Before attending X. to his home, I fortified myself with a glass of wine, a ham sandwich, and read a
chapter of old " Burton's Anatomy of Melancholy." I likewise placed in my pocket a copy of " Mother Goose," a
Noah's Ark, and a pound of Stuart's broken candy, — for,
somehow, I thought they would serve to amuse and instruct
" Little Paul," — but, bless you, Barry, I found he knew
absolutely nothing about our light literature, was fearfully
benighted regarding the event of the flood, and, I believe,
sucked something quite different than candy.

Of course X.'s topic of conversation, on the way to his
modest domicile, was the baby. He mentioned its weight,
which either was nine ounces or nine pounds, I 've forgot-

ten which; and he told me of its hair, which would one day, he said, be either white or red; as yet, the family — his wife's family — could n't decide which. X.'s, you may remember, is decidedly red; and I judged, after seeing the child, from that particular color prevailing to an alarming extent, that it would probably be like our friend X.'s. He said something, too, about little X.'s teeth, and wished to know who was my dentist, together with sundry other questions that have escaped my memory.

When we had reached the house, X. led me cautiously into a darkened room, and up to the side of the bed, within which I discerned a little heap of flannel; softly he raised the covering till I caught sight of a very bald head and the tip of a remarkably little nose. "There," said X. exultingly, "did you ever see a boy like that before?" As it had never been my luck so to do, I could, with a good conscience, answer No! "Look at his hands," he continued, — and he placed in mine a chubby little fist that felt like velvet and looked like a crumpled rose-leaf, — "are n't they beautiful?" And then he showed me the child's feet, very broad at the toes and very narrow at the heel; and if the nurse had n't come up just as she did, I verily believe he would have continued his researches for my benefit very much farther.

As I stood regarding minor X. with about the same feeling of wonderment as possessed me when looking at the mummied cats in Abbot's collection, not knowing what I was expected to do next, whether to kiss him, or go away without kissing, he stirred the tip of his nose a trifle and breathed quite hard. So I said to great X., "Don't you think small X. has a cold?" "Oh, no!" he answered, patronizingly, as if pitying my ignorance, "that 's snoring, — he 's snored more or less all of his life." Then the baby began to cry: the father said it was caused by wind; the nurse said I had better be going; and so, depositing my offerings at the baby's feet, I took, I trust, my last look of

X.'s baby, and departed. As I descended the stairs, I thought I heard X. singing the ditty of " Rock-a-bye, baby."

With feelings of deep commiseration, **my dear Barry,** **for** your unfortunate situation, I remain,

Your bachelor **friend,**

CLARENCE.

It is evident to me that Clarence knows little or nothing of babies. What has X.'s child got to do with mine, I should like to know!— so far as I can see, absolutely nothing. What does he mean, then, by writing to *me* such a letter? I am afraid that there will be trouble between Clarence and myself, unless he explains matters. To think of comparing my infant son with X.'s baby! The thing is highly preposterous and insulting. I feel it a duty which I owe my infant son to call Clarence to an account.·

CHAPTER XVI.

My Bachelor Friends pay their Respects to the Baby. — Their Offerings. — My Speech. — Proceedings at the Barn. — John. — Cultivating Catnip. Lines to our Baby. — His Disappearance. — Our Anxiety. — His Return.

Y bachelor friends visited Hillside lately, for the purpose of paying their respects to the new baby. They marched up here in procession. The baby was prepared to receive them. He was neatly, not gorgeously, arrayed in a new bib and tucker. I had, moreover, requested the nurse to curl his hair. She complied, I believe, with my request, as far as practicable. Each of my bachelor friends, it gives me pleasure to state, brought with him some little present, as a birthday offering to my infant son. The offerings consisted, principally, of juvenile toys; and comprised two sets of corals and bells, a wooden trumpet, a drum, a sword, a top, a tin horse, an A-B-C primer, five India-rubber teething-rings, a rattle, and a silver toothpick; together with a pair of mittens, a volume of the "Star-Spangled Banner," a wooden spoon, a pair of moustaches, a quantity of popped corn, and a dozen cinnamon-scented cigars. In returning thanks for these favors received, which I did in behalf of my little boy, I remarked that many of them were not only ornamental but useful; and that they were quite sufficient in number to set him up handsomely in the world. In conclusion, I said, that I trusted my friends would soon give me an opportunity to reciprocate, in a like manner, the obligations they had placed me under. At this point several of my friends cried, "hear! hear!" being, apparently, favorably impressed with what I had said. I then closed with the following sentiment: —

“Bachelors and Babies, — though thoroughly antagonistic, each, seemingly, striving to put the other down, yet by the magic of a golden ring often become closely and fondly united.”

On account of the young gentleman’s nerves, my bachelor friends were admitted, one at a time, within the sacred precincts of the nursery, and there, in the presence of the nurse, were severally introduced to my infant son. The child behaved exceedingly well, and showed to good advantage, until my thirteenth friend, who sports a moustache, looked upon him, when he became frightened and immediately commenced crying, — which, I am ashamed to confess, he kept up during the remaining presentations.

After the introductions were over, — to the satisfaction, I believe, of all, — my friends, headed by the black boy, proceeded to the barn, where a cold collation was spread. In consideration of Mrs. Gray’s delicate state of health, I selected the barn, as being the more proper place than the house, in which to entertain my friends. It was, perhaps, well that I did so; for, towards the conclusion of the feast, several speeches were made and songs sung, which elicited considerable applause. There was, also, a degree of excitement at one time, which threatened to destroy the harmony of the occasion. It arose from a desire, on the part of each of my bachelor friends, to be honored with having the baby for a namesake. They even went so far as to ballot for a name. On examining the votes I found that each present had cast a ballot in his own favor. The result was as follows: The votes on which were inscribed the name John, amounted to three. All the other names received but one each. This result arose from the fact that there were three Johns present. Hereupon my friends, with the exception of the three Johns, violently protested against the legality of the whole affair; and, finally, at my suggestion, concluded to leave the matter with Mrs. Gray; — which, under the circumstances, I consider a wise and prudent course.

I am sorry not to be able to give a report of the speeches which were made on this very interesting occasion. Unfortunately, only a brief synopsis of my own speech, as above recorded, was preserved. The little black boy — who, I am happy to state, has entirely recovered from the brandy-peach-stone illness — sung a song, the words of which, I believe, may be found in the unabridged editions of "Mother Goose," beginning and ending in this wise: —

> "Rock-a-bye, baby, upon the tree-top,
> When the wind blows the cradle will rock,
> When the bough breaks, the cradle will fall,
> Down comes lullaby baby and all."

Thus triumphantly ended the ceremony of the presentation of my bachelor friends in the nursery, together with the festal proceedings afterwards enacted at the barn.

The baby already begins to notice things. To stare, with his great blue eyes, at the blazing lamps, seems for the present to be the height of his ambition. He cries, too, I have discovered; cries o' nights, I understand. But this concerns his nurse, however, more than it does me. He has thus far, as I have been confidentially informed, passed through life without suffering from those "little diseases" to which infant flesh is heir. That we may be prepared, however, for all exigencies, I have instructed the black boy to devote a small part of his garden to the cultivation of catnip, saffron, and such like simple herbs.

I took the liberty, one Sunday afternoon, during the absence of the nurse in the village, to "*tend baby.*" From certain observations I made at that time, I am satisfied that he is considerable of a boy. Mrs. Gray says that he is a very handsome child, — handsomer, she seems to think, than the general run of such articles. To me, he appears to be very much like other babies. In fact, I think his resemblance to them is striking. The same excess of brilliant coloring is displayed in him, which my friend, from "Over the Bay," mentioned as prevailing to an alarming extent in X.'s baby. Time, however, Mrs. G. assures me, will remove my objections in this particular.

Ever since the arrival of my infant son, Mrs. Gray has not ceased to importune me to address some verses to his little lordship. As soon, therefore, as I could bring my mind into a proper state for verse-making, I did so, and composed these lines : —

TO OUR BABY.

Little allspice, pepper, pickle !
Baby, changeable and fickle,
Lying in your nurse's arms,
Safe from everything that harms ;
Full of smiles, and full of tears,
Full of joys, and full of fears,
Are you mortal or divine ?
Tell me, little baby mine !

Little rabbit, cricket, robin !
Baby, whimpering and sobbing,
Sleeping on your mother's lap,
Dreaming, 'whiles, of sweetened pap,
Pleased with chirping, pleased with song
Quieted by nothing long,
Care you most for milk or wine ?
Tell me, little baby mine !

Little monkey, lemon, clove,
Baby, fruit of wedded love,
Seated on your father's knee,
As wide awake as you can be,
Striving, while you clutch the air,
To pull his whiskers or his hair,
Think you not you 're something fine ?
Tell me, little baby mine !

Little poppy, saffron, thistle,
Baby stilled with chirp and whistle,
Nestled in your cradle small,
Like a little waxen doll,

Do you in your slumbers view
Spirits hovering over you, -
Angel spirits half divine?
Tell me, little baby mine!

Little cherub, sunshine, star,
Baby, comfort of mama,
Welcomed to this world with kisses,
Crowned with love and earthly blisses;
Dimpled darling, blue-eyed boy,
A future hope, a present joy;
Why thus round my heart entwine?
Tell me, little baby mine!

I am sorry to say that Mrs. Gray considers the above lines not exactly the thing. She thinks that I address the baby by improper titles. In short, she evinces considerable disappointment in regard to them: but I have promised her, one of these days, to write some others of a more pleasing character.

We missed the baby this morning from his cradle. He was not to be found in any of his accustomed haunts. At first, I thought some one of my bachelor friends had come up to Hillside and stolen him. Mrs. Gray was fearfully agitated about it. The nurse was very angry, and vented a good portion of it on me. She declared I had hidden the infant. For my own part, though I expressed considerable anxiety in regard to the young man's movements, yet I confess I was secretly pleased at his absence. I wondered if he would stay away forever. I fervently hoped that we would have no more little boys — nor little girls either, — simply for the reason that I don't like to have a nurse in the house. The house, generally, was in an uproar. I was afraid at one time that the ceilings would fall. After a while, the new cook, taking me aside, told me, in a sepulchral whisper, that she suspected the dog had devoured the baby. She had seen him, it seems, very composedly licking his chops, out on the green in front of the house.

The suspicion, however, was much too horrible for me to entertain. If I had not remembered the story of Beth-Gelert, I might have killed the dog. Nevertheless, I called Watch to me and examined his mouth; but I saw nothing which would indicate that he had breakfasted off of our baby. When I showed him the empty cradle and said, " Baby!" he barked violently and ran towards the door. It seemed to me that he understood what I meant. As I have often heard of the sagacity of dogs, I resolved to follow wherever he might lead, in the hope that thereby I might discover the lost baby. As soon, therefore, as I opened the door, he started for the stable, stopping in his progress to ascertain if I were following. Having satisfied himself in this matter, he would bark encouragingly and lead on. When we reached the stable, I discovered, much to my astonishment, indignation, and joy, the little black boy seated on the sorrel horse, holding in his arms, safe and sound, our baby. To my question how he dared to carry off the baby, he replied, that he guessed the baby wanted to see the pigs, and horses, and turkeys, and hens, and the " new red." I did not stop at that time to lecture the ebony lad, but I resolved to do so at no very distant day. Taking the baby, I hastened into the house, and placed him in the arms of his almost distracted mother, who seemed quite happy to receive him. When I told the nurse where I found him, her eyes flashed, and she straightway left the room. A few minutes thereafter I heard Mr. Black Boy making considerable of an outcry; and it is my private opinion that the nurse gave him a whipping. Oh! a monthly nurse is a terrible being!

CHAPTER XVII.

Plans for the Fourth. — Old Soldiers. — Fireworks. — My Oration. — National Hymn. — American Flag. — The Baby. — My Audience. — Dinner. — Cat and Crackers. — In the Evening. — Barrel of Ale. — Good-night.

MRS. GRAY, myself, and the little black boy celebrated the Fourth of July at Hillside in a most proper manner. For a week preceding this national anniversary, I was busied in making preparations for its coming. If it would not be considered altogether improbable by my friends, I would state that my best energies were devoted to getting up the celebration in a patriotic style. I held long conversations with Mrs. G. o' evenings, seated on the front piazza, on the subject. My confabs with the little black boy on the same momentous question were not limited either to time or place. Mrs. Gray advocated strongly the plan of having Mr. G. deliver an original address, or, as it pleased her to term it, an oration, on the occasion. At the same time she herself offered to sing one of Morris's "National Hymns."

The little black boy, however, cared nothing for anything of this kind, and "went in strong" for a lot of fireworks and a drum; and especially did he insist on having a cannon and a tar-barrel. So far as my own wishes went, I was desirous not only of celebrating the occasion in accordance with Mrs. G.'s and the little black boy's plans, but of doing something more in honor of the day, which, like Christmas and Paus, comes but once a year. I wanted to give a dinner to some old friends of mine: not my bachelor friends, for I knew Mrs. Gray would object to it; nor yet to any of the young lady pupils of the college, for to this, too, I felt that my wife would be warranted in raising serious objections; but to four old soldiers, — men who saw service in the war of 1812. Poor and disabled they are, too : one with a leg missing, another an arm, and the other two feeble and white-haired.

When I mentioned to Mrs. Gray my wishes, she came forward in what I call a noble and patriotic manner, and promised me that she and the cook would both stand by me in getting up the dinner, and she doubted not but the old soldiers would have a good one.

This point being satisfactorily arranged, I could give my attention solely to writing the little address which, to please Mrs. G., I purposed delivering. The fireworks I left — after giving some slight directions in the matter — exclusively to the care of the little black boy, to whom I gave an order on the village pyrotechnist; and I must say that my ebony friend obtained a very magnificent assortment of fireworks. It appeared to me, when I received the bill for said fireworks, which was politely handed me the day after the Fourth, that the little black boy had made his purchases regardless of expense. I asked the firework man, when he tendered me the account, if fireworks had n't risen lately? He replied they had gone up rather high the previous evening, but that they were fallen low enough now.

Hereupon he laughed, as if the matter was a capital joke ; but I confess I saw nothing funny in it. I offered to return him — provided he would place the same to my credit — some of the fireworks that would n't "go off." But he refused to receive them, and said that there was no demand in the market for them at present. He advised me, however, to keep them over till the next anniversary of the day, when, perhaps, I might dispose of them to advantage. I don't think I shall allow the little black boy to purchase fireworks on my account again, for he buys "not wisely, but too well." I have since understood that, on account of his extensive purchase, the villagers generally were rather "short" in the matter of fireworks. I know, now, why so many visitors came to Hillside in the evening; it was reported in the village that I had bought up all the fireworks that were for sale, and they came, doubtless, to witness the display.

A few days previous to the Fourth, I drove out with Mrs. Gray to call on the old soldiers above mentioned, for the purpose of inviting them to Hillside. We found it quite impossible to make short calls, as they each had so much to say, that we were, perforce, constrained to sit quietly and listen till their stories were ended. Our first visit, which was to the one-armed veteran, consumed the better part of the day, and it was only by skilful management on my part that we succeeded in getting through with the remaining ones by nightfall. It was no difficult task, nor required much diplomacy, to obtain from each a promise to honor Hillside with his presence on the approaching Fourth. To tell the truth, they all appeared very anxious to come, and kept sending me word every day thereafter, until the Fourth, that I must be sure and remain at home, and not go away to celebrate the day elsewhere. They were very fearful that I would forget my engagement made with them, and, I believe, took turns in watching the road that leads from Hillside. The little black boy was stopped every time he passed the blacksmith's shop, where these old soldiers kept watch, and was put through a very severe cross-examination in regard to the preparations at Hill-side.

When the evening of the third arrived, everything, I am happy to state, was in proper train for the next day. My address was completed, and I had practised delivering it, in the barn, before the little black boy. Mrs. Gray had succeeded in setting the national hymn to appropriate music, and ever and anon was singing it softly to herself. The cook, despite the heat of the weather, had the most important part of the dinner prepared for the oven. The little black boy, with assistance from one of the hired men, had erected, on the hillside opposite the house, a stand for the fireworks, and had obtained not only a cannon and tar-barrel, but a bass-drum. Just at sunset, the wooden-legged veteran made his appearance, bearing with him the American flag. He said that he kinder guessed, seeing as how the little black boy had n't said nothin' about it, that I had n't " nary " a star-spangled banner on the premises, so he thought he 'd just bring along an old one which he used for a spread on his bed to home.

As he had brought his bed's covering, it did not surprise me at learning that he intended to remain all night, " so as to be on hand," he remarked, " in the morning." And what is more than this, he has been " on hand " ever since, nor evinces any desire to take up his bedclothes and walk. He and the little black boy managed to keep awake till midnight, when they startled all the household by the report of their cannon. I think they fired thirteen guns at that time, but will not be positive, for our baby, awakened by the report, cried so loudly that it was almost impossible to hear them. After performing this feat, the two heroes and the baby, I think, must have gone to sleep, for there was a lull from that time till sunrise. Then the cannon-ading again commenced, with the additional noise of the drum, both of which were kept up pretty well through the day.

When I made my appearance on the lawn, shortly after sunrise, I found all my old soldiers were ahead of me. They had come early, they said, " so as to make a day of it."

As soon as we finished breakfast, I thought it would be well to get through with my address before the heat of the day came on. I mentioned as much to Mrs. Gray. She agreed with me in the matter, and only regretted the ab-sence of a larger audience. I replied that, as it was to be

my maiden effort at a Fourth of July oration, it were, perhaps, as well not to desire an increase of hearers. She
declared that I was too modest by half, and wished, at least,
to dispatch the little black boy for the parson, that he
might have the pleasure of listening to me on the occasion.
I, however, objected seriously to this, but told Mrs. G. she
might ask a few of the neighbors to be present. So she
straightway sent the little black boy to invite them. Two
of them returned answer that they were going down to the
village to attend the circus; while the third sent word that
he did n't care anything about hearing Mr. Gray preach,
and besides, he wanted to plough his corn. I think Mrs.
G. was slightly disappointed at the refusal of her invitations.
I believe, even, that she would have consented to have had
my bachelor friends present for the sake of an audience.

It was with considerable trouble that I got my few hearers collected together in the shade of the elms, at the front
of the house. I do not think they wanted to listen to me.
Only my wooden-legged friend appeared to care anything
about it ; and he absented himself so long when he went
to call his companions, that I was obliged to send the little
black boy after him. The lad not returning, and the old
soldiers failing to make their appearance, I was forced to
go for them myself. I found them all collected below the
barn, pitching quoits. When I came among them, however, they ceased their sport, and said they were just on
the point of coming as I turned the corner of the barn.

Then, as if to provoke me, at the moment I rose to commence, the baby began to cry ; so my wife had to enter the
house to get him. While she was gone, the cook thought
she smelt something burning on the stove ; so she departed
to see about it. Then one of the old soldiers was thirsty,
and went down to the well, just beside a stone jug which
stood there, to get a drink. Then the rest of the old soldiers were thirsty, and followed suit. So only the little
black boy remained ; and as I was afraid that he also would

give me the slip if I waited longer, I commenced my address. I think my sable friend rather "admired" being my solitary hearer, for he straightened back on his chair, pulled up his shirt-collar, showed his ivories, and exclaimed, "Hear, hear!" before I had concluded my first sentence.

As soon as I made my voice heard, one by one my audience returned. First came Mrs. Gray and the baby; then the cook, bringing with her a pan of peas to shell; then my four old soldiers, rather the worse for their visit to the well, near the old stone jug; and lastly, the farm-dog. Watch.

Had my audience been less select than it was, I should doubtless have been flattered by the applause with which they greeted my speech. As it was, they applauded its feeblest parts and allowed its most striking points to go unnoticed. I discovered, too, that my old soldiers took their cue from the little black boy, and clapped their hands whenever he did.

After a while — when, too, I was in the most eloquent part of my oration — the baby cried again; so Mrs. Gray was obliged to carry him back into the house. Then, no longer kept in awe by his mistress' presence, the little black boy commenced his pranks. My address was not written in the most legible hand, and as I am near-sighted, I was obliged often to hold the manuscript close to my eyes to enable me to decipher it. At such moments the little black boy would take the liberty of throwing crackers on the stage where I stood, which, exploding, caused me much indignation and dismay. I think that the old soldiers were rather pleased to have him do so, and encouraged him in it, notwithstanding a reprimand I administered.

At last two of the old soldiers fell asleep, and the little black boy having slyly managed, without my having perceived it, to get my wife's favorite cat and a pack of lighted crackers together into a barrel, thereby causing quite an excitement, I abruptly brought my oration to a close. I sup-

pose it will be published entire when my works are collected in book-form, after my death. Till then, however, unless surreptitiously taken therefrom, it will remain, unknown to the world, in a corner of my writing-desk. When Mrs. G. had succeeded in quieting the baby, she made her appearance on the platform by my side, and sung the "National Hymn" spoken of above. I greatly regretted at the time, and still do, that the soldier-poet who composed the hymn was not present to hear it sung. My old soldiers roused themselves from their drowsiness, and beat time to the music with their crutches. My thrifty neighbor, who did n't care to hear me preach, left his plough standing in the furrow, and hastened across the fields to listen to this song. At its conclusion, they would not be satisfied till Mrs. G. once more sung it through. They did n't ask me, however, to repeat the oration, and I must confess I was glad they did not.

To please the old soldiers, who were accustomed to early hours, dinner was served at exactly twelve o'clock. In regard to it, I will simply say that it was got up under the direction of Mrs. Gray, who was ably supported by the cook herself. Consequently it was one the merit of which has never been surpassed at Hillside. After the cloth was removed, several speeches of a somewhat rambling character were made by the ancient warriors, and the little black boy sang an original song, composed by himself, to the air of "Oh, hush!"

Directly after dinner the old soldiers complained of being drowsy, so I showed them into the large room where the farm-hands sleep, and left them to their naps. They charged me, however, before I went from the room, not to allow them to sleep later than the tea-hour. I gave the little black boy strict injunctions not to set off any fire-crackers, nor to beat the drum, nor make any unnecessary noise. He promised me he would not. No sooner had I laid down, however, than I was aroused by a terrible outcry

in the yard. On hastening thither to learn the cause of
the disturbance, I found that the little black abomination
had made an unhappy family in a hogshead, by placing
therein the cat, dog, and five packs of lighted crackers.
After I had restored peace by liberating the animals, I
returned to my couch ; but it was vain for me to seek to
sleep. No sooner did I get into a doze than a greater disturbance awoke me. Now it was the cannon ; then the
drum ; and afterwards the old soldiers themselves, into
whose pockets the black boy had inserted several serpents,
pin-wheels, and other species of fire-crackers, which he had
set off. So the afternoon wore away, and at last tea was
ready. Then visitors from the village arrived. My bachelor friends, on horseback, came " for the purpose," as my
" Arbor " friend expressed himself, " of staying all night
with me." The editor of the " Star-Spangled Banner,"
accompanied by his " lady," rode up in a gig.

When the night came, and the young moon had hidden
herself behind a bank of heavy clouds which lay in the
west, the rockets, and Catherine-wheels, and blue lights,
and Roman candles, and fiery serpents, together with various other kinds of fireworks the names of which I do not
know, were " set off," and elicited from the crowd assembled considerable applause. After the fireworks had gone
off, and a barrel of Taylor's Aster ale had been broached
for the good of the public, Mrs. Gray, in a whisper, asked
me if I would not like to deliver my oration again. She
had alluded to it, she said, in a little conversation she held
with my tall friend Christopher, who had expressed much
regret at not having heard it. I might never have the
opportunity again, she added, of delivering it before such
an assemblage. I pleaded weariness, however, and begged
of her, if she loved me, not to mention the subject again,
either to me or to any of my friends.

Late in the night, after all the ale had disappeared, we
lighted the tar-barrel, and by aid of its blaze my visitors

found their way from Hillside. But my old soldiers were too wearied to go home, so they remained with me till after breakfast the following morning, and one, as I have before mentioned, remains a fixture at Hillside to this day.

I nearly forgot to mention that the little black boy managed, during the evening, to get slightly blown up. He went up on a bunch of rockets to which he accidentally set fire, and, much to his surprise, found himself, a few seconds thereafter, on the roof of the barn. He descended to the ground by the lightning-rod, however, and was particularly careful, during the remainder of the evening, how he handled the rockets. He reported having passed two rocket sticks coming down as he went up, and when himself returning, encountered three balls from a Roman candle. With the exception of being made very bald, — his hair having been entirely singed from off his head, — he suffers no inconvenience from his trip.

CHAPTER XVIII.

An Anniversary. — Mrs. G. slightly astonished. — I refer to my Bachelor
Days. — Apology of the Little Black Boy. — Duels. — Fire-Eaters. –
Mrs. G. and the Baby. — The Happy Occasion. — Judge's Address. –
John's Speech. — Serenading.

HE first anniversary of my wedding-day occurred
a short time since. It gives me pleasure to be
able to mention that Mrs. Gray was very gracious
on the occasion. Immediately after dinner on that day,
Mrs. G. suggested to me the propriety of asking a few of
my bachelor friends to pass the evening at Hillside. At
first I said very decidedly, No! but when I perceived that
my wife had set her heart on my having them come, simply
because she thought it would give me pleasure, I consented. We were in the library at the time, and Mrs.
Gray was examining, with delight, a little present I had
just made her. It was a framed engraving — Ary Schef-
fer's Dante and Beatrice. It may be that this little circumstance had something to do with her graciousness.

When Mrs. G. asked who of my friends I desired to invite, I took pencil and paper and wrote down their names
I then handed the list to Mrs. Gray for her approval. After perusing it, she said she feared that the house would
not accommodate so many. She hoped that I would not
think of asking more than five or six of the thirty-eight
whose names she had read; "besides," she added, "I fear
that the thought of being obliged to entertain so many
persons, Mr. Gray, would bring on one of my nervous
headaches."

I should be very sorry to have Mrs. G. troubled again in this manner. I said something to her to that effect. She replied that she was happy in hearing me say so, but supposed that it would be a matter of perfect indifference to my friends if she were sick or well. I assured her that such a supposition wronged them; for I had repeatedly, on various occasions and in different places, drank the health of Mrs. Gray, when the same had been proposed by one or another of them. This seemed slightly to astonish her; but she recovered in a few moments, and remarked that she hoped, for goodness' sake, I did n't go about the village drinking that toast with every good-for-nothing bachelor I came across. She trusted, too, that I was not falling into any evil habits. I assured her, in reply to each of these, that I did and was not, and that moreover I had got rid, during the past year, of many habits which, though not really evil, and perhaps even well enough in a bachelor, were yet considered by her unbecoming a married man — "and," added Mrs. G., smiling, "a father."

"True, my dear," I said; "a father." And I looked through the open door into the chamber beyond, where that father's little boy was slumbering in his crib; and a heart-born though silent prayer rose heavenward for his peace and happiness through life.

"Yes," I continued, after a minute's pause, "have n't I given up the pipe my German friend sent me? do I look at the 'weed' now, except semioccasionally? do I ever sit up with a sick friend? do I stay out late o' nights, unless when business demands it? do I ever serenade young ladies? do I go fishing? have n't I almost forgotten where the Female College is situated? does any one ever meet me in the 'Arbor,' or at the 'Red Jacket Garden,' save when you, my love, are with me? what has become of my night-key?"

Here Mrs. Gray interrupted me by saying that it was with the bunch of keys I gave the baby yesterday to play with. Not heeding her, however, I continued, "And **my** boxing-gloves?"

Mrs. G. pointed to the little black boy, who just then passed across the lawn with his hat filled with my choicest cherries.

"And," I exclaimed, as I dashed out of the room after my colored friend, "what has become of my liberty? and following up the subject, when I found myself out of Mrs. Gray's hearing, "my right to go and come unquestioned? the jolly days and jollier nights of bachelorhood? my old sweethearts? my lady correspondents? my games of whist? my"— but having reached the little black boy and the cherries, I left the sentence unfinished.

I think that I accosted that boy somewhat roughly. I know I frightened him, else why did he commence crying? When I told him he did very wrong to steal my cherries, he said he was ready to apologize. As I did n't want his apology, I set him to weeding the garden. He is not partial to the business—he complains of its making his back ache. I am glad I have at last found how to make it ache; for a year past I have endeavored to discover some way of effecting this result, but without success. I already begin to feel sorry for that youth, as there is a great deal of land on the farm that will bear weeding, and when he gets through with that, if he lives long enough to do it, I will set him to picking up the stones that encumber the fields.

When I returned to Mrs. Gray's presence, I had forgotten my grievances, and thought only of the proposed bachelor party for the evening. So when Mrs. G. asked for the names of the five or six whom I intended to invite, I was quite ready to name them to her. I confess, however, that I was disappointed. I could not but think how foolish it was in me to run the risk of offending thirty-two of my old friends simply for the sake of making five happy; and even their happiness was problematical. At first I did n't think I could do it. I said so to my wife. She merely remarked, in reply, that she would assume all the responsibility in the matter. After this I could make no further objections; but I took care, in selecting my company, to choose only such of my friends as possessed the most choleric and fiery dispositions; and who would be the most likely to resent any slight which they might imagine rested in a non-invitation. I did n't care to get involved in a quarrel with any one, which might possibly terminate in a duel. I don't approve of duelling, unless I and my antagonist stand on equal ground. When I was a bachelor, the thing was different; but now, for me to fight a duel with an unmarried man, nobody's husband or father to speak of, would not, I think, be altogether the fair thing. To avoid a duel, then, was my reason for selecting the men I did. When I repeated their names to Mrs. Gray, she termed them a set of fire-eaters, and wondered at my taste; but, nevertheless, said they would do.

Straightway, then, I had the little black boy harness the horse, and rode down to the village. I first called on my friend Smith. Mr. S. is a very fierce man, and carries one of Colt's revolvers constantly with him. He says it is because he is afraid of highwaymen. For my part, I think he is more fearful of dogs. When I asked him to go to Hillside, he replied that the distance was so great, and the night so dark, and the watch-dogs so numerous on the line of the road, that he should not like to promise affirmatively. When I informed him that, being the height of the dog-days, the canines were kept chained, he hesitated no longer, but said he would go.

Then I saw my friend John, of "Arbor" proclivity, who, unlike Mr. Smith, is n't afraid of dogs, but, on the contrary, is rather partial to them, and, I believe, keeps a fighting-dog, which, however, he endeavors to make the public think is simply a greyhound. When I told him that Mrs. Gray would be pleased to see him at Hillside that evening, he said he was sorry, but an engagement already made would prevent him from accepting her invitation. He felt afflicted beyond measure that it so chanced to be; for he would any time go out of his way a mile for the sake of meeting with Mrs. Gray. His compliments, therefore, deep regrets, and all that sort of thing, he trusted I would deliver to her. Just as I was leaving him, I chanced to mention the beverage which would take the place of coffee on this occasion: — so soon as I had uttered the word, he exclaimed I need say no more, for he would go to Hillside that evening, in spite of everything; — and he came.

Frank, the Judge, and my tall friend P., all gave me to understand that nothing short of an earthquake would prevent them from honoring Hillside with their presence. Only Fred, of all the invited guests, did n't come; possibly some young lady held out greater inducements than I offered, which influenced him to stay away.

After I had made some few purchases necessary for the evening's entertainment, I turned homeward. When I came in sight of Hillside, I saw evident signs of rejoicing going on. The old soldier, who is yet spending the Fourth with me, had taken the liberty of spreading to the breeze his star-spangled banner. The cannon, too, which had deafened us on the National Anniversary, was placed on the lawn in front of the house, ready for action. As I rode into the yard, I noticed that the little black boy had on my highest standing-collar, and was, moreover, gorgeously arrayed in a crimson waistcoat which reached to his knees. The old soldier, also, had given more than usual attention to his toilet. He had evidently been using somebody's razor, and blacking-brush, and had rubbed up the tarnished buttons on his well-worn regimentals. He stood beside the cannon, and as I rode by he saluted me in a stiff and military fashion.

Within the house, too, I found evidences of joy. Mrs. Gray, more charming than ever, appeared in her bridal attire ; and the baby, rosy and smiling, was half smothered in laces and ribbons. There was evidently a wish in my wife's heart to make the occasion one of pleasure. She looked back, I trusted, with no small degree of satisfaction, on the past year. For my own part, I could recall a great many red-lettered days in the twelve months gone by. Some of them, to be sure, came while Mrs. G. was visiting her mother ; but the greater portion of them occurred when my wife was at home. Thinking of these things, then, was the reason why, when I encountered Mrs. Gray, I saluted her in a very hearty manner.

In the evening, after the cannon had been fired thirteen times, my bachelor friends made their several appearances. It was a very pleasant thing for me to meet my old companions once more around the social board. When I winked over my glass at one of them, during a temporary absence of my respected spouse from the dining-room, it seemed to me as though I were still a bachelor. I am sorry, also, to say that, for one moment or so, I forgot all about Mrs. Gray and the baby. It happened just at the time when I proposed the toast of " We, seven jolly bachelors — long may we live !" Mrs. G. recalled me to my senses by remarking that but five bachelors were present, while the balance of the company consisted of Mr. and Mrs. Gray. I immediately begged my wife's pardon, and hoped that she would overlook, on this happy occasion, any little mistakes of which I might be guilty.

Of course there were several speeches made by my friends present : many of them complimentary speeches, extremely flattering to Mrs. G. and myself. The Judge made an unusually grave and sound address, in the course of which he charged his bachelor companions to follow my example. Circumstances, he said, purely of a private nature, would prevent him from living up to the advice he so freely gave. My friend John — who, by the by, was rather too attentive to Mrs. G. during the evening — got off quite a flippant speech, in which he had the audacity to assert that, had the farm contained one hundred acres more than it does, he would himself have married Mrs. Gray. This result, however, I have good authority for saying, could never have occurred under any circumstances. Frank spake sundry witty things, which flashed and sparkled like the beads on the champagne. Mr. Smith told some funny stories, and imitated perfectly the barking of a dog; while my tall friend P. sung several sentimental songs, which were much applauded, and which — either the applause or the singing — caused the baby to wake.

After a while, just before the party broke up, my old soldier marched into the room with his star-spangled banner wound around him, and informed the company that their mirth so disturbed him he could n't sleep, and he begged them, if they honored old soldiers, to go home like good boys; which advice, as the large hay-wagon at that moment drove up to the front-door, ready to convey them in safety to the village, they concluded to follow.

I am informed on good authority, viz. by the man who drove the party away from Hillside, and who failed to return home till after daylight the following morning, that my indiscreet friends were not willing to go to their several boarding-places until they had disturbed with a serenade every available young lady in the village, and the inmates of the Female College in particular. They drove no less than eight times around the college grounds, and sung twenty-nine different songs, before they were satisfied that the thing was effectually done. They were all very hoarse the next day, and on the following Sabbath there was a preponderance of bass voices in two of the churches.

As for myself, I was troubled, the ensuing day, simply with a headache, the result, I told Mrs. G., of my partaking, late in the evening, of raspberries and cream.

CHAPTER XIX.

I join a Literary Society. — Extra Meetings. — Cymbals *vs.* Symbols. — Impertinence of the Little Black Boy. — My Singing. — His Music. — The New Charter Oak. — The Old Soldier's Wish. — Mrs. G. is Jealous. " Ina, of Lakelawn." — How I came to write these Sketches. — Shaking Hands. — My Wicked Remark.

HAVE lately joined a literary society in the village. I was encouraged to do this by Mrs. Gray, who thought that thereby, some day or another, I might have an opportunity of redelivering my Fourth of July oration. I do not, however, intend that such an opportunity shall ever occur. I have not spoken thus decidedly to Mrs. Gray, in relation to this matter. I am willing that she should live in anticipation of such an event. If she thought I did not intend to distinguish myself, as she expects, I fear she would not consent to my going so often to the village of evenings as I now do. What with regular meetings and extra ones of the society, I manage to reach the village about three times a week. This is an agreeable episode to my Hillside life. Not that I am becoming weary of my home, although the baby does cry a good portion of each day and night, but simply because it gives me an opportunity of gaining much useful information, and at the same time enables me to meet my bachelor friends. Sometimes, too, after I get to the village, I learn, much to my surprise, that the extra meeting, to which I was duly notified, will not take place. When I inquired of the secretary of the society — who, by the by, happens to be my friend Frank — how he came to send me notice of such meeting, thereby forcing me, as it were, away from the bosom of my affectionate family, he answered that it was "simply a mistake; and besides," he added, "I wished to see you on particular business."

What that "particular business" is, I am not at liberty to state. In fact, I do not even mention it to my wife. She considers it very odd, however, that the extra meetings should extend so much later into the night than the regular ones. I account to her for this in two ways. First, that the subjects introduced for discussion are of a more private character, and, consequently, require more deliberation; and, secondly, that, as we are not limited to the fifteen minutes' rule in speaking, which is strictly enforced at the regular meetings, the speakers are apt to be rather lengthy in their remarks. This explanation, I am happy to say, satisfies Mrs. Gray. I hope she will remain satisfied with it. I should not like to be questioned too closely as to our proceedings. One thing, however, Mrs. Gray insists on knowing, — which is, why I take the little black boy with me to these extra meetings. For the reason, I tell her, that horse-thieves are prowling about the village, and I have him to sit in the buggy to keep watch during the society's meeting.

For her part, she remarked, she should not consider the guard which he would be likely to keep as amounting to anything; for if he should fall asleep, — and it would be just like him to do so, — any one might steal the horse out of the shafts, and ride off without the lad's dreaming of waking.

"In that event, Mrs. G.," I said, "we would have the carriage left us."

"I am not so certain of it, Mr. G.," replied my wife; "for it would not be at all strange if the next robbers who came along should take a notion to the carriage, and, perhaps, run away with it and the black boy besides."

"If they should do this, my dear," I remarked, "I fully believe you would not object to losing the horse and buggy, for the sake of getting rid of the little black boy, since I believe you consider him a 'great pest.'"

"If he would make less noise, Mr. Gray, and not be so continually waking up the baby whenever the nurse or myself get him to sleep, I should not think him a *pest*, and would even like to have him live at Hillside all his life ; for he is a smart lad, and does a great many 'chores' ; but he makes a deal of disturbance, one way and another, in the house, which annoys me exceedingly. Moreover, he lately has taken to playing a pair of cymbals. To me, Mr. Gray, subject as I am to nervous headaches, it is an intolerable nuisance to hear them : in my opinion, they are symbols of unrest ; for the moment they are struck, I have to run immediately to the baby."

"Your remedy, my love," I replied, "is simple. You have only to strike the little black boy in return for his striking the cymbals, and the matter resolves itself into a nut-shell."

"It is a 'nut-shell,' Mr. G., which I do not care to strike. Where," continued Mrs. Gray, after a slight pause, "the little wretch could have gotten these brazen instruments, I cannot, for my life, imagine. He produced them for the first time, I noticed, the morning after you had taken him to one of the extra meetings of your literary society. When I asked him where he had found them, he replied that he 'found them over the left.' For this impertinent speech I set him to scouring the knives and the steel forks the men use, and then I made him rub the brass andirons ; and after he had finished them, as if to provoke me, Mr. Gray, he, of his own accord, scoured up his abominable cymbals."

"That was certainly too bad, my dear. I think," I added, "that he must have a good deal of brass in his composition."

"But where," exclaimed Mrs. G., "do you imagine those cymbals came from ? "

"Perhaps," I replied, "he purchased them of the tin pedler who was along here the other day."

"But they are not tin, my dear ; they are brass : and besides, I never heard," said Mrs. Gray, "of a tin pedler, or any other description of pedler, carrying such articles about the country."

" No, my dear," I replied, " nor I either."

" Besides, Mr. G.," added my wife, " he neglects his work shamefully. He does n't even feed the young chickens, and the ' new red' shows how little he is taken care of; and all because the little black boy, forsooth, is practising on the cymbals. He passes the greater part of each day in the barn, where he beats those pieces of brass together most fearfully. Have n't you ever heard him, Mr. Gray? Why, it was only this morning that I really thought, my dear, I heard you singing, out there, while the little black boy beat the time."

" Pshaw ! Mrs. G.," I said ; " you know I have no voice for singing. Why, when a boy, I could never whistle ' Yankee Doodle '; and I was dreadfully mortified, after I became a young man, at being turned out of the church choir in my native village, because I could n't sing ' Old Hundred.' The fact is, my love, I don't belong to a musical family, though I have no hesitancy in claiming for it the title of a ' happy family.' "

" Very happily expressed ; but have you never heard," persisted Mrs. Barry, " the sound of those cymbals ? "

" It is possible, Abeline, that I have ; but, doubtless, I supposed the sound to proceed from the wind soughing through the pines."

" If that is the case, Barry, I fear that you are getting deaf ; for the two sounds are entirely dissimilar.

" There," exclaimed Mrs. G., as a most barbarous noise broke on our ears, — " there ; now do you hear it ? "

I confessed that I did. " But," I suggested, " may it not be three or four locomotives on the railroad, angrily whistling ? "

Mrs. Gray laughed contemptuously, and said, " No, no ! " and there the conversation ended ; for I, taking my hat and riding-whip, started for the barn and the little black boy.

What passed between the black youth and myself, when we met within the barn, it is not my purpose to relate. Enough that my readers should know that, since that time. the darkey beats his cymbals only on the extreme verge of the farm, — one hundred acres distant, at least, from Mrs. Gray and the baby, — and where, I understand, he keeps them in a hollow oak, which he chartered from me for that purpose. The old soldier, who is still keeping the Fourth at Hillside, terms it " the new charter oak "; so that the country, he says, may not be without one, although the original has fallen. The same old soldier is very anxious to obtain a staff from the old Charter Oak, to support his tottering steps. He has, for a week past, constantly importuned me to write to some person at Hartford to send him a piece. When I informed the old veteran that I possessed no acquaintance in the place, he replied that then I had better write to the mayor and common council of the city, and he doubted not that, if his case was properly represented, they would accede to his wishes. I promised him I would mention the matter in my next Hillside Sketch ; and as this chances to be it, I feel that I can do no less than fulfil my promise. I trust that some one, I don't know who, that has lived within sight of the old oak, will forward him what he so much desires. To use the words of the crippled veteran, " I wish no better tombstone to mark my grave," he said to me one evening, as he sat smoking his pipe under the apple-tree back of the house. " than such a staff would be, thrust into the earth above my breast ; nor a more decent winding-sheet than the old and tattered flag would prove."

I think Mrs. Gray is jealous : jealous, too, of some one whom I doubt whether she or I have ever seen, — of one who, judging from what she writes, is even now passing to the spirit-land. Young, and doubtless fair, she is, but fading like a broken lily. I try to impress this sorrowful fact on Mrs. Gray, but to little purpose. Sometimes I think I have succeeded, — for, while I speak, tears dim the brightness of my wife's dark eyes; but the next moment they are unclouded and I hear her say, " No, no, Barry, it won't do. I cannot submit to having even an invalid young lady speak of you as 'Dear Mr. Barry Gray,' and 'longing to grasp you by the hand.' If Miss 'Ina, of Lakelawn,' would confine her attentions to your bachelor friends, I should not mind it one bit; but I protest against her making love to you. And it all arises, Mr. Gray, from the fact that I was rash enough to give my consent to your publishing these foolish Sketches; but you coaxed me so persistently, Mr. G., and declared so decidedly that they were in you and would come out, that I could not avoid saying yes to your entreaties; and now I see the result. I might have known it; but I was blind, Mr. Gray, — blind. Did n't you win me to be your wife, Mr. G., with your pretty stories, and the sentimental rhymes you addressed me? And are other ladies less susceptible than I?"

" But, my dear," I remarked, "you are laboring under a mistake. Miss Ina is not in love with me; she only desires to grasp my hand, and also the hands of my bachelor friends. So far as I have heard from my friends since her note was published, they, to a man, are anxious to accommodate her, if she will only let them know where to find her. My tall friend P. said he 'd ride the pony fifty miles for the sake of meeting her."

" Is there any one, Mr. G., — any young lady, I mean, — whom they would object to grasping by the hand? Did n't they, on Commencement Day at the Female College, go through the entire building shaking hands with each young lady within the walls?"

I told Mrs. Gray I was not aware whether they did or did not.

" But I know, Mr. G.," she said; "and if they grasped the young ladies' hands with as much cordiality as they do mihe when they visit Hillside, why, all I can say is, that I should be sorry to have a daughter of ours educated in that institution, — at least if your bachelor friends visit it often."

" Well, my love, it will be time enough," I wickedly remarked, " to speak of that when we get a little daughter. Perhaps before that period arrives my bachelor friends may all be married and have little daughters of their own. At present, you know, we have only a little boy ; but when a daughter comes "—

" There, Mr. Gray, that will do," interrupted my wife ; " I think I hear the baby crying : now be a good husband, and go rock his cradle ; for you know, love, the nurse is gone to the village."

So I kissed my estimable wife and went up-stairs to the nursery ; but the baby was sleeping peacefully, and I do not think had thought of crying. I took a book, therefore, and, seated beside him, sought to read, but I could not ; for somehow what Mrs. Gray had said of the way my bachelor friends shake hands was foolishly occupying my mind. I don't think it a good plan for married ladies to shake hands with bachelors. Strange I never thought of this before ; but — well, well ! the next time those old bachelors come to Hillside I'll watch them closely ; and after that visit, maybe, I won't ask them to come again.

CHAPTER XX.

The Baby wakes. — At Breakfast. — Life's Sweets. — The Troubadours. --
Two Little Black Boys with Cymbals.— Mrs. G.'s Promise. —A Prisoner.
Hints to my Bachelor Friends.

URING the past few days I noticed that Mrs. Gray had that on her mind which, apparently, she desired to communicate to me. For reasons of my own, I avoided giving Mrs. G. an opportunity of so doing. She essayed to speak of it, however, the other night, after the light was extinguished, and proceeded as far as to utter these ominous words, — " Mr. Gray, I am astonished,"— when, fortunately for me, the baby, who sleeps in his cradle within arm's-length of my side of the bed, commenced crying.

I could not imagine what caused " our baby " to cry just at that moment ; for, to all appearances, only a minute before he was sleeping most soundly. Mrs. G. wondered at it, and asked me, in an accusative tone of voice, whether I had touched him. Of course I was indignant at her question, and would make no reply. Afterwards I said, however, that I thought a mosquito must have bitten him, as I had heard the singing of one. It was some time before the child became quiet : when he did, I am happy to state that, to all intents and purposes, I was soundly asleep. I know that I was soundly asleep, from the fact that my estimable wife asserts that she spoke to me no less than six distinct times without eliciting a word in reply.

One can't always sleep soundly, however ; and the next morning, at breakfast, Mrs. Gray recommenced the attack in this wise : " Mr. Gray, I am astonished that a man of your age,"— I involuntarily thought of the few gray hairs which, prematurely I am certain, appeared in my whiskers, —" a husband, too, and a father,"— Mrs. G. lays great stress on the fact of my being a father, —" should allow himself to be led astray by a set of incorrigible bachelors from the path of rectitude, as, I have good authority for saying it, I understand you have been."

While Mrs. Gray was speaking, I resolved in my " heart of hearts " to give the little black boy a beating. When she concluded, " My dear," I said, reaching towards her my cup, " I will thank you for a little more sugar in my coffee. Life's sweets, Mrs. Gray," I added, after a trifling pause, " are not found always in one spot: the bee, although his home may be in the midst of a beautiful garden, and though honeysuckles and jessamines may wreath them- selves over the hive he inhabits, will yet wander far away in search of foreign sweets, and when he returns home, will bring with him, gathered perhaps from some despised and neglected bachelor's button, uprising by the roadside, as pure and sweet a drop of honey as any in the hive : and thus, my dear, is it with man ; though he may possess the greatest joys and delights of life, in and around his home, yet for all this — loving home none the less — he likes sometimes to wander from the Eden in which he dwells, out into the great and busy world, where, among his bachelor companions, he will be enriched with many a bright fancy and kindly thought, to take back with him to gladden and adorn his home."

" All that is very well, Mr. Gray," said my wife, " pro- vided he walks out in the broad sunshine, and don't seek those ' bright fancies ' by starlight."

" Well, well, my love," I exclaimed, " I dare say you are right ; and, as the poet says, ' the rainbow of' "—

" Never mind, Mr. G., what the poet says," interrupted my wife ; " I am not to be put off in that way. See here what the newspapers say about you." And, raising the

salver in front of her, she drew from beneath it a copy of
the "Star-Spangled Banner," opening which, she read from
its columns the following article.

THE TROUBADOURS.

"We congratulate the young ladies of our village that
there exists in our midst a company of amateur musicians
known as the Troubadours. To these choice spirits our
fair ladies are indebted for the many delightful serenades
which, of late, have called them from their soft couches
and sweet slumbers, to listen to music (both instrumental
and vocal) such as it seldom before has been their lot to
hear.

"Of course the names of the parties engaged in this dis-
tribution of sweet sounds, it would hardly be the fair thing
in us to divulge. We feel, however, that, without mentioning names, we may be permitted to allude complimentarily
to two or three of the band. We consider the low notes
of the short gentleman who sings bass to be very low indeed; while the high notes of the tall gentleman who sings
the air, we consider to be very high. We may be incorrect
in both of these criticisms, but we think not. The execution of the young gentleman who performs on the French
horn strikes us as being very favorable; while the little
black boy [here Mrs. Gray read very slowly] who throws
himself on the cymbals is inimitable, besides producing
music slightly deafening in its character. We should really
like on some stormy night — if the little black boy could
make it convenient — to receive a serenade solely from
him.

"With the exception of one gentleman, who resides a
short distance out of the village, the Troubadours are
bachelors. More than this, we understand that they are
looking for wives: not other men's wives, but wives for
themselves. This is as it should be. Girls set your (night)
caps for them."

When Mrs. Gray had finished reading this scandalous article, she handed to me the paper, and asked if I could give her any explanation of what was therein set forth.

I replied that I could not; and added, I considered it very singular that there existed another little black boy than ours, who possessed a pair of cymbals. I had not failed, however, to notice, I remarked, that the negro race was partial to noise, and that undoubtedly it was a common occurrence for little black boys to own cymbals.

Mrs. Gray thought otherwise, and wished to know who I imagined the married man was, spoken of in the newspaper.

I told her it was impossible for me to say, for my acquaintance with married men was very limited; and further, that I knew of only two persons who would be likely to unite in any such "tomfoolery," and even with these, there were prudential reasons which I should think would deter them from pursuing such a course.

Mrs. Gray hoped I would name these persons to her. She would like to know on whom my suspicions rested. She trusted they were none of her acquaintances. If she would not mention the matter, I said, to the parties themselves, I would reveal their names. She promised never to say a word to either of them regarding it. So I told her that I thought our parson the likeliest man to engage in such an affair, and after him a gentleman named Barry Gray.

"As regards our good clergyman, Mr. G., I do not believe it possible; but for yourself, I fear it is only too probable. Yes, Mr. Gray, I have no doubt but you are the married man referred to in the 'Star-Spangled Banner,' and I must say that I consider the whole proceedings most shameful; and if it were not for that sweet little baby, I'd write immediately to my mother to take me home, and "—

"Mrs. Gray," I interposed, "you promised if I would tell you whom I considered the two likeliest persons to engage in such proceedings, that you would never mention the matter to either of them. I now claim the fulfilment of your promise."

This, Mrs. G. said, was adding insult to injury ; but, inasmuch as she had promised, why — well — she struggled hard to keep back a smile that would come, however, and which, when I perceived it, caused me to rise from my seat, and to walk round to where my wife sat, and to place my arms about her neck, and to kiss her on the lips held up for that purpose.

But I shall not attend any more extra meetings of our literary society. The little black boy's occupation, too, is gone. While the general impression among the Troubadours will be that Mrs. Gray has discovered the affair. None of them, either, will dare to come near Hillside for the next month, unless they should ride up on horseback, under the especial protection of some amiable young lady. It would be safer, too, if the young lady were a member in good standing of the same sewing society to which Mrs. G. belongs. It would also be well to send me a note through the post-office, specifying the hour of the intended visit, so that Mrs. G. and the baby might be in proper " trim " to receive them. Mrs. G. does not " admire " being taken by surprise. With these few preparations, any one of my bachelor friends might venture, without much risk, to give me a short call. It is n't a very pleasant thing to be a close prisoner, even on one's own estate ; and the face of a friend seen now and then is cheering to the heart. I do hope that some of them will visit me, that I may know what the news is in the political, literary, and musical portion of the world contained in " our village."

CHAPTER XXI.

Green Corn Pudding. — Nantucket Fashion. — Neighbor Pound. — Eggs.
The lost Dinner.—Hungry New-Yorkers.—Tempest in the Kitchen.

THINK, my dear," I said to Mrs. Gray, one fine morning, as we walked down the lane leading past the cornfield, "that it would be a good plan to have a corn-pudding for tea."

"A corn-pudding!" she exclaimed.

"Yes, a corn-pudding," I answered. "Perhaps you do not know what a corn-pudding is?"

"Well," she replied, "perhaps I do not; but I know what a johnny-cake is, and a bannock, and corn-bread, and mush, and hominy, and an Indian pudding. Now, if it be neither of these, I must confess my ignorance."

"You are, then, most certainly, my dear," I answered, "in a most benighted state of ignorance, and in this instance ignorance is far from being bliss; and, furthermore, it is not folly to be wise. Allow me to say a few words about corn-pudding, — green corn-pudding, — my dear, and you will then perceive your total ignorance of the matter. Many persons, my dear," I went on to say, seating myself on the top rail of the fence, and looking admiringly across the field of waving corn, with its sword-like leaves, its tufts of silvery silk, its upright ears, and tasselled tops, — "most estimable persons, too, know nothing about corn-puddings. There be thousands, doubtless, down in the village, who have never eaten of it. It is a satisfaction, however, to me, to know that I am not of that number. My knowledge of corn-puddings dates from infancy. When my great-grandfather removed from the island of Nantucket to the mainland, and built one of the first dwelling-houses in the city, now known as Hudson, but which was then, in 1783, called Claverack Landing, — Claverack is, I believe, the Dutch for Clover-reach, — he carried with him the knowledge which enabled him — or rather the women-folks of the family — to concoct corn-puddings. This was the best thing, I think, that he took away with him from Nantucket. The 'filthy lucre' which he had amassed there in the whale-fishery business, I count as dross. Succotash, however, is not a bad dish, and my esteemed grandmother — may Heaven rest her soul!" — here my wife piously crossed herself — " knew how to make that in perfection. She also knew how to prepare codfish chowder and make pumpkin-pies.

" But I find myself wandering slightly from the subject." My wife said she thought I was, but added it was excusable. " Some persons," I continued, not heeding her interruption, "especially those who are of Nantucket birth, believe that corn-puddings can be made nowhere in perfection except on the island. ' Harry Franco,' my dear, an out-and-out Nantucketer, having the blood of the Coffins, and Mitchells, and Macys, and ever so many others of the people of the island in his veins, and who, you may recollect, wrote that curious poem about sheep-shearing, in which the refrain

> " 'T is tu I can't, and tu I can,
> All the way from Shearing Pen "

occurs," — Mrs. Gray shook her head dubiously, — " he, I say, — good authority in these matters, — so thought, until one day in my bachelorhood, I asked him to partake at my rooms of a corn-pudding. He replied, in his usual cynical manner, that he would go, but that he did not believe I would be able to give him any corn-pudding. He had not, he said, eaten any worthy of being so called since he had left Nantucket, (which, according to my computation, must have been at least fifty years ago, if not longer,) and he had no faith in those of foreign make. When I told him, however, that I inherited the gift of making them from my grandfather, and the recipe from my grandmother, and, moreover, that I made them myself," — here Mrs. Gray looked up at me inquiringly, from her seat on the mossy stump below me. — "Yes," I said, answering her interrogatory look, "I make them, my dear." "Oh!" she cried, — "he said that he would try and have faith, but that, after all, the proof of the pudding was in the eating. Well, to make a long story short, I am happy to say that he was entirely satisfied with the dish I placed before him, and acknowledged the Nantucket skill evinced in its concoction. In the fulness of his appetite, however, he made a rash vow, which was, that if we both lived till 'chowder-time,' he would invite me to his house to partake of a genuine codfish chowder, such as only Nantucketers or their descendants can make. Many 'chowder-times,' my dear, have come and gone since then, but not an invitation have I received to such a feast; and as 'Harry Franco' — as well as myself — is getting quite gray, and the years are stealing upon him, I fear I may never taste a spoonful of his chowder."

Mrs. Gray here said that it would be a pity if it should so turn out. "But have you nothing further to tell! me," she continued, "about corn-puddings?"

"I have," I answered; "and as many other persons besides 'H. Franco' may like to eat of corn-puddings, and as I know you will be likely to circulate the account through the sewing circle," — here Mrs. Gray looked vexed, — "I will give you the recipe for making this truly delectable dish, which is of Indian origin, improved upon by the Quakers, and which, when eaten, should constitute the sole repast of what is known in Nantucket under the name of 'tea.'

"Take four dozen full ears of sweet green corn," — here I got off the fence, and began to pluck the ears, — "score the kernels, and cut them from the cob. Scrape off what remains on the cob with a knife. Pound the corn cut off in a mortar. Add a pint and a half, or one quart of milk, according to the youngness and juiciness of the corn. Add four eggs well beaten, a half tea-cup of flour, a half tea-cup of butter, a table-spoonful of sugar, and salt *quantum sufficit*. Bake in a well-greased earthen dish, in a hot oven, two hours. Place it on the table browned and smoking hot, eat it with plenty of fresh butter, and be thankful.”

Having by this time picked the necessary number of ears, I gave Mrs. Gray to understand that we would go home, and that I would immediately proceed to make the pudding, which, much to the indignation of the cook, and the intense delight of the black boy, I did. My wife, when we came to eat it, declared it was equal to anything of which she had ever partaken, and declared that if I would only go to New York and open a corn-pudding shop, I might make my fortune.

We have neighbors near Hillside. Everybody, I suppose, has neighbors. They are not, however, all alike. Some are good Samaritans, — such we love ; others are simply nuisances, and try one’s temper exceedingly. Of all annoyances, a borrowing neighbor is the greatest. We have such an one near Hillside. He stands ready to borrow anything, from a span of horses down to a carpet-tack. Nothing, in fact, comes amiss. There is never a day passes but neighbor Pound wishes the loan of a portion of our personal property. It would not surprise me if some day he should ask for a part of the real estate, — a bit of ground off the northwest corner of the farm, — or the well, or the gravel-pit, or almost anything.

He is constantly borrowing eggs, in the height of the egg season, and when they are scarce. He got so at one time that he borrowed them directly from under the hens ; and finally he borrowed the hens, and that without mentioning the circumstance to me. The only way I stopped this, was by shutting up the hens and locking the hennery door. If he had not kept hens himself, which would come

into the garden and scratch up all my wife's choice flower-
seeds, I would willingly have lent him all the eggs he could
have eaten ; but he wanted his own eggs, so he informed me,
to sell.   He was n't so well to do in the world, he said, as
was I, and besides, an egg now and then would n't be missed
by me.   I think, too. that he used to sell my eggs ; for one
day a market-man informed me, quite confidentially, that my
neighbor Pound did n't bring nearly as many eggs to town
then as he did formerly.   After which remark the dealer
in eggs winked and laughed.   A bad feature in my neighbor's case is, that he invariably forgets to return the articles
he borrows. This greatly aggravates me. One reason why
I keep the black boy is, that I may have somebody at hand
to run for borrowed property when it is wanted.

Once he, or his wife, — 't is all the same, — borrowed our
entire dinner, from the roasted turkey down to the currant-
jelly. Mrs. Gray and myself had just seated ourselves at
the table and I had asked a blessing. when in rushed
neighbor Pound's wife : " Such an unfortunate woman as I
am, Mrs. Gray!" she exclaimed. " Here now, I 've visitors
come, relatives of Mr. Pound's, from the city. Of course
they 're most starved, — people from the city always are,
when they get into the country, — and we 've not a morsel
of meat in the house to give them. ' Here now,' I said to
Pound, when he asked what in the world we would do ? —
' here now, I 'll go right over to Gray's, and ten to one I can
borrow their dinner.' " — As she said that, I thrust the carv-
ing-fork into the turkey. — " I remembered of seeing this
black boy, here now, killing a turkey early this morning,
and I knew what kind people you were, and that if I could
only get over here before you began eating, why you 'd
accommodate me. So that 's what I came for; and, here
now, I am."

As she saw me place the point of the knife close under
one wing of the doomed bird, "Oh, Mr. Gray," she exclaimed, " don't carve it ; " then turning to my wife, " could

we, would we, spare our dinner for that day; only think, visitors, — New-Yorkers," — as if New-Yorkers were of more consequence than Hillsiders; "and nothing decent in the world to offer them; here now, do lend it to me." The woman really cried as she gazed on our well-spread table; she would, I have no doubt, have gone down on her knees, had not my estimable wife, overflowing with pity and kindness, granted her request.

Mrs. Pound did n't wait for another word. Her basket was ready, our dinner quickly disappeared within its capacious mouth, and the next moment it was borne triumphantly away.

After it was gone, Mrs. Gray wept with vexation; the cook fairly raved, slashing things about in the kitchen at an awful rate, and declared to the black boy that she would leave her place if she was obliged to cook for the neighbors. The black boy nearly sprained his wrist stoning "old Pound's fowls" out of the garden. For myself, I endeavored to find consolation in mixing and imbibing a strictly private beverage, in the library. In thinking over the matter, I must say that I deeply regretted having performed the little devotional act over that turkey, when we sat down to the table, which I did.

I seldom meet Pound now without thinking of that lost dinner; for, of course, it never came back in any form whatsoever. He looks to me, always, as though he yet had that dinner somewhere under his waistcoat. I have no doubt but that he grew fat on it. I believe, too, that his dogs did; for I noticed him, the next day, feeding them with turkey-bones; and if anything is good to fatten dogs on, it is turkey-bones.

CHAPTER XXII.

Neighbor Pound's Daughter borrows "our Baby." — The Chase. — The Rescue. — Triumphal Return Home. — Our Fountain. — My Fish-pond. — Hydraulic Rams and Sheep.

THOUGHT, when my neighbor Pound borrowed our dinner, that, as regarded cool assurance, nothing could go beyond it. But this morning I found out my mistake. During a temporary absence of Mrs. Gray from the nursery, which, with the baby, was left in charge of the maid, who has been with us but a few days, Mrs. Pound's eldest daughter, a young lady on the shady side of thirty, called, and, without ringing the door-bell, — such kind neighbors are not apt to be formal, — proceeded direct to the nursery, where she found the new maid, whom she told that her mother had sent her over to borrow the baby for a little while. Then, without another word, she plucked my young son from his cradle, where he was peacefully sleeping, and before the nurse could interfere, had passed out of the house.

I was engaged writing in the library at the time, and my attention was only called to the occurrence by beholding Mrs. G., apparently half distracted, darting, bonnetless and shawlless, across the lawn, as if in pursuit of her shadow. The next moment she passed through the great gate, — leaving it wide open behind her, so that stray cows and pigs could enter the garden to destroy it, — and disappeared down the public highway. While I wondered what it all meant, I heard a "hubbub" in the kitchen, and presently the cook issued forth after Mrs. G., armed with a broom-stick; the nursery-maid followed close behind, weeping and wringing her hands ; and over in the orchard (where he passes a great deal of time since the apples ripened) I heard the black boy whistling for Watch.

The affair, I now thought, had become quite enough complicated for me to investigate. As I threw up the window and stepped out on the side piazza, I perceived, far down the road, Pound *fille*, streaking it along towards her house at a two-forty gait, with (it was impossible for me to be mistaken, even with my short-sightedness) our baby in her arms. Mrs. Gray was behind her but a few rods, and travelled, I thought, at a little faster rate. Had the course been say the sixteenth of a mile longer, Mrs. G. — I would have been willing to wager any amount — would have won the race. Every moment the affair, to a simple looker-on, grew more exciting — especially after the cook, nursery-maid, little black boy, and Watch, made their appearance. The old soldier was confined to his room with "the rheumatics," or else he would have hobbled after.

I am sorry to say that Mrs. Gray and party were beaten ; for Miss Elmira Pound not only reached her own home ahead of Mrs. G., but, most provoking of all, seated herself at an open window, where she danced little baby up and down directly before the eyes of his disconsolate mother, approaching the house.

Of course, Mrs. G. did n't, on this occasion, stop for ceremony ; and, not waiting to ring the bell, walked firmly into the house, and without speaking a word, — the fact is, she was too tired to utter a syllable, — took immediate and unresisted possession of "our baby," and, retreating instantly, marched, with flying colors, — I refer to the ribbons on her morning cap, which fluttered gayly in the breeze, — escorted by the entire company, back to Hillside.

I met the party at the great gate. The meeting between Mrs. Gray and myself was truly affecting : she placed the baby in my arms, and, half weeping, half laughing, clung about my neck, — she must have been very weary, I think,—while she asked me if I would n't arrest all the members of the Pound family for stealing our baby. After Mrs. G. had somewhat rested, and had refreshed herself with a glass of water, which the little black boy brought from the well, we moved up the gravel walk, and entered the house.

In regard to Pound *fille's* case, all I feel at liberty to say at present is, that she had better not venture to visit the domicile on Hillside, for some time to come, without bringing with her three or four of her father's dogs for her protection.

One more incident in which my neighbor figures. I had been trying various experiments with hydraulic machines. Mrs. Gray desired a fountain on the lawn. She thought it would improve the appearance of the place greatly. "Artificial fountains and stumps, my dear," I said, "do not seem exactly suited to each other." Thereupon Mrs. Gray made an observation concerning a savage and enlightened state, which, as I did not properly understand at the time, is my excuse for not more fully dwelling on at this moment.

At all events, more to please Mrs. G. than myself, I built a fountain. Of course, it proved a failure,— artificial fountains always fail,— and our fountain turned out to be simply a syringe in disguise. The little black boy, one evening when we had company, got up an opposition fountain with a hollow piece of alder a foot long, and a string wound about a stick for the piston,— the performance of which, under his direction, quite threw into the shade its more pretentious rival. Since that eventful night, we have taken little care of our unfortunate fountain, and, as a natural result, it passed into the hands of the little black boy, who has suffered it to go to decay.

I seldom behold that fountain now, without wishing to call my wife's attention to it, terming it " Mrs. Gray's folly "; but I am withheld from doing so by the remembrance of a little folly of my own, which, just about that time, I perpetrated, with a like amount of success as attended the fountain business. In short, I wished a fish-pond close by the house, where it would be convenient for me to cast my line before breakfast. To accomplish this, I purchased a hydraulic ram, and went to considerable expense in the matter. The whole concern, however, turned out badly. My fish-pond, somehow, would n't hold water. It allowed it to run out nearly as fast as the hydraulic engine poured it in. I sometimes fancied that the bottom of the pond was a great sieve. Then, too, the hydraulic ram failed to work well. It got choked up with green apples, which Tomothy thrust into the fountain end to see if they would come out at the other.

Provoked, at length, beyond endurance at my ill luck, I gave the whole thing up, and have ever since been contented to catch my fish from the small trout-stream which runs through my meadow at the foot of the hill, and to gaze, with Mrs. Gray, at such fountains as it pleases God to give us in the shape of mountain torrents and roaring brooks.

But I came near forgetting my neighbor Pound. One day — during the height of my hydraulic excitement — he called on me to borrow some article, when I chanced to ask him if he had any hydraulic rams on his farm.

"Not a blasted ram," he replied. "Why, here now, Gray," — the "here now," I believe, is peculiar to the whole family, — "those rams and sheep — for they 're all the same — are just the tarnelest critters for going over fences that ever was ; and you can't keep them, either, even if you build an eight-railed fence, staked and ridered all around ; because, here now, my dogs would kill more of your dratted rams and sheep in one night than you could buy in a week, sarch Alleghany county clean through ; and then I 'd like to know who 'd want to pay for your mutton. So, here now, Gray, I give you fair warning that, if you should stock your whole place with rams and sheep, I won't pay a single copper for any my dogs kill."

I assured Pound that I had not the remotest idea of stocking my place with sheep, or any kind of horned cattle that would be likely to break down fences and stray away; that, for my part, I had as much as I could do to keep my fowls at home, and prevent them from trespassing on my neighbor's grounds; and that I should be rather " scary " bow I ventured to invest my dollars in such nimble-footed animals as sheep, especially while he lived near, and kept such a race of curs about him.

I think my neighbor took a slight offence at what I said; for he immediately got off of the saw-buck on which he was sitting, and said he guessed as how he 'd better be jogging along: and more than this, he did not come near Hillside for three days thereafter.

CHAPTER XXIII.

My Parole. — Studying Chinese. — Weeding Carrots. — My Cousin's Father
"Our Lizzie."

T is nearly two weeks since I was in the village. I
may as well confess — for all my bachelor friends
have guessed it — that I am on my *parole d'hon-
neur* not to venture within the corporate limits of the village, for yet two weeks to come. I wish it understood,
however, that I made such a promise to Mrs. Gray of my
own free will. I am sorry, now, that I did; but Mrs. G.
has lived up to the promise she made, and I will to mine.
Of course, my time is not all occupied with the business of
the farm. I have many leisure hours on my hands. Formerly, those hours were passed in the company of my bachelor friends, within the village ; now I devote them to reading, writing, and studying. I am reading up my classics ;
I am pursuing with renewed vigor the study of Hebrew,
which, of late, I have greatly neglected ; I am, also, to a
limited extent, puzzling my brain over the Chinese language. It is, I find, a very difficult language to speak. I
am not certain that my pronunciation of it is altogether
correct. The little black boy, however, — who, with the ex
ception of the baby, is the only person that has heard me, —
thinks it is very good Chinese. In acquiring it, I labor
under several disadvantages : the chief one is the lack of
books. I am learning it solely from off a lot of old tea-
chests which I fortunately discovered, one rainy day, stored
out of the way in the garret. Mrs. Gray, I am sorry to
state, does not in the slightest degree encourage me to pursue it. She says it will only be labor thrown away. She

suggested to me that, in lieu of studying it this afternoon, I should address to our baby some lines, founded on the attempt made by Miss Pound to steal our infant, which would please her; or else write a short sermon on the text, " He was lost and is found," based on the same occurrence, and send it to my grandmother.

I said "No!" to both of these propositions of my wife's, and added that I wished to write one of my Hillside Sketches. She replied I had better cease writing any more of those silly articles ; that half of them were not true, and the other half simply scandalous; and that, instead of spending my time in that way, I had much better be out in the fields weeding carrots.

I answered that I had enough weeding carrots when I was a very young man, and went courting a cousin of mine who resided on a farm. Her father — foolish man that he was — somehow did n't fancy me, so he used to get me to go down into the field with his boys to weed carrots. I was no fonder of weeding carrots then, Mrs. Gray, than I am now; and though I liked courting my cousin well enough, I was not, I confess, partial to the carrot business. And so, to make a long story short, Mrs. G., that was the course my cousin's father took to break off any little matrimonial engagement which, perhaps, existed between us, and (for stooping over in the hot sun made my back ache abominably) he succeeded.

" Did your cousin, Mr. Gray, ever marry? " asked my wife, somewhat anxiously, I thought.

" Certainly, my dear," I replied ; " and she has long been a happy mother. Her eldest son — she is blest with two, besides one daughter — is named after me, and possesses a silver cup presented by me as his godfather."

" Which is more, Mr. G.," said my wife, somewhat excited, "than you have done for your own son."

"That little affair, my dear," I replied, " rests entirely with our boy's godfather and not with me."

Thereupon followed a discussion between Mrs. G. and myself relative to the child's baptism, which, as it was purely of a private character, I will not here repeat.

After a while, when I thought Mrs. Gray was so absorbed in her needlework as to have forgotten all about my cousin and the carrots, she quite surprised me by hastily asking what was the character of my cousin's husband.

I answered, "I cannot positively say, but her father one day informed me — I remember we had been drinking ale that day together at dinner, his voice pendulating somewhere 'twixt joy and grief — that Mr. Jones was no more partial to weeding carrots than I."

"Which meant, Mr. Gray, I suppose," chimed in my wife, "that he was a lazy man!"

"I do not know, my dear, what it meant," I replied; "but let me tell you that it is very hard work to weed carrots. And now, my love," I added, let us go into the orchard and gather some apples." And we went.

When we reached the orchard, Mrs. Gray asked me what number of female cousins I possessed?

"They are countless," I answered, "as the leaves in Vallambrosa!"

"Where, under the sun, Mr. G.," asked my wife, "is Vallambrosa?"

"In the sunny South," I replied, "and it is a country of which the poets love to speak."

"Do your cousins, my dear," asked Mrs. G., "reside there?"

"No!" I answered; "some are nearer home; others are in Utopia; and there are still others whose mortal remains are in Greenwood, but whose souls are, I trust, in 'mansions not made with hands, eternal in the heavens.' Come, my dear," I continued, as we reached the shade of a venerable apple-tree, evidently the patriarch of the orchard, — "come, 'let us sit upon the ground and tell sad stories of the death of kings.'"

"No, my dear," she replied, " better sit on this large, flat stone, and tell me of your cousins in Greenwood."

" Well, as you please," I answered, " 't is nearly the same thing, — kings or cousins, — for, if beauty and worth are emblematic of royalty, and should meet with due reward, my cousins would all have been crowned queens."

Mrs. Gray smiled a sad, sweet smile, and I continued: " You may have observed, my love, during our wedded life, that I often express great partiality for my cousins, especially such as are of the gentler sex. I love those who are living; I love those who are dead; and of these last, — the most precious of them all, perhaps, though it is hard to say who is the most precious of the well-beloved dead, — is one who rests in Greenwood, and on whose tombstone you will find simply these words, ' Our Lizzie,' and 't is all-sufficient : we who knew her ask for nothing more, — name, date, and words of praise are alike unnecessary, — all these are inscribed on our hearts; while to the mere stranger these two words will touch a chord in his heart, and make a pulse vibrate to a hidden memory, which a score of graven sentences would have failed to awaken.

" A wife she was, too, — a wife of barely six short months. In May, just six years gone, her bridal was ; but ere the autumn fled, with the last flowers of the season, she perished. She did not, like flowers that die upon the stalk, wither day by day, but as one plucked will droop and fade within the circlet of an hour, so she, so full of life and love and joy, one hour, was, in the next, all cold and still and dead.

" Struck down by the grim destroyer, almost in an instant, ere her fond husband could reach her side, her pure spirit. loosed from its mortality, winged its rejoicing way to paradise. The husband — so joyous before — from that day was seldom known to smile. Mourning and broken-hearted, he went through life, performing faithfully and well the duties required of him as a man and a Christian.

Such was his life ; until one day, a year ago, God sum-
moned him to lay aside his earthly tabernacle, and, thank-
fully obeying, he passed from earth, hoping to meet her
who was so dear to him in life. And then that which remained of him was laid gently down by her side in Greenwood, there to sleep till those who die in Christ shall rise."

I looked at Mrs. Gray and found her weeping. I took
her hand and said such occurrences were common to our
race ; they were every day happening about us. Such
events we were all likely soon to meet.

" They are none the less touching and sorrowful to think
of," she replied, " for all that."

" True, my love, none the less," I answered ; " then let
us strive to meet with fortitude — the fortitude that only
the Bible can yield us— that day when the separation
shall come, and which even the most loving hearts must
know. But see," I continued, " how the long shadows go
creeping through the aisles of the orchard. The dew, too,
is falling, and it is time for us to enter the house and take
a look at baby."

Since we came in, the lamps have been lighted ; the tea
partaken of ; the baby placed in his cradle for the night ;
the little black boy severely reprimanded for feeding
several of the cows on ears of " hot, hot corn, piping
hot," which he stole from the kettle where they were boiling for the men's supper ; the cook fully posted in regard
to the morrow's breakfast ; Mrs. Gray has been engaged
in reading a new novel, and I have been allowed to write
this Hillside Sketch.

CHAPTER XXIV.

The Caravan. — Wide Awake. — Miss Smith. — An Uncomfortable Household. — Another Visitor.

MRS. GRAY and myself have not yet been on our picnic for the reason that we have been troubled with company. The company came the very day we had "fixed on" for our party. It consisted of an elderly young lady, with a King Charles spaniel, two trunks, three bandboxes, a jar of geraniums, a shawl, and an umbrella. This caravan arrived about daybreak on a rainy morning, long before Mrs. G. or myself even dreamed of rising. I think I must have been disturbed by the grating of the carriage-wheels on the gravel walk as it drove up to the door, for just about that time I dreamed I was at work making a macadamized road, with a chain and ball attached to my ankle. While I was thus laudably engaged in the service of the State, a bell rang for breakfast or prayers, I could n't tell exactly which, when I discovered, much to my chagrin, that the chain was made fast to a stone pillar, so that I could not possibly get away. The bell continued ringing, however, for me to go to breakfast or prayers, and I pulled with all my strength to get free, when suddenly the pillar fell with a loud crash towards me, and I, leaping aside to avoid it, found myself standing in the middle of the chamber, the bedclothes grasped in my hands, the cradle overturned, the baby crying on the floor, Mrs. Gray sitting up in bed shivering with fright and cold, while the most confounded rapping and knocking and ringing was going on down-stairs at the hall-door that was ever heard.

"*What* can it be?" asked Mrs. G.

"*Who* can it be? you mean," I replied, in no very good humor; "the *what* is evident enough."

"Perhaps it's the Judge, from the city," suggested Mrs. Gray; "you know, when last here, he half promised to make us a visit."

"But he, or any sane man," I answered, "would n't come at such an unseasonable hour; nor would he create such an abominable disturbance. No; you may depend on it, it's some inconsiderate woman."

"Perhaps it is my mother," she replied, "or yours, Mr. Gray."

"Nothing more likely," I answered.

"Well, Mr. G.," said my wife, as a fresh supply of knockings took place, "why don't you go down-stairs and open the door, and see who it is?"

"If you 'll be patient, my dear," I exclaimed, "till I get on a stocking or two, I 'll go; but look at me," — Mrs. G. positively declared that she would not, — "am I in a fit state to go down to the front door?"

Mrs. G. then urged me to hurry, and, at the same time, wished me to pick up the baby and give her some portion of the bedclothes. I complied with Mrs. G.'s reasonable request, and then, slipping on my dressing-gown, I proceeded down-stairs and opened the door, when in marched the caravan alluded to above.

The lady was an entire stranger to me, but as I presumed she was, at least, a first-cousin of my wife, I ushered her, with great politeness and cordiality, into the parlor; saw, myself, that all her travelling-furniture was safely housed, and then, telling her that I would send Mrs. Gray immediately down, I went up-stairs. I had entirely forgotten to ask the stranger's name; so when my wife, the moment I entered the room, wanted to know who it was, I was obliged to confess that I could not tell her. Mrs. G.'s curiosity was greatly excited, and she declared that she would n't go down-stairs until I had first inquired the visitor's name. To please Mrs. G., therefore, I did so. When I came up again, I found Mrs. G. leaning over the banisters, at the head of the stairs, trying to spell the lady's name from the card tacked on the end of her trunk, which, by chance, was upside-down. She, however, failed to decipher it, nor was her curiosity much allayed when I mentioned that the lady's name was Smith. Thereupon Mrs. G., after considering a moment, remarked that very likely it was her cousin Mary Ann, from Oakland. When, however, Mary Ann's portrait was drawn very graphically by Mrs. Gray, I immediately declared that the inhabitant of our parlor was not that personage. Mrs. G. knew several other Smiths, but none whose personal appearance, in any way, corresponded with "our early bird." It was some time before Mrs. Gray would go down-stairs, though quite prepared so to do. She seemed to enjoy wonderfully enumerating, for my benefit, the many Smiths whose acquaintance she possessed, and guessing which of them all was our visitor.

At last she left me, when I arranged myself comfortably for another nap. I was soon, however, disturbed by Mrs. G.'s return, who astonished me with the alarming information that she had never, until that morning, encountered the Miss Smith who had come to visit us. Mrs. Gray had heard of her, however, through her mother. In fact, the visit to us was based on the ground of her acquaintance with my wife's mother. Miss S. had once visited Mrs. G.'s mother. She had passed a winter with her. My estimable wife, at the time, was from home at boarding-school. Mrs. G. remembered, however, hearing of Miss S.'s visit. She was aware, too, that Miss S. devoted her life to visiting among her acquaintances. On the slightest pretext she would pay you a visit. One word of welcome given her would ensure you a month's visitation. With two words, you might be certain of her staying half a year. And further encouragement would keep her with you a lifetime, provided you were not absolutely uncivil towards her.

When Mrs. G. had duly given me this information, I told her she had better inform the " morning herald " that there were many admirable hotels in the village, and recommend to her one of them. Tell her, too, that we are overrun with visitors; that there is a dearth of milk and honey in the house; that the cook takes snuff; that the baby is teething; that there is no lightning-rod on our cottage; that I am a — I could n't think of anything bad enough to suit me, so I asked Mrs. G. what I was: she suggested " miserable sinner," which was evidently a quotation. Yes, I continued, a miserable sinner; and tell her, too, that I am expecting a horde of old bachelors to pass a week with me: not that I exactly expect them, my dear, at least not till you visit your mother again ; but, then, they might possibly come, you know.

Mrs. G. said, incredulously, " Yes," she knew they might, but that, for her part, she did n't believe that any old bachelor could frighten off Miss Smith. Indeed it would not surprise her if she were partial to them.

" Then," I said, " I guess she 'll prove another old soldier, and pass the winter with us." Mrs. Gray thought not. She would treat her, she said, so politely that she would be glad to beat a retreat.

The concluding words of Mrs. G.'s remark showed me that she had listened to the old soldier's phrases to some purpose. My wife's tactics were admirable. She gave the strange lady the run of the parlors and one chamber ; she debarred her access to either the nursery, the sitting-room, or the library. She even went so far as to have the black boy take each meal to her, which was served in the parlor. This was done under plea that the dining-room was being painted. I set the painters to work the day the caravan arrived. It was the beginning, so Mrs. G. said, of the fall house-cleaning : and from that day till Miss

Smith "beat a retreat," five days thereafter, there was a continual scrubbing and rubbing, painting and mopping, washing and slopping, going on throughout the house, till at last the whole establishment was cleansed, with the exception, Mrs. G. informed Miss S., of the parlors and one chamber. This hint was sufficient. The next morning Miss Smith and suite took the first train going South. Mrs. Gray said, at parting with her, that she hoped she had been comfortable. There was about that time a "cold term," which lasted a week, not more to our visitor's discomfort than to Mrs. G.'s, who, with doors and windows open, was superintending, in person, the house-cleaning operation. There were no fires, save in the kitchen, where the cook reigned supreme; in the nursery, where the baby dwelt; and in the library, where I confined myself. Shawls were in requisition both by Miss S. and Mrs. G., and it is very doubtful to my mind whether, under the circumstances, our visitor was as comfortable as Mrs. G. hoped. One source of annoyance to our morning belle was the little black boy. The tricks he played on her "sweet little spaniel" were innumerable, and I think had great weight in influencing Miss S. to take her departure. After she had left, house-cleaning continued one day longer, and then ceased. Somehow Mrs. G. managed on that occasion to take a severe cold, which continues with her to this present time, and will, I fear, prevent us from going on our contemplated picnic, until, at least, another summer arrives.

CHAPTER XXV.

A Caller. — " The Editor." — An Epic wanted. — Mrs. Gray's Mistake. — Her Rebuke. — Mysterious Disappearance of the Little Black Boy. — Roasting Chestnuts.

THE editor of the " Star-Spangled Banner " called on me a few days since. He was quite down in the mouth. His newspaper, he feared, was running to seed. He was afraid he would himself, should he be obliged to " shin out " much longer. He wanted me to assist him. I, he said, could do it. He mentioned exactly how I could accomplish it. I should like to have accommodated him, but I was so circumstanced that it would have been impolitic in me so to do. Indeed, it would have been a dangerous thing for me to have attempted. I told him so. He appeared much disappointed. At first I was fearful he would immediately go and destroy himself. I am happy to state, however, that he finally went away from Hillside in good spirits.

The following day I bethought me of a plan by which I could benefit him. I would write some striking verses for his newspaper. Thereupon I composed the following lines. If anything will cause his paper to sell, I think that they will. They set forth his case in a very strong and proper light. After reading them, I trust his old subscribers will immediately pay up, and that new patrons will forward their subscriptions. He has a note, I understand, to pay early next month, and any assistance rendered him before that time arrives will be doubly acceptable. I have allowed myself the privilege — an author's privilege — of forward-

ing the lines to the "Home Journal" for publication prior
to their appearance in the "Star-Spangled Banner"

THE EDITOR.

He came to me, just five feet high,
  A gentleman in dress and manner,
Who ne'er was known to tell a lie,
  Yet edited the Spangled Banner.
In politics he is *non est*,
  Conservative as any parson,
Did vote for "Harry of the West";
  Would like to vote for old Kit Carson.

But to the present he was blind,
  Cared nothing for its men or measures,
Said that republics were unkind,
  And sought for peace in household pleasures.
He 'd been in office once, and knew
  What 't was to truckle to a party;
He 'd tried them all — each thievish crew —
  And now, he said, he cursed them hearty.

He 'd had advances made of late,
  To him by men of either section : —
One offered him a set of plate
  To use his paper till election ;
Another promised him a place
  Within the Custom-House, for "sartin."
He answered him, with laughing face,
  Yes, " in his eye, and Betty Martin."

And still another said, that they
  Would make him consul at some island
In the Pacific, — far away, —
  With sunny shores and verdant highland.
He thought the latter rather green,
  To offer him such situation ;
He 'd like to call on England's queen,
  Or go to Russia's coronation.

He had his price, he said, but then
  He had n't found a decent bidder;

He went for money, not for men, —
  Besides, his wife might be a " widder ";
And he would like to have it told,
  If he should die before election,
That he had left his spouse some gold —
  'T would show the world he had affection.

He felt, though, that the times were hard ;
  His best subscribers failed to pay him.
Butter had " riz," and so had lard,
  And eggs, and eke the hens that lay 'em.
A literary sheet, he said,
  Was something that the people needed ;
But if it would n't bring him bread,
  He 'd let their dulness go unheeded.

He trusted though that they would change,
  And give him — say a grand donation ;
And then — he should n't think it strange
  If he should give them an oration.
He 'd deem it quite the handsome thing,
  If his subscribers would sustain him ;
If not, no more to them he 'd bring
  His paper, and they could n't blame him.

Nothing was stirring now, he said,
  Save only scheming politicians ;
The troubadours had gone to bed,
  Or, worse, had gone on foreign missions,
Electioneering through the State,
  And making many foolish speeches.
'T were better they, with SUE and KATE,
  Were home, and eating cream and peaches.

He wished — upon his word he did —
  That I would give another dinner ;
He 'd come, if only he were bid,
  Or else he were a perfect sinner.
Then such an article he 'd write,
  For his judicious Spangled Banner,
As ne'er before had seen the light : —
  Thought I, myself, you are a planner.

"'T would sell the number sure, he said,
  And start again its circulation;
'T would hit the right nail on the head,
  And re-create the old sensation.
" Come, my dear fellow-mortal, come,
  You 'll much oblige me if you 'll do it."
"I would, but Mrs. Gray 's at home,
  And, oh, my eyes! how I should rue it."

He took his hat; he took his cane;
  He said he felt much disappointed.
He wished to gracious it would rain;
  He 'd like to see the world disjointed.
He took a step towards the door,
  He looked, indeed, quite broken-hearted;
He dropped his hat upon the floor,
  He picked it up, and then departed.

But scarcely had he gone a rod,
  When I recalled his looks so fearful,
Oh! how significant his nod
  Was of the grave and all things tearful.
I oped the door, — I called him in,
  And asked him if he 'd have some whiskey?
He said he would. It made him grin;
  And then he went away quite frisky.

As soon as I had completed the above lines, I called to
me the little black boy, who was diverting himself by
swinging on the great gate, and ordered him to take the
MS. to Mrs. Gray, in the nursery, for her perusal. I did
not see Mrs. G. till tea-time. I thought during the meal
that she would speak to me regarding them; but, to my
surprise, she did not. As a general thing, Mrs. Gray does
not pass over my productions in silence. She is apt to
criticise them severely. She wishes I would omit such and
such lines, or introduce such and such expressions. She
suggests many changes and alterations. She would like
to have me write one poem, at least, in accordance with her
plans. I gather by her conversation, delivered principally
on rainy Sundays, that she would have me compose an epic,

something after the style of " Paradise Lost," — something grand and solemn, worthy, Mrs. G. says, of a place on the shelves of the Astor Library, and which would be read with satisfaction in future times by future generations. Simply to keep my wife in good-humor, I tell her that I am turning the idea over in my mind, and that one of these days I expect to produce something noble.

She quite alarmed me the other day, when I mentioned that I was turning the matter over in my mind, by remarking that a rolling stone gathered no moss, and she feared my " turning ideas " would prove but rolling stones. Knowing, therefore, Mrs. Gray's tendency to speak freely in relation to my writings, I was astonished that she failed, during the tea-hour, to discuss the merits and demerits of my last production. Afterwards, therefore, when we were gathered about the library fire, Mrs. G. engaged in re-buttoning my last winter's overcoat, and I " munching," squirrel-like, some October chestnuts, I asked my wife, as I peeled off the fresh brown shell of one, how she liked " The Editor " I sent her that afternoon.

She wished to know if I referred to the short, seedy-looking individual whom she noticed zigzagging across the lawn, in a sort of dog-trot, yesterday morning; for if it were him I had sent to her, she was thankful that she had not seen him; and what could have possessed me, she would like to know, to send to her such a man as that.

I told her that she misunderstood me. I simply meant the verses entitled " The Editor," which I sent to her by the little black boy. She had neither received the verses, she said, nor seen the colored child.

It was strange, I replied. Then I rung the bell for the black boy to make his appearance. He failed, however, to do so. At the second ringing of the bell, the cook made her appearance. She informed me that he had gone away about four o'clock, and had not yet returned, though supper, she said, was over, and everything cleared away, and mighty little of anything to eat· would that boy get till the next morning. It was strange, she continued, what had become of him. She had never known him to be absent before at meal-time.

To tell the truth, I was myself a little alarmed. His absence from supper was a bad feature in the case. "Something out of the common course," I said to Mrs. Gray, "must have occurred to detain him. 'T is no small matter, you may depend on 't, which keeps him this night away from his mush and milk and sweet potatoes. It would be a little singular, my dear," I continued, "if, though so late in the season, you and I should yet go a black burying."

"Mr. Gray," said my wife, very solemnly, "never allow yourself to joke on serious subjects. It is an evidence, not only of a shallow mind, but also of a wicked heart. If any accident has happened to the little black boy, Mr. G., you will be sorry for having thus lightly spoken in regard to him."

After this rebuke from Mrs. Gray, I said nothing for five minutes, but applied myself most industriously to roasting a few large and choice chestnuts, on the shovel placed over the live embers, and wondering — if the black boy had indeed given up his lease on life — what had become of the verses I had intrusted to him. While I was occupied in this profitable speculation, there came a ghost-like tap at the door, which so startled me, that I dropped the shovel and chestnuts into the fire, and hastily turning around, beheld young ebony himself. I was on the point of blowing him up sky-high, — losing my chestnuts as I did, aggravated me a good deal, — when Mrs. Gray commenced the attack, opening her battery of small fireworks by saying, — "Now, Mr. Black Boy, I want you should give an account of yourself. I should like to know where you 've been, and where that paper is Mr. Gray sent by you to me."

The lad looked like a black sheep before the slaughterer.

He would n't do so again, he said.

"Do what again ? " asked Mrs. G.

"Why, go off," he replied.

"Where? go off where?" insisted Mrs. G.

"Why, down yonder," he continued.

"Come, sir," I said, losing patience, "tell me all about it."

So he proceeded to inform me that he had been down to the blacksmith's shop at the corners, where he had been reading my verses on "The Editor" to the company there assembled. He read it, he said, five times to crowds of people, who were very much tickled with it, and who gave him three cheers. He told them that Mister Gray wrote it, but that he himself helped on a good deal of it.

If ever there were a proud little black boy, he stood before me. He wanted to know if I would like to have him read it to me. I replied affirmatively ; whereupon he mounted an ottoman, and read in a very clever manner — I taught the boy to read, you 'll remember — the verses in question.

When he had finished, Mrs. G. gave him a slice of cake and a sip of wine, and the cook took him into the kitchen and treated him with a large piece of pumpkin-pie. Before he left the library, however, he asked me what I thought of his going about the country the coming winter, delivering poems. I replied I thought favorably of it. He appeared quite delighted with my answer, and went out, to get his pie, in high glee.

"Mrs. Gray," I asked, after the black boy had retired, "how do you like my verses?"

Mrs. G. did not like them at all. She thought they lacked both wit and originality. I admitted the former, but denied the latter accusation.

"But don't you think, my dear," persisted my wife, "that your writings bear some resemblance occasionally to Mr. Chickweed's ?"

"Not a bit of it," I replied; "they are no more alike, my love, than cherries and gooseberries. What poem of Chickweed's," I continued, "do my verses resemble?"

Mrs. G. said she did not know, but that they sounded somewhat like something she had somewhere read. She did not, however, allude particularly, in her present remarks, to these verses. She referred, generally, to my prose. It was imitation, not the real article; German silver, not the pure ore.

"If you please, Mrs. Gray," I remarked, "we will here let the subject drop, for it is one not entirely agreeable to me."

"As you like, Mr. G."

And thereupon the conversation ceased.

CHAPTER XXVI.

I get up a Picnic. — Kissing the Baby. — Vanity. — The Advantage of
Picnics. — Prim and Bustle.

AM going on a picnic. My wife and baby are to
accompany me. As the picnic is gotten up solely
by myself, I could do no less than invite Mrs.
Gray to join it. To be candid, she is the only one whom I
have invited. I should like to have asked a few of my
friends ; but when I mentioned to Mrs. G. this desire of
mine, she gave me so distinctly to understand it would not
be agreeable to her, that I incontinently gave it up.

" Because," said she, " of course we shall be obliged to
take the baby with us ; and how do you suppose I can take
proper care of the child if any of your bachelor friends are
prying about ? "

I don't profess to be a very " smart " man, but I instantly
perceived how inconvenient it would be to increase the
number of our party. Babies, after all, I thought, are great
annoyances, especially in assemblages where bachelors are
present. Their proper places are in the nursery. I said
so to Mrs. G., and suggested the feasibility of leaving baby
at home. She replied that such a thing was not to be
thought of, and wondered at my desiring it. Then I
laughed, and said I only suggested it to tease her. Then
Mrs. G. laughed, and said it was shameful in me to do it.
Then we both proceeded to the nursery to look at the baby,
who lay in his cradle asleep. Mrs. Gray kissed him, and
wanted me to do the same. I refused, however, and told
my wife it was all nonsense kissing babies, for they did not

appreciate it, and that, for my part, I 'd rather kiss a pretty girl.

"Don't, Mr. G.," my wife replied, — "don't say so, for it pains me to hear you speak so slightingly of the precious little darling. See how prettily his hands are folded across his bosom! Is n't he a handsome child, Mr. Gray?" and the fond mother stooped over him, ostensibly for the purpose of arranging his pillow, but really to once more kiss him. I suppose she felt sorry that I refused to do so. Just as we were leaving the room, and Mrs. Gray's back was turned, I bent down and kissed the youngster very softly, without, as I thought, its being perceived by Mrs. G.

When we reached the library, my wife remarked that she thought I did love the child, notwithstanding I permitted myself to allude to him oftentimes in a light and thoughtless manner; "for," she added, "I noticed, my dear, in the mirror, that you kissed him."

I don't think it a good plan to have a mirror in the nursery. I believe the nurse spends much time which should be devoted to taking care of the baby, in arranging her hair, and otherwise adorning her person. I should be sorry to be the cause of creating, even indirectly, in any one's mind a regard for vain and frivolous things. Vanity is a sin which lies at the foundation of many a blasted reputation. I spake all this to Mrs. Gray, and requested her to remove the mirror from the nursery. Mrs. G., I am sorry to say, absolutely refused to grant my request. If it were not that the baby might chance to be harmed thereby, I would order Tomothy to throw — quite accidentally, of course — a stone into the open window at the tale-telling mirror. As it is, I shall request our parson to preach a sermon against vanity.

After a while, when reference was again made to the picnic, I said, addressing Mrs. Gray, "Nothing, my dear, can be better in summer time than a picnic. It is better than a party or a ball. It is better than going to the the

atre or the circus " — Mrs. G. here interrupted me to say
that she never went to such places, and she really hoped I
never did.

" Sea-bathing," I continued, not heeding my wife's remarks, " is undoubtedly pleasant ; but even on a picnic
one is generally sure to have the benefit of a bath before
he gets home. And here let me add, my dear, that you be
particular to remind me to carry with us an umbrella. A
picnic, too, is a healthful diversion, even under the most
unpropitious circumstances. Should it rain in torrents —
should the chicken-pie be forgotten and left at home —
should the spoons be lost or stolen — should we be chased
by dogs or ferocious horned cattle — should we tear our
clothes scrambling through bushes or climbing over rail
fences — should we miss the tide, if we go by water, and
thereby have to row the whole distance, both going and
returning, against the current — should we find, when we
are ready to return home, that the boat has floated from
its moorings — or the oars been used, by the young lady
who personates the cook, for firewood — or, quite as bad,
what once happened to myself and party."

Thereupon Mrs. G. said that she would like dearly to
know what it was to which I referred. To please Mrs.
Gray, I opened my writing-desk, and taking therefrom a
journal of some years' standing, read from its pages the
following account of the matter, — first, however, prefacing
the story with this introduction : —

" You know, my dear," I commenced, " Prim and Bustle, whom we met at my old home at Rivertown, whither
we went on our wedding-tour?" Mrs. G. nodded an as-
sent. " But you do not know, my love," I continued, " tha'
my friend Clarence and myself seldom failed closing a
summer or a winter day without passing an hour or two —
perhaps it were more, for time flew on swallow's wings
during that halcyon period of my life — in the society of
those two sunny maidens."

Mrs. Gray hereupon observed that she did not; but it in no wise surprised her to learn that such was the case.

"Ah!" I continued, half soliloquizing, "those were cheerful nights we passed around the centre-table in the corner, when, the solar lamp lighted, and the shades dropped at the windows, and, if it were winter, a fresh scuttle of coal cast on the cheerful fire, heeding little the storm going on out-of-doors, we sat with loved ones within their dear old home."

Mrs. G. looked up inquiringly from her work, and exclaimed. "Indeed!"

"There was Prim," I went on, "so precise and dignified, sitting erect in her high-backed chair, busily sewing on some useful garment; and Bustle, on a low stool, daintily stitching a bit of ruffle; and the Gemini — they were wild girls in those days — occupied, more or less, with their school-lessons, while the good mother, — God bless that mother, Abeline!" "Yes," said A., "God bless her!" — "with pleasant smiles and gentle words, sought, in the basket beside her on the sofa, her own necessary work; while Clarence and I alternately read aloud from some entertaining book."

"What books were they, Mr. Gray?" asked my wife.

"Oh, there was the Encyclopædia Britannica, in twenty volumes, to commence with," I replied; "and the autobiography of Mahaloo Doolah, an African princess, in ten octavo volumes; and the wonderful history of Abou Ben Adhem, a Mahometan, whose tribe increased" —

"There, Mr. G.," interrupted my very matter-of-fact wife, "that will do: please to continue your narrative."

So I went on. "Prim and Bustle, my dear, still sit, as of old, around that magic table; the Gemini, somewhat sobered down, crochet and net, instead of studying; and the good mother yet plies her housewife's needle: but Clarence and I are not there to join them, though others, doubtless, have stepped into the places we once occupied, and the circle remains complete."

"But what has all this, Mr. G., got to do with your story?"

"Story! Why, bless me, my dear," I replied, "I had quite forgotten it, though I remember now all about it." So, turning to my journal without further delay, I read what will be found in the next chapter.

CHAPTER XXVII.

A Picnic on Rocky Island. — Not exactly Poetry. — Rowing. — Securing
the Boat. — Ebb Tide. — In the Mud. — Carrying the Girls. — Our
Reward. — The Wager. — Home Again.

ET'S get up a picnic?" said I to Clarence.
"Agreed! agreed!" said he. "Who shall we
ask?" said I to Clarence. "Why, Prim and
Bustle," said he. "Who else shall we ask?" said I to
Clarence. "The Gemini," said he. "And their cousin
from Montreal," said I. "With their cousin S.," said he.
"Quite a family party," said I to Clarence. "Yes, very,"
said he to me.

"Mr. Gray," interrupted my wife, "is that poetry which
you are reading?"

"No, my dear," I replied, "not exactly poetry."

"I thought it was," continued Mrs. G.; "but whatever
it is, for goodness' sake don't read me any more; it will
weary me to death if you keep on longer in that strain."

"But, my dear," I replied, "if I am to read the story to
you, I cannot do so otherwise than as it is written."

"Could you not, however, manage, Mr. Gray," persisted
my wife, "to omit repeating so often the ' said I ' and ' said
he '?"

"Perhaps I could," I replied; "to please you, I will endeavor so to do."

"Thank you, my dear," added my wife. Then I continued the narrative as follows: —

"The evening of the day on which the above conversation occurred between Clarence and myself found us, as
usual, gathered about the round table, discussing the sub-

ject of the intended picnic. It was a matter of doubt for some time as to where we should go. A portion of our party was in favor of visiting Bash-Bish Falls. This would have been very pleasant; but the distance, I urged, was so great that the whole day would necessarily be consumed in going and returning. I added, also, that the place was noted for the numberless rattlesnakes which infested it. That alone was sufficient, and not a young lady of them all was courageous enough, after learning that fact, to express even a wish to go there. Besides, I whispered to Clarence, what with horses and carriages, the party would cost much more than it was worth. Considering these things, then, it is no wonder that we concluded to visit Rocky Island.

On the following morning, therefore, we went. Clarence and myself rowed the boat the whole distance, — some five or six miles. Of course, the tide was dead against us. Of course, too, his hands were blistered. Mine would have been, only, when quite a lad, I came near going on a whaling voyage around " the Horn," and the simple thought of all I might have gone through so hardened their palms that working the light sculls had no effect on them. Clarence, however, ungenerously said that my schoolmaster hardened them for me; while Bustle thought they became so in my vain efforts at weeding carrots. Prim thereupon looked very grave, and desired Bustle to desist; and just at that moment my oar — accidentally, of course — slipped out of the rowlock and spattered water on the two detractors.

In due time we reached the island in safety and good spirits. We passed the day there pleasantly enough. At sundown we started to return, — that is, we went to the spot where we had left our boat. We had taken particular pains to secure that boat, either from drifting away or being stolen. We had fastened the painter, with a padlock, to a tree that grew near the water's edge. We had cast over the stern of the boat a rope, with a large stone attached, for an anchor. We had carried the oars with us into the woods. We had unshipped the rudder and hidden it in the bushes. We had even taken out the thole-pins, and had placed them in our pockets. In short, we had taken every imaginable precaution to secure, for our own use, that particular boat when we should wish to go home. When, therefore, we went to the place where, in the morning, we had left our craft rocking in six or seven feet of water, we had no difficulty in finding it, safe and secure as we expected, but, to our surprise, there was no water within half a mile of it. There had evidently been a great falling off in that particular article. The boat lay in a bed of soft mud. The tide was out. It was still going out. The buoys within sight all pointed down the stream. How much longer it would continue to ebb I was not sailor enough to know. I thought that in the course of an hour or so it would turn, and then in three or four more the boat would float. When I mentioned this to the young ladies, they remarked it was painful to think of. At that rate it would be ten o'clock at night before we could leave the island; "and you know, Mr. Gray," said Bustle, "you two youths are not the best oarsmen in the world, so it will be midnight at least before we get home; and won't my good mother," she added, "be worried about us; and won't you two catch a scolding for keeping us out so late?"

"It is too bad," I said, "but it can't be helped, that I see." So we seated ourselves in the boat, which no one had stolen, and which had n't floated away, and watched the receding tide. Suddenly, Clarence, who had been silent for several minutes, surprised us with the information that it would not be flood-tide till six o'clock the next morning. He had just calculated the whole thing, he said, by the rule of three, in his head, and knew that it was so. While we were pondering on this frightful information, and wondering if it were true, the cousin from Montreal appalled us by stating that she also had made a calculation based on the time of the moon's rising, and that she was certain, if we waited for the tide, we would not get away under two days.

Then it was that we began to feel quite low-spirited. There was no game except squirrels on the island, and who of us was spry enough to catch them! The only house within sight was the Mountain House, full twelve miles distant in a bee-line. But from the sojourners there we could hope for no assistance. The provisions which we had brought with us had been consumed. There was n't even a drop of comfort to be extracted from any jug or bottle in our possession. We felt exceedingly Robinson Crusoeish. We spoke of building a hut and going to housekeeping. "Two huts," said the girls; "one for you, the other for us."

"What if it should rain?" asked Prim.

"Look at the clouds," said Cousin S.

"Is that sound thunder?" asked the Montreal cousin, who, perhaps, had been reading "Ion."

"See the mountains, how dark they are!" exclaimed one of the Gemini.

"And hear the wind, how it shrieks," added the other.

"Nonsense," said the redoubtable Bustle; "listen to what I have to propose." And she proclaimed her plan for our delivery. It was sufficient. The next minute Clarence and myself were standing, minus shoes and stockings, in the yielding mud, by the side of the boat. "Now, then, my hearty," shouted Clarence, "shove!" and he and I placed our shoulders to the stern of the boat and shoved with all our strength. But not an inch did it move.

"Try again," said the girls, encouragingly.

Once more we united our strength. "There she glides," exclaimed Bustle, as our feet, sliding backward through the soft and slippery mud, brought us upon our faces.

"You 're mistaken," said Prim.

Bustle acknowledged she was.

As we raised ourselves up, the girls laughed and said we resembled canal-diggers. We were muddied, but they ought not to have laughed at us. Were we not laboring like true knights in their behalf? We resolved, then, to have our pay for this mistimed pleasantry.

" Lighten the boat," said I.

" Passengers ashore," shouted Clarence.

Then once more we tried. Slowly but surely the boat moved from her bed. On we went till a dozen feet were between the boat and the bank, where stood our party.

" Good-bye, my dears," said I. " Any word for your fond mothers ? "

" Come back, oh! do come back for us," exclaimed the frightened maidens.

" Farewell, beloved ones, farewell!" said C.

Cries of grief, prayers, entreaties, wringing of hands, mingled with some scoldings, occurred among the shore party. But the boat kept steadily on her way. The distance from our forlorn damsels increased. The water was near. We reached it. The boat floated. We could barely hear the forsaken ones. We saw, however, scarfs and 'kerchiefs waving for us to return. We perceived, too, one venturous maiden on the way to join us. We let go the anchor ; we left the boat swinging in the current, and waded shoreward. The young lady hastening to meet us suddenly retreated. We marked her white feet plashing through the mud. We gave chase ; she won the race, however, and stood panting on the green bank as we came up.

They all appeared glad to see us, but not enough so as to welcome us with kisses. We thought we ought to be paid in this coin. They, however, obstinately refused. They would kiss us when we had returned them safely home. We thought it doubtful ; but they were resolute : so we yielded.

Then, with crossed hands, we made a chair, and carried thereon each, one by one, to the boat. 'T was a slippery walk, but we were full of daring and chivalry, and minded it not. Surrounding the boat the water was some two feet in depth. The opportunity was too good to be lost. So we said to the first fair freight we carried, " Bustle, dear, we can't wait till we reach home ; be kind and smile on us, and while your white arms are clasped about our necks, grant our guerdon — a kiss ; or else we fear we may drop you in the water."

It was too bad, she exclaimed ; we could not be gentlemen, thus to take advantage of weak woman.

" How very wet, Clarence," I remarked, " the water is this evening."

" Yes," he replied, " very wet."

" But," said B., " you won't drop me ? "

" Certainly, we will, Miss Bustle," I replied.

" Well, then, you 'll never tell — promise me that — if just this once I kiss you."

" Never, dear Bustle," we replied, — " never."

Oh, they were soft, those kisses — very soft, but sweet withal, — sweeter, so thought C. and myself, as we walked shoreward for another burden and another kiss, than any we ever before received.

" And I believe, my dear," I said, addressing Mrs. Gray, " that Clarence thinks the same to this day."

" How is it with yourself, Mr. G. ? " inquired Mrs. Gray.

" Madam," I answered, " until I kissed my wife I thought as Clarence does."

" Enough, Mr. Gray. Please to read on."

Fair burdens and kisses were ours till all, save the English girl, were deposited in the boat.

" You 'll never," said Bustle, " dare ask our cousin for such reward as we so foolishly have granted."

" Or if you do," said Prim, " she 'll never grant it."

" I 'll wager you, Yankee lasses," I cried, " that we 'll get two apiece from the English lady."

" Done," said Bustle ; " you shall have five from me, besides, if you succeed ; but should you fail, the kisses shall be changed to boxes on the ears."

" Agreed," we cried ; " agreed."

Then all the others wished to make the same rash wager.

"Clarence," said I, "this thing is getting serious. Should we succeed, kisses with us will be as common as strawberries in June."

"But should we fail?" he asked.

"It must not be," I answered: "no English girl must be more resolute than our Yankee maids."

Bustle was fearful of this, so she dared us to the attempt. She did not want her English cousin lording it over her.

If ever there were a woman afraid of water, it was "our cousin from Montreal." When, as we moved with her to the boat, we told her of the wager we had made, she said she'd rather give us ten apiece than have us drop her in the water.

Just by the boat we stopped: quickly she kissed us then, on each our cheeks, and thrice the same repeated.

Some persons never pay their debts of honor. This is shameful and exceedingly wrong. Had we lost, we, doubtless, would have suffered for it; and as it was, it were near the same, — for then, and many a day thereafter, I never parted with Prim or Bustle without tingling ears and a tendency to headache.

"And it served you right, Mr. Gray," exclaimed my wife; "your and your friend's conduct was atrocious."

"The very words, my love, which Bustle often used," I said, "in alluding to the subject."

"What hour was it, Mr. G., when you reached home that night?" asked Abeline.

"Nine o'clock, or thereabouts," I answered. "Once afloat, and passengers aboard, Clarence and I, on the top of the flood, made speed in going home."

"And now, Mr. Gray," said my wife, "when shall we go on our picnic?"

"Why, to-morrow," I replied, "unless it should rain; and in that case, the first pleasant day thereafter."

CHAPTER XXVIII.

I go to the Village. — Frank's Case. — Temptation. — The Editor wants
my Obituary.

AM no longer a prisoner at Hillside. My month
of probation has passed. This event occurred
three days since, much to my satisfaction, but, I
think, greatly to Mrs. Gray's regret. I had walked so cir-
cumspectly during the month, that Mrs. G. began to entertain fond hopes of my reformation. Even I myself began
to entertain similar ones. I thought how pleasant a thing
it would be to sustain the character of an exemplary husband. "An exemplary husband, Mr. G.," said my wife,
"is sure to make an exemplary father, and set his children
a good example." I quite agreed with Mrs. G., and fully
resolved to become one. I think I should have succeeded
if my quarantine had not come to an end. The very day
it ended, I went, accompanied by the little black boy, to
the village. Of course I met my bachelor friends. They
were all delighted to see me. They feared I had gone to
foreign parts. They wanted to know what I had been
doing. I replied that I had been attending to the business
of the farm, — the amount of fall work which I had seen
to was enormous, but I thanked fortune I was through with
it now, and should have a little leisure time which I could
call my own.

Thereupon my friends said they were very glad to hear
it, and wished me to remain with them till evening, and
after a light supper at the "Arbor," to accompany them
on a serenading party. In short, they said the Trouba-

dours were going to be around that night, and they wanted me to assist them. Frank, they told me, quite confidentially, had returned from the city, where he had been for the purpose of renewing some " slight attentions " which he had paid, during the summer months, to a lady promenader of the Fifth Avenue, who had sojourned at the " water-cure," in the village. He had come home, apparently in very low spirits, and it was with the hope of cheering him that the Troubadours proposed taking the field again. The speakers, too, who had been off electioneering, had returned to vote, and expressed a willingness to turn out on this occasion.

As Frank is a general favorite with the community, this melancholy intelligence has excited the sympathies of all. Especially have the young ladies of the village endeavored to console him. He has received no less than seven anonymous letters, written in delicate handwriting, on tinted note-paper, the writers asking permission to alleviate his sorrow by sharing in his confidence. Three pair of worked slippers have been sent to him, as also several bouquets, a bottle of cologne water, and one copy each of the " Mourner Comforted " and Baxter's " Call to the Unconverted." These circumstances I learned from Frank himself, so that my account can be depended on as truthful. I scarcely need to say, that my own feelings were deeply enlisted in F.'s behalf; and it was with difficulty that I could refuse acceding to my bachelor friends' wishes to join them on this occasion. My desire to divert Frank from his grief was very great, but I had promised Mrs. Gray, when I left home, that I would return to tea without fail; and I determined to do so. When I informed my friends of my decision, they one and all declared it was shameful, and that I was a very foolish man for making such a promise; and, furthermore, they would advise me not to regard it, but to remain in the village, and they would stand by me, and see me safe through any difficulties which might arise. I told them they spoke very bravely, but that they did not live at Hillside, as I did; besides, it was a matter of principle with me. When I said this, they replied, "Oh, if it were a matter of principle, why they had nothing more to say." And so our interview ended.

As the black boy and myself rode through the village, on our way to Hillside, I said to him, "It is a great thing to resist temptation." He answered, that he reckoned it was. "Did you," I inquired, "ever resist temptation?" The sable youth replied that he never had. "Then I can assure you, my young friend," I continued, "that you do not know what it is to possess an approving conscience." He said he guessed not. "With no temptations to resist," I proceeded, "men can lead very virtuous lives. Simply abstaining from evil courses, when there are no inducements tempting one to pursue such, amounts to nothing. What he resists is a better test of a man's rectitude than his failures are proofs of his wickedness. If we knew both the sides of some 'sad dog's' life, we might, after all, strike a balance in his favor, and find him not so great a sinner as we had thought."

"That's so," exclaimed the black boy, the moment I ceased speaking.

Just as the little black boy closed his remarks, we arrived opposite the office of the "Star-Spangled Banner," the editor of which hailed me from his open window, inviting me to alight and enter his *sanctum*. Not having, at that moment, the fear of Mrs. Gray before my eyes, I did so. He received me like a brother. His cordiality was excessive. He informed me, exultingly, that the lines I had sent him had been the means of rejuvenating his newspaper. They had set him up amazingly. The day after the poem had appeared in the columns of the "Star-Spangled Banner," his subscribers, with the exception of one "old file," had come forward, like gentlemen, and paid up their subscriptions. Several new names had been added to his patrons. He had taken the liberty, he said, in his last issue, of placing my name in his list of regular contributors; and he trusted I would not be displeased thereat. I informed him that he could " reckon " on me occasionally, but that engagements of various kinds would necessarily debar me from giving him that constant assistance to which his wishes and my pleasure pointed. I regretted it very much, I added, but I could not gratify him unless I neglected my lady correspondents; which was not to be thought of.

Of course, he said, if that was the case, he would not ask for a weekly contribution.

Then he showed me various articles he had had sent him as donations, including three hats, lithographic portraits of each of the Presidential candidates, a firkin of butter, and a basket of eggs; together with a mysterious jug, which he kept in a left-hand cupboard, convenient to his inkstand. He poured out for me some of its contents into a very uncleanly appearing tumbler, and more of it into a still uncleanlier glass, for himself, and then exclaiming, " Here 's luck! " drank it off. I must confess that either the appearance of the tumblers, or a doubt as to the quality of the refreshment offered, deterred me from following his example, and my glass remained untouched, till, chancing to turn my face for a moment in another direction, I was surprised, on looking back, to find the glass empty, and the editor smacking his lips on the further side of the room.

Afterwards he informed me he would be very happy to write my obituary for the columns of the " Banner "; and he hoped I would note down, for his use in compiling the same, the principal events of my life. I had no objection, I told him, to his writing it, but I trusted that it would be long before he had occasion to use it. After I were dead and buried, I added, the thing might answer; but as for publishing my obituary at present, I should object to it, and should continue to object, so long as I could stand up and walk. The principal event, however, in my life, up to this time, if he desired to know it, was, I thought, my marrying Mrs. Gray. In all other respects, my life had been unnoticeable.

His request, I confess, somewhat surprised and startled me. I did not know but that he meant to " use me up," and had, after all, taken offence at my verses, but had kept down his wrath till he had me alone, meaning to slaughter me, and then write my obituary. For a moment I wished myself safe out of his office. It occurred to me that it might possibly be his practice to murder a person for the sake of getting an obituary for his paper. I looked at the mysterious jug suspiciously. Could it, I asked myself, contain poison ? The editor, noticing where my eyes rested, poured more of its contents into the uncleanly-looking tumbler aforesaid, for me ; and a further supply into the still uncleanlier-looking tumbler, for himself. Then, without hesitation, he drained his glass, smacking his lips as the last drop disappeared, and informed me, in a confidential tone, that the " stuff " was " old rye," and that mine host of the " Spread Eagle " had sent it to him. Thereupon I came to the conclusion that it was not poison, so my confidence and courage returned. Afterwards, when I came to consider the matter, I made up my mind that my editorial friend meant my biography instead of obituary.

CHAPTER XXIX.

The Circus. — It rains. — Naughty Black Boy. — Spangles. — Motley. — Babylon. — Mrs. Gray's Friend. — What the Sultan does in Ispahan. At Breakfast.

AS I was leaving the editor of the " Star-Spangled Banner," he presented me with a ticket of admission to the travelling circus, which was to open, on the village green, in the evening. I thanked him, and accepted the ticket, intending to give it to the black boy. When I reached the street I looked at my watch, and discovered, much to my surprise, that it was long past my tea-hour. Mrs. Gray, I said to myself, has doubtless given up watching for me from the library window, and has, ere this, taken her vesper meal in silence and sorrow. I began to feel sorry for Mrs. G. ; I also began to feel sorry for myself. 'T will do no good, I thought, for me to hurry home now. So I stopped the horse and got out, — telling the colored youth, at the same time, to be a good lad, and remain in the buggy till I returned, — and set off on a stroll through the village. Somehow, my steps led me towards the green, where stood the white tent of the circus, in which the band was already playing the last popular melody. I saw that the canvas doors were open, and persons were beginning to pass in. Many years had elapsed since I had been to an entertainment of this description. I wondered if the present one equalled those of my boyhood. Was the clown as funny as the olden clowns ? Was the ring-master as entertaining, or the company, generally, to be compared with those of yore ? I quite wearied myself, too, wondering whether there were a young lady, very beautiful and very graceful, in a pink or blue gauze dress, covered with spangles, who enacted the fairy queen and flying sprite, within the tent before me. I determined, after a long cogitation, to satisfy myself in the matter. So, producing my ticket from my waistcoat-pocket, and giving it to the man at the tent-door, who eyed me suspiciously, I passed in. The moment I entered, I recognized the tan and sawdust smell, mingled with the smoke of tallow candles, which I had known in my days of wilfulness. There was the same pea-nut eating, the same drinking of soda and spruce-beer, the same whistling, shouting, and stamping going on in the motley assembly there collected, which is, doubtless, always found at such places. Seating myself high up on the tier of benches, I sat quietly watching the crowd before me, marking their various peculiarities. As my eyes wandered over the pit, scanning those persons who, full of eagerness, crowded closely up to the ring, I espied, much to my astonishment, the physiognomy of the black boy. At first I could not credit my senses. What business, I thought, has that lad to be here? He ought to be ashamed of himself. Of all bad places, a circus is the worst: it is a species of entertainment the lowest; none but the ignorant and foolish delight in it. It is a mark of a depraved taste in any one to visit it, and it was very wrong in him, I soliloquized, to come here. I resolved to speak thus to the little black boy when we should ride home; but, after considering the subject a few minutes, viewing it in its various lights and shades, I concluded, that, under the circumstances, it would be wiser in me to keep quiet. Just then two men dressed in red, tooted on a couple of brass horns, quite distractedly and the next moment two score of gaudily dressed knights on horseback sprang into the ring, and rode three times around it very furiously, making the tan fly into the eyes of those closest about them. Then the two score of horsemen went through a sham-fight, in which they managed to get mixed up very badly, though I think no one was injured

Then they rode out from the ring, and into their private tent. Then a very old boy, with white jacket and pants, walked into the ring, lowered a triangular frame, set round with lighted candles, to the ground, and after snuffing them, raised it to its place. Thereupon the crowd cheered him very heartily, when, much to their surprise, he threw a somerset in the air, and came down on his feet, minus his white jacket and pants, a very comical appearing clown. This feat was accomplished something after the Ravel style, and promised well, I thought, for Motley. Then the young lady, whom I had not seen in twenty years, made her appearance, looking not a day older, and wearing the same spangled, pink dress she did when first we met. She went through the usual feat of standing first on one foot and then on the other upon the horse, till everybody was satisfied she could do it, when she, escorted by the clown, who was very polite and ceremonious to her, disappeared into the side-tent. Then the band stationed in the triumphal car played either " Love not " or " Sweet Home," I could n't make out exactly which. That, somehow, caused me to think of Mrs. Gray, and made me wish myself at Hillside. It was then, too, I first became aware that I was sitting in a little pool of water. I felt, also, that quite a rivulet was making its way down my back. Of course I looked upward to see whence it proceeded, when a very respectably sized stream poured into my face. There was a dull, heavy sound on the canvas roof over my head. It was at once evident to me that it was raining. I moved a few feet from the place I had been occupying, in the hope of avoiding the leak. The leak, however, proved to be a very extensive one. The water followed me up wherever I moved. I thereupon came to the conclusion that a circus-tent, during a heavy rain, was not exactly the spot in which to keep dry, and so I immediately resolved to go home. I looked for the black boy ; he was engrossed in watching a man support an anvil, while two others industriously beat on it with heavy sledges. I resolved then, if I were obliged to drive home alone in the rain, to give him a severe lecture for his disobedience, and, if feasible, to further punish him for going to the circus.

So I left the tent and the little black boy behind me, and walked in the rain down the dark and silent streets to where the horse and buggy were. I tried to think of some excuse, as I walked on, to say to Mrs. Gray, for having stayed away from her so long; but it rained so hard and I made so many missteps, that I could not keep my mind long enough on the subject to frame one which would appear to her plausible and satisfactory. I was greatly surprised, when I reached the buggy, to find Master Black Boy in it, and, to all appearance, fast asleep. If he were not so wet, as I discovered he was, I should have thought that, possibly, I had been mistaken in seeing him at the circus. As it was, I made up my mind that he had seen me there, had marked my departure, and straightway hastened after me.

I said nothing to him, however, during our ride home, for my mind was busy with another matter. I was thinking of Mrs. Gray. I feared she had been very lonesome during my absence. I hoped she had found some entertaining book to read. I wondered if she would scold me. She never had scolded me, though she came very near it when she discovered the Troubadour business. I am very much afraid of a scolding. When I was a boy, every one scolded me except my grandmother, and she used to whip me. I was always thankful to her for pursuing this course. I hold her in great esteem for it to this day. It is very tiresome listening to a "good scold,"— she is apt to be so lengthy. I fervently trusted that Mrs. G. would not, on this occasion, be disposed to scold. It did not seem to me — wet, hungry, and wearied, as I was — that I could stand it. "No," I said to myself; "if Mrs. G. shows any symptoms of scolding when I enter the house, I'll not listen to

her, but go straightway to the barn, where I'll pass the
night in the hay. This will probably cause Mrs. G. to feel
badly, and she will, moreover, be sorry for me; and in
the morning, when I enter the house with my hair full of
hay-seed, and straws among my whiskers, she'll be glad
enough to see me, and won't say a word about my staying
out, and will make me a cup of delightful Mocha coffee."

When I had reached thus far in my silent soliloquy,
the black boy disturbed me by remarking that Hillside
was pretty well lighted up. On looking forth, I found it
was even so. I discovered lights gleaming, not only from
the windows of the sitting-room and library, but also from
the parlors and guests' chamber above.

"Black boy," I said, "make that black horse travel a little faster up this hill."

He applied the whip. Who, I wondered, has come to
Hillside during my absence? I wished the circus in
Babylon. I must have expressed this wish aloud, for the
little black boy immediately mentioned the fact that he
had caught crabs close by that town. I remarked that he
had best stop talking to me, and added that I meant a good
deal older Babylon than the one of which he knew.

Thereupon the young man held his peace till we reached
the house. On entering the tea-room, I learned, greatly to
my surprise and indignation, that a tall gentleman was in
the parlor with Mrs. Gray. He had arrived — so the nursery-maid informed me — early in the afternoon, had remained to tea, and, she believed, intended staying all night
I had my suspicions that he was the same person who, in
the spring, accompanied my wife when she returned from
visiting her mother. When I entered the parlor, I found
that my suspicions were correct. I welcomed the stranger
with much cordiality. He was, apparently, very glad to
see me. Mrs. Gray did not appear to be as glad to meet
me as I imagined she should have been. In fact, she did
not seem to care at all that I had stayed away. She had

passed a delightful evening, she said, with her old friend.
" Her old friend " declared that he had passed a delightful
evening with Mrs. G. When I casually mentioned the
hour, they both expressed great surprise at learning how
late it was, and remarked to each other how very short the
evening had seemed. Thereupon I looked at Mrs. G.'s
tall friend, and wished the evening had seemed as long as
he was. What business, I thought, had he, a married man,
to be visiting my wife ! What if he were one of Mrs. Gray's
old beaux ; was that any reason why he should be at Hillside while I was absent ? I decidedly thought not. I said
as much, after the gentleman had retired, to Mrs. G. She
did not exactly reply to me, but simply desired to know
where I had been passing the evening. I was silent.
Had I been to a meeting of the Literary Society ? she
asked. " It would have been a good night for the Troubadours, only it rained rather heavily," she added. " Or, perhaps, Mr. Gray," she continued, " you have been calling on
some of the young ladies in the village."

" No, my dear," I answered, " I never leave my wife for
the sake of visiting old sweethearts. It was business, Mrs.
G.,— business, too, of an important nature, you may be
assured, — which kept me from your side this evening.
And you must excuse me, my love," I continued, " if I decline saying anything further to-night regarding my absence from tea." Mrs. Gray replied, " Very well," and
retired to the nursery. And I immediately marched into
the library, where, seating myself at my writing-desk, I
indited the following lines, which I gave to the black boy,
telling him, before he went to bed, to slip them between
the door and the sill into the chamber which the tall
stranger occupied.

WHAT THE SULTAN DOES IN ISPAHAN.

[BARBAROUS.]

When the Sultan Shah-Zaman
Goes to the city Ispahan,
Leaving behind him ROSE-IN-BLOOM,
Weeping within his favorite room;
As he passes the thirtieth palace gate,
He yields himself to toward fate;
And strokes his beard, and a moment prays.
Allah! Bismillah! is what he says.
Then he counts his camels as they go by,
Loaded with spices of Araby,
And silks, and satins, and all things rare,
Fit to adorn some Persian fair;
With vessels of silver, and vessels of gold,
And gems and jewels of worth untold:
For he means to purchase an hundred maids, —
Samarcand's beautiful dancing-girls,
With moon-like bosoms and cloud-like curls, —
When the Pet of his Harem's beauty fades:
And while he is gone to Ispahan,
He knows 't will fade, does Shah-Zaman.

Then, when the Sultan Shah-Zaman
Reaches the city Ispahan,
He goes straightway to the mart where stand
Slaves from many a foreign land, —
Circassian maids, and Turkish girls,
Tartarian damsels with teeth like pearls,
And India's daughters with jetty curls.
There, on the ground, his carpet spread,
He seats himself, and bows his head,
Charmed with the sight which meets his eyes,
And fanned by a fan of a thousand dyes:
Gravely he smokes his narghila,
And drinks sherbet, and shouts Allah!
Then chooses from the frightened throng
The dancing-girls and the girls of song.
That's when the Sultan Shah-Zaman
Reaches the city Ispahan.

Now, when I mark my neighbor start
For the great and gay commercial mart, —

> When I see him seated in the cars,
> Smoking his rarest and best cigars;
> And view the contentment which fills his eyes,
> And the smiles that rise in lieu of sighs, —
> I know as well as I know to swear,
> I know as well as I can or dare,
> *That the glorious Sultan Shah-Zaman*
> *Goes to the city Ispahan,*
> Designing there to vary his life,
> By slyly wooing some husband's wife.

The following morning, while seated at the breakfast-table, the tall gentleman mentioned having found a narrow slip of paper on the floor of his chamber, containing some lines which he had taken the liberty of reading. He wished, he said, that I would allow him to retain them; he should like to send them to his wife after he reached the city. (It seemed he was on his way to New York.) He should like, too, to know the author's name.

Thereupon Mrs. Gray suggested the propriety of his reading aloud the lines to which he referred, when, perhaps, she would be able to give him the information he desired.

Then Mrs. G.'s tall friend read aloud the above lines. During their reading, Mrs. Gray appeared absorbed in reflection. Once she looked at me inquiringly, as if she expected I would assist her in determining the author, but I was so busily engaged with the side-bone of a chicken, on my plate, that she received no encouragement in the matter.

When, however, the reading was ended, my wife remarked that she certainly had seen that poem, or a similar one, in the "Knickerbocker Magazine." Mr. Gray, she continued, remembered about all these things, and she had no doubt I could tell everything concerning them. "Is n't it, Mr. G.," she added, turning to me, "in the last 'Knickerbocker'?" I replied that I thought not. "Then it is in one of the late 'Home Journals,' Mr. Gray; now is n't it?" she persisted. "I have never seen it there, Mrs. G.," I replied. Mrs. Gray reviewed the matter again in her own mind. After a moment's silence, she exclaimed she was certain that it was in both of the publications she had mentioned. So she sent the black boy to the library for the " Knickerbocker." The lad returned with the October number. " Now, then, my dear," said Mrs. G., as she turned to the Table of Contents, " for once in your life you will have to allow that I am right, and that my memory is better than yours." " We shall see," I remarked. " So we shall," said my wife, and read aloud this heading, — "' When the Sultan goes to Ispahan.' There, Mr. G.," exclaimed my wife, triumphantly, " are you satisfied ? " I was not. I pointed out the difference in the titles. Mrs. G. began to be slightly astonished. I read aloud the Knickerbocker poem. While I read, my wife grew more and more astonished. When I had finished, " Ah !" she cried, " that, Mr. Gray, now sounds something like poetry."

" Yes, Madam," replied the tall gentleman, " one can readily perceive in it true Oriental ideas ; there is a beauty and a finish to it, which the manuscript does not possess. Am I not right, Mr. Gray ? "

I replied, " I believe you are, sir." Then, turning to my wife, " My dear," I said, " what do you suppose our neighbor Pound thought when he saw the extra lights flaming from the parlor-windows last night ? "

Mrs. Gray answered, very innocently, that she did not know ; but supposed he thought we had company.

" Ah !" exclaimed the tall personage, " if the printed lines are applicable to Mrs. Gray, then I fear those in manuscript are applicable to me."

I said they were. Then he laughed till he nearly strangled. I almost wished he had. Instead of being angry, and calling for his hat, and overcoat, and rubbers, and cane, and umbrella, and brown paper parcel, as I hoped he would, he seemed more at home than ever.

It was I who got angry ; but I straightway solaced my-

self with an extra cup of coffee. It is astonishing what
effect coffee has on me! It quiets my nerves; it cools my
blood; it warms my heart; it awakens my conscience; it
strengthens my mind; it kindles my fancy; and fills me
with charity. On this occasion it had the effect of causing
me freely to forgive the tall gentleman who had passed a
short evening with Mrs. G. for all he had said. It caused
me, too, immediately after we left the breakfast-room, to
ask him to ride down to the village. As he intended leaving, he said, in the ten o'clock train, for "the great and gay
commercial mart," he would accept with pleasure my invitation.

To tell the truth, I was glad to learn that he intended
bidding good-bye to Hillside and Mrs. Gray; besides, it
gave me an opportunity of seeing my friends in the village.
So when the black boy had got the horse up, he made his
adieus, and then we departed.

CHAPTER XXX.

Frank and his Washerwoman. — " The Camp-meeting." — The F. F. V.'s.
Hymns of Zion. — Lord of the Treasury. — The Shanghai. — Gabriel.

MY friend Frank went to a camp-meeting during
the past summer. It was under the control of
the sable sons of Africa. I do not know why
Frank went. I am inclined, however, to believe it was out
of respect to his washerwoman, whose husband is a colored
preacher. and who, doubtless, figured at the meeting aforesaid. If I had a washerwoman who owned a preacher for
a husband. I should feel it my bounden duty to attend all
the camp-meetings he did. Not having a washerwoman
thus situated in life, however, I have never been to such
meetings. Therefore, when Frank informed me that he
had seen the whole affair, and had thereby been much edi-
fied, I requested him, in a very polite manner, — after having first invited him to partake of a bottle of Scotch ale, —
to write for me an account of the same. After many urg-
ings and remindings on my part, accompanying the same
with sundry bottles of ale, I obtained at last from my modest friend the following description — which I read aloud
to Mrs. Gray — of

THE CAMP-MEETING.

" I heard there was a negro camp-meeting in Van's
woods, and never having seen a sable conventicle, I determined to go. The camp was five or six miles distant, with
a choice of two conveyances, to wit: on foot, or in the
'Shanghai stage.' The Shanghai stage is a great institu-

tion; in capacity, somewhat over Noah's ark. It plies between our village and the neighboring town, freighted with all sorts of animate and inanimate burdens. It is as proverbial for regularity in its departures and returns as the town-clock. My boarding-house-keeper depends on it instead of the clock, — which, being around several corners, cannot be seen from our house, — and calls us to breakfast, dinner, and tea, just when it goes by. Once the Shanghai stage broke down, and was two hours behind time; and, though dinner was quite ready, yet our landlady would n't allow the bell to be rung till the stage came along. If that stage should cease running, I think our boarding-house would have to be closed."

Mrs. Gray interrupted me at this point in my reading, by remarking that she thought my friend Frank boarded at the " Spread Eagle " tavern.

I answered Mrs. G. that she was right; " but in the height of the summer's travel, Frank is obliged to go into other quarters, so that the transient guests of the 'Spread Eagle' may be accommodated." Thereupon, my wife ejaculated "Oh !" and I proceeded with Frank's narrative, as follows : —

" It was at the faded end of a summer evening's twilight that I plunged into the unknown abyss of the Shanghai, heard the driver sing out ' All right !' from the bow of our craft, and went rolling through clouds of dust to the camp-ground. The vehicle started before I had fairly gotten my seat; consequently, I found myself, much to my surprise and secret delight, plumped bodily into the arms of half-a-dozen gay-hearted damsels, occupying the seat facing mine. The introduction being of a rather pleasant nature all around. I — after being extricated from the entanglement in which I had fallen — sandwiched myself between two fat men in my seat proper, and proceeded to prosecute with ardor the acquaintance thus happily commenced. I found the damsels were some of the F. F. V.s, (first families of the village,) and were bound to the camp-ground, under the superintendence of a solemn bachelor uncle to three of them, who sat with the driver, for fear of sea-sickness.

"Considering the fact that we were going to 'meeting,' we were, I think, rather lively. 'Wait for the Wagon' may have been very applicable to the Shanghai, but it did not then, nor does it now, seem to me altogether an appropriate hymn with which to open the exercises. In due time, however, we reached the camp-ground — a pretty piece of woods, with a stream running through one corner of it. The *tout ensemble*, as we entered the area of the camp, was exceedingly picturesque. Vehicles of every description, from the elegant carriage to the coarsest 'lumber-box,' filled the outer circle. The horses were, many of them, 'unhitched' from the wagons, and were either tied to neighboring trees, or else were fastened securely to the wagons themselves. Passing this equestrian circle, through which the venders of pea-nuts and candies were apparently doing a thriving trade with the 'outsiders,' we came to what may be considered the camp proper, — a collection of rough sheds, forming the arc of a circle, enclosed the spot where the exercises were held. These sheds, or 'tents,' as the preachers termed them, were for the use and convenience of the assembly, and comprised the preachers' tent, the sisters' tent, and the kitchen and dining tents. Within this penetralia, seats formed with rough boards held a portion of the audience ; the remainder either sat on the ground, or else were perched amid the trees. Between these seats and the preachers' stand was an open space, where the brethren could assemble for the closer exercises of a prayer meeting.

"The evening services had commenced, when the bachelor uncle and myself, accompanied by the light brigade of damsels, entered the camp-grounds. Having, after some difficulty, obtained desirable seats, we turned our attention to the novel scene about us. At least one half of the as-

sembly was of the Caucasian race, and had come there,
like ourselves, simply from curiosity. If any were attracted
by a worse motive, — with a desire of mocking those simple-
hearted worshippers, — we will trust that they 'who came
to scoff, remained to pray.'

"We saw before us the long bench in the pulpit filled
with a row of ebony St. Paul's; one of whom was discoursing to the people below. The ground was lighted by
fires. placed at suitable intervals, and we might readily have
imagined we beheld the turfy altars of the Druids prepared
for sacrifice. The fitful glare of the wood fires had a weird
effect on the swart group within the circle, interspersed
with here and there a white face. Though we came not
to laugh or scoff at the worshippers, yet now and then
something would be said or done of a nature so ludicrous,
that gravity of demeanor was, for the time, out of the
question. Their eloquence, if not Athenian, was, at least,
practical, direct, and simple, and seemed fully appreciated
by the assembled audience, as their oft-repeated 'amens,'
and 'yes, brother, yes,' testified. But their main reliance
appeared to be in the singing; and their strange hymns
filled the wide woods, and were echoed back from the hill-
sides with wonderful distinctness. Such hymns and tunes
as 'The Good Old Way,' 'We'll soon have done with
Trouble here,' and 'Mary, ring dem bells,' were the favorites. The felt hat circulated freely for the odd coin of the
spectators. Indeed, the campers seemed to rely on their
music for obtaining the sinews of war; and, as one dusky
gentleman was passing around a borrowed hat in his bland-
est manner, the preacher, who was lining the hymn from
the pulpit, suddenly stopped, and declared he would not
sing another line until he saw a bill put into the hat.
Whereat the hat-bearer was more pressing in his solicita-
tions; and, some misguided youth having finally dropped
in a counterfeit note, the singing was renewed with increased spirit. When the lord of the treasury neared my

stage acquaintances, they wished me to request the singing of a certain camp-ground melody. Accordingly I made the proposition to the purse-bearer, that I would place so much silver in his hand if the company would sing the suggested piece. With an ivory smile, that reached from ear to ear, he promised it should be done. The pieces of silver were paid over, and, with many bows and smiles, on moved the dusky treasurer. For an hour or more longer, the preaching and exhorting continued, — prayers were uttered and hymns sung, — but my request was unattended to. I feared I should not get the worth of my money, and I thought my fair neighbors looked on it as a bad investment. At last prayer-meeting was called, and I was about to remind my colored friend of his promise, when I saw him ascend the pulpit in a very dignified manner, and make proclamation in these words: ‘Dear brethren and sisters, a dear brother in the audience has given us some money to sing one of the good old songs of Zion. You will, therefore, please to form two by two, and march round the camp-ground, singing, ‘Play on the Golden Harp.’ ”

Here Mrs. Gray asked me if I thought this golden harp was at all like the “harp of a thousand strings,” which had been so often rung of late? for if it were, she should not care about hearing it.

I said it was not. Then I continued: “There must have been fifty verses, at least, of this popular melody, of which the following verse is a specimen : —

> “ ‘ If you want to make old Satan run,
> Play on the golden harp !
> Just shoot him with the gospel gun,
> Play on the golden harp !
> Play on the golden harp ! play on the golden harp !
> I want to go where Mary ’s gone,
> And play on the golden harp.’

“The enthusiasm of the singers went beyond description. They leaped and danced, and swayed their arms and bodies as they marched, as if they were passing through a whirl-wind. One Herculean African required two men to hold him, so triumphantly was he borne along on the tide of song. Bass, tenor, falsetto, soprano, numbers one, two, three, up to a dozen, all commingled in one accord, was poured forth, till every leaf of the forest trembled on its topmost spray. The fifty verses were finally accomplished, and, fully satisfied with my investment, we reluctantly — the Shanghai's driver was blowing his horn by the road-side — bade adieu to this primitive church in the woods, and, by a bright starlight, were again on the homeward road. Long after the camp-fires had disappeared, we heard the sound of singing, as it came rolling over the green meadows that intervened between us and the camp-ground. By and by, the singing ceased, and then we in the Shanghai told stories, and laughed, and the solemn bachelor uncle reproved us, and went to sleep in his seat in the corner; and just as he had got into the middle of his first dream, the driver tooted on his great tin horn, which so frightened 'our uncle,' that he suddenly awoke, and, rising on his feet, asked where was Gabriel. There-upon his nieces, and all in the Shanghai, laughed at him ; and then, much elated, we drove into the village."

When I had finished reading the above account, Mrs. Gray asked me if I knew who were the young damsels referred to. I told her I did not, but doubtless she could learn their names by inquiring of my friend Frank.

Thereupon Mrs G. said, that if I thought she were going to spend her time asking any such question of my bache-lor friend, I was much mistaken, as she would not do it for all the damsels in creation, and that, for her part, she did n't care the least bit in the world who they were. And then Mrs. Gray's needle flew faster than ever. Neverthe-less, I think my wife would like very well to know the names of those same young ladies ; therefore I have made a note in my memorandum-book to examine Frank on the subject.

CHAPTER XXXI.

Fishing. — Gunning. — Fiddling. — Gardening. — Walking in the Garden. — Invent a Table. — Its Shape. — Its Legs. — Its Magic Spring. — An Ugly Trick. — Thanksgiving Dinner. — "A Bachelor's Bacchanal Lyric." — Anacreontic. — Our Mahogany. — After Dinner.

MRS. GRAY is desirous that I should totally give up troubadouring and circus-going, and devote my time henceforth to some employment more profitable to my purse.   Somehow, though, nothing exactly " the thing " has turned up for me to do.   I engaged in fishing, but without any great success.   I thought this might be owing to the style of hook I used; so I consulted an old fisherman in the matter.   He agreed with me, and very kindly advised me to try a new hook — one with a Limerick point and an O'Shaughnessy bend.   I purchased five hundred of them, at an exceedingly high figure, and afterwards gave them all a faithful trial, but, I am sorry to say, with no apparent improvement in my success as a fisherman.   Thereupon I gave up fishing, and took to gunning. I pursued this sport effectually, but never, I am happy to state, caused the death of any bird or animal.   Once, however, I came very near to shooting a squirrel — a gray squirrel, with a bushy tail.   My shot struck the limb of a tree, just one moment after he had left it.

When I narrated this circumstance to Mrs. Gray, she said she was very thankful that the squirrel escaped; and she trusted that I would no more follow the cruel business of gunning.   So, to please my estimable wife, who is tenderhearted, I disposed of my gun, and bought with the proceeds a violin.   I had often heard Mrs. Gray speak admiringly of Ole Bull and Vieuxtemps, whose concerts she had attended when at boarding-school, and I thought of the pleasure she would derive in listening, through the long winter evenings, to my playing. Besides, I thought it would serve to quiet and amuse the children; and, moreover, I trusted that it would prove a source of comfort to me. When I brought the violin home, tied up in a green bag, and laid it at Mrs. Gray's feet, she was slightly astonished. She wished to know what I intended to do with it. I answered that I intended to play on it. She asked if I was acquainted with the use of the instrument. I replied that I was not, but that I could soon introduce myself to it. Then I endeavored to play a certain air, that I used to sing to my excellent wife in our courtship-days, but without accomplishing my purpose. In fact, I rather made a failure of it. I believe I sadly frightened the baby by the discordant noise I drew forth, for he set up a painful cry. Mrs. Gray begged me to desist, and said that I needed "practice" before I could succeed as a player. So I gave for several weeks my whole mind to the instrument, practising in private, in my own apartment at the top of the house, till at last I ventured to play " Days of Absence " in Mrs. Gray's presence. She was very much affected by it, and remarked that she had never heard Ole Bull play like it. And I do not believe that she ever had. I think that in time I should have been able to play Yankee Doodle, for I practised it incessantly, — but, unfortunately, the music gave Mrs. Gray the headache; so I, just as I began to be able to play an air through, hung up the fiddle and the bow, and turned my attention to gardening. So I went to work and planted various kinds of seeds. Then I watered the garden every day, if there were no rains. I contrived, also, an awning to shade it, which I could draw over it when the sun shone too hotly; and then I waited very patiently for the seeds to germinate and the green leaves to put forth. After a while the plants, etc., came on. They

came on, indeed, finely. My wife and myself found much
pleasure in watching them. Day by day they progressed.
At last my wife, the baby, the nurse and I, took a walk
together in the garden. We went for the purpose of ascer-
taining the names of our garden's productions. An alpha-
betically arranged catalogue of plants, vegetables, etc., I
carried opened in my hand. By the aid of this valuable
book I learned the names of all the green things contained
in the garden. I discovered that the ornamental and the
useful were strangely united. Flowers and vegetables
grew side by side. Out of a mass of mignonette the slender top of an onion appeared ; potatoes and poppies were
mingled together ; roses and radishes were inseparable ;
tulips and tomatoes were united forever ; and peas, peonies,
and petunias were preëminently perceivable. In short,
our garden was clearly overstocked. It never produced
anything, either in the flower or vegetable line. And so
one day, most unexpectedly to us, it went to seed.

It being summer, and the weather quite warm, I kept
myself, most of the time, in the house. I thought deeply
upon a great many things. I pondered upon the steam
engine ; I revolved in my mind the mechanism of the
printing-press, and I wondered at the construction of the
cider-mill. Then I set to work and invented a dining-
table, in the form of St. George's Cross, that I " rather
calculated" would prove the means of adding to my pecu-
niary resources ; but, strangely enough, the sale of it was
quite limited. A tailor, a friend of mine, to whom I was
slightly indebted for sundry articles of clothing, was my
sole purchaser ; and he, I think, took one out of sympathy
for the table, which had twelve legs, and, what was a little
curious, they folded together under the body of the table,
if a certain spring, situated on the surface of it, near the
centre, was ever so lightly touched. Mrs. Gray objected
to the table on account of the quantity of legs it possessed ;
but I thought this unfair both towards the inventor and

the table itself. I said as much to Mrs. Gray, but she, nevertheless, refused either to withdraw the offensive observation or to apologize for uttering it. Another little objection which my esteemed wife raised against my table *à la* St. George, — which objection, well founded I must confess, proved ruinous to the sale of my patent right, — was, that it possessed an ugly trick of folding itself up in the twinkling of an eye, while my family and myself were seated around it, if a dish was, through accident or carelessness, placed on the magic spring, and straightway depositing our entire dinner, or whatever the meal might be, upon the floor. I will do my amiable wife the justice to say she endured this little mischance several times without finding any very great fault with the construction of the table; but after it had broken, by this doubling-up process, three distinct china dinner-sets, and crowned its ill-mannered conduct by collapsing on the occasion of the parson taking tea with us, and thereby breaking certain ancient pieces of antique china family heirlooms, descended from my wife's great-grandmother, Mrs. Gray denounced its acts, and exiled it forever from the dining-room, greatly to my dismay and sorrow. Then, for a while, I became low-spirited, and took to reading Burton's "Anatomy of Melancholy." I was only restored to comparative cheerfulness, however, by the arrival of Thanksgiving-day. I will simply state, in regard to the Thanksgiving-dinner, that it was of the New-England pattern, stuffed with turkeys, and mince-pies, and other delicacies of the season Furthermore, after the cloth was removed, — one of Mrs. Gray's best damask ones, which she keeps in a drawer redolent with lemons, — a bottle of Longworth's sparkling Catawba was placed upon the mahogany, and partaken sparingly of by Mrs. Gray, but liberally by myself. It was while imbibing this wine, and during the intervals of rest my nut-cracker enjoyed, that I composed the following verses, afterwards published in "The Wine Press":—

A BACHELOR'S BACCHANAL LYRIC.

Come, oh! come, my well-beloved,
  With me to that sunny clime,
Where the purple grapes are blushing
  'Midst the olive and the lime.

There, among the merry viners,
  In the vineyards we will walk,
Grapes in large and luscious clusters
  I will eat, while you may talk.

You may tell me sweetest story,
  Either love or fairy tale,
Till we reach the vineyard's limits,
  Till my appetite shall fail.

Seated then within the shadow
  Of an overarching vine,
You may sing me festal lyrics,
  While I quaff the ruby wine:

Wine of rare and olden vintage,
  Worth its weight in precious gems, —
For a pipe of which would princes
  Sacrifice their diadems.

Like a Bacchus I will gayly
  Overflowing beakers drain,
Whilst the light guitar you finger,
  Waking many a dulcet strain.

You may crown my brows with roses,
  Mixed with leaflets of the vine,
While your health, in flowing numbers,
  I will drink in cups of wine.

In a cup Cellini modelled,
  From a mass of virgin gold;
Oh! a cup by such a master
  Only wine like this should hold!

More than blest, my well-beloved,
  You would find your future life, —

> Blest now, while you are a maiden,
>   Blest when you become a wife.
>
> Do you ask the why and wherefore ?
>   You are careless of your bliss !
> Know you nót you must be blessed,
>   Toasted thus in wine like this !
>
> There, my fairest, seated by me,
>   You may brim my cup with wine,
> Till, the golden flagon emptied,
>   I shall deem myself divine.
>
> Deem myself a godlike hero,
>   Braver than earth's bravest ones,
> While I quaff the blood of vineyards,
>   Warmed to life by fiery suns.
>
> You may tempt me, too, with olives,
>   Squeeze for me the juiciest limes,
> Spread my board with figs and melons,
>   When the bell for vesper chimes.
>
> Let us hasten, then, beloved,
>   To that fair and sunny land,
> Where, 'mong vines and olive orchards,
>   We may wander hand in hand.

After reading this lyric to Mrs. Gray, I asked her if she did not think it highly anacreontic. She confessed her ignorance of the term used, but added that she thought it very pretty. And with this praise from Mrs. G. I was well contented.

No one could enjoy more than I did my Thanksgiving-dinner. But it was after the good things of the feast had disappeared, and while yet my wife and I were seated around the mahogany, that my enjoyment reached its flood. And here let me speak of our mahogany, which has witnessed the festive gatherings of my family for generations past. Rather an antique affair it is, with carved feet and rounded corners, but grand, massive, and substantial, like

my brave ancestors — sea-kings — who in days of yore
stretched longer, and stouter, and comelier legs than are
mine, beneath its leaves. I am pleased to be able to state
that it came to this country, not in the " Mayflower," as
did the larger portion of the old furniture found in the
New-England States, but it reached our shores in company
with Sir Walter Raleigh's colony, and after passing a century at Roanoke and in its immediate neighborhood, travelled north, till it found itself one day, much to its surprise
and indignation, among my Quaker ancestors, on the island
of Nantucket.

At least, this is the account with which I favored my too
credulous wife on Thanksgiving evening, when she asked
for its history. Of course I could not substantiate my
statement by positive proofs, but I am happy to say that
my simple assertion to this effect appeared perfectly satisfactory to Mrs. Gray. And why, in the name of all old-
fashioned furniture, I wonder, should it not, when never
a splinter of any, said to have been brought hither in
the " Mayflower," has anybody ever dared to call in question?

Perhaps it was from the many pleasing associations connected with this ancient table, brought forcibly to my mind
through my wife's inquiry, that my enjoyment arose. Perhaps my Catawba wine had something to do with it. Perhaps the prattle of my two children; or, more likely than
aught else, as being the cause of my deep enjoyment, that
mother's trusting look turned on me, the sweet tones of her
voice as they fell on my ear, and the gentle pressure of her
hand in mine. Perhaps it was — but why weary myself
with conjectures? Enough that I was happy. And so,
with the fire blazing on the hearth, the shadows dancing
on the wall, the wine sparkling in my glass, the dark mahogany glowing with the heat, the little one playing on the
rug at its mother's feet, and my precious wife, with her
hand resting on my arm, beside me, singing me songs or

listening to my idle tales, did Thanksgiving night close around us.

Before the fire smouldered on the hearth, or the wine had lost its flavor, the midnight came, and I, at peace with all mankind, bade Thanksgiving-day good-bye.

CHAPTER XXXII.

An Original Remark. — " The Married Man's Plaint." — Mrs. Gray's Opinion of it. — My Defence. — Pranks of the Black Boy. — About the Circus. — The Black Boy's Accident.

"MRS. GRAY," I said one morning, while I still lingered at the breakfast-table, though she, seated in a rocking-chair near by, was selecting some work from her basket, "if you will allow me, I will read you some verses which were sent to me a few days since." "Verses !" exclaimed my wife ; " who, I would like to know, has been sending you, Mr. Gray, verses? I should as soon think of sending a cargo of ice to the inhabitants about the north pole."

That this was an entirely original remark of my wife's, I am perfectly satisfied; for when I added — " or coals to Newcastle," she said that, as to that matter, she could not say, not being well informed as regarded the coal business in that town.

When I attempted to explain the matter to her, she remarked that she had rather I would not, for she was anxious to hear the verses to which I alluded. " But you did not," she continued, " answer my question as to who sent them."

" Nor can I," I replied, " simply for the reason that I do not know. They came to me through the post-office, enclosed in an envelope, without the name of their author, or any clue whereby I could trace their parentage. I am inclined to believe, however, that the editor of the ' Star-Spangled Banner ' knows of their existence, and sent them to me in exchange for my verses written for him."

"But do you think he wrote them, Mr. Gray?" asked my wife.

"Not he," I replied; "though it were easy for some one else to write them for him. If he thinks they are in the least applicable to me, I would assure him he is much mistaken. But you shall hear the verses, and then you can the better judge as to their applicability." So I read aloud

THE MARRIED MAN'S PLAINT.

In days of yore, when I was gay,
  And careless, free, and single,
Of many friends, each festal day,
  I chose with whom to mingle.
They all were glad to have me come, —
  I 'd scores of invitations, —
And little rose to keep me home
  Among my poor relations.

I knew who brewed the strongest punch;
  I knew whose wines were rarest;
I cared but little for their lunch,
  Nor who had maids the fairest.
I went where Bacchus would have gone, —
  I felt it was my duty, —
I feared the rosy god would mourn,
  Should I leave him for beauty.

But now, when wife and I, to dine,
  Politely are invited,
I dare not ask about the wine,
  But go, though quite benighted.
And we must dress in festive guise:
  My wife in silks and feathers;
While I — the tears oppress my eyes —
  With feet in patent leathers.

I cared not once a whiff of smoke
  About my gloves or collars,
Nor felt the weight of fashion's yoke,
  Nor measured men by dollars.

I wore then coats of easy fit.—
  My tailor was most clever,
And never pinched me in a bit:
  To *suit* was his endeavor.

I used to dine with men of mind,
  With others who were funny,
And those who'd share with all mankind
  Their dinners and their money.
We talked of authors, old and new;
  We criticized the critics;
We re-reviewed the last review,
  And praised our friend's " Prismatics."

We sometimes pledged a poet's health
  In overflowing glasses;
But ne er — unless the maid had wealth —
  Would stoop to pledge the lasses.
We never mentioned love nor wife;
  Nor dreamed of baby faces;
Nor thought we'd find our paths in life
  Strewn thick with bows and laces.

We scarcely knew what marriage meant,
  Knew naught of bills for bonnets;
And thought the bills physicians sent
  Were similar to sonnets.
(I found this trifling error out
  While Master Bob was creeping:
For 't was the doctor's bill, no doubt,
  Which kept me nights from sleeping.)

We used to drink good liquor then,
  And tell some clever stories;
We were, I think, the best of men,
  And fresh as morning-glories.
We knew full well where lemons grew,
  What sugars were the sweetest, —
And how great bowls of punch to brew,
  In just a way the neatest.

. We could strike up a lively air
  At proper times and places:

" Crambambuli," with " Sweet and Fair,"
  And " Drink, ye Solemn Faces ! "
Champagne from cider we could tell ;
  Esteemed a glass of brandy, —
Nor called for water from the well,
  If something else were handy.

No one e'er asked me where I 'd been,
  When late abroad I tarried ;
Nor rose from bed to let me in, —
  For then I was n't married.
I bought a latch-key for my use, —
  Latch-keys are great inventions, —
I gave it up — I was a goose ! —
  To show my good intentions.

But things have changed since days of yore
  I have a wife to chide me,
A boy who tumbles on the floor,
  And one sweet girl beside me ;
I mark the hairs, amidst my beard,
  Which Father Time is growing ;
I told my wife the gray appeared
  Full ripe enough for mowing.

A few brief years, perhaps, may pass,
  Before old Time comes reaping ;
Till then I 'll slyly drain my glass,
  And laugh instead of weeping.
I know my wild oats all are sown,
  My friendly comrades banished,
And I, alas ! am forced to own
  My jovial days are vanished.

The shadows lengthen on my path ;
  The sunset is approaching ;
While I, about the household hearth,
  Some idle tales am broaching.
Perhaps, it I should reach threescore, —
  Could death so long be parried, —
I might forget the days of yore,
  And bless the day I married.

When I finished reading the above, Mrs. Gray said they were scandalous, and that the author, whoever he were, ought to be ashamed of them.

"To think," continued my wife, as she placed her hand trustingly in mine, — "to think that any man, possessing a heart, would write such naughty verses, is scarcely creditable. Believe me, my dear, no father, or even husband, could write thus; only some disappointed bachelor — who, after all, is more to be pitied than scorned — could have composed these lines. What!"—and here Mrs. G. dropped from her hands the little white merino robe she was embroidering, and, rising from her chair, walked to and fro the room, — "what! can any man prefer, to the pure companionship of woman, the society of the bottle and those who pass it! I cannot believe it; for sweet humanity's sake, I would not believe it, if I could." And thereupon Mrs. Gray paused in her speech and walk, as if desirous of having me make a reply; but as I remained silent, lost in admiration of my wife's remarks, she continued, — "The vein of humor that runs through the verses by no means balances the evil they inculcate. They wrong man's nobility; they grievously wrong woman's devotedness and affection."

"But," I rejoined, "they were, doubtless, written in jest."

"Neither in jest nor earnest should they have been written," exclaimed Mrs. G.

"Besides," I added, not heeding my wife's interruption, "there are, you must allow, some good things in them." — Mrs. G. said "No." — "They point out some of the follies of life; they call forth our smiles; they even are, in some slight degree, pathetic; and, in spite of ourselves, we feel our sympathies enlisted in behalf of the sufferer." — "Nonsense!" ejaculated my wife. — "And," I continued, "they even inculcate a moral."

"What moral, Mr. Gray, I should like to know," asked Mrs. G.. somewhat incredulously, "do they inculcate?"

" That," I replied, " of leaving well enough alone."

" Pshaw ! " exclaimed my wife ; and resuming her seat and work, she plied her needle industriously in forming a white rose-bud out of floss.

After a while, — my wife remaining silent, and apparently giving all her mind to the formation of rose-buds, — I concluded to drive to the village ; so I rang the bell for the black boy. The sable youth, however, did not come. At last I asked Mrs. Gray if she knew where he was ? She replied that she did not, but added, " He is, doubtless, engaged in some act of mischief, as usual. Every day he grows worse. I don't think I can much longer put up with that child's actions. I fear, Mr. G., you will have to send him away from Hillside. I am half inclined to think he is slightly demented ; for latterly he has kept himself, during his spare time, literally turned upside-down. If he goes to the well, he holds the pail by his teeth, and rolls over and over, like a cart-wheel without tire or felloes. He frightens the cook in the kitchen, by standing on his head on the table for minutes together, till his face changes from black to purple, and his eyes roll fearfully. He watches his opportunity, too, and, slipping into the nursery while the maid is absent, wakes the baby from the soundest of naps, and then amuses him by walking around the chamber on his hands, with his feet elevated in the air. Yesterday, while my cousin, Mrs. Day, and Mrs. Judge Chitty, were calling, I heard a knock at the parlor-door, and, supposing it to be Nora, with the baby to show to the ladies, I opened it, when, to my fright and mortification, in fell Master Black Boy, feet first. When, after my friends departed, I called him to me, and inquired what he meant by such conduct, he replied he meant ' nothin,' but he guessed he was an India-rubber boy.' His answer quite puzzled me, and I resolved to ask you its meaning."

I told Mrs. G. I was as much in the dark as she regarding it.

"I forgot to say," added my wife, "that he has been full of these pranks ever since the night it rained so hard, and you and he remained so late in the village, on 'particular business.'"

"The evening," I remarked, "your tall friend passed with you?"

"The same," she answered.

"Ah! well, really," I stammered, "I can't imagine what could have brought on him such an attack of eccentricity."

"What kind of an attack did you mention, Mr. Gray?" inquired my wife.

"Eccentricity," I repeated; "for I can imagine nothing more eccentric than standing on one's head."

"True, Mr. G.," said my wife; "but have I not heard of a class of persons who make their living by performing such eccentric acts?"

I knew then that Mrs. Gray had, somehow, learned about the circus; but I merely answered, "Possibly: I believe the Ravels are addicted to something of that nature."

"No," she answered, "the Ravels are celebrated artists, — men of genius, — and not to be placed on a level with circus-riders."

"Well, then," I remarked, "it must be the circus-riders themselves of whom you have just spoken."

Mrs. Gray bit her lips, but said not a word.

"I am often surprised, my dear," I continued, "at your uncommon quickness. Now, I should, doubtless, have puzzled my brains, for a whole day at least, striving to think of the particular class of persons you asked about, when, seemingly without any exertion of mind on your part, pop — just like a cork out of a champagne bottle — comes forth the very name, from your own mouth, of which you were asking me. The thing is wonderful, my dear, — wonderful."

"Mr. Gray," said my estimable spouse, striving hard to

keep back the smiles from her lips, "you are an extremely provoking man, and, more than this, you go to
circuses."

"Occasionally," I replied,—"once in twenty years."

"But you take the black boy there," she said, "and he
comes home with his mind filled with somersaults, and
tight-ropes, and India-rubber boys, and what not; so that
't will be months ere he forgets these things, and during all
that time he 'll keep the whole house, as well as himself,
upside-down."

Mrs. Gray had evidently mounted a somewhat spirited
horse, and was riding around the ring full tilt. I managed,
however, to say, while she drew rein a moment to breathe
her charger, that I did not take him there, but he "hooked"
in under the canvas. Mrs. G., though, paid no attention
to my remark, and, starting afresh, said, — "There was
that cymbal business: he nearly drove me distracted, and
kept the baby awake, for hours together, with the noise he
made practising on them, so that he might accompany that
atrocious band of Troubadours in its nocturnal wanderings.
I suppose "—   Here Mrs. Gray, who was walking the
room, suddenly paused, and said that, if I wanted the black
boy, I had better call him, as she could see him, she thought,
among the trees in the orchard.

Glad of an excuse to take my departure, under the plea
that the lad was too far distant to hear my call, I seized my
hat and left the house. It was very lucky for him — regarding the affair through my near-sighted and contracted
vision — that I did so, for, had a few more moments elapsed,
doing "chores" about Hillside would no longer have been
the black boy's occupation. "For how," as I said to Mrs.
Gray, in narrating the occurrence to her, in answer to her
inquiry of "Why not?" —"for how could a black boy, who,
accidentally, had hung himself," —"Hung himself!" exclaimed my wife, greatly horrified, —"yes, hung himself,"

I repeated, " until quite dead, have done any more ' chores about Hillside ? " — " But he is not dead, Mr. G. ? " my wife said, interrogatively.

" No," I replied ; " but he doubtless would have been, had a few more seconds elapsed in my reaching him. The little rascal, my dear," I continued, " in trying to perform some feat he had witnessed at the circus, suspending himself by the chin with a piece of rope attached to a limb of an apple-tree, thereby making a pendulum of his body, in some way managed to get the rope twisted about his neck, and there, when I came up, he was, dangling in the air. So I immediately proceeded to cut him down, not being desirous of having a deceased black boy on my hands."

The individual alluded to, who had stood by my side while I was narrating this occurrence, shaking as if he had the ague, and looking several shades whiter than ever before, exclaimed, " I reckon, Mister Gray, I 's glad myself that you come along ; and so, when I tell her of it, will be dis child's mother." And the tears stood in his eyes, and the big drops rolled down his dusky cheeks, as he thought of his mother. And tears stood, too, in Mrs. Gray's eyes, and in the old soldier's eyes ; and then the cook, taking him under her especial protection, carried him in her arms — though he loudly protested, and exclaimed he could walk there ; and, as he had walked from the orchard to the house with me, I think he could have accomplished it — to the kitchen, where she fed him with several large pieces, each, of mince and pumpkin pie, and then made him bathe his feet and go to bed.

In justice to the black boy, I must say that his appetite appeared quite as good, if not better, than usual, and that he said going to bed — it was about eleven o'clock A. M. — was a good deal nonsensical. The cook, however, — a very determined woman, — persevered, and had her way in the matter ; though the boy got up at dinner-time with a re-newed and improved appetite.

Mrs. Gray says that the " accident " — in speaking of the occurrence, she calls it " the little black boy's accident " — has had the good effect of causing the child to give up practising circus-tricks, and she hopes, too, it will prove a lesson to me not to attend any more circuses.

CHAPTER XXXIII.

Cold Meats. — Mrs. Gray's Opinion of Christmas. — Its Antiquity. — My
Astonishment. — A Delightful Book. — Christmas Eve. — Santa Claus's
Visit. — The Old Fathers. — Christmas Day.

ROM Thanksgiving night to Christmas eve is little
more than a span. The former day is but the
forerunner of the latter, and the mince-pies and
roasted pig of the Thanksgiving dinner, if you have any
remaining on hand, will answer to warm up for the Christmas feast." I uttered these words to Mrs. Gray as we sat,
Christmas eve, beside the round table in the library, —
she engaged in doing a butterfly with colored silk floss, on
a circular piece of white satin, and I looking over the
photographs illustrative of the Miles Standish poem. In
reply to my remark, my wife simply ejaculated, "How
absurd!"

"What is absurd?" I asked; "the style of butterfly
which you are embroidering?"

"Mr. Gray," answered my crinoline half, regarding me
somewhat sternly, "it is a *bouquet*, and not a butterfly,
which I am working: and I cried 'how absurd!' in regard
to your speech. Don't you know, Mr. Gray, that Christmas
is a much older and holier festival than Thanksgiving;
and that it would be almost sacrilegious to permit the cold
meats of the one to do service at the festal board of the
other?"

"Older, Mrs. Gray!" I asked, with an incredulous tone
"are n't you mistaken? I thought that Thanksgiving day
was as old as Plymouth Rock itself, or, at least, as old as
the Pilgrims who landed upon it."

" But Christmas, Mr. Gray, is still older."

" What! older than the Pilgrims, my dear!" I exclaimed. " Older than the eleventh of December, 1620, old style! Our New-England friends will not believe that, Mrs. Gray."

" You are too absurd, Mr. Gray. You know as well as I do that Christmas day is as old as Anno Domini, and neither more nor less."

I simply laughed in reply, for I was not certain that Mrs. Gray was in error, and I resolved to satisfy myself before answering.

" Oh! you may laugh, my dear," she added; " but you know it is so."

And as I did not deny it, our conversation came to a break, and stood still for a while.

" What a delightful book this is!" I at last remarked, as I turned over its cream-colored leaves containing the descriptive text. " These photographs, my dear, are admirable,"

" Yes," lisped Mrs. Gray, in a school-girlish way.

" Yes," I replied, pleasantly; " and this courtship scene, my dear, (showing it to her,) reminds me of a similar occurrence between ourselves."

" It is pretty and suggestive," my wife answered.

" It is more than that, my dear; it is very truthful," I remarked.

" Perhaps it is," she replied; and then followed a little sigh from Mrs. Gray, a smile from me, and straightway the book was closed and the embroidery laid aside, while Mrs. G., bringing her little chair nearer to mine, laid her hand confidingly on my arm, and I, in low, sweet tones, spoke of the Christmas eves of long ago, and of one not so distant wherein I wooed and won her.

By and by my wife said, " It is time that Santa Claus should fill the children's stockings." So, rising from her chair, she proceeded to the closet and presently came back bearing a basket containing toys and confectioneries, which she placed upon the table. "Now, be quiet, my dear," she said, as I reached forward to take her hand, "and content yourself with looking at Santa Claus."

So I was quiet; and while watching Santa Claus, it struck me as being odd that the old saint should appear wearing a head-dress, hoops, and a pair of gaiter-boots, — but I said nothing, — and Santa Claus proceeded to fill a pair of brief, red worsted stockings, till they were stuffed so full that they looked like very badly-shaped little legs that had been exposed to the cold; a tiny pair of white cotton socks — the baby's — were also filled, and then both were duly hung beside the wide-mouthed fireplace. "But whose," exclaimed Santa Claus, taking up a pair of larger and yarnier ones, "are these, Mr. Gray?"

"I do not know," I answered; "perhaps they belong to the little black boy. He was in here not long since, and asked me if I thought Santa Claus would come down the library chimney. As I told him I thought that he would, it is probable they belong to the black boy."

"They appear to be too large for the little black boy, — are n't they yours, Mr. Gray?"

Before I had time to reply, the library door was opened a trifle, and the little black boy's voice exclaimed, "Them stockings, if you please, Santa Claus, is mine, and no Mister Gray's;" and immediately the door was closed, and the black boy's feet pattered through the hall.

"Well, I declare," said Santa Claus, "that is a saucy little black boy of yours, Mr. Gray; but I suppose I shall have to fill his stocking; will you assist me, sir?"

Straightway I produced, from under the table. enclosed in the identical green bag which it wore when I laid it at Mrs. Gray's feet, the fiddle which used to give my wife the headache.

"Just the thing!" said Santa Claus, "only we can't get it into these colored stockings; but we'll hang it beside them, and place this red morocco porte-monnaie in one stocking, and some candies in the other." There was a subdued chuckle outside the library door, and immediately a pair of colored feet pattered down the hall again. Santa Claus paused and listened, shook her head, and then came and sat down in the chair beside me.

Softly and silently Christmas eve faded away, and Christmas morning brightly arose. Mrs. Gray and I, as a matter of course, attended service at the church in the forenoon. I am happy to be able to state that I went there purely from principle. I fear, however, Mrs. G. went simply because it was becoming so to do, and, moreover, was expected of her. I think Mrs. Gray was afraid I would wander off to the village before church-time, and thereby fail to drive her, wrapped in buffalo robes, to the sanctuary. To prevent such " meandering " on my part, she suggested, immediately after breakfast, the propriety of my examining carefully what the " Old Fathers," of the first and second centuries, had to say concerning Christmas. To please Mrs. Gray, I did so. I posted myself, to a limited extent, in the matter. In the midst of my investigation my wife informed me that it was time to start for church, and the horse and sleigh were in readiness. So I put on my overcoat and hat, and went towards the door. Mrs. Gray, however, stopped me in front of the bow-window, to scrutinize my dress, for the reason, she said, that it was Christmas, and she wanted me to appear neatly.

I replied to Mrs. G. I was very well aware it was Christmas ; and did she know, I continued, that Jerome, one of the early writers, speaks of " the ancient and universal tradition concerning the observance of this festival ? "

Mrs. Gray said she did not; but, doubtless, Jerome was correct in what he wrote.

" Yes," I added, quoting almost *verbatim* from the volume I had been reading, " though the direct evidence of the keeping of this festival in the first century is less than that of many others, still there is every reason to believe that it is primitive, if not Apostolic, and that, with few exceptions, it has always been observed on the 25th day of December, and consequently it is older, as you remarked last evening, than Thanksgiving-day."

I think I slightly astonished my estimable wife when I made the above remark, though she said nothing, but employed herself, during my utterance of it, in picking off a few white shreds clinging to my coat, and at the same time took the somewhat unnecessary trouble of retying my cravat in a more fashionable knot than I had tied it, and also placed my hat at a little different angle on my head.

Then Mrs. G. desired me to look at her, and tell her what I thought. And my wife walked majestically across the room. So I told Mrs. Gray my thought was of Augustin, Bishop of Hippo, another of the early fathers; and was going on to quote from his writings, but my wife said she wished not to hear anything more about him; besides, she did n't believe there had ever existed such a person as the " Bishop of Hypo."

" Hippo," I said, — " not Hypo ; " and offered to go for the book containing my authority, but Mrs. Gray replied, " Never mind ; " and added, " Now do, my dear, tell me if I appear to advantage, and let me know what you think of me."

Thereupon my wife walked majestically back again.

To speak the truth, I was very much struck by Mrs. Gray's appearance. She had gotten herself up with good taste, — velvets and laces, feathers and furs, and all that sort of thing ; besides, she looked charmingly, and had, altogether, a Christmas air, as if she actually saw the star in the East. She seemed to be, too, surrounded by delicate perfumes, as odorous as the frankincense and myrrh of the wise men.

I said as much in my reply to my wife, who straightway shook her head at me, and termed me "a flatterer," together with other undeserved epithets of a like nature.

When I drew on my gloves, she begged of me, as a particular favor, not to take them off while in church, for the reason, she said, that to do so was not fashionable. What fashion-plate Mrs. Gray has been studying to learn this, I do not know. The when and where she obtains her knowledge of many matters, greatly puzzles me to tell. Heretofore I have had no rule to guide me in wearing my gloves. I took them off and put them on as my fancy or desires prompted. But now, having learned it is fashionable not to unglove in church, I shall on no account violate the fashion. Not that I myself care aught about it, but I shall wear them simply to please Mrs. Gray. As a general rule, I like to please my wife, and am accustomed to adopt in my dress and manners any little additions or improvements it may please her to suggest. I interfere very little with her adornment of my person. If she chooses to tie a red ribbon about my hat, or a blue ribbon in my button-hole, I never object to her doing so. If she should say to me, " Mr. Gray, I should like to have you walk Spanish this morning ; " or, " You will oblige me by sitting in the Turkish style this evening," I would endeavor, so far as possible, to accommodate my estimable spouse in the matter. It is something of very small moment to me how I am attired, or walk, or sit. To have Mrs. Gray satisfied, and kept in a pleasant humor, is what I particularly aim at. Of course I have an object in this. I confess I am not entirely unselfish. I have discovered that my morning cup of coffee, in its different degrees of excellence, is governed entirely by the gradations of happiness which fill my wife's heart. To keep, then, my coffee up to the standard of the first cup, (made for me by Mrs. G.,) in point of exquisite flavor, is one of the great objects of my life, and often influences me to yield to many of Mrs. Gray's whims.

And so, while turning over the glove business in my mind, I deposited Mrs. Gray within the sleigh, and, seating myself beside her, proceeded towards the village.

CHAPTER XXXIV.

Going to Church. — My Erudition. — Moslems and Mosques. — Chateaux.
At the " Arbor." — Race with the Parson. — The Wrong Pew. —
Mrs. G.'s Presence of Mind. — Greens. — More Learning. — Geoffrey
Crayon. — Chancel-Windows. — Memory. — Change of Subject. — An
Untold Anecdote.

WHILE on our way to church, on Christmas morning, I added to Mrs. Gray's astonishment by a still greater display of erudition. " My dear," I remarked, as I drew rein at the foot of a long hill we were about ascending, " I would be pleased to have you give me a moment's attention, while I say a few words more in regard to the NATIVITY, or, as it is now termed, Christmas."

Mrs. G., having informed me that she would give me the attention I desired, settled herself deeply amidst the buffalo robes, buried her face, except her eyes, which shone brightly, behind her muff, and evidently made up her mind to receive a large amount of information. Thereupon I remarked that Chrysostom, who lived about the year 390, says this festival was one of great antiquity and long continuance, — the most venerable and tremendous of all festivals, — being famous and renowned in the Church from the beginning, far and wide, from Thrace to the Gaddes, in Spain.

Here my wife interrupted me to ask who Chrysostom was.

I informed her he was Bishop of Constantinople as long ago as Anno Domini 398. " It were a pity," she said, " that he did not convert the Mahometans and mosques to Christianity and churches."

" I have no doubt, my dear," I replied, " he would have done so, had Mahomet or his followers existed at that early period. It was not, however, till about the year 600 that the Prophet and the Koran arose, and at that time the good bishop was undoubtedly a saint in heaven."

Mrs. Gray having echoed my words, " in heaven," in a somewhat abstracted manner, and being apparently engaged in building a castle in the air, I incontinently dropped the subject, and commenced erecting a little *chateau* for myself in the neighborhood of my wife's. I was so busily occupied moulding some Gothic arches, that I quite neglected to guide the horse, who, not knowing we were on our way to church, — probably he was aware it was not Sunday, — suddenly stopped, much to my surprise and my wife's mortification, in front of the " Arbor Saloon."

When Mrs. Gray perceived where we were, she very quickly gave me to understand that it was not the place she wished to stop at.

" Nor I, either, my dear," I replied.

" Then, why not drive on ? " queried Mrs. G.

" Because," I answered, " the horse will not budge, notwithstanding I whistle and chirrup for him to ' get up.' "

" Whip him, then," whispered Mrs. G., now quite distracted, for every one on their way to church was gazing at us, and smiling.

" I would like very well to perform that little act," I replied, " but I fear the whip is lost, as I cannot find it."

Then Mrs. Gray and I searched the straw in the bottom of the sleigh for it, but without success. So at last I was obliged to get out — I knew exactly why the horse was waiting — and enter the " Arbor " for a moment ; when, so soon as I stepped into the sleigh again, the rascal started. As ill luck would have it, our parson, on his way to church, saw me come out, and cast on me, as he bowed, a look made up of inquiry, surprise, and disapprobation.

This unfortunate occurrence was the one straw which

broke the camel's back : and Mrs. Gray, pressing a high-priced lace handkerchief, odorous of frankincense and myrrh, to her eyelids, held it there till we reached the church-door.   Having handed my wife out, I told her I would join her in the vestibule as soon as I had blanketed the horse.   She waited for me a few moments, but seeing the parson coming, she hastened in.

I, for my part, joined the reverend gentleman at the middle gate of the church-yard, and wishing him a merry Christmas, which compliment he very solemnly returned, walked a short distance by his side, up the broad and beaten path, till he, just before we reached the porch-steps, diverged into another and narrower path on the right, leading to a private door at the rear of the edifice, of which he carried the key.   I watched him till he opened the little door, when I thought I 'd see who would get into church first.   In my haste I managed to run against two ladies, who were pluming their feathers in the vestibule, preparatory to making the grand entrance with the organ accompaniment.   I also tripped up the sexton, who had just finished tolling the bell ; and then stepped on the senior warden's gouty foot.   When I reached my pew I was quite out of breath, and glad to get a moment's rest.   On looking around me, I was surprised not to find Mrs. Gray beside me.   It occurred to me, that, aware of my wife's musical abilities, the choir had invited her to join them in singing the Christmas anthem.   So I turned my head around, — which act, owing, I think, to my new necktie, was one of great difficulty, — and gazed into the organ-loft, but without beholding Mrs. Gray.   As I twisted my neck back again, some one in the rear pew touched me on my arm with a prayer-book.   I looked and saw it was Mrs. G., and at the same moment the senior warden opened the door of the pew in which I was seated, to let in his wife, his wife's two maiden sisters, and himself.   It having become, by this time, very evident to me that I was in the wrong pew, I resolved to retreat; but the senior warden's family had commenced filing in, and egress through the door was cut off. My next idea was to step over the back of the pew into my own, as being the quickest way of extricating myself from the dilemma. To tell the truth, I had no desire to be shoved into the far end of the slip, with two maiden ladies, another lady, and the senior church-warden between me and the door. What, it occurred to me, would I be able to do in case of fire! The thought was unendurable, and I was on the very point of getting into my pew the shortest way, when Mrs. Gray, with great presence of mind, suggested to the incoming ladies the propriety of making room for me to pass out. The only way they could "make room," was by first going out themselves, which they did, much to their annoyance; and then I took my hat and followed them.

I found, after I was safe in my own pew, that I need not have been in so great a hurry to get into church, for the parson did not make his appearance until some minutes thereafter. I occupied myself, therefore, in the interval, with quietly gazing around the church, scanning the assembled multitude. Even after the services were commenced, I was, I might say, called to order several times by Mrs. Gray, either with a rebuking look, a serious shake of the head, or a firm touch of a little moccasined foot, reminding me of the place I was in, and recalling my wandering thoughts from the study of the various Scriptural mottoes, " done in greens," placed here and there about the church, to the contemplation of something equally as good, contained in my prayer-book. I cannot refrain, however, from saying I was much pleased with the manner in which the church was adorned. Evidently some person of taste had superintended the arrangement of the evergreen festoons and wreaths; and if it were not that the tiny leaves of the cedar-wreath, which was wound round the column beside which I sat, kept dropping into the back of my neck each time I knelt in prayer, thereby causing considerable irritation. I should have enjoyed, with greater zest than I did, the Christmas services.

Of course we had a very excellent sermon. Christmas sermons, usually, are excellent. Perhaps, as a general thing, they are better than any other sermons of the year. I said as much, during our ride home, to Mrs. Gray. She replied that she thought they were. Then she asked me if I could repeat the text of the morning's discourse. I was obliged to confess I could not. Whereupon Mrs. G. said she was not at all surprised at my ignorance of it; for she had noticed I was engaged, during its delivery, in counting the various colors in the chancel-window. I was much surprised at my wife's knowledge, and feared that I had numbered them aloud. But she assured me it was simply from my fixedness of gaze, and the motion of my lips, at the time, by which she had arrived at the truth. Then I wondered whether the parson knew it, or any of the congregation. Afterwards I quite delighted my wife by speaking as follows :— " The services of the church, my dear, about this season are extremely tender and inspiring. They dwell on the beautiful story of the origin of our faith, and the pastoral scenes that accompanied its announcement. They gradually increase in fervor and pathos during the season of Advent, until they break forth in full jubilee on the morning that brought peace and goodwill to men. I do not know a grander effect of music on the moral feelings than to hear the full choir and the pealing organ performing a Christmas anthem in a cathedral, and filling every part of the vast pile with triumphant harmony."

When I ended, Mrs. Gray remarked that what I had just said was as perfect as anything I had ever uttered. I replied that I thought it was; but I forgot to tell her where she might find the identical remark. Afterwards, when she had time to recall my words, she desired to know when and where it was that I had heard a Christmas anthem performed in a cathedral. So I told her that it was while I was travelling in England with Geoffrey Crayon, author of the " Sketch-Book "; and that probably she could find an exact transcription of all I had uttered somewhere in the pages of that volume. Thereupon my wife wished to know the exact year in which I was abroad.

" It was the year," I replied, "just previous to our marriage, and while I was a resident of Utopia."

" Of course it was," said my wife; and then our conversation ceased for a while. During the pause I busied myself finishing my *chateau*, which I made very grand indeed, by filling it with chancel-windows of stained glass, illustrative of gorgeous Oriental poems; figures of Georgian slaves pouring from tall and slim-necked flasks lucent syrups; Circassian maids, wonderfully draped, standing in dancing attitudes; and various other highly wrought Eastern scenes, — none of which were exactly appropriate, perhaps, for illuminating chancel-windows, but which differed, after all, from the figures in the church-window very slightly, — the difference, indeed, being more in the description of the emblems than in the character of the emblems themselves. At last Mrs. Gray brought my architectural work to a close by remarking she thought it quite strange that the horse should have stopped, as he did, at the "Arbor."

" Not so very strange," I replied, " when you recall to mind that it is the identical horse which one of my bachelor friends, who had a proclivity for stopping there himself, used to ride when he visited me at Hillside, during your absence at your mother's."

" Oh ! " uttered Mrs. Gray, in an incredulous tone; " but all that, my dear, occurred long ago, and you do not expect me to believe that the horse remembers it at this day ? "

" Indeed, I do," I replied. " Horses, let me tell you, have excellent memories, and never forget the spot where they once were in the habit of stopping. Let me tell you, my

love, a little anecdote about a physician's horse, which "—
but Mrs. G. interrupted me by saying, —

"Never mind concerning the anecdote, Mr. Gray; but
allow me to inquire which horse it is you usually drive
when you go to the village, and where it is you generally
stop?"

I was obliged to confess that this was the horse; "but,"
I added, "it is to the post-office I go, and not to the 'Arbor.'"

Mrs. Gray hoped it was so; but I could perceive that
she was considering the matter, and so, to break the thread
of her thoughts, I again essayed to tell the little anecdote
about the doctor's horse, but no sooner did I attempt its
narration than she declared that to hear it would make her
head ache; "indeed," she added, "my head, Mr. Gray,
already aches."

"Caused," I remarked, "by the parson's sermon, I have
no doubt."

"Mr. Gray," she exclaimed, "do you forget the day? —
are you a heathen, that you speak thus of that good man's
discourse?"

"No, my dear," I replied, "but"—

At this moment we reached the door of our cottage, for
which I was extremely thankful, as our arrival brought
to an end a painful conversation. Though, had it proceeded, I should still have insisted upon the excellent
memory our horse possessed, and, further, should have told
the anecdote I was so anxious to relate.

CHAPTER XXXV.

My Exit. — Anniversaries. — Freedom. — In the Snow. — Frank. — My
Breakfast. — A Serf. — Female Collegians. — Blue and Gold. — My Old
Friends. — The Editor. — " Sherry Time." — Apple-Jack. — Going
Home. — Mrs. G.'s Company. — A Safe Ride.

N New-Year's day I took my hat and went down to
the village. I performed this feat early in the
morning. I did not even wait for breakfast, but
departed before Mrs. Gray made her appearance in the
breakfast-room. The fact is, I had promised to make sundry calls with my friend **Frank**, and I knew that it would
be almost impossible to break from the attraction of my
wife's presence if I waited for my matutinal meal. Besides,
Mrs. G. would not only have disapproved, but seriously, perhaps resolutely, objected to my leaving her at all. I am attached to my wife. I think she is an admirable little woman.
I pass a great deal of my time in her society. I spent the
whole of Christmas with her. We ate our Thanksgiving-
dinner together; we picnicked side by side on the Fourth
of July. I drank her health many times, and was happy
to do so whenever, during the year, we celebrated together
certain anniversaries, — our betrothal, our espousal, her
birthday, my birthday, **each** of the children's birthday,
also her mother's, her grandmother's, and my great-grandfather's. Mrs. Gray said it was all nonsense celebrating
my great-grandfather's, who died at least fifty years before
I was born, but for whose memory I entertain the highest
respect ; not that I ever heard or knew much about him,
save what I have learned from his monument, — which is
a very costly affair, and gives him a very good character.

Besides the aforesaid anniversaries, I keep, with my estimable wife, all the feast and fast days imposed by our
Mother the Church. Moreover, I remain at home with Mrs.
Gray whenever she has her little headaches, and whenever
I am sick myself. I thought these matters over, as I lay
awake one night, just after Christmas, and resolved that I
would, on New Year's, indulge myself with a day's freedom
— join my bachelor friends, and, as far as practicable, become one of them again. So, as I have already stated, I
took my hat, just before the hour Mrs. Gray usually makes
her appearance down-stairs, and departed for the village.
I left with the little black boy, for Mrs. G., a very elaborate
note, written the night previous, stating the case, and ex-
cusing, as far as I was able, my early flitting. I felt very
sorry for Mrs. Gray, as I wended through the snow on my
way to the village, when I thought of the disappointment
she would experience in not finding me in the breakfast-
room. When she, looking so fresh and charming, and with
such a blithe, happy New-Year's greeting on her lips, should
enter, my absence, I feared, would be a great shock to her.
She will, doubtless, I said to myself, refuse to partake of
breakfast, will weep bitterly, and, it may be, utterly disheartened, will wander forth and perish in the snow. These
thoughts caused me uneasiness, and I wished I was home
again. Besides, my appetite was improving; and a three
miles' walk through deep snow, with last year's stomach
unprovided for, was no pleasant affair. I encouraged and
consoled myself, however, with thinking how pleased Frank
would be to see me, what a rare breakfast we would take
together, and with what delightful conversation we would
enliven it. But somehow, when I entered Frank's gorgeous apartments, he did not appear as pleased to see me as
I had anticipated. He had taken breakfast, he said, and
he more than intimated that he did not desire another; so,
quite disappointed, I sought the " Arbor," and partook of my
New-Year's breakfast in solitary grandeur. During its prog

ress I thought, several times, that it would have been better for me to have remained at home, even if it had fallen to my lot to have been asked by my wife to search the writings of the Old Fathers, for evidence relating to the antiquity of the day, which must be older than Anno Domini, if not coeval with the beginning of the world. I knew it would have proved a fruitless task ; but still I believe I could so far have accomplished it as to have satisfied Mrs. Gray, and, afterwards, with her approval, have ridden down to the village in time to make my annual calls. It was, therefore, in no very exuberant spirits that, after my meal was ended, I again entered Frank's rooms. To my surprise, his serf — a youth whom he had imported from Russia expressly for his own service — informed me that his lord had departed for the Female College, where he would be pleased to meet me. Of course, my going there was out of the question, and Frank knew it very well. He was aware that Mrs. Gray had interdicted it from me, simply for the reason that the last time I was there, at a meeting of the Sophia Society, I was slightly enamored of a sweet little girl, clad in blue and gold — like one of Ticknor & Fields's miniature volumes of poems. Mrs. Gray said I talked of her in my sleep — which I don't think I did. However, my wife learned all about the affair, and read, in the " Star-Spangled Banner," where they were published anonymously, the six or eight sonnets, songs, poems, etc. which I had thoughtlessly, but innocently, addressed to the azure and gilt young woman. I would not offend Mrs. G. again, by visiting that enticing institution, for fifty young ladies, even if they were decorated with all the colors of the rainbow. Not wishing to make calls alone, I undertook to find John, formerly of " Arbor " proclivity, who, having become engaged to be married, would not, therefore, think of venturing to such an alluring place. To my astonishment, however, I learned that the innocent John had been induced by Frank to accompany him. I failed in finding any of my old friends

who would or could go with me. My tall friend, P., did
not make calls. Fred and John, of the moneyed institution, were already making calls, and could not be found.
Another of my friends had been seeing the old year out,
and was in no condition for making calls. He, however,
presented to me the following parody, — which he had
written and sung the night before, — and insisted on warbling it to me while standing in the street, in front of the
" Spread-Eagle " tavern. When I say that his " warbling,"
as he himself termed it, was more appreciated by the crowd
which gathered around us than by myself, I speak the
truth. My musical friend was no other than the editor of
the " Banner."

SHERRY-TIME.

Come to me in sherry-time,
　When the old year closes ;
We 'll have a Tom-and-Jerry time
　Among the ruby noses.
While the wine is flowing fast,
　And our glasses jingle,
Grief afar we 'll sternly cast,
　Only *smiles* we 'll mingle.

When the night is fading out —
　Just before the dawning,
" Happy New Year! " we will shout,
　And " Won't go home till morning."
Then come to me in sherry-time,
　As the old year closes ;
We 'll have a Tom-and-Jerry time
　Among the ruby noses.

After leaving my dulcet-tongued friend, I essayed to
make a few calls, but met with ill success. Only one of
the eight or ten families at whose door-bells I rung, received callers. At this one place, however, I remained
five hours, and enjoyed myself exceedingly. The apple-
jack brewed there was excellent ; and when, just at dusk,
I found my way out of this hospitable mansion, I decided

that it was time for me to return home. Fortunately, just as I started, I met the little black boy coming into the village with the horse and sleigh, who, for a consideration, was willing to turn the horse's head and return with me; though he had come down to the village, he said, to keep New Year's day. I suggested that it was quite too late to commence keeping it. He could n't help that, he replied, for Mistress Gray had so much company, that it kept him running to the door all the while, a-letting them in and out.

"But Mrs. Gray, in my absence," I said, "did not see any one, I trust, — did she?"

"But she just did," answered the little black boy.

"Has she not been troubled with a headache?" I inquired.

"Not that I knows of," he replied.

"My little black boy," I said, "tell me the names of the gentlemen who have called on Mrs. Gray."

"Can't remember them all, sir; there 's bin so many. Oh, Mister Frank and Mister John, they is there now. They 've bin there most of the afternoon."

"Alas!" I thought, "my treacherous friends!" Then I applied the whip to the horse, and we reached the cottage just as the two gentlemen were departing. I was very polite to them, — very cordial indeed, — and invited them to remain all night — to stay even for a day or two, and go out shooting deer with me on Monday. They both declined, however, and Frank had the impudence to say that they had been hunting *dears* all day. Then I wished them a safe and pleasant ride down to the village, bade them "good-night," and went into the house. Mrs. Gray, the maid said, had just retired. So I sent to her, by the servant, the compliments of the season, stirred up the fire in the library, and made myself comfortable. I thought of Frank and John. I knew the night was dark, and the snow sadly drifted over the road. I did not envy their "safe and pleasant ride," for I believed they would meet

with many upsets on their way home. It was only the little
black boy's knowledge of the road that saved me. The
next day I heard that they had upset no less than ten times,
and were bruised and half frozen besides. I am sorry to
say this account gave me pleasure.

CHAPTER XXXVI.

Mrs. G.'s Remarks by-and-by. — Peace-Offerings. — The Hut. — My Occupation. — A Violinist. — A Compliment. — An Unaccepted Offer. — "Some Poetry."

SEVERAL weeks have elapsed since New Year's, and in that time neither Mrs. Gray nor I have said aught concerning our separate celebration of the day. I have waited, with much anxiety, for my wife to allude to the subject ; but to this moment her lips remain sealed. That she will, however, express her feelings in suitable words, I am most positive. I am too well acquainted with Mrs. G. to doubt it. By-and-by, when I am least expecting it, she will give me to understand that five hours are too many for a married man to invest in a single call on New-Year's day ; or, indeed, as she will take occasion to add, on any other day. She will, further, express her disapproval of apple-jack as a beverage, and finish by inviting me to " warble ' Sherry-Time.' " Till this little affair is settled, I shall continue to be very uncomfortable in my mind. This matter has already been a source of much expense to me, and will, doubtless, continue to be so. I often feel quite timid, after an absence from home of a few hours, when I reënter the house, lest my wife should have something to say about New Year's. I avoid, as far as possible, any allusion to the day. I invariably carry home with me a peace-offering for her when I return from the village. I have in this way presented Mrs. Gray with a coffee-urn, a carpet-sweeper, a pair of French boots, a canary bird, three white mice, a photograph of " Rosa Bonheur," a dozen bottles of Delluc's " Choice Extracts," a bouquet of japonicas, a sewing-machine, and a superb crinolinish arrangement that resembles a trellised summer-house. My deserving wife receives these propitiatory gifts with a calmness of demeanor delightful to witness. I think she clearly understands why I bring them, and has resolved, so long as they make their appearance, to let the New-Year's affair rest in silence. But this course cannot be pursued forever. My bank account will not permit it. Another week will run the thing into the snow, and then —— well, I will not anticipate domestic trouble.

There are a number of matters about the farm that, at present, greatly engage my attention, and take me from the family circle. I am building a long line of rail-fence, and superintend personally the splitting and laying up of the rails. In the woods, where the men are at work cutting down the trees, I have erected a stone hut, and roofed it with hemlock-boughs. It contains a cooking-stove, a pine table, and three or four roughly constructed benches. It is a place in which one can make himself quite comfortable. Plenty of pine knots strew the ground just outside the door, and a spring of water bubbles forth not far off. A demi-john stands in one corner of the hut ; and though lemon-trees do not flourish near by, nor the sugar-cane grow on the premises, nor the kettle always sing upon the stove, yet are lemons and sugar and hot water easily procurable. Occasionally, when my bachelor friends come up to see me, as they did last week, they find these items without difficulty. I am happy to say that Mrs. Gray never visits the place. I doubt if she be aware of its existence. No one at the cottage, save myself and the little black boy, has ever been there. Nor do I deem it necessary that any should. In case of an insurrection in my household, it appears to me that the hut would prove an available place of refuge. Not that I really anticipate aught of that nature, but allude to it simply as an event which might possibly occur. I am indebted to my friend Frank for the suggestion that impelled me to build this lodge in the wilderness, and I really consider it as very kind in him. Besides, I find it a most convenient and comfortable spot wherein to write my letters, — letters purely of a private character, and in no way interesting to Mrs. Gray, — and where, too, I may possess the society of my bachelor friends, and enjoy dreamlike reveries undisturbed by the noise of children. When, after being absent all day superintending the workmen, Mrs. Gray says to me on my return, " I am sorry, my dear, that you are obliged to stay out in the cheerless woods thus, day after day, exposed to the cutting winds and the drifting snow. I fear you will take cold, and fall sick ; be careful, my love, and do not expose yourself more than is absolutely necessary,"— I assure her that I am careful ; that I am not so much exposed to the inclemency of the weather as she thinks ; that it is quite mild in the woods, and the choppers have huge fires burning, where I can warm myself. But I say nothing about the hut and its accessories. Why should I ? It is there that the little black boy practises on the violin which I gave him at Christmas. I confess that I am surprised at the progress he makes on the instrument, especially since his teacher is but an indifferent performer. I think little black boys take naturally to violins. When he comes to perform before Mrs. Gray, I am inclined to think she will be slightly astonished. She will wish to know when and where he learned to play, and who was his instructor. Then, I am fearful, the story of the hut will come out. The moment my estimable wife learns this circumstance, I think she will conclude that my superintendence of the workmen is not as arduous a duty as she imagined.

I have lately been invited to join a fire-engine company. Excelsior, I believe, is the name. I have been offered the situation of secretary of the company, if I will accept it ; and, as a further inducement, promised that the little black boy shall receive the appointment of torch-bearer. It is,

of course, very gratifying to my feelings to be noticed in
this way.   It evinces a spirit of kindness, on the part of the
members of the company, for which I was not prepared.   I
confess that I should like to see myself arrayed in a red
shirt, and with " Excelsior" printed, in gilt letters, on the
front piece of the leather hat upon my head.   I should
further like to wear my trousers inside of my boots, and
bawl myself hoarse, for once at least in my life, with crying
" Fire!"   But I have a regard for the feelings of Mrs.
Gray.   I think, in the first place, that she would object to
my wearing a red shirt; and in the next place, she would
be most decidedly opposed to my leaving her, — say, in the
middle of the night, — to go down to the village to assist
in putting out a fire.   I should myself object to this part
of the business, and should not appreciate, either, working
the brakes.   Taking these things duly into consideration, I
thought it my duty to decline, respectfully but firmly, the
invitation.   The editor of " The Star-Spangled Banner "—
who is foreman of said company, and who composed the
committee that waited upon me with the above offer —
was much pained, he said, at my refusal.   The company,
which he had the honor to represent, would be greatly disappointed.   He trusted that I would reconsider the matter, and if I should conclude to join, he would resign his
own post in the company in my favor.   Would I accept
the office of foreman?   With my present limited knowledge
of fire-engine tactics, I told him, I rather thought not;
and though I fully appreciated the compliment paid to me,
yet owing to certain domestic circumstances, which could
not be overcome, I must decline the honor intended.   I
requested him, however, to thank the company for their
kindness, and to say that I should be greatly obliged if they
would accept from me, — say on the twenty-second of
February, — as a slight testimonial of my esteem, a silver
trumpet.   Thereupon the editor of " The Star-Spangled
Banner," and foreman of " Excelsior Engine Company,"

gave me to understand that he would take the responsibility of accepting, in behalf of said company, my offer. As he was on the point of leaving me, he placed in my hands for perusal, and publication, if I desired, the following choice verses, which he composed a few years since, while an humble member of the New-York Fire Department. The lines are entitled —

SOME POETRY;

BY THE FOREMAN OF MINNEHAHA, NO. 40.

I goes some days a-takin' walks, —
  Some days jest after dinner, —
Adown Broadway, I say, I stalks,
  Along with saint and sinner.
I sees the sights as may be seen
  From Union Square to Battery;
I notices each painted quean
  As ruined was by flattery.

I observes, too, the dandy crew,
  With whiskers and moustaches;
I likewise notices a few
  Young gals a-sellin' matches.
I mixes right among the crowd,
  I shoves the aristocracy,
And lets 'em see, though they be proud,
  I 'm prouder of democracy.

I wears a red shirt, all ablaze;
  Hi, hi! I runs with "Forty";
I goes to fires nights and days,
  And goes by name of "Shorty."
I 'm foreman of a crack masheen,
  Its house is in the Bowery;
And when it plays, as I have seen,
  Yer 'd say 't was rather showery.

There 's Liza-Ann, as keeps a shop,
  And deals in cake and candy,
With whom, when there a'n't fires, I stop,
  And finds her place quite handy.

And she is jest the nicest one, —
  No Broadway gal is healthier, —
And when she gets her purties on,
  I reckon none is wealthier.

And as I goes a-takin' walks
  With Lize, jest after dinner,
I tell yer what, the way she talks
  Would make yer glad to win her.
I shows her all as can be seen
  From Union Square to Battery,
And then I says, says I, "My queen!"
  Says she, "Go 'long with yer flattery.

CHAPTER XXXVII.

The Old Soldier's Present. — Charter Oak. — Thimble-Case. — Toddy-Stick.
Frank and John. — Polishing the Cane. — Prayer for the Donor.

THE old soldier has been wonderfully " set up "
lately. He has had that presented to him which
makes him appear younger, by ten good years,
than he is in reality. The request I made in his behalf, a
short time since, has met a kind response. The staff from
the Charter Oak, for which the ancient patriot so much
wished, to support his tottering steps, is even his ; and it is
the possession of this which has so set him up. He is indebted to the generosity of the Hon. J. W. Stuart, of Hartford, on whose grounds the old oak stood, for this memento
of that tree whose heart was the casket in which the liberty of Connecticut was preserved.

The staff arrived at Hillside late one Saturday evening,
after the old soldier had hobbled off to bed ; but as I knew
he was desirous of seeing it, — he having heard, by letter,
from the donor that the same was on its way, — I told the
black boy, who had brought it from the village, to take it
to the old soldier's room, and, if he were awake, to deliver
it to the brave veteran. The old soldier chanced to be
asleep, and the black boy, without my approbation or consent, proceeded to stir him up with the Charter-Oak cane,
much to the soldier's discomfort and displeasure. In fact,
he left on his person almost as many bruises as there are
scars. At first, on being aroused, my old pensioner was
inclined to show fight ; and addressing the little black boy
as an " imp of darkness," seized his crutch, standing at the
head of the bed, with an evident intention, then and there,

of demolishing the youth.   But he is a spry boy, — seeing
what he did at the circus improved him somewhat, I think,
in the article of spryness, — and he easily avoided the old
soldier's attack, and darting under the bed, raised it up,
thereby casting its enraged occupant, wrapped in the
American flag, out upon the floor. Fortunately, at this moment, I made my appearance ; or else the war, doubtless,
would have been carried into Africa, much, perhaps, to the
little black boy's sorrow. As it was, I had great difficulty
in calming the old man, and making him understand the
affair : it was only by placing the staff in his hands, and
shouting, at the same time, " Charter Oak ! Charter Oak ! "
that I succeeded. When, however, he clearly comprehended
the case, his joy was very great ; he freely forgave the
black boy, and would, I believe, have embraced me, had I
allowed him to do so. Then he examined the staff carefully, and measured it with a six-inch rule he carries in his
pocket, and made the ebony youth set down the figures, as
he called them off, in chalk, on the foot-board of his bedstead. Then he hobbled across the room with its assistance, and retold to him, for the twentieth time, the history
of the tree, from the period when a deputation of Indians
came to the steward of Governor Wyllys, as he was cutting
away the trees, preparatory to erecting a residence for his
master, and requested him to spare the old hollow oak.
" For it has been," they said, " the· guide of our ancestors
for centuries, as to the time of planting our corn. When
the leaves are of the size of a mouse's ear, then is the time
to drop the seed into the earth ; " — its history from this
period, I repeat, did the soldier relate, down to the day of
its fall. When I left his room he was in the midst of his
story, and I think he kept the boy up, listening to revolutionary stories, and tales of 1812, during the remainder of
the night; for when I awoke, very early in the morning,
j1st when the " new red " in the barnyard was signalling
daybreak, I could hear the treble of the old man's voice.
even through the deadened walls which divided us.

Thereupon I woke Mrs. Gray from a sound sleep, that she might hear the old soldier. I do not think my wife was altogether pleased because of my awaking her. In fact she said as much. She would like to know, she exclaimed, what I meant. I told her to listen to the ancient warrior. She spoke something about a fig in connection with my warlike friend, and then immediately fell asleep. Of course she was asleep; for though I addressed her eight or ten times, calling her "Mrs. Gray," she failed to hear me, and consequently made no reply. So I, wearied out, and waiting for "the light to thicken in the east," lay and listened to the old soldier, who, five rooms off, "shouldered his crutch, and showed how fields were won."

In connection with the old soldier and his present, it may be proper for me to mention that Mrs. Gray and myself received, at the same time, from H. B. Beach, Esq., mementos of the fallen tree. Mrs. G. was honored with a thimble-case, in the form of an acorn, made from the wood of the old tree, and which case contained within it a very perfect sample of the natural fruit of the Charter Oak. This natural acorn Mrs. Gray is intending to have mounted with a golden cup and enamelled oak-leaf, and to wear it as a scarf-pin. The only trouble Mrs. G. has in the matter is the fear that the jeweller, with whom she may trust the precious relic, will be tempted to substitute for it an acorn of less noble birth. She is even suspicious of the little black boy, and is quite afraid that he may take it into his head to change the acorn before the jewellers have an opportunity. It would be like him, she thinks, to do so; especially now, while his mind runs on the Charter Oak and its acorns; and his pockets are filled with similar ones, gathered from the "new Charter Oak," where he still keeps his cymbals.

For my portion of the old tree, I received what the worthy donor was pleased to term "a very suspicious-looking specimen for these 'Maine-law' days." He presumed, however, that it would be " acceptable, and prove a useful institution at the social gatherings of my bachelor friends." My excellent correspondent presumed rightly, as Frank and my friend John, of " Arbor" proclivity, can bear testimony. Of course, I do not care to state what it was I received. I refrain from naming the article purely out of delicacy to my friends' feelings. I believe they would not like to have it known that they ever used such article. Though they each remarked to me, quite confidentially, as they were practically testing the same, that they would like very much indeed to possess similar ones. I may as well mention here that the little black boy, when he first saw my memento of the Charter Oak, supposed it to be a drumstick, and asked why Mr. Beach sent me a single one. When I told him that it was a stick of another sort, and immediately — after stepping to the library closet, where I keep demijohns and bottles, and lemons and sugar, and nutmegs, and such like concomitants, and then to the kitchen, where the cook keeps hot water — showed him, by a practical illustration, its goodly use, he said it was just the kind of thing I needed, but that, for his part, he had much rather have a pair of drumsticks, which he thought would please him most of anything.

The old soldier spends a good deal of time over his cane. He is bringing it to a high state of perfection. The different polishing processes he has put that staff through is astonishing. He has oiled it and boiled it, steamed it and smoked it, sand-papered it and pumice-stoned it, filed it and scraped it, rubbed it with a preparation which resembled honey, and then sprinkled it with a powder that looked like India-rubber and cork pulverized; and immediately afterwards sunk it in the well, where it remained one night, and gave to the water a very pungent taste, together with a brownish tinge. It has been rubbed with flannel and with velvet, with chamois skin and with kid, with sheep's wool and an old silk handkerchief; and still the work goes on.

Every night, with two exceptions, — once when it was in the well, and again when the black boy slept with it,— since it came into the possession of the old soldier, has he carried it with him to bed. He fairly loves the cane, and he loves the donor of it. He actually prays for him, and that, too, aloud, and in the church. I noticed he did so the first Sunday in which he carried the staff to church with him; and he has continued the practice ever since, notwithstanding my telling him of the impropriety of so doing. Instead of praying, as he ought to do, in accordance with the service of our church, for " *the President of the United States*, and all others in authority," he, not being altogether favorably disposed towards the Buchanan administration, drops Mr. President, the cabinet, etc., and substitutes therefor the names of our gracious donors of Charter-Oak memorials.

When the old soldier first came to Hillside, he was in the habit of praying for me and all my bachelor friends, in lieu of the President. He afterwards dropped us, at my earnest solicitation, and took up, of his own accord, " the Directress of the Sewing Society, and all its members," because they had made and given him a couple of shirts.

CHAPTER XXXVIII.

Mrs. Gray's Valentine. — Her Sarcastic Remark. — Slippers. — Embroidering. — Oh! — Letter from Clarence. — The Old Saint. — Mrs. G.'s Approval.

T. VALENTINE'S DAY, which is set down in the almanacs as occurring on the fourteenth of February, was celebrated at Hillside slightly in advance. As early as the tenth of the month Mrs. Gray received, through the post-office, an original valentine. I may as well here confess that I was its author. By a private arrangement which I made with the postmaster at New Orleans, the valentine bore the official stamp of his office. Mrs. G., having no acquaintance in that part of the world. is somewhat at a loss to know from whom it came. She, however, suspects my old friend Steel, who there resides. I have increased this suspicion in Mrs. Gray, by informing her that my friend is engaged in the pursuit of literature, and is decidedly of a literary turn of mind. I have had less hesitation in saying this, than I otherwise would, were I not aware of his being in the " book-trade."

MRS. GRAY'S VALENTINE.

(Air — "RORY O'MORE.")

The pride of her husband
  Is Abeline Gray, —
His comfort and glory
  Through life's thorny way ;
She is joyous and merry,
  But not over-gay ;
And the pride of her husband
  Is Abeline Gray.

She keeps his house tidy
  From May until May ;
And seldom from home,
  For her pleasure, doth stray, —
As this gadding about
  Among neighbors "don't pay."
Oh, the pride of her husband
  Is Abeline Gray.

She clothes herself neatly, —
  She loves not display, —
She loves but her "gude mon,"
  And him to obey ;
For she knows it is foolish
  To have her own way.
Quite the pride of her husband
  Is Abeline Gray.

And when she goes shopping,
  Not long does she stay
From her spouse and her baby,
  Lest gossips should say,
That fashions and follies
  Have led her astray.
Oh, the pride of her husband
  Is Abeline Gray.

To church she goes weekly, —
  In Lent every day, —
Where, humble and tearful,
  She kneels down to pray :
That her prayers are accepted,
  Ah, who shall gainsay !
Yes, the pride of her husband
  Is Abeline Gray.

She 's all that her consort
  Can hope for or pray :
She 's good, and she 's handsome,
  She 's witty and gay.
She loves him the fonder
  As life wears away ;
And the pride of her husband
  Is Abeline Gray.

After Mrs. Gray had perused her valentine, she handed it to me to read; at the same time asking me who I supposed was the author. Then it was that I mentioned my friend Steel, as above narrated, and continued the conversation in this wise : "I must say, my love, that I consider it very polite in my old companion, thus to send you a valentine; being a stranger to you, it is certainly an act worthy of note."

Mrs. G., however, did not agree with me. She thought it rather impertinent than otherwise for a stranger to send her such verses. Then she decried the poetry, and declared it was not equal to a valentine which I once sent her. She wished I would write her such another; and I half promised her so to do.

My friend Clarence, who lives afar off in the woods, thousands of miles distant from any womankind, and where I had no idea that Valentine days ever came, has sent me the following letter, which he wishes to palm on me for a valentine. "If I can't," I said to Mrs. Gray, " have a better valentine than this foolish epistle, — one from a lady, either married or single, I care not which, — why, I 'll stop writing any more valentines myself." — " Could you not manage, Mr. Gray," said my wife, " to have something else than poetry sent you, for valentines? You know you are well supplied with poetry, and possess all you need; but there are certain articles, quite as necessary as poetry, of which you sadly stand in want."

" A pair of slippers, for instance," I suggested; " and a new dressing-gown ? "

" Nonsense ! " uttered Mrs. G.

" Before I was married, my dear," I continued, " I had any number of slippers presented me : blue velvet slippers embroidered with gold braid, and others worked with silk floss; and still others of stronger materials, more durable and useful. But now, when I wish a pair of slippers, I am obliged to purchase them, or else go without.

I tell you, my love, I take no comfort or delight in the wearing of slippers which I buy. The ones you denounce as 'horrid, ugly-looking yellow things, fit only for steamboats and hotels,' which I am now wearing, answer my purpose full as well as any I could purchase. They are a change from the close boot, and, therefore, are preferable to it; but they do not possess that cosiness of fit, that peculiar warmth and softness, that cushiony feeling of repose, which one finds in slippers worked by the fair hands of some sweetheart or friend. Oh, my dear," I continued, appealing to Mrs. Gray, "if you would but work me a pair of slippers, how pleased I should be."

Mrs. Gray, however, gave me to understand that her time was fully occupied in embroidering robes for our "blessed baby." "And," she added, "it was not slippers nor dressing-gowns of which I was about to speak, but things much more important, which I fear you, Mr. Gray, will never possess." I looked at my wife inquiringly. She continued : — "Instead of poetry, seek to have the valentines you receive freighted with modesty and humility, or almost any of the cardinal virtues, and, I doubt not, you will be the better therefor."

After my estimable spouse had delivered herself of this somewhat pithy and sarcastic remark, — doubtless caused by my allusions to sweethearts and velvet slippers, — she remained silent, notwithstanding my ejaculation of "Oh!" uttered in a way to incite her to continue her remarks.

Then, after waiting a few moments, I read aloud this

LETTER FROM CLARENCE.

"There may be holier saints, Barry, in the calendar than ever Valentine was, but I doubt if there are any better disposed to make mankind happier than this same Saint Valentine. As I understand it, — though it is possible I may be in error, — he is the patron saint of matrimony, and wherever he finds a man unmated, or a woman in a like condition, it becomes his mission to bring them together, and, if possible, make them husband and wife. Whether this be altogether a wise proceeding on the part of the old saint, is, to me, extremely doubtful. I have known, even in my short experience of life, many married persons who were mated, to be sure, but mated with an *ill* before it.

"There is an old adage — none the less true for being old — that says, 'Leave well enough alone.' Now, as a bachelor, I am contented with my lot, and I should be but risking my present moderate degree of happiness in seeking change as a married man. I am satisfied it would never be my good fortune to obtain for a wife such a true woman as — well, say Mrs. Gray, for instance ; no one who would be to me all that she is to her husband, — no one who would welcome me home with such pleasant smiles and cheerful words of greeting as she does him, — no one half so fair-looking, nor half so gentle in her manners, — no one half so clever a housekeeper, nor half so good a woman. I fear me, Barry, my wife, if I ever obtain one, will seldom be without a frown on her brow, and will often utter those ominous words, 'My dear, where have you been ?'"

"Poor Clarence!" exclaimed Mrs. Gray, "how I pity him! If I had only seen him, Mr. G., before I married you!"

"Well, if you had," I asked, "what then ? "

"Why, then," answered my wife, slightly hesitating and blushing, "why, then, I should have seen him."

"And is that all ? " I inquired.

"Yes," replied Mrs. G., "that is all," — adding, however, after a pause, in which she appeared to be considering the matter, "perhaps."

Then, very solemnly, I continued the reading of Clarence's letter : —

"Still, I do not like Saint Valentine's Day to pass, without writing something like a valentine in honor of the day itself; for I have heard that, if any unmarried person neglects to do so, the old saint feels hurt and sorrowful ; and, as he is a good-natured old fellow, though essentially wrong in his notions regarding happiness, I like to humor him, as far as I can consistently. So if you, Barry, married man though you be, will receive this as a valentine, it will greatly oblige me, and, at the same time, delight the venerable saint.

" I know full well that you are a good churchman, and regard with reverence and esteem all those holy saints the Church so loves to honor ; but, at the same time, I think you cannot object to remember with me this day — albeit Saint Valentine be not niched in the walls of ' our Mother the Church.'

" Protestant, Romanist, and Jew, alike send pleasing missives to their lady friends on each recurring anniversary of this day ; and, provided such practice ends not in matrimony, I, for one, am in favor of its being sustained. True it is, that, like everything else in this world, the privilege is liable to be abused ; but let us not condemn it on that account, for, if the custom be followed in a proper spirit, it is a cheerful and a joyous one, and, though it accomplish no more than the gladdening of children's hearts, it is sufficient. But it effects more than this : it often calls forth the purest and best emotions of our being ; it ' makes a sunshine in a shady place.' It is like the quality of mercy, blessing both the giver and receiver ; and, if one of its missives stir the heart, if memories are called forth out of the past, — and there are blessed memories, Barry, in every one's heart, that should not be carelessly forgotten, — or if hopefulness for the future be aroused, is it not enough to warrant us in perpetuating alike the day, the custom, and the saint? Let us, then. my friend, give thanks to Saint Valentine for instituting this festival. Let us celebrate it as a red-letter day in our life ; and may the birds in the tree-tops, on each recurring anniversary of the same, while they woo and wed, emulate each other in singing cheerful songs of praise unto his pious memory."

"Mr. Gray," said my wife, when I had finished reading the foregoing, "that is a better valentine than the one I received, although it be not written in rhyme, nor transcribed upon lace-edged paper."

And I think Mrs. G. is correct.

CHAPTER XXXIX.

1be Donation-Party. — The Old Stone Parsonage. — A Debate. — Novel Crinoline. — The Company. — The Good Shepherd. — His Travels. — His Book. — His Portrait. — His Excellences.

MRS. GRAY and myself attended, not long since, a donation-party. This pleasant affair came off at the old stone parsonage with the Gothic windows. It was gotten up, in fact, solely for the benefit of the inhabitants of said parsonage. It strikes me that a donation-party must prove, to those most interested in it, a very convenient event. I have sometimes thought I would like extremely well to be a parson myself, especially about donation season. The day itself must appear to the recipients exceedingly like an overgrown Thanksgiving. I believe the observance of this custom is not confined exclusively to villages, but is, to a limited extent, followed in sundry cities. Nowhere, however, as in the country, is it so happily sustained. Here it is observed from a sense of duty as well as for the pleasure derivable therefrom. Quite often, too, the greater part of the country pastor's year's support depends, almost entirely, on the donations given him at these annual visits. With others, however, who receive regular salaries for their services, it is given as a " *bonus,*" — a something over the legal seven per cent. interest to which they are alone entitled. But, whether it be the all-in-all, or simply a " makeweight " to the minister, to the congregation and inhabitants at large it ever is a joyous occasion. Church feuds and animosities are, for the time, forgotten. The vestry and the choir, the parson

and the sexton, meet with the congregation, in friendliest
relations. Little differences are put aside : and high and
low, rich and poor, stand on a common level. The parsonage is looked upon as neutral ground, and the parson
himself the worthy pacificator of all enmities.

The donation-party under consideration opened at an
early hour in the afternoon, and continued in session till
late at night. The " old folks," especially those who resided some distance from the village, attended in the afternoon, and the " young people " in the evening. It being
a matter of some doubt in my mind as to which of these
two classes Mrs. Gray and myself belonged, the settlement
of it afforded us a subject of considerable debate. My wife
spoke very feelingly on the junior side of the question ;
while I, remembering the gray hairs in my whiskers, was
disposed to favor the senior. After much arguing, *pro* and
con, we finally decided the matter amicably, by going to the
party some time between daylight and dark. But though
we went thus early, we did not return home until quite late.
And I had several times to appeal feelingly to Mrs. Gray,
before I could gain her consent to depart, — she being much
engaged during the evening in promenading the rooms
with certain well-appearing gentlemen who had known her
previous to our marriage.

On reaching the parsonage, we were ushered up-stairs
by our black boy, — our parson not possessing a black boy,
had borrowed him for the occasion, — who showed us to
separate attiring rooms, where we disrobed ourselves of
out-door garments. I confess I was much astonished, when
we passed down the stairway to the parlors, to perceive
how much more space Mrs. Gray occupied than when ascending, though enveloped in numerous shawls and man-
tles. Her increase in breadth and circumference was wonderful to behold. I discovered that a large portion of the
ladies present appeared to be equally expanded. At first
I thought it arose from an optical delusion on my part ;

then I feared some one had stolen my near-sighted glasses from their frame, and substituted for them lenses of great magnifying power. Thereupon I took off my spectacles, and examined them very carefully, but found they were unchanged. Afterward I came to the conclusion that Mrs. G. had been consulting some high-toned fashion-plate, and had modelled her dress in accordance with its requirements. I will here remark that Mrs. Gray continued in this expansive state through the entire evening, and only collapsed, as it were, when we came to go home.

I could not avoid noticing, when I glanced about me, the apparent harmony and good feeling that prevailed among the assembled guests, who, as a general thing, are inclined to be slightly at "loggerheads" with each other. Perhaps the spirit they evinced was owing, in some measure, to the associations connected, not only with the festival of Christmas, just passed, but also to those with which the incoming Lenten season was surrounded. Whatever it was, I am certain that Christian feelings pervaded the hearts of all who that evening met within the walls of the old stone parsonage.

The roguish young man, so apt to annoy the precise maiden lady, occupying the slip in front of his, by placing his hat in her cushioned pew, and who has several times taken it therefrom sadly crushed, through her skilful management in seating herself upon it, I saw enjoying a *tête-à-tête* with the very lady in question, who put on the same airs with which she had sought to bewitch the youth's father thirty years before.

The old gentleman who uses tobacco, and expectorates so liberally on the church-floor, notwithstanding the sexton's repeated remonstrances, was standing in the hall arguing with this latter worthy regarding the comparative durability of marble and red sandstone for monumental purposes, — the old gentleman advocating marble, and the sexton sandstone. The sexton almost made himself out to be another "Old Mortality," so well posted was he in all relating to ancient tombstones.

The leader of the choir, a tall young man with a moustache, came down a few notes, and condescended to hold an animated conversation with the young lady dressed in black — between whom and himself there is perpetual discord — who plays the organ in a very scientific manner.

The first and second bass singers — who are continually making light of each other's baseness — were occupied in turning over, together, a copy of the "Women of the Bible," lying on the centre-table, and discovering very striking likenesses, in the portraits therein, to many ladies who are honored with their acquaintance.

The old allopathist doctor and the young homœopathist physician, who own pews on opposite sides of the church, and are invariably, whenever they come to church, called out just before the sermon commences, by our black boy, — who is paid quarterly, as he informs me, for this service, — and, moreover, are as divided in their religious principles as in their form of practice, one favoring High and the other Low Church doctrines, were, for once, united on a case, and played the agreeable to a fair widow — patient to neither of them, but a sojourner at the water-cure — seated between them on the sofa.

The venerable lady so regular in her attendance at church, and who takes snuff so freely as to keep her neighbors, within six pews' distance of her, on every side, continually sneezing, — greatly to their annoyance, but to the secret amusement of the other portion of the congregation, — I noticed, radiant with smiles, and gay with colored ribbons and bows on her cap, meandering through the rooms, her snuff box open in her hand, and inviting every one she encountered to "stop and take a pinch, — won't you?" Of course, on this occasion, every lady accepted her invitation, and, as a natural consequence, nearly all present were, more or less, engaged in sneezing.

The editor of the "Star-Spangled Banner," who has a "Religious Column" in his newspaper, wherein is noted the texts, at least, of each of our village clergymen's Sunday sermons, and where, sometimes, he slashes, with very Herod-like zeal, the discourses of our worthy parson, — and who, moreover, sets himself up for an evangelical critic, — was, to use his own expression, " on hand, on this very interesting and highly satisfactory occasion," and waited very patiently, seated on the stairs leading to the dining-room, for the announcement of supper.

As for the parson himself, he moved among his flock like a good shepherd, with a kind word for this one, an encouraging word for that, and even a gentle reproof for any he thought deserving it. Our parson is not simply a village priest, and "passing rich with forty pounds a year," but something more. He is quite an extensive gun in the ecclesiastical world, and, I have heard, makes splendid speeches at the conventions. He has published a volume of sermons, very Melvillish in style, to which is prefixed his portrait, engraved after a painting by Huntington. Any one can obtain the portrait, without the sermons, framed and glazed, — in an oak frame, exquisitely carved, representing a Gothic archway, — by stopping the colporteur when he chances to be passing their way.

Our parson's parishioners — of whom I am the humblest — sent him, a few years since, on account of ill-health, to Europe and the Holy Land, where he passed several months in travelling, and afterwards returned, much improved in his bodily health, and with his mental faculties wonderfully increased in their "powers of persuasion." The winter following his return home, he delivered an interesting and instructive course of lectures in the chapel of the Female College, on the subject of " *Travel; its Advantages and Disadvantages, as exemplified in a Trip to the Old World.*" I understand, from a private, but, I think, reliable source, that our parson is negotiating with the booksellers at the

sign of the " Golden Harp," in Cliff Street, for the publication of his " Text-book of Travels in Primitive Lands."
The volume itself is to be illuminated and printed in colors, in the ancient missal style, and profusely illustrated
with views " taken on the spot." This book will, doubtless,
be the identical one of which we have all read in the newspapers, under the appellation of the " book of the season."

Our parson — so his parish solemnly believes — is, in
every respect, a most proper personage to be made a bishop ;
and I am certain that two thirds of it pray devoutly for
such consummation. Altogether, our good doctor of divinity has the appearance of one who is well satisfied with his
share of the good and pleasant things of this world, and
unconsciously, perhaps, evinces by his manners a belief
that even better things are in store for him in the world
to come. And I, for my part, believe that there are.

It is certainly very refreshing for one like myself to encounter so exalted and excellent a personage as our good
clergyman. I am usually the better for such interview. I
carry about with me, for several days thereafter, an air of
sweet contentment, and regard with thoughts of supreme
indifference everything relating to earthly honors. I even
feel quite ashamed of myself for having written any of
these foolish " Hillside Sketches," and fully resolve never
to write another.

Our parson, besides his other goodly qualifications, possesses a strong will, great energy, and an indomitable perseverance. His zeal and industry, in all matters connected
with his church, have become proverbial amongst his brother
clergy. Whatever seems to him right and proper to pursue, however out of the beaten track it may be, that will
he do, nor stop till all he sought for is accomplished.
Armed with no buckler, nor helmet, nor breastplate, only
holding in his hands the cross of Christ, personifying in
himself alone the Church militant, he enters any battlefield where sin is to be fought, and, after a brief combat,
retires victorious.

CHAPTER XL.

A Praiseworthy Incident. — Ringing the Bell. — The Old Soldier. — An Appropriate Text. — A Slight Mistake. — "The Parson." — The Silk-webbed, Self-inflating Skirt.

HE church in which our valiant shepherd — spoken of in our last chapter — labors, is situated on the summit of a slight elevation, and fronts a small open space of ground known as the village green, from which three streets diverge. The church-porch commands an excellent view of the same, and, by stepping forward a few paces, to the centre of the green, near the flag-staff, a further view may be obtained, looking down other two streets, that run parallel with the sides of the yard enclosing the church. I am thus particular in describing the local position of the sacred edifice, that my readers may the better appreciate the following

PRAISEWORTHY ANECDOTE.

At the beginning of the season of Advent, our parson thought it advisable to open the church, of which he is the worthy incumbent, for daily service. This was something unusual in our village, but for a time, being a new thing, was well observed by the congregation, — the attendance some days being very large, though after a while — it pains me to mention it — it fell off greatly. The zeal of the parishioners cooled with the weather, and finally froze up when the thermometer stood at zero. The following morning the mercury, falling five degrees lower, no one — not even the deaf old woman who nods her head approvingly at all the parson says — appeared at the church;

only the sturdy, big-hearted parson himself was present. He proved himself, however, to be a man equal to the emergency; and, after ringing and tolling the bell — I suppose the exercise kept him warm — the requisite number of minutes, — the sexton being engaged in secular duties through the week, can only take his place at the bell-rope on Sundays, — he passed from the tower into the vestry-room, and so into the chancel ; but finding no one present, he, in his white surplice, returned to the tower and retolled the bell. Then, after a few minutes of this exercise, he walked out to the flag-staff on the "green," and gazed wistfully up and down the several streets, in hope of seeing some one or more of his truant flock coming churchward. But in vain did he look. Only the wind and the snow were abroad ; so he returned sorrowfully, but not disheartened, to the church, and again, for the space of five minutes, tolled the bell. Then out to the flag-staff for an observation, when the wind seized upon his surplice, and, winding it about his head, completely blinded him. On his third visit to the " green," he beheld the old soldier hobbling up to the rescue. So he and the parson marched into church together ; and, though the ancient veteran is not much of a reader, nor, indeed, can scarcely see to follow the church service, as set forth in the book, yet the two managed to get safely through the proper duties of the sanctuary. Then my old soldier, arm-in-arm with our resolute parson, marched down the slippery streets, holding his cane of Charter Oak in one hand, to the old stone parsonage, where he dined with the parson, and, on account of his age and infirmities, was treated to a glass of aged port.

On the ensuing day, though the weather exceeded in coldness the preceding one, yet, because of the above praiseworthy anecdote having been noised abroad, the daily morning service was fully attended, and the parish recovered its former tone of sanctity.

But, to return to the donation : Every one who was anybody was present ; and all, it is to be presumed, brought an
offering of more or less value, proportioned to their means
or disposition. I, for my part, being somewhat of a literary
Bohemian, and possessing nothing of any value to give the
parson, wrote for him, on sermon paper, the following lines.
My modesty being in the way, prevented me from presenting the same to him before the assembled company. Therefore it was that I placed them between the pages of his
next Sunday's sermon, which was lying on the outside of
his writing-desk in his study. Perhaps the text on which
that particular sermon was written — "If *we* have sown
unto you spiritual things, is it a great matter if we shall
reap *your* worldly things?" 1 Cor. ix. 11 — may have had
weight with the parson, and influenced him to leave the
sermon itself in the somewhat careless place it occupied.

I may as well here mention that the worthy man, being
doubtless fully occupied during the two days intervening
between the donation and the Sabbath in counting up his
gains, and therefore having no time to devote to studying
his sermons, did not come across my effusion till the following Sunday, when midway in his morning's discourse.
Being written on sermon paper of a size corresponding to
that he used, it did not arrest his attention until he raised
his eyes to the top of the page, when he paused a moment,
as if somewhat in doubt, but thinking, I suppose, it was a
poetical quotation which he had himself selected, read the
first two lines of it aloud, then suddenly stopped, appeared
perplexed, run his eyes over the writing, shook his head
negatively and solemnly, and, after carefully placing the
MSS. between the leaves of the Bible beside him, proceeded
with his own original discourse.

Mrs. Gray, to use her own words, was " extremely mortified and shocked, horrified and frightened," when she heard
our parson deliver, with great emphasis, my somewhat un-
classical lines, for she was well aware that I was the author.

For my own part, I came very near choking, though my danger arose, as Mrs. G. said, "from wicked glee, instead of penitential grief." As for the rest of the congregation, they were rather amused at the circumstance, though some were in doubt as to what it all meant; while the old lady who takes snuff termed them "very fine lines, so far as heard from."

The following day I called on the learned doctor, and made an humble apology, which he accepted, and at the same time laid a portion of the blame on himself, for not reading over, as he was accustomed to, his sermon before he went into church. I think he will not fail henceforth to perform this little act.

THE PARSON.

Our parson is a model man,
  And by the church he lives,
And, like a good Samaritan,
  To all who ask he gives.
He freely gives them bread and wine —
  Upon communion days —
And goodly precepts, line on line,
  And for each sinner prays.

Our parson 's short; our parson 's fat;
  His hair is rather gray ;
He hides it underneath his hat,
  And oils it every day.
Most seemly gloves and boots he wears,
  Black coats and pantaloons ;
And little heeds he worldly cares,
  But naps it afternoons.

A learned man he is, forsooth !
  And Greek and Latin knows ;
He studied Hebrew when a youth,
  As many a sermon shows.
And at the college, where he passed
  Four long and studious years,
Much other knowledge he amassed,
  Of which his parish hears.

So apt a scholar ne'er was seen
  Within the college walls;
Yet did he wear a modest mien
  When walking through its halls.
No pride nor scorn e'er filled his breast,
  But humbly on his way
He went, and honors round him pressed
  At each Commencement Day.

And when his college course was run,
  The Faculty agreed
He was his Alma-Mater's son —
  Her favorite indeed.
They also prophesied that he
  Would as a preacher shine;
And, afterwards, a grave D. D.
  They made the young divine.

But thirty years have passed away
  Since he took up the cross,
And those who never heard him pray
  Can't estimate their loss.
For when he reads the daily prayers,
  So pleading is his voice,
Each sinner loses half his cares,
  Each mourner doth rejoice.

And when, — this is no idle tale,
  But just the simple truth;
Nor ever was it known to fail
  With any maid or youth, —
And when the marriage form he reads,
  That joins two loving hearts,
Down the broad aisle, with frantic speed,
  Full many a couple starts.

But having reached the chancel-rails,
  Their guardian angels come,
So prudence over love prevails,
  And they, unwed, go home.
But Cupid hovers round their way
  Until the angels sleep,

And then the parson wins the day,
  And then the angels weep.

Our parson married late in life, —
  The fault was all his own, —
But he declared he 'd take no wife
  Till he was " let alone."
For twenty mothers — maybe more —
  Full twenty years had stood,
And praised their daughters o'er and o'er,
  And called them fair and good.

Until at last, quite wearied out,
  And getting rather thin, —
Perhaps he felt a twinge of gout,
  Or something else akin, —
Hoping to end his days in peace,
  He gathered up his clothes,
And packed them in a small valise,
  Then left his female foes.

But where he went nobody knew —
  Not even Mrs. Spy,
Who is a gossip, and a shrew,
  And sees with half an eye.
Though when two weeks had gone around,
  She said that he was dead :
But this was false, for soon she found
  That he was only wed.

And wisely had the parson done,
  And goodly was his choice ;
No woman 'neath the blessed sun
  Could more his heart rejoice.
And there within the parsonage,
  In peace they 've dwelt ten years ;
Now may they reach a ripe old age,
  All free from grief and tears.

It was a late hour that Mrs. Gray and myself bade good
night to the dwellers in the old stone parsonage and their

few remaining guests. The black boy drove us home.
After we reached there, I noticed my wife's diminished
figure, and requested her to explain to me the mystery.
She answered by remarking that there were some things
of which gentlemen should not know, and this was one of
them. And so, disappointed, but still wondering in the
matter, I retired to rest. I had a frightful dream in the
night. I dreamed my estimable spouse was changed into
a huge balloon, and one evening, as we were walking out
together, she left me and went up to the moon.

A few days afterwards the whole affair — I mean the
mystery and the dream — was explained. I overheard,
quite accidentally of course, my wife ask her cousin, Mrs.
Day, whether she had yet seen the " silk-webbed, self-inflating balloon skirt," that a very ingenious member of the
" Sewing Society " had invented. Her cousin, fortunately,
had not. So Mrs. Gray took from her work-basket an
article resembling in appearance a lady's netted silk bag,
not much larger than my hand, and, placing it on the floor
before her, it expanded, balloon-like, without any assistance,
until it attained the shape of an immense pear. The whole
contrivance appeared to me so very wonderful, yet ingenious and simple, that I could not refrain from walking
into the apartment where Mrs. G. and her cousin were, to
examine the " thing " more closely ; and at the same time
addressing Mrs. Gray, I remarked that this was a decided
improvement on every kind of hooped skirt heretofore
produced. No sooner, however, was my voice heard, than
my amiable wife lifted the miraculous skirt from the carpet,
and turning it upside-down, it dwindled, almost instantly,
in size to the dimensions aforesaid.

When I saw the " silk-webbed, self-inflating balloon skirt "
shrink away as it did, I could not avoid asking Mrs. Gray
whether, at all times, in all places, and under every circumstance, it would thus " perform," simply by being inverted ;

for, if so, I should entreat her not to put herself within its treacherous embrace.

Thereupon the cousin gave a little scream, and my wife, in a very dignified manner, desired me to leave the room ; with which desire I immediately and considerately complied.

CHAPTER XLI.

Mrs. G. and I take a Journey. — "The Hamlet." — March Winds. — Old
Particular. — "Mudlark." — Birds. — "The Sugar-Cane Green." —
The Hostess. — Fires. — Shenstone. — Up the Mountain. — A Fine
View. — The Mountain Home. — "The Angler's Song."

MRS. GRAY and I have been on a journey. We
were absent from Hillside a month and over.
Where we went no one, outside of the select circle of my bachelor friends, will ever exactly know. I will
say, however, that we passed, on our way to this almost
unknown place, sundry flocks of bluebirds, and other feathered harbingers of spring, flying north. We also noticed,
growing in open gardens, snow-drops, hyacinths, jonquils,
and various other plants in flower, making the air redolent
of summer. We likewise saw, edging the roadside, patches
of grass; and, in sunny nooks, violets, anemones, and strawberry blossoms. And, moreover, when we arrived at the
end of our journey, were regaled with brook trout and
green peas.

I have no idea that the name of "The Hamlet"— it is
simply a cluster of houses, with a wooden church in the
midst, built rather carelessly as regards regularity, in a lit
tle valley up in the mountains, where we pitched our tent,
not literally, but figuratively, I mean — is to be found on
any State or county map. Whether it is or not, I suppose,
matters very little either to its inhabitants or to the readers
of these sketches. Nor is it of any consequence to me or
to mine. But, sequestered and unknown as it is, and of
little note in this great world, yet did it answer exceedingly
well our purpose. We found there exactly what we sought,

namely, mild weather and blue skies: we escaped all we endeavored to — the clouded heavens and boisterous winds of March.

These March winds put on rather high airs, and talk loudly among the tall pines and broad oaks that grow about Hillside. It is not altogether pleasant for Mrs. Gray to hear them. She remembered what they had said to her a year ago, and therefore she resolved not to listen to their savage remarks again. This it was, and nothing else, that caused Mrs. B. G. and myself to put our spring clothing together in one trunk, and, on a sunny morning towards the last of February, to depart in quest of a milder clime. I said Mrs. Gray and I: let me add, moreover, the baby, the baby's nurse, and, for my own especial comfort and delight, the little black boy. The old soldier, assisted by the farm-dog Watch, we left behind, to keep watch and guard over Hillside. For other and good reasons, too, the cook remained, sole mistress of the kitchen and its environs.

"The Hamlet" was recommended to us by a convalescent friend, who had sojourned there a season, as the only place within three days' travel of Hillside where we could find the climate we so greatly desired to encounter. To reach it, we took the cars — after riding from Hillside to the railroad depot — and went due south. We changed cars several times during that day and the following. We ate, or attempted to eat, several tedious beefsteaks and sundry portions of salted ham and eggs, during the same space of time. We also regaled ourselves — or, at least, I did — with various native teas and coffees, concocted, I imagined, from curled peach-leaves and roasted peas; though Mrs. G. absolutely refused to partake of either of these beverages, and turned her attention exclusively to my private stock of "old particular," (*vintage* 1822; *exceedingly choice and delicate,*) which, for greater safety, and through fear of sudden illness, I carried in my overcoat-pocket. We likewise slept, during the journey, on any number of feather-beds, very warm and yielding, but not equal, I think, and so does Mrs. G., to hair mattresses.

The third day we rode, in a westerly direction, three hours, in an old-fashioned stage-coach drawn by four horses, driven by a black boy who was at least fifty years of age. Just at noon we arrived at a little town called " Mudlark."

" Singular name, this," I remarked to Mrs. G., when our black boy, who, stretched out on the top of the stage, leaned over its edge, and thrusting his curly pate into the opened window, had duly apprised me thereof, — " but, doubtless, appropriate."

" Yes," she replied, " so far as the mud goes it is ; " that particular commodity being up to the hubs of the wheels of our conveyance, as we passed into town ; " but regarding the lark I am not so certain."

" But I am, Mrs. Gray," I continued. " That they have larks here, of one kind or another, I am sure, though they may only sing at night."

" Do larks sing at night, Mr. G.?" asked my wife. " Are n't you thinking of nightingales ? "

" No, my dear," I answered ; " nor of whippoorwills either, of which General Morris pipes ; nor of the skylark, of which Shelley warbles ; nor of Robert of Lincoln, of which Bryant sings ; nor yet of the Poland rooster, of which Mr. Sparrowgrass chirps, — nor, indeed, of any bird of which the poets speak ; but one, my love, of very different plumage from either of these."

" Oh, yes !" exclaimed Mrs. Gray, very cheerfully, " I know now — you mean a night-owl ? "

" A night howl ! Mrs. G.," I shouted, — " a night howl ! that 's the species of lark to which I refer."

Luckily for Mrs. Gray, — luckily, perhaps, for me, — at the moment I ceased speaking, the stage stopped, after making two great crescents in the mud, where the wheels' tracks on each side of it, had first radiated and then converged, when, on a short gallop, we swept round a corner of the tavern, before the low door of " The Sugar-cane Green." and we and our family immediately deserted the places we occupied, and stepped on the soil of Mudlark.   I said *on*, but I should have said *into ;* for once there, and we became almost fixtures.   Any one riding past at railroad speed would doubtless have taken us for Mudlark's wax-works, and thought well of the taste the town displayed ; or that we were ornamental figures done in *terra cotta*, and placed, through the munificence of its landlord, in the open space fronting the " Sugar-cane Green " inn.   It was act-ually, to me, a source of great anxiety to know whether Mrs. Gray had not become as immovable as was Lot's wife. Happily, though, this was not the case ; and after a reason-able time, Mrs. G. — as also the remainder of my family, including myself — was, through the assistance of a dozen spry darkies, released from the unpleasant position, and received — somewhat exhausted and faint, perhaps, but otherwise in fair condition — under the dingy (caused by the smoke from burning pine-knots and tobacco freely in the bar-room) roof of " Sugar-cane Green."

The hostess, — a tall, dark-complexioned woman, with dark eyes, and dark hair, and dark-colored teeth, and wear-ing a dark calico gown — gored in the skirt to give it an extra fulness — which, " hooked up " in front, though the hooks, evidently, were gone, and across whose shoulders a gay-colored bandanna, folded triangularly, was thrown, the ends of which, falling down beneath her chin, served in lieu of the hooks, — the hostess (I must be permitted to repeat the word) took Mrs. Gray immediately, and literally, to her bosom and her hearth.

Such another fire as was blazing in the deep chimney of the " best parlor " was only surpassed by the one that glowed in the bar-room.   I do not believe their equals, in the matter of intense heat, could be found on the earth ; nor yet, it may be, in any other spot.   The whole house was like an oven. I wondered whether or not they were baking feather-beds in the chambers. My curiosity was such, that I took the liberty of ascending the stairs to examine into the matter. I found that they were. The beds seemed to be nearly done. They appeared to be puffed up with heat, and were, apparently, as light as buns. I would not have slept in one of those peculiar institutions for numerous plantations. I should have turned out in the morning as brown as a mummy. What between "Monongahela" and hot feather-beds, "mine host" looked like a copper image of some ill-used saint. Of course, it was impossible for us to stay in such a spot longer than an hour; so, after partaking, to a limited extent, of a half-burned loaf of cornbread, an overdone beefsteak, and cracking a few hard-boiled eggs, we ordered private conveyances, two mules and a donkey, and prepared to go on our way rejoicing.

"Mrs. Gray," I asked, as we sat toasting ourselves pretty brown in the parlor, just before our departure, "have you ever read Shenstone's poems?"

Mrs. G. had not.

"That he was a truthful writer, my dear, I am," I continued, "this day convinced."

Thereupon Mrs. G. desired my reasons.

"Listen, then," I replied, "while I repeat certain lines of his which were favorites with Dr. Johnson." I then repeated, very feelingly:—

> "Whoe'er has travelled life's dull round,
>   Where'er his stages may have been,
>   May sigh to think he still has found
>   The warmest welcome at an inn."

When I ended, Mrs. Gray gave me to understand that she should never sigh to think that she received such a warm welcome at the "Sugar-cane Green."

"But with whom," she asked, "did you say the lines were favorites?"

" Dr. Johnson, my dear, — Dr. Samuel Johnson," I answered, — " not Dr. John Johnson, of our village, but the celebrated Dr. Johnson, the *Ursa Major* — the great bear, whose life has been written by a very wonderful man named Boswell."

" Oh, yes !" said my learned spouse, " I 've heard of him."

" Heard of who ? " I asked.

Mrs. G. said, " Boswell."

Of course it was Boswell.

The distance from Mudlark to " The Hamlet " is a trifle over five miles. The only road, a narrow mule-track, creeping up the side of the mountain, scarcely wide enough for a wheelbarrow. At last we started. The black boy, on foot, led the procession ; then followed Mr. Gray, on mule number one, bearing in his arms " our baby " ; after him came Mrs. Gray, on mule number two ; who was, in turn, succeeded by Nora, the nurse, on a stumpy little donkey, long-eared and ragged, carrying before her a well-filled carpet-bag. Our trunk we were obliged to leave at the " Sugar-cane Green " till the following day, when it reached the Mecca of our pilgrimage, escorted by four stout negroes, and showing, by signs not to be mistaken, that it had passed through a course of ground and lofty tumbling since we had parted company with it the previous day.

It occurred to me, as we rode through the streets of Mudlark, on our way to " The Hamlet," that we were making rather a fine appearance. I was convinced of this when greeted by cheers from three small boys, who met us as they were going to school. Our course lay — I like to be particular in my accounts, for perhaps somebody might desire to visit " The Hamlet " — in a direction a little south of east from the village of Mudlark. The way was all up-hill, and the path filled with large, loose stones, which made the travelling, especially for our four-footed friends, extremely uncomfortable. But they were doubtless accustomed to it, and picked their way upward very carefully. Mrs. Gray and I sat our animals wonderfully well, nor met with a single mishap; but Nora, poor girl! was in a great deal of "throuble." She was continually falling off of her charger; sometimes going over his head, sometimes over his tail. She declared her misfortune was entirely owing to the black boy, who, in spite of all my orders to keep in advance, was constantly slipping behind, "and," she said, "was casting bits of rocks at the beast, which made him unruly-like." Of course, when I asked the boy why he did thus, he denied the whole thing, and said it was just the donkey's own friskiness, and he guessed 'twas because he felt his thistles. And I believe it was, for I afterwards saw him applying a bunch of thistles to the animal's rear.

There are numerous fine views to be obtained from various points on the shelving mountain-road, embracing many characteristics of land and water. A grand old forest of tall pines stretches from the base of the mountain, in a southerly direction, as far as the eye can reach, showing a heavy mass of dark-green foliage, interspersed occasionally with trees whose leaves are of a lighter shade. Hugging the forest in its silver folds is a narrow river, that glistens brightly in the sunlight as it passes onward to the sea. A level plain, showing already tender sprouts of green, spreads westward, from the opposite bank of the river, miles and miles, till lost to sight in the dim distance. Scattered at intervals over this plain are large mansions, with small houses and great red barns clustered about them, the centres of wide plantations. And also humble villages, composed of white cottages, lay here and there, looking like great pearls on the lap of mother Earth; while far off, near where the river, grown broad and deep, bears up huge ships, the towers and spires arise of a great city. Beyond the city, where the horizon dips down into the ocean, a mist hangs low in the air — a veil between sea and sky. To the north-

ward, gray mountains rise majestically, and keep back the
cold piercing winds and Arctic snows.   Three small lakes,
looking fair " dimples on the face of earth," lie, half hidden
in spring's young foliage, on the plain.   At times, dark
shadows come sweeping over the picture, giving it a sombre
appearance, until chased away by bright streaks of sunshine,
that seem to sink into the earth, warming and strengthening
her great bosom, till each tree and bush, plant and flower,
fibre and seed, on and in it, feels a genial glow, and gains
thereby more life, and strength, and beauty.

I spoke somewhat thus to Mrs. Gray ; she said I had
better cease talking, and give my attention solely to the
baby, as she feared, unless I did, that, while making such
poetical remarks, I might forget the child, and some accident befall him.   Consequently, I said nothing more to my
matter-of-fact wife regarding the scenery, but gave to him
my attention, as she desired. Mrs. G. afterwards apologized
for having addressed me in this manner, and added, that
she was prompted thus to speak through fear I might let
the baby fall.

We reached " The Hamlet" shortly before sunset, and
found, at the " Mountain Home," — where our journey
terminated, — cheerful rooms, a well-spread table, gentle
attentions, and a quiet house.

" Mrs. Gray," I asked, while we were partaking of our
tea and toast, " what do you think of ' The Hamlet ' ? "

Mrs. G. replied that she thought well of it.

" It is not the Hamlet, my dear," I continued, " of whom
Shakspeare makes mention," — Mrs. G. looked up inquiringly, — " not the royal Dane who loved the fair Ophelia."

Mrs. G. said she knew, quite as well as I, that it was
not.

" Well, my dear." I replied, " since you know it, we will
say no more about it."

And so our conversation ceased, together with our tea
and toast.

The following morning, while enjoying some speckled trout cooked in the most approved style, I remarked to Mrs. Gray that I was reminded, through the fish, of some lines our worthy parson had sent me, just previous to our leaving Hillside, in return for the verses I had given him on the occasion of his donation.

"Ah!" exclaimed Mrs. G., reproachfully, "and you have let me know nothing of them until now; how shameful!"

"I have scarcely had an opportunity," I replied; "but if you would like to hear them, I will read them aloud."

Thereupon Mrs. G. gave me to understand that she would like to hear them; "but, I am not aware," she continued, "that the good man is addicted to writing poetry."

"Oh, yes," I replied, "like Crabbe's Vicar,

> "'Music and fishing are his arts; at times
> He alters sermons, and he aims at rhymes!'"

"But the verses, Mr. Gray," asked my wife, "what are they entitled?"

"The parson, my dear," I replied, "termed them an 'Ode to Hail!'"

"Did he mean," inquired my wife, "the Mrs. Hale who compiled a cook-book, containing directions in regard to frying trout?"

"No, my dear; and, as I considered the title inappropriate, I took the liberty of altering it, and also inserted an impromptu verse from my 'facile pen.'"

Thereupon, without further remark, I proceeded to read

THE ANGLER'S SONG.

BY OUR PARSON.

> Hail to the spring-time and the hills!
> Hail to the meadows and the fog!
> Hail to the gorges and the rills!
> All hail the trout 'neath yonder log.

> Have good care,
> That 's his lair ;
> Heigh-ho, hop,
> Flip, flap, flop.

> Hail to the shocking old straw hat,
>   Second-hand trousers, coat, and boots,
> Box of gentles, lively and fat,
>   All hail your hook in those old roots.
>   Careless man,
>   Mad as bran,
>   Neither snap,
>   Nor flip, flap.

> Blessed and calm the smiling morn ;
>   Birds sing wheresoe'er we roam ;
> Flowers the fields and woods adorn ;
>   All hail my line 'midst dancing foam.
>   Gentle one,
>   This is fun ;
>   Now then stop,
>   Flip, flap, flop.

> See my slender, tapering rod,
>   How it bends above the brook ;
> Firm I step upon the sod,
>   For a fish is on my hook.
>   Now, look out, —
>   Silent stand, —
>   And a trout
>   Will kiss my hand.

> Hail the graceful silver gleam !
>   Lo! a trout with sudden spring
> Forms a spray-bow o'er the stream,
>   And is added to my string.
>   Do not stop ;
>   Fishes flop,
>   Verbum sap,
>   Flip, flop, flap.

When I ended my reading of the above lines, Mrs. Gray
said that she thought she preferred the parson's sermons to
his poetry ; but, she added, they certainly are original.

Whether she meant his sermons or poetry, I do not know, for a servant making his appearance at that moment with a fresh dish of trout, I gave my undivided attention to them, and forgot to ask my discriminating spouse to which her expression referred.

CHAPTER XLII.

Our Landlord. — Frank's Letter. — A Whippoorwill. — The Black Boy's
Nimbleness. — His Aptitude for Business. — Selling Eggs. — Paas Eggs.
" On Easter Day."

THE landlord of the " Mountain Home," where Mrs.
Gray and I sojourned during the month of March,
is a noteworthy character.   He is a tall, gray-
haired, stout old man, about sixty years of age, and wears
a flowing beard, a blue coat with gilt buttons, a buff waistcoat, black knee-breeches, with silk stockings, and low-
quartered shoes, ornamented with silver buckles.   On Sundays and holidays he adds to this — his usual costume —
an elaborate shirt-frill, and ruffles at the wrists. He carries
a cane formed from some portion of " Old Ironsides "; and
from his fob, where dwells a gold repeater, massive seals
— antique and of strange device — are pendent. He is,
withal, somewhat learned, quotes Shakspeare and the older
poets aptly, and interlards his conversation with scraps of
Greek and Latin. Each day he reads the Bible, Plutarch's
Lives, and Froissart's Chronicles; admires the characters
of Don Quixote, Sir John Falstaff, and Baron Münchau-
sen, but entertains doubts concerning the truthfulness of
the last-named personage ; considers Milton a bit of a wag ;
terms old Burton — not New York's favorite Burton, but
he of the " Anatomy of Melancholy " — a humorist ; and
calls the divine Watts a gay fellow. He believes in Washington, Jefferson, and Calhoun ; thinks the public men of
to-day have sadly degenerated from those of old, nor can he
perceive any prospect of improvement in the coming ones.

His theology is simple : the Bible is his guide. He endeavors to live in accordance with the golden rule, and holds fast to the Ten Commandments. I should also mention that he is seldom without a copy of Isaack Walton in one pocket, and a book of flies in another. Of course he is addicted to angling, which he considers one of the fine arts, and is never weary of discoursing thereon. When I informed him that my worthy cousin, who resides at Maple Hill, pos sessed an admirable portrait of old Walton, copied, I believe, from an original, he manifested great desire to see it ; and, one evening, over his silver punch-bowl, gave me to understand, that, if he had a letter of introduction to my cousin, he would take pleasure in visiting him, for the purpose of examining the above-mentioned portrait. So much for mine host of the " Mountain Home." Now for the house itself.

There may be finer hotels in the country than the " Mountain Home " — hotels better supplied with fresco and gilding, with plate-glass and cut-glass, with silver and china, with foreign dishes and foreign wines, and with servants and annunciators. Indeed, I know that there are. I recall to my mind several which, in the days of my bachelorhood, when I frequented them, greatly surpassed, in the particulars above enumerated, — as also some others not mentioned, — aught of a similar nature to be found at the " Mountain Home."

But at none of the grand hotels of the country can you find such white table-cloths and napkins, such lavendered sheets and snowy curtains, such appetizing food and pure wines, such conscientious bells and civil servants, or a more gentlemanly landlord, — not even among the Cozzens or Coleman families, — than Mrs. Gray and I found at the " Mountain Home." The building itself makes no pretensions to architectural display, but is a simple, unostentatious structure of one story, making up in breadth what it lacks in height, — it being spread over a large tract of ground,

forming the four sides of a square, with an open court-
yard in the area.   Above the main entrance to the house,
and half hidden by a climbing vine, are inscribed the following lines : —

> " All the comforts of life in a tavern are known :
>   'T is his home who possesses not one of his own ;
>   And to him who has rather too much of that one.
>   'T is the house of a friend, where he 's welcome to run.
>   The instant you enter my door, you 're my lord,
>   With whose taste and whose pleasure I 'm proud to accord ;
>   And the louder you call, and the longer you stay,
>   The more I am happy to serve and obey."

" With such a motto over the doorway," I said to Mrs.
Gray, " we must surely find comfort and pleasure within."
Nor were we, I am happy to say, disappointed.

My time was passed principally in fishing and shooting,
eating and sleeping, riding and walking, talking with mine
host, and giving good advice to the black boy. Mrs.
Gray generally accompanied me in my walks and drives,
and at other times was engaged in various feminine occu-
pations.   What with the summer-like weather, the absence
of cares, and change of scene, the roses came back to her
cheeks, the bloom returned to her lips, and light shone
from her eyes.

My friend Frank wrote me once during my absence from
home, and it affords me pleasure to lay his communication
before my readers.

" Within the Shadow of the Female College.

" MY MARRIED FRIEND, — The almanac tells me that
it is nearly time for me to look for your return to Hillside ;
but as I promised that I would write you a letter during
your sojourn abroad, I will even fulfil it.

" Since you left, affairs in the village have progressed
slightly. Breadstuffs and whalebones have advanced. Veal
is coming in ; likewise eggs and maple-sugar.   So much

for the market. In politics there is but little occurring: politicians have apparently gone to seed, — though we have had an election here, and run in our candidate for the office of President of the village. He is pledged to sustain the Troubadours ; to put down street-beggars and gas-pipes in the principal thoroughfares ; to give a large and fashionable party ; and to subscribe for your Hillside volume. It was doubtful, at one time in the forenoon of the election day, whether we could elect our man ; but we managed to buy, for a mere song and a bottle of champagne, the editor of the 'Star-Spangled Banner,' and his afternoon edition of it, over to our side, — which threw such a damper upon the old fogies' ranks that it enabled us to bring up to the polls with a rush, our Anglo - Celtic, Anglo - Franco, and Anglo-Germanic friends, who, going in for their rights, in an unparalleled manner swept everything before them ; and our worthy townsman was returned by his constituents to the tune of Old Hundred, — that is, by one hundred majority. The following day the 'Star-Spangled Banner' lost fifty-six subscribers.

" Of course the party, which our new President is pledged to give, will not come off until after the season of Lent, of which we are now, I regret to hear, only in the middle. Speaking of Lent reminds me that some of the 'blue-lights,' in the meeting-house over the bridge, assert that you left here simply to escape keeping Lent faithfully They think, too, that you have lost your religion. This is simply slander, and I mention it only that you may know what the gossips are saying. Try to be home by Good Friday; for we can't tell how soon after that period the party will come off.

" I have news to tell you concerning our bachelor friends. John, of ' Arbor ' proclivity, has, I am pleased to state, entirely reformed, and thinks of becoming a candidate for some foreign consulship.

" Our tall friend P has been chosen one of the Examining Committee of the pupils at the Female College **for** the approaching Commencement. He is quite elated by the honor, and is so occupied in 'cramming' himself with the classics, mathematics, and other studies preparatory to assuming his high duties, that he finds no time to go out with the Troubadours. We regret this the more as he has a fine bass voice, which we **need.**

" The Judge is, as usual, full of wise saws and speeches. Our remaining friends — Fred, one or two other Johns, and the balance of the Troubadours — are slowly but surely approaching the threescore-years-and-ten of man's life, with hearts filled with faith and hope.

" As for myself, I am, as usual, paying devoted attention to sundry young ladies, and in the interim am settling up my affairs preparatory to starting for Japan, where I propose taking up and following earnestly the business of a wandering minstrel.

" Yours, slightly *sub rosa,*   F RANK.

"*Postscriptum.* — The grass has made its appearance on the village green; I also hear the croaking of frogs, just at nightfall, in the marshes. Please present my respects to Mrs. Gray.   F."

Of course, after reading what my friend Frank had written, I could not do otherwise than be at home on Good Friday. So it came about that Mrs. Gray and I, one day early in April, bade good-bye to the residents of the " Mountain Home," where we had passed nearly six weeks of genial rest, and rode the mules, made ready for us, down the mountain, to Mudlark; and from thence onward, by stages and rail-cars, did we return home.

But we need not to have been in so great haste to get back, for, though now the last of April, our new President has not yet redeemed his pledge with a party; nor, so far as I can learn, does he propose giving one. I sometimes think that Frank invented the story for the purpose of bringing me home. I am certain he invented the fable concerning the grass on the village green, as patches of snow linger there even now; and further, regarding the croaking of frogs, I am quite doubtful as to its truthfulness. I believe he heard some other voices of the night, perhaps the waul of some stray grimalkin on the house-top, calling for his love.

We actually have, however, in the woods at Hillside, which is some little distance south of the spot where Frank dwells, a whippoorwill. What this singular bird can be doing in this latitude at this season of the year, is more than I can tell. I have consulted Audubon on the subject, without any satisfactory result. Whippoorwills, he says, cannot be expected to arrive in this part of the country much, if any, before June.

Mrs. Gray, having never seen a whippoorwill, is extremely desirous of beholding one. To please Mrs. G., therefore, I have sent the little black boy no less than five different times, on as many evenings, to capture said bird. He returns, I am sorry to say, unsuccessful from each expedition. My patience is quite exhausted.

"What is the use," I asked my wife, "of possessing a little black boy, unless he can catch whippoorwills?"

Mrs. Gray suggested that, peradventure, they are not easy to catch.

"With one's hands alone, of course not, Mrs. G.," I replied; "but remember, if you please, the extent and variety of weapons the lad possesses wherewith to capture the bird. Have not I taken great pains in fitting out that boy as a sportsman? Have not I given him almost everything, in the way of artillery, that he has asked for? Is n't his bedroom a perfect arsenal? There is the old revolutionary sword which belonged to your great-uncle, the general; and the bent harpoon which was owned by my grandfather, the sea-captain; and the dirk presented to me by our cousin, the midshipman, just before he sailed for the coast of Africa; and the new hatchet with which the little rascal cut down my choicest cherry-trees; and the fish-lines and hooks, and the landing-net that my friend the parson gave me; and the rusted musket that I carried when a corporal in the State Militia, together with a basket of fresh salt, some bullets, and a powder-flask."

"What on earth, Mr. Gray," inquired my wife, "did you carry a basket of fresh salt for when a corporal?"

"Pshaw! my dear, don't pretend that you do not understand my meaning: you know I referred to the little black boy's possessions, and not to what Corporal Gray carried. And now permit me to ask you, Mrs. G.," I continued, "who would desire more than these weapons simply to enable them to catch whippoorwills?"

Mrs. Gray thereupon replied that she really could not say if any one would, "but," she added, after a pause, "would it not be well to furnish the black boy with a ladder?"

"No," I replied; "that boy is just as nimble as a squirrel. I have seen him ascend a tree, where the smoothness of the trunk was unbroken by branch or spur for thirty feet, with the greatest ease; and then, after reaching the limbs, up he would go till the topmost bough bent and swayed beneath his weight, as if a strong wind was stirring it. Oh, a fine sailor-boy was spoilt, Mrs. Gray, when that lad came to Hillside to do 'chores.'"

But for all this, up to this time, he has signally failed in his attempts to catch the whippoorwill.

The little black boy, one way and another, has become the proprietor of a dozen or more of hens; and for their eggs, he finds a purchaser in me. A few days after Paus he came to me with nearly four dozen, which I immediately bought, paying for them the highest market-price. The following day the cook had occasion to use some eggs. She took such as she wanted from the lot purchased of him. The first she broke proved to be a hard-boiled one; the second was even harder boiled than the former; and the third turned out even harder than the others: in short, the eggs had all undergone the process of boiling. They proved to be eggs that he had won from the square-shaped boys at the Dutch settlement over the hill at Paus, by pinking or cracking eggs with them.

I could not help wondering whether or not the egg the black boy used — for he told me he won them all with one — would not, if it had undergone incubation, have pro duced a most wonderful gamecock. I even asked him his opinion in the matter. He replied he guessed 't would have hatched out a foreign bird of the China breed, because 't was made of porcelain. I have come to the conclusion that the boy is a smart lad, and I told him so; but at the same time I gave him to understand that if he sells me again with his eggs, he will himself be used in a very unpleasant manner.

But it is not always that I am so unfortunate in my speculations. Sometimes I have an unprecedented run of good luck, — often, too, without any exertion or risk on my own part. Easter proved itself to be, for me, a red-letter day. Not only did our matin eggs make their appearance at the breakfast-table, stained a deep-red color, — typical thereby of the blood shed for us by our Saviour, — but, while Mrs. Gray and I were preparing ourselves for church, a robin-redbreast lighted at our chamber-window, and poured forth a very Easter-hymn of joy and thankfulness. And as if this were not sufficient to make the day memorable, after church the black boy, who — unknown, of course, to me — had returned to Hillside by way of the express-office, brought with him a box which he had found there, with my address upon it, containing half a score of presents from my esteemed and generous friend Rowley.

Under the influence, perhaps, of that contained within one of the above-mentioned presents, I indited the following ballad-like verses, which, with my thanks, I afterwards sent to the well-beloved donor.

ON EASTER-DAY

At Hastings dwells a friend of mine;
He raises grapes, and he maketh wine.
There came a knock at my outer door,
  On Easter-day, on Easter-day,
While one exclaimed, " Here 's half a score
  Tall bottles for you, bold Barry Gray."

I took the gentle strangers in ;
To keep them out were a deadly sin ;
I stood them up in a formal row,
  On Easter-day, on Easter-day,
And brush'd their coats from ice and snow,
  Then shouted aloud, " Sweet Mistress Gray !"

The lady came with quiet speed :
" Can I do aught for my good lord's need ? "
I bade her look at the oaken floor,
  On Easter-day, on Easter-day.
She viewed the strangers o'er and o'er,
  Then, " Are they for you, dear Barry Gray ? "

" They are for me, my love," I cried ; —
My voice had a tone of boastful pride ; —
" My friend who lives on the Hudson's shore,
  On Easter-day, on Easter-day,
Has culled them from his choicest store,
  To gladden our hearts, fair Mistress Gray."

Each bottle bore a dainty crest,
And coat of arms upon its breast,
On which appeared, in a golden fráme,
  On Easter-day, on Easter-day,
The year of vintage, and the name
Of grape from which the good wine came,
  To warm the blood of Barry Gray.

And while I read, a foolish pain
I 'd conquered time and time again,
Stirred in my breast to its inner core,
  On Easter-day, on Easter-day ;

For there appeared, in a ruby score,
The name of one who, years before,
  Had moved the heart of Barry Gray.

My lady spoke, " I pray you tell
The rich grape's name ? " — " 'T is the Isabel."
Nor dared I venture to utter more,
  On Easter-day, on Easter-day ;
But when the wine I slowly pour,
My thoughts fly to the Hudson's shore,
  Though I toast aloud sweet Mistress Gray.

18

CHAPTER XLIII.

Death of the Old Soldier. — His Obituary. — His Funeral. — The Black
Boy's Grief. — Leaving Hillside. — Wild Oats. — Letters.

HILLSIDE is Hillside no longer. Its glory is departing. The old soldier has finished his Fourth-
of-July visit. He has ended his race upon earth.
He has gone, covered with scars, and wrapped in his tattered flag, to the grave. The aged warrior, alas! is dead
and buried.

He had been ailing for some weeks, but was about much
as usual, attending to little out-of-door affairs until within a
few days of his decease. The night previous to his death
he requested my presence at his bedside, when he told me
that he felt the blood growing cold in his veins; that he
was a'most done with the things of earth; that he had
fought the good fight, and, he hoped, not in vain; that he
knew his hours were numbered ; that his name, before the
morning watch, would be added to the long list of soldiers
who had marched before him, and that when the roll was
called at daybreak in the other world, he would be there to
answer.

These were the last words the old soldier spoke. I sat
beside his bed through the night, musing upon his somewhat eventful life, and watching, with great anxiety, each
change in his countenance. He slept very peacefully,
waking but twice during the night, and then remaining
awake only long enough to sign for a glass of wine to
moisten his lips. Nature seemed in him completely exhausted ; but I entertained hopes that by good nursing, and
keeping up his strength with gentle stimulants, he might

yet be restored to health. Just before dawn, however, he awoke, and I instantly perceived that the hand of death was on him. He strove to raise himself up in bed, but was too weak, and before I could reach him he had fallen back upon his pillow, and the spirit of the old soldier had " returned to God who gave it."

The following obituary, which I cut from the columns of the " Star-Spangled Banner," contains all that will interest the readers of these Sketches concerning the old soldier.

OBITUARY.

ANOTHER REVOLUTIONARY HERO GONE.

DEATH OF EBENEZER BABCOCK. — We were pained to learn of the death of the old soldier whose name is placed at the head of this article. He expired on Tuesday morning, April 28th, at Hillside, the residence of Barry Gray, Esq., in the ninety-second year of his age. His funeral obsequies took place on Thursday afternoon, at four o'clock. He was buried with military honors. The " Continentals '76," of which corps he was an honorary member, escorted his remains to their last resting-place. The three old soldiers — Samuel Sampson, Job Ripley, and Joseph Thompson, his companions in arms — who reside in the village, appeared on the ground as chief mourners. The Freemasons also turned out to do him honor, he being, at the time of his death, a member of Saint John's Lodge. The procession which followed him to his grave made rather an imposing appearance. The number of people assembled was quite large. The President of the Village, the Editor of the " Star-Spangled Banner," the Sheriff of the county, " Mine Host " of the " Spread Eagle," the proprietor of the " Red Jacket Garden," Jones of the "Arbor," Mr. Gray's bachelor friends, and numerous other distinguished characters, were present.

The old soldier had himself selected the spot wherein to

be buried. It is on the Hillside farm, but nearly a half mile distant from the dwelling-house, under the spreading branches of a noble oak-tree, known as the " New Charter Oak." The ceremonies which took place, both at the house and grave, were of a very interesting and imposing character. The body, up to the time it left the house, was in possession of the Masons, who, we understand, took upon themselves the charge of defraying the funeral expenses. The Grand Master of the order made some feeling remarks. He began by speaking of the age of the deceased brother, who lived longer than the usual time allotted to man. He alluded to his having fought and bled for his country, and, indeed, gave quite a little sketch of his life. From his remarks we learned that Ebenezer Babcock was a native of Vermont. That he was born on the first day of April, 1766, near Bennington. That his father was killed in one of the earliest battles of the Revolution; and he himself, though a lad during the war, was in several of its engagements, and received a gunshot wound at the battle of Eutaw, which disabled him for further service during the continuance of the war.

He was with General Stark at the battle of Bennington, and acted as drummer-boy on that memorable occasion. He remembered distinctly hearing Stark make the noted little speech, relative to his wife sleeping a widow; and recalled with pleasure the feeling of courage with which those few words had animated the soldiers.

When war broke out in 1812, he was among the first to rally around his country's flag. He fought in many of the principal battles of that war, being several times wounded, once taken prisoner, and once left for dead on the field. His life had been a hard one. He had for some years past, however, been in receipt of a pension, which had enabled him to live in comfort. He had never married; nor had he a single relative, that he knew of, living. He had great regard and honor for General Scott, whom he resembled

somewhat in appearance. The Grand Master closed by
hoping that the ancient veteran had at last found rest
within one of the many mansions in his Father's house.

At the close of the remarks the military received the
body, and the procession being formed, proceeded with it
towards the grave. At the entrance of the field the clergyman, from the old stone parsonage, commenced reading
the burial service, as set forth in the service of the Episco-
pal Church. After its conclusion the " Continentals '76 "
fired a volley over the grave ; and then, deeply impressed
with the uncertainty of human life, the assembly dispersed
to their proper homes.

I have but little more to add, except that the black boy
made his appearance at the funeral, with a weed of crape
attached to his cap, over a yard in length, that trailed almost
on the ground behind him as he walked. He also proceeded to the old soldier's resting-place in the evening,
after the burial, taking with him his rusty musket, and there
passed more than an hour firing volleys over the grave. It
was his intention to have fired as many times as the old
man had passed years, but his powder giving out, he was
obliged to postpone a portion of the salute until another
season. No one at Hillside, or elsewhere, I dare say,
mourns for the old warrior more deeply and truly than the
little black boy. They were warm friends, and the soldier
enjoyed nothing better than sitting by the kitchen-fire o'
winter evenings, telling stories of Revolutionary times to
him ; and he, in turn, liked nothing better than listening to
them. The old patriot left to the lad all of his wealth,
comprising nearly a hundred dollars in gold, and his well-
worn suit of regimentals ; which last the boy takes great
pride in wearing, notwithstanding they are acres too big
for him. The cane of Charter Oak he bequeathed to me,
with strict injunctions never, so long as I lived, to allow
it to pass from my possession.

I began this chapter with saying, Hillside is Hillside
no longer. This is even so. After to-morrow it will have
passed into other hands than mine. Its broad acres, its
tall trees, its fields and meadows, even the old soldier's
grave, will belong to another than me. Another mistress
than Mrs. Gray will preside over its household; other babies perchance than ours will laugh and cry in its nursery;
and another little black boy will be doing " chores " for its
new possessor. Various circumstances induced us to dispose of the place to the highest bidder. We had plans
that could not be consummated while dwelling at Hillside.
I am not at liberty to state what their nature is. Furthermore, we wished to educate our son in a proper manner.
The advantages in the vicinity of Hillside for learning are
not of a satisfactory nature. The schools are very far from
being all we desire. To be sure, the lad is still young, and
there will be ample time for educating him, even if we
should not leave Hillside for the next half dozen years;
but then, too, we ourselves desire different society from that
we find around us. Mrs. Gray does not think Neighbor
Pound a fitting associate for me; neither do I consider his
daughter, Miss Elmira Pound, who stole our baby, a proper
companion for my wife. The village is too distant for us
to see much company, especially as the road is bad and accompanied with much up-hill. It would not do, however,
for us to go into the village to reside. My bachelor friends
would each prove, so Mrs. G. thinks, a separate temptation,
inducing me to neglect my family, and become not only an
enthusiastic Troubadour, but a goer to circuses and wild-
beast shows, — and, possibly, a frequenter of the "Arbor"
saloon. Once, and but once, I suggested to Mrs. Gray the
propriety of our removing to the village; but she negatived
the plan so energetically that I was contented to say nothing further about it, and left the matter entirely with my
estimable spouse to decide as she might consider best.
Had it pleased her to remove to Turkey, or to the interior

of Africa, I should have said never a word against it, but would instantly have set about preparing for such removal.

Singularly enough, however, Mrs. Gray decided to go to my old home on the banks of the Hudson. She might better go into the village. I possess a score of bachelor friends at Rivertown, who will be pleased to have me once more among them. They will be glad to show me the new lions, and go around with me considerably. My lady acquaintances there, too, are numerous. Some of my old sweethearts, I understand, remain unmarried to this day. There is no telling what may occur when I meet them. I do not know what olden memories may arise to stir the chords of my heart. I cannot consider it wise in Mrs. G. to venture with me there. Had she deigned to ask my view of the matter, I should have told her the truth. I would have advised our seeking some other locality. I am afraid, too, that Mrs. Gray may hear of some "performances" of mine, while a youth, which may not be altogether pleasing to her ears. If she should take it into her head to look over the fence, into the field where some of my wild oats were sown, she would be considerably astonished at the magnitude of the crop therein growing. I fervently hope that her steps may never go by those acres. I fear, though, that some very kind friend of mine will lead her that way, and carefully point out the field of my enterprises. I wonder if Madge and Lucy are unmarried? I should like to see Prim and Bustle — and, indeed, twenty others whom I could mention. Ah! it is foolish for Mrs. Gray to go to Rivertown. For my own part, I would not "admire" to have Mrs. G. seek her old home for a residence. She, doubtless, has old beaux there. The tall man, I know, resides there; and his wife, I understand, is a feeble woman. Commend me to new places and new faces.

The black boy has just brought me a note from my
bachelor friends, the contents of which, being somewhat of
a flattering character, I cannot forbear transcribing, for the
perusal of my numberless readers.

"THE ARBOR SALOON.

" DEAR SIR, — Your worthy bachelor friends, hearing
with regret that you are about to bid farewell to Hillside, —
where they have at different times partaken freely of your
well-known and generous hospitality, — have deputed us,
a committee appointed for the purpose, to tender you, before
your departure from their midst, as a slight testimonial of
their respect and regard for you as a gentleman, a scholar,
and a boon companion, a complimentary dinner at the 'Arbor Saloon.'

" We would respectfully suggest that Wednesday, the
sixth instant, at eight o'clock P. M., if it suits your convenience, would be an appropriate day — being the anniversary of the formation of the Troubadour Society — on
which this pleasant affair should come off.   Cordially
yours,

" FRANK, Secretary of Troubadours,
" JOHN, formerly of ' Arbor' proclivity,
" JOHN, of the Moneyed Institution,
. " Committee.

"To Barry Gray, Esq."

MY ANSWER.

"GENTLEMEN, — Your invitation is before me. In reply,
it will afford me much pleasure to meet my bachelor friends
at the place and time suggested therein. Believe me when
I say I highly appreciate the compliment you are pleased
to offer me ; and only regret that my intended departure

has called forth this expression of regard from you.   With
feelings of great respect, I remain, gentlemen, yours faithfully,   BARRY GRAY.
" To Frank, Secretary of Troubadours;
     John, formerly of 'Arbor' proclivity,
     John, of the Moneyed Institution,
                         "*Committee.*"

CHAPTER XLIV.

The Dinner. — My Deportment. — Outside Expenses. — A Clean **Breast.**—
" Star-Spangled Banner's " Report. — Speeches. — " The Song." — Finis.

HE complimentary dinner, of which mention was
made in the preceding sketch, " came off " at the
place and time therein specified. My modesty,
however, is of such a nature as to prohibit me from describing, as fully as I otherwise should, the affair wherein
I sustained a most prominent place. Still, I do not feel
that the matter should be passed over in entire silence.
It is, indeed, due to my bachelor friends, especially that
portion of them who are connected with the Troubadours,
that some mention should be made of the same. Their
modesty in no wise stands in the way. They have no wives
who will rise up and chide them for having engaged in said
performance. They have no children who are in the least
liable to be injured by the example set them. Neither will
their consciences ever trouble them for having thus in-
dulged. In consideration, therefore, of all these circumstances, I feel in duty bound to make some reference to
the farewell dinner at which I was the honored guest.

During the time that intervened between the receipt of
my invitation and the dinner itself, I occupied a great many
leisure moments preparing an address, which I intended
to deliver on the occasion. Furthermore, I spent a large
portion of time before our largest mirror practising striking
attitudes and graceful gestures. When I thought I had
become quite perfect in these, I invited Mrs. Gray to witness
my evolutions. I am sorry to say that she laughed out-

right at them. She wished to know if I had Saint-Vitus's-dance. I reminded her, she said, of a dancing-jack. Thereupon I told Mrs. G. that her presence, as a witness to my proceedings, was not required. So Mrs. Gray majestically retired. Afterwards, while still engaged in getting up my deportment, I heard a smothered laugh and a chuckle proceeding from an adjoining room; on opening the door leading thereto, I caught the little black boy, with his eye at the keyhole. I am very positive that there was no more laughter from him that afternoon. For several days I visited quite regularly a colored barber, who took more than usual pains in dressing my hair and trimming my beard and whiskers. I even ordered a new, white Marseilles vest from a fashionable New-York tailor, and "went in" for the adornment of my outer man in a decidedly liberal style. I had several private interviews with many of my bachelor friends, who assured me, quite confidentially, that it was a very great honor they were about to do me, and that the affair would cost a considerable sum of money. They trusted, too, as the times were hard, that I would be a little generous in the matter, and give some small amount towards defraying various outside expenses. What these expenses were they did not tell me, though I think that the proprietor of the "Arbor" could give, if he chose, a correct account of the same. For my own part, I know it is a very expensive thing to be the "honored guest" of a complimentary dinner. I think that hereafter I shall decline — respectfully, of course, but decidedly — all such invitations. Judging from what this little affair cost me, I have come to the conclusion, that he must be a very wealthy man indeed who can afford to accept from his fellow-citizens a service of plate. I would much rather be asked to subscribe to building a church, erecting a lunatic asylum, or founding a hospital for decayed beggars.

The evening on which this affair came off, I gave Mrs. Gray to understand that I should be away from home, attending to business of importance connected with the building of our new church now in process of erection, — something, I told her, in the way of a vestry meeting. Thereupon Mrs. G. desired to know if I were one of the vestrymen. I told her no, but that I meant to be a candidate next year, if anything should prevent our contemplated removal from the village.

"Then, Mr. Gray," exclaimed my wife, "allow me to say that you will have to reform considerably before that period comes round, if you would hope to stand any chance of an election."

I know it is very wrong in me to attempt to deceive Mrs. Gray, as I sometimes do, because I am always certain to be found out. Even if Mrs. G. did not discover my little inaccuracies, I am still inclined to think that it would be morally wrong thus to act. I endeavor faithfully, by precept if not example, to inculcate in the black boy a love of truth. I punish him severely whenever I know of his deceiving me. He has learnt by heart the story of Ananias and Sapphira. I was in hopes that when he knew of the fate which befell them, it would cure him of his fault. I am not certain, however, that it has had any effect on him.

When on the point of leaving Hillside for the scene of festivity, Mrs. Gray suggested to me the plan of taking with me the black boy, for fear I might be weary after the meeting, and require some one to drive me home. I thought Mrs. Gray spoke rather ironically, so I declined his companionship, and expressed my ability to take care of myself under any circumstances.

Then she advised me not to get into argument with any one composing the vestry, in regard to church-affairs, for excitement brought on through debate was not good for me; "and be sure, my dear," she added, "to return home as soon as the meeting is adjourned."

I promised to bear in mind all Mrs. G. advised, and, if possible, to act in accordance with it. So, after bidding her good-evening, I took my departure. I cannot say that I carried away with me a very light heart. I felt that I was doing wrong in thus deceiving Mrs. Gray. Indeed, I did not feel certain that she was deceived. From her manner and tone of voice when we parted, I began to suspect that she might, after all, be informed of my intentions. I felt decidedly uncomfortable about it, — I mean the deceit I was practising on my trusting wife. Look at it in whatever light I would, and from the most favorable point of view, it did not seem to me that I was doing right. By the time I reached the foot of the hill, I had decided what course to pursue; and, therefore, turning my horse about, I retraced my way to the house.

I found my wife in the nursery, seated beside the crib wherein our little boy was sleeping. I do not think there were tears upon her cheeks, though her eyes were moist and a sigh trembled on her lips. She expressed surprise at my return, and said she supposed that I had forgotten my handkerchief — though she had laid one on the dressing-table for me. I told her it was for no handkerchief I had come back, but to tell her truly where it was, and for what purpose, I was going. Then I told my sweet one all about it, and showed her the letters that had passed between the committee and myself, and read her the little song I had written for the occasion, and kissed her, and was sorry that she could not accompany me, to be present at the dinner. And all the time she looked so happy, and smiled, and pressed my hand at this confidence on my part, that really it would have given me more pleasure to remain at home with her through the evening than to have gone down among my bachelor friends. But I was expected by them, and at last, entirely to please her, and at her earnest request, for the second time I bade her good-bye, and drove away. It was astonishing how different a man I felt. There was no weight on my heart any longer. I had nothing to conceal, and should not be expected home till late in the night.   I confess that the feelings I experienced were altogether new, strange, and delightful.   The perfect security I felt of not being found out — having nothing to hide — made me laugh aloud.   The idea of my riding down to the village in the evening for the purpose of attending a dinner, given by my bachelor friends, while Mrs. Gray was cognizant of the whole thing, and had actually, as I may say, indorsed it with her approval, was in itself so strange that I could scarcely realize it.   Henceforth, said I to myself, I will do nothing without first informing Mrs. G. of my intentions.   I will no longer hide anything from her; and who knows, I thought, but that next year I may so far have reformed as, after all, to be elected a vestryman.

The accompanying account of the dinner appeared, a few days since, in the " Star-Spangled Banner," and as it contains a full description of the affair, I take the liberty of embodying it in the present sketch.

THE PUBLIC DINNER TO BARRY GRAY.

It becomes our duty as an impartial journalist — one who records all matters of interest going on in our midst — to describe the brilliant affair which took place on the evening of Wednesday, May the 6th, at the " Arbor Saloon."   We refer to the complimentary dinner given to Barry Gray, Esq., previous to his leaving our vicinity, by his bachelor friends, and particularly that portion of them which constitute " The Troubadours."   We OURSELF, though not a bachelor, nor yet a " Troubadour," — albeit we have an excellent voice, and lead one of the church choirs, — received, in our capacity of editor of the " Star-Spangled Banner," an invitation (through politeness of committee) to attend, and which, our better half being absent, we cordially accepted.

To any one acquainted with Jones, of the " Arbor," we need only say that, for style in getting up the provender and putting it on the table, it surpassed anything of the kind we had ever seen. The bills of fare used on the occasion were not, however, as showy as we would have got up in our office, had the job been given us. They were struck off at the office of " The Teetotalist," the temperance paper, and of course were done in a slovenly manner. The names of many of the wines were spelt wrong: for example, Heidsieck was changed to Headsick, Mouton to Mutton, Rudesheimer to Ruddy Shiner, Nesmeli to Nose-mellow, and Burgundy to Blue Monday. Such important typographical errors as these could not possibly have occurred in the printing establishment attached to the " Star-Spangled Banner." Our compositors are too well acquainted with good wines ever to make such stupid blunders. We bear no ill-will towards the proprietor of the " Arbor"—on the contrary, we esteem him a clever fellow, for he has, on various occasions, sent us pickled oysters ; but we must say that it was a shame to place such an appearing bill of fare before Barry Gray, Esq., and his worthy bachelor friends. Of course we shall let the matter drop here, nor say any more about it ; and if an attack is made on us, through " The Teetotalist," for what we here say, we shall in dignified silence pass it by without notice.

We have little more to add regarding the dinner, except that the cloth covering the table was not removed when the wine was placed on it, — the committee having lately learned that it was no longer in good taste to do so. The proceedings, after the wine made its unlimited appearance, were convivial in the highest degree. Speeches and addresses were got off by many present, to all of which Barry Gray responded in his usual felicitous style. Frank made a very witty and telling speech, in which he feelingly, and at the same time gayly, alluded to the departure of Mr. Gray. John, formerly of " Arbor " proclivity, told several anecdotes, and wound up towards the latter part of the evening with a temperance address.

The Judge sung a comic song, written by a young lady in the village, entitled, " Come and take Tea in the Arbor," which elicited rounds of applause, and was encored.   Fred got off some original conundrums, which told remarkably well.   Mr. Gray's tall friend, Christopher, made a few remarks, — something like the farewell speech the man makes who is about to put his head in a noose, — and shook hands with all his bachelor friends at parting.   John, of the moneyed institution, made no speech, though he performed a very handsome act: at a late hour, just before the party broke up, he offered to exchange, with the company present, any Spanish coin which they might have in their possession, for American currency, — giving for the Spanish or Mexican two-shilling piece our American quarter.

Many toasts were proposed and drank.   We, OURSELF, was toasted tremendously, and responded in a very delectable speech of an hour's length, — though it was not all delivered, owing to the lateness of the hour. To gratify our numerous readers, it will, however, appear at length in our next week's issue.   Copies of the same can be obtained at the counter, — price six cents.

The whole thing, with the exception, as we before remarked, of the bills of fare, was a most gorgeous and splendid affair.   Convivialities were kept up till the " wee, sma' hours " of the night, — the other side of the twelve, — and everything passed off very harmoniously.   We trust that somebody else, we don't care who, will soon be leaving us, so that another dinner, like the above described one, may take place.

We close our notice of the festivities by giving the words of the song written by Mr. Gray for the occasion, and sung with much spirit during the evening by the Troubadours. We obtained them for publication through the politeness of Frank, the Secretary of the society.

THE SONG.

Once more, my trusty friends, we meet
   Around the festive board;
Once more each other kindly greet
   While fast the wine is poured.

Once more the merry song is sung,
   The jovial story told,
Till we, who are no longer young,
   Forget we're growing old.

Once more we gayly smile and laugh;
   Once more we drain the glass,
And health on health we lightly quaff
   To many a sunny lass.

We gild the minutes as they fly,
   Inlay the hours with song,
Till Time himself, in going by,
   Moves tenderly along.

Then fill the glass with ruby wine,
   And while it sparkles high
We'll drink a toast almost divine, —
   "God Bacchus, you and I!"

Before bringing these "Hillside Sketches" to an end, I will simply add that Mrs. Gray's hopes of seeing me reform are not in the least shaken, but are each day strengthened by noticing my endeavors to become all that she can wish.

Of my bachelor friends I am able to declare that, up to the latest date, they were individually and collectively doing as well as could be expected. The little black boy is pursuing, under a somewhat stricter discipline than he has heretofore known, his agricultural studies, in the neighborhood of Hillside, and bids fair to become a very respectable darkey. The dog Watch barks on the same farm where the former hoes corn, but, I understand, has lately been caught killing sheep. If so, his days, very likely, are even now numbered.

Mrs. Gray, the baby, and I, are dwelling peacefully together in my old home at Rivertown ; and though Mrs. G. has taken sundry walks, and gazed, standing on tiptoe, over many fences, she has not as yet discovered the lot wherein my wild oats are growing. My friend Bustle, however, has offered to guide Mrs. Gray to the exact spot, and as she is very well able to do so, I have no doubt but she will take great pleasure in performing this act. And now, sadly but truly, I say it, Hillside is Hillside no longer.

THE END.